Final Drive

By Shelly Hess
As told to Vivien Kooper

First published by Dog Ear Publishing
4010 W. 86th Street, Ste H
Indianapolis, IN 46268
www.dogearpublishing.net

ISBN: 978-160844-994-1

This book is printed on acid-free paper.

Printed in the United States of America

*This book is dedicated
to my amazing children, Dylan & Payton.
All my love forever, and remember…
Make good choices.
And to Bud. Rest in peace and keep your
watchful eye on us. You'll always be in my heart.*

Acknowledgments

A very special recognition of my children, Dylan and Payton: I love you dearly and I'm always here for you. Sticking together has gotten us far and it will continue to keep us going.

To my parents, Jeanne and Ray: I'm blessed to have you as my parents. This project wouldn't have come true for me without your support. All my love always.

To my best friend, Randa: I love you and I will always be by your side.

And, a special note to my mom and Randa: Thank you for all the time you generously gave as you listened, encouraged, and loved me through this journey.

To my brother, Mitch, and my sister-in-law, Theresa: Thank you for being there and somehow always keeping my glass full when I needed it.

To Denny: Thank you for your support, and all the professional help and advice.

To Maggie and Ann, my two "reality" friends: Thank you for always keeping me grounded.

To Kenny: I have no words for how much I appreciate all you have done for the kids and me throughout this difficult time. Thank you for being my friend. There are so many years to catch up on.

To Bill, Sr., Judy, Jeri Ann, and Michael: Thank you for everything, now and over the years. I love you all.

To Jan: I wish you the best. Time will help us all heal.

To coach Lisa, Scott, and all the Gym Quarters girls and their families: The kindness and support you showed my family is tremendously appreciated.

To Dan and Penny: Thank you for listening and understanding.

To Beth: Thank you for your wisdom and kindness as my friend, and for your listening ear when I needed it. And, a special thank you for your insights in reading through the manuscript.

To my writer—and new friend—Vivien Kooper: I would like to express the deepest appreciation to you for helping me get my story into words. Your warmth and wise insight made our sessions in preparing this book just the therapy I needed.

To all my other family members and friends: Thank you for supporting the kids and me throughout the trying times.

And last, but not least, to Bill: Thank you for our love, our children, our twenty-four years together, and all the memories—good and bad. We learned so much together, and our time contributed to the person I am today. You will always be in my heart.

PART ONE

THE RIDE BEGINS

Foreword

At the beginning of 2009, I knew I would be facing a monumental year—a year filled with milestones.

I knew I would be turning forty on January 4th, and starting a new job on the 5th. On May 19th, my oldest child, Dylan, would turn sixteen years old. And, on May 20th, my husband Bill and I would celebrate our twentieth wedding anniversary.

That is how life goes, isn't it? We look down the road and anticipate what is to come, as if we could predict such things with certainty. For example, I know that summers here in the Midwest are hot and humid; every autumn, the leaves turn and fall from the trees, leaving a beautiful quilt of colors underfoot; the ground freezes every winter; and, spring eventually arrives, bringing new beginnings, just in the nick of time.

I also know that what they say here in the Midwest is true: "If you don't like the weather, just wait an hour or so. It's bound to change."

Life is the same way.

We stand at the beginning of a new year—or a new relationship, a new job, or even a simple drive out in the country—and we imagine the road ahead, as if we could see clear and straight. As if there were no bends in the road that seemingly come out of nowhere.

~2009~
June 17th
Family Vacation

"Don't neglect your family...
Everything depends on
How much we love one another."
Excerpted from "The Joy in Loving"

~by Mother Teresa

E very year, we took a family vacation. Usually, we went either to the beach or to Disneyland. In June of 2009, we took a family vote and unanimously agreed that we wanted to do something different. The kids had never been to the Pacific Northwest, the place where Bill and I started our lives together, got married, and spent our first two years as husband and wife.

Bill loved our time there. We were so young then, and didn't have a lot of communication tools yet, so we could have really made a mess of our new marriage. But, being too far away to run home to Mom and Dad, we had no choice but to find a way to work it out. I will always believe that we survived our first two years of marriage because we were so far away from home and family.

Taking the kids back there was a really big deal. They were both very excited to see where Bill and I had gotten married. It didn't hurt that the movie *Twilight* had recently come out, and our daughter was a huge fan of the film (which was set in the Washington area). There was also the fact that my kids grew up in the cold Midwest, and had never set foot in a mountain range where the weather was mild enough to wear shorts. So, all the way around, they were very excited about the trip.

On June 17th, we flew to Seattle. The trip was such a joyful experience. Bill and I got a huge kick out of seeing the kids so excited, and we took advantage of every opportunity to stroll down memory lane.

Bill made sure the entire trip was documented in photographs. He had the kids take our picture at the spot where we got married, and he stopped strangers to take pictures of the four of us whenever we arrived at a place that was meaningful to our family. We all had a great time, laughing and enjoying ourselves.

You are walking down the road of your life, hand in hand with your best friend and partner, having no idea what is running through their head…

~June 30th~
Separation

O n June 30th, a little more than a month after our twentieth wedding anniversary, and six months after my fortieth birthday, I happened to be returning home from one of my bi-monthly trips to Louisville, Kentucky. In my position with my new company, I handled home health and I.V. billing, as well as accounts receivable. Part of my responsibilities involved traveling to Louisville twice a month.

There was nothing remarkable or memorable about that particular trip. So, when the plane landed and I collected my things and proceeded to drive home, I had nothing more spectacular on my mind than seeing my kids and husband, and relaxing in my own home.

Opening the front door, I walked inside our house. Bill was already home—and yet the house felt strangely empty. Our twelve-year-old daughter, Payton, was gone for a full week at gymnastics camp, and our sixteen-year-old son, Dylan, was out and about with friends, busy being a teenager. But, their absence didn't account for the eerie stillness I sensed.

Something was off—but what?

Bill did not seem particularly happy to see me, and barely acknowledged my return home. He did not engage me in conversation about the trip, or fill me in on the goings-on at home while I'd been away. In fact, he didn't have much to say to me at all.

What I wanted to say was, "Well, you sure seem to be in a mood, so, fine—have it your way." What I did say was, "I'm going upstairs to take a shower and get ready for bed. It's been a long day."

I had taken a late flight, and was looking forward to getting out of my work clothes and climbing into my own bed.

I let the hot water run over me, called it a day, and went to bed. As I drifted off, I was vaguely aware that something was going on with Bill, but I was too exhausted to really give it any thought. I slept soundly, and didn't awaken when he came to bed.

Wednesday morning July 1st dawned like any other, except that, for some reason beyond me, Bill was barely speaking to me. He muttered "Good morning" and "Have a good day."

I did the same, and off we went to work, with me scratching my head, clueless. Unlike our usual routine, where Bill called me at some point during the workday—either during lunch, or when he was out in the field, doing utility work for the City of St. Peters—I didn't hear a peep out of him all day.

When I got home from work that night, Bill was still very standoffish, and clearly in a strange state of mind. As for me, I was done waiting for him to open up. I was not about to go through another night of the cold shoulder, especially when I had no idea what I'd done to provoke it. As I've mentioned, only one week prior, we had been on our family vacation, and everything had been perfectly fine. We hadn't been arguing or anything, so I was completely in the dark.

I said something to the effect of, "I come back from out of town and get the silent treatment? What is your problem? Have I done something?"

Bill was sitting at the computer in the family room, which connects to the living room, where I was sitting. He turned away from the computer and faced me.

After a loaded silence, he finally said, "It's over. I want a divorce."

Divorce? The word did not register. I was dumbfounded, and just stared at him.

"I can't believe that just came out of your mouth," I said.

To my way of thinking, if someone is unhappy in their marriage, they don't suddenly blurt out, "I want a divorce." That is the last resort, after trying everything else under the sun to remedy the problem!

"You're serious?" I said. "You want a *divorce?* Just like that?"

"Yes," he said. "I want a divorce."

This great wave of hurt, disbelief, and anger washed over me. I started crying.

"What happened? Why, all of a sudden, do you flat out want a divorce? It doesn't make sense. If we are having problems, why can't we do some kind of counseling or something? Don't you want to try to work it out—whatever is bothering you?"

"No," he said firmly. "We are past that point. I've made up my mind. I just want to move on."

"Move on? You want to move on? How can you say that?" I asked.

"I'm unhappy!" he said. "What else do you want me to say? I've never been on my own before, and I just want to move on."

"But, I don't understand!" I said. "Don't you love me, anymore?"

"Of course I love you," he said. "I love you...as a friend. We haven't had anything in common in a long time. We don't really even have anything going on sexually anymore. We're more like friends."

His words were daggers in my heart. This looked like my house, and this looked like my husband, but it was as if I had stepped into some strange world. I just wanted to step back into my own reality.

"Friends?" I said. "If this is how you treat your friends, I'd hate to be your enemy. A friend wouldn't just drop this on me without being willing to talk about it or go to counseling."

A long time ago, we had started out as friends. Had we really come full circle? Had our marriage turned back into a friendship when I wasn't looking? And, was our marriage really so awful that, in order to escape, he was willing to do this not only to us but to our kids?

"What about the kids?" I asked.

Bill said, "I'm sure the kids will be happier knowing that I am happier."

I'd heard stories of horrible marriages, and that wasn't us. But, I knew there was no point in trying to remind Bill of how happy we had been. It was clear that he was hell-bent on this course of action.

Our kids had always been so proud that, unlike the parents of many of their friends, their parents were still together. How could he do this to them?

"So, what is your plan?" I asked. "Where are you going to go? What are you planning to do? How is this all supposed to play out?"

"I don't know," he said. "I just know I want out."

I am very organized. I always have a plan, even with simple things like a trip to the grocery store. And even when people are not naturally organized like I am, when they are considering leaving their spouse, they suddenly get very organized, and start planning like crazy.

In fact, I had several friends who had gone through a divorce, and *all* of them had given a great deal of advance thought to where they were going to go, and what they were going to do. They *all* had an escape strategy.

Even if I hadn't been someone who personally knew people who had left their marriages, I had read enough books and seen enough movies to know that, at the very least, the spouse who is leaving has arranged in advanced to stay with friends, or go to a hotel. *They have some kind of a plan.*

But, Bill had no answers. It just didn't add up. It was as if he had decided to leave his wife of twenty years, and break up his family, on a whim.

"You honestly have no idea what you're going to do next," I said in disbelief.

"Nope," he said. "Not really."

"There's something you're not telling me," I said. "There has to be. This doesn't make sense. *This just isn't you!* Is there another woman or something?"

"Don't be ridiculous," he said. And that was it. He had nothing more to say to me.

We were married in our twenties, and we knew we wanted kids before we turned thirty—but no more than two. That was *our* plan. It was a good dream, and we had been living it for twenty years—twenty good years. And, as far as I was concerned, we were happy. Of course, we had our differences. We weren't perfect. But, family, friends, and loved ones always said, "Those two will go the distance. It will be Bill and Shelly all the way."

And it's true—the Bill I knew probably would have stayed with me forever. But, this guy was a stranger to me. Who was this man, anyway? I had known him for over half of my life, and yet I'd never felt more alienated and disconnected from another human being.

I was upset, confused, and lost. I just couldn't wrap my brain around the concept of getting divorced. My heart was breaking as I made my way upstairs to gather my thoughts. I could not understand what was going on, or how any of this could be happening one week after we returned from vacation. What had I done? What had I missed?

I started reviewing the recent past, looking at it from all angles. I started with our vacation, mentally going over every step of that trip. It was inconceivable to me that my husband was contemplating divorce at the very moments that we were revisiting our past. Was it his way of saying goodbye? Washington was where we began our married life. Maybe it seemed fitting to him that it end in the same place.

Even though a part of me understood that warped logic, it was difficult to grasp. How could a husband take his whole family on vacation, give no indication whatsoever that he is unhappy, and then one week later, announce that he wants a divorce?

I was able to come up with a couple of things that seemed significant in hindsight.

The first had to do with the book Bill was reading while we were on our trip—"Into the Wild." It was a book I enjoyed, and I had suggested it to him.

"I can really relate to this book," he commented more than once. "I actually understand that desire that someone might have, to totally cut themselves off from the world, and check out."

It was rare that Bill got into books. Yet, with "Into the Wild," he devoured most of it on vacation, and finished it on the plane ride home. I couldn't help but wonder if he'd gotten caught up in the story. Did the book plant a seed inside of him? Did he, too, go looking for his soul—and get lost along the way?

The second incident happened a few days after we returned from our vacation. It was Saturday, June 27th—the day before our daughter was leaving for gymnastics camp, and I was leaving on my business trip to Kentucky. Bill and Dylan were going to be home by themselves for a few days.

That Saturday evening, Bill's cell phone rang. When he picked it up, he found out that Payton's gymnastics coach, who was on vacation in Florida, was stranded. Sunday, the coach—with the help of some of the parents—was planning to transport the girls in a caravan of mini-vans, SUV's, and an RV, to gymnastics camp in Tennessee.

Now the coach was not going to be able to get back in time to drive the RV to camp. He asked Bill if he would be able to take his place driving the RV to Tennessee on Sunday morning.

Typically, Bill would have been not only willing, but excited, to make that drive.

There were years during our marriage when we had driven kids all over the country, and Bill loved every minute of it. We had even talked about retiring someday and buying an RV. So, I figured he would have been a happy camper (no pun intended), to be behind the wheel of a big RV, with the girls in the back, and the open road before him.

Instead of being excited, he was livid.

"How could he expect me to do this?" he ranted. "It is so irresponsible of him. And besides, what kind of person makes their travel arrangements like that? Who leaves so little margin between arriving home at night and having to leave again the following morning? I can't believe he cut it so close!"

I looked at him like he'd lost his mind, and said, "But, what's the big deal? You drove kids all over the U.S. for four years—and loved it!"

Bill kept repeating, "It was just so irresponsible of him!"

True, it was going to be ten straight hours of driving—five hours there, and five hours back. Then, he would have to go into work on Monday.

"Well," I said, "you have about twenty vacation days saved up. Couldn't you just use one day? This is your daughter we're talking about here. And, the coach would not have asked you if he wasn't in dire need. Obviously, he trusts you to do this."

I was really confused by Bill's reaction to the coach's request. He lived for his kids.

Bill had told the coach that he needed to talk to me before he could make a decision.

"In the meantime," the coach said, "let me work on things on my end, and I'll call you back."

The coach called back with an idea. "Listen," he said. "I understand you need to get back to work on Monday. If you can drive one way to Tennessee, I can fly you back home. You will still be gone the entire day on Sunday, but at least you won't have to drive both ways."

The coach's plan made perfect sense to me. Sure, it was still going to be a bit inconvenient for Bill, but it would not only be helping his little girl, but the families of the others girls, as well.

Bill didn't like the plan at all. He walked in and out of the house with his cell phone, pacing and talking.

Bill's reaction to the coach's request seemed totally out of character. I couldn't understand why someone who was such a giving man, and lived to help people, was so put out by having to drive his daughter and her teammates to Tennessee.

"Okay," he announced, stepping back inside the house. "I'm not going. He got somebody else to do it—thank God."

"I don't understand," I said, feeling very frustrated. "What the hell is your problem with doing this?"

"Well," he said, "it's supposed to be a really nice day on Sunday, and I have other plans."

I said, "Other plans? What other plans could be more important than your daughter?"

He said, "A few of us are going for a ride on our Harleys."

Marriage is all about compromise, and Bill's motorcycle was one area where I compromised, big-time. I understood that in every relationship, each partner has their likes and interests—things that they do on their own. Bill's bike was his solitary place, his sanctuary, his baby. You didn't go near it, and you sure as hell didn't touch it, which was fine with me.

It wasn't unusual for Bill to go on weekend rides with his friends. And, he often went to the annual week-long motorcycle festival in Sturgis. I never threw a fit, and I didn't object to the financial cost of him owning a motorcycle. It made me happy to see him happily involved with his passion—but I was not happy that he wanted to go on a ride instead of taking his daughter to camp.

"Seriously?" I said, now furious. "You are going to put your need to go for a ride with your friends above the needs of your child? I don't even believe you!"

"I just need a break," he said. "Anyway, it all worked out fine."

I just shook my head and walked away, saying, "You are losing your mind. I don't know what's wrong with you."

"Nothing," he insisted. "I just need a break."

So, Bill went off with his friends for a ride, Payton left for gymnastics camp, and I boarded a plane for Kentucky.

That Sunday, I was taking a group of our employees to Churchill Downs for employee appreciation day. It suddenly occurred to me that I had not heard from Bill. He had not checked in since the morning, when he called to say, "I just dropped Payton off with the gymnastics team, and she's on her way to Tennessee. Dylan is with his buddies, and I'm going riding now."

I said, "Okay, great. Just check in with me at some point and let me know that everything is okay." That was my only request—and he was used to it. Whenever he would go for a motorcycle ride without me, I always asked him to check in and let me know he was okay.

It was getting later and later, and I still hadn't heard from Bill. I was starting to get a little bit worried. I knew that because it was a nice day, they would be riding on the back roads, where it was likely to be windy.

I tried dialing his cell phone, but he let it go to voicemail, which completely threw me. Clearly, he could see that it was me calling. Why didn't he pick up?

My mind started playing games. Finally, around four o'clock in the afternoon, when I couldn't stand it anymore, I broke down and called Dylan.

"Have you heard from your dad?" I asked him. "He hasn't checked in, and I don't know where he's at. He's not answering his cell."

Dylan said, "Oh, Dad called me about an hour ago…"

I said, "Really? What did he tell you?"

Knowing that Bill had managed a call to Dylan, I was no longer worried—just upset. Dylan didn't need to hear me say anything disrespectful about his father, so I was careful with my words.

"Well," Dylan said, "he said he's going to be really late. He told me I should go home and feed the dogs, and I'd see him tomorrow morning."

Now, my mind was really imagining the worst. What was Bill doing? Where had he gone? Whenever he went for a ride, he always stopped to return a call to me.

The night before, Bill had been acting strangely concerning the coach's request that he drive the RV to Tennessee. Now, he couldn't bother to check in and tell me that everything was okay?

Back at my hotel, I turned off my cell phone and went to bed.

When I woke up in the morning, I had a voicemail. Bill had called at three o'clock in the morning, saying, "Sorry, Hon, I got delayed…"

He went on to say that there had been an accident on a back road they were taking, and the road was closed, so they had to backtrack. "We didn't get home until late. I'm really sorry. Give me a buzz when you wake up…"

I was not happy, and I did not call him back that morning. Now that I knew he was okay, I was in no rush to talk to him. When I did call him that afternoon, he could tell I was angry. He apologized for not taking my call, saying he had just gotten caught up in having fun. I didn't think twice about the fact that he'd called Dylan at three o'clock in the afternoon, but he hadn't called me until three o'clock in the morning.

He then repeated, verbatim, everything he had said in his phone message. Of course, I believed him. He had never given me any reason not to believe him.

I said something along the lines of, "Fine, whatever. I'll see you Tuesday when I get home," And, before we hung up, I gave him the "please don't ever make me worry like that again" speech.

How does a man wake up one day and suddenly walk, talk, and act like someone else? And how does a wife live with her husband for twenty years and never see it coming?

This was the same man who, year in and year out, for as long as I could remember, had been my husband, my partner, my best friend—my everything. We had slept beside each other, shared meals, made love, talked, laughed, danced, played, volunteered, parented, built a family together, and shared our hopes, fears, and dreams.

Inside and out, I knew him as well as I knew myself—or as well as we can ever know another human being.

The Beginning

"Sing with me,
Sing for the years,
Sing for the laughter,
Sing for the tears,
Sing with me now,
If it's just for today,
Maybe tomorrow, the good Lord will take you away.
Dream on, dream on, dream on,
Dream until your dream comes true."
"Dream On"

~by Steven Tyler (Arrowsmith)

I f you had known Bill as I knew him—as this devoted, loving, attentive husband and family man—you wouldn't have believed the man who sat there that night, completely detached. It was pure science fiction—like a movie in which the character undergoes a personality transplant or has their body taken over by aliens.

To give you a better sense of the Bill I had always known, let me take you back to 1985, when I was sixteen years old. That was when life took an unexpected turn, and put me on a road I would travel for over two decades.

It all began that summer when I was working at Dairy Queen, and got it into my head one night as my shift was ending that I should surprise my boyfriend by bringing him some food. As I presented him with the food, he rewarded me not with a kiss, a hug, or a heartfelt "thank you," but with an announcement that he was dumping me!

Completely distraught and outraged, I hopped into my car and immediately zipped across the street, where I'd noticed that some friends of mine were hanging out. As I made the short drive, I was already rehearsing in my head what I was going to say about the horrible treatment I'd just received.

That is how I came to meet the man I would marry. He happened to be hanging out with some friends of mine in a parking lot of a Seven-Eleven.

In the course of conversation, it came out that this stranger—Bill—had graduated from high school that year. I was about to go into my junior year. I don't remember learning much about him that day, but for all that I was paying attention, he could have said he had grown up on the planet Pluto. My mind was focused on the now ex-boyfriend, and my story about getting the Dairy Queen food thrown back in my face.

As I sat there, sitting and talking with my friends, and giving them the blow-by-blow, Bill was essentially ignoring me. I was milking my story for all the sympathy it was worth, and I found it annoying that he didn't have enough sense to feel sorry for me. Couldn't he see that a person needed their hand held when they were going through a terrible ordeal? True, we had just met, but the least he could do was put on a compassionate face.

Nope. Bill wanted nothing to do with the conversation. He did not make a great first impression on me. Only later did I find out that I had also failed to knock his socks off. For years afterwards, whenever the story of our first meeting would come up, he would tell people, "At first, I thought she was a stuck-up snob!"

It was not exactly love at first sight.

So, you might wonder how it was that we became inseparable. Bill was friends with my group of friends, and whenever we did things together as a group, he came along. Once we got to know each other, the conversation between us flowed.

Over the summer, I began dating a friend of Bill's. Whenever I wanted a guy's perspective on whether my boyfriend was acting like a jerk, I would sit Bill down and give him the details. And, unlike my female friends, who just agreed with everything I said, Bill would give me his honest opinion, and help me see things from a different angle.

It wasn't just my romantic problems that filled our conversations. He was happy to talk about whatever might be on my mind. That was just the kind of guy he was—very giving. If you were lucky enough to have him as a friend, you could count on the fact that he always had your back.

I worked later hours during the summer at Dairy Queen than I did when school was in session. Whenever any of us were working the night shift, we would keep the doors locked, but we would sneak our friends inside. Bill always showed up to visit me at work, and whenever I was feeling down, or simply had a bad day, he would bring me a Hallmark card to cheer me up.

They were always the friendship cards, with a message like, "Just to let you know I'm always here for you."

Sometimes he brought me a single rose—or a pickle. He knew I loved those big dill pickles sold by the piece from a huge jar, so he would stop by the deli and show up with a pickle.

I was totally taken aback by those gestures. The guys I usually dated were so consumed with their own lives, it simply would not have occurred to them to do something thoughtful for me. So, whenever Bill extended himself in that way, it intimidated me a little bit. I just couldn't get over him.

In September of 1985, the dynamic between us took on a different feeling. It became obvious that Bill wanted to be more than friends with me. One day he said, "I'm tired of listening to all the problems you have with these guys. If you would just go out with me, we could be happy together!"

"Go out with you?" I said, horrified. "Are you kidding me? Absolutely not!"

His face fell.

I quickly explained, "You're too good a friend!"

He still looked crestfallen.

I went on. "Do you know how hard it is for a girl to find a good guy friend? It's next to impossible! If we get involved romantically, and it doesn't work out, we could end up losing our friendship."

I wanted no part of Bill's plan to turn me into his girlfriend—but he was relentless. He left love notes saying, "I can't imagine living the rest of my life without you. You're making a huge mistake!"

To which I would reply, "You're not going to live the rest of your life without me. We'll always be friends." Of course, I knew full well that it wasn't the same thing.

He left roses on my car at school and at work, and promised he'd never hurt me. I started to realize, my God—he really is not going to give up! In the end, all my female friends convinced me that I was insane to continue saying no. After all, I wasn't the only one—none of us had ever been treated so well.

So, at the end of September, I gave in.

Bill had come over to my house to extend another invitation to dinner and a movie. "Okay," I said, "I guess we can try this dating thing and see how it goes. But, I'm scared to death of losing you, so you have to promise me, if it doesn't work out, we will still try to be friends."

"That is absolutely fine," he said. "If things don't work out between us, we can still be friends… But, don't worry," he said, flashing one of his signature grins at me, "that's never going to happen. You'll see… it is all going to work out great!"

During the entire time he'd been pestering me to accept a date from him, he had been saving his money, just in case I said yes. So, when I finally caved in, he had quite a savings stored up.

"I want to take you somewhere really nice," he said. "Somewhere special—maybe a steakhouse."

A steakhouse? I was a lacto-vegetarian, someone who eats dairy, but never meat or fish. It had all started with a family meal of cube steak. It tasted to me like it had rubber bands in it, and I almost gagged. Another time, my mom tried to make me eat fish sticks, and I ran away from home to avoid them, hanging out at the local VFW hall until I got scared and went back home.

"Listen, Shell," my mom said to me, "this is not a restaurant. I will be cooking one meal a night. If you don't like what I'm cooking, you don't have to eat it. But, you're going to get awfully sick of making yourself cheese sandwiches."

I never did. To this day, I still love cheese.

Anyway, there I was, trying to get out of a steak dinner with Bill without hurting his feelings. "Actually," I said, "Pizza Hut sounds great!"

"Pizza Hut?!" He was in shock—but he wasn't about to argue. He had waited long enough for me to agree to date him.

So, we saw our first movie together—*Rambo: First Blood, Part II*. And we shared our first romantic meal—cheese pizza for me and pepperoni for Bill. After dinner, we went to Westport Plaza, an outdoor shopping mall with a lake in the center of it.

Bill hit all the right notes with me, and didn't do anything out of line. Standing there with my dear friend as the night lights reflected off the water, everything seemed right with the world. We were already comfortable together, so there were none of the usual first-date jitters.

We survived our first date beautifully, with no damage to our friendship at all. We seemed to have found the perfect balance between the excitement of romance and the ease of friendship. I knew the big finale was still ahead of us, and I started to feel a combination of nerves and excitement. Were we really going to do this? After so many hours spent together as friends, were we actually going to *kiss* each other?

I was still living at home at the time, and Bill walked me to the front door. With a slight end-of-summer chill in the air, we stood on the porch together, ready to say goodnight. So many mixed emotions were going on inside me, I was shaking a little bit.

Then, this guy I had come to consider my rock and my best friend gave me the perfect first kiss to top off the perfect first date.

I stepped inside the house and shut the front door. I couldn't believe how well the evening had flowed. The whole thing could have gone horribly wrong. Not only was I concerned about ruining our friendship if things didn't pan out romantically, but I was skeptical because we came from such different backgrounds.

Where I came from, there was no divorce at all. It was family first—relatives were always around, always there for you, doing whatever they could. Everyone spent birthdays and holidays together, and you always knew your family had your back. I treasure my great family, and it hurts me to think that not everyone is as lucky.

Bill came from a broken home. I have always had a lot of compassion for the underdogs, so it wasn't surprising that my heart went out to him.

When Bill was a teenager, he ran away from the home he lived in with his mother and second stepfather. Bill's mother, Jan, and biological father, Bill Sr., had been teenagers when he was born, and when they divorced, they were still teenagers—not even nineteen years old. After the divorce, Jan seemed at a loss as to what to do with this small child. She was still really only a child herself.

Bad choice after bad choice followed, and by the time Jan married Bill's second stepfather, Bill was reaching the end of his rope. He just did not get along with his stepfather, whom he saw as controlling, and whom he resented for trying to fill the shoes of his real father.

Bill longed for a closer relationship with his real father, who lived two hours away in Cuba, Missouri, and whom he saw only a few times a month. It wasn't until later, after we were married, that Bill would finally enjoy the close bond with his father that he so longed for when he was young.

Anyway, as a teenager, Bill made a break for it, and ran away—to the home of his grandparents. Strangely, his grandparents didn't send him back home to his mother, and Bill's mother never came for him, either. She did call and try to persuade him to return home, but she never showed up, put him in the car, and said, "Come on, let's go home and work this out."

Her failure to physically go get him and bring him back home wounded Bill deeply. How could his mother just leave him there, like he didn't matter? In Bill's eyes, his mother chose her husband over him. He never got over the pain of what he saw as a betrayal, but despite his heartache, he definitely loved his mother.

Anyway, that was the sad background of my old friend and new sweetheart.

As I was drifting off to sleep, I thought, gosh, I sure do hope this works out. I had never had a relationship before where the guy was both a good friend and my boyfriend, and I was very excited about that possibility.

~1985 to 1986~
The Courtship

"You are my sunshine, my only sunshine,
"You make me happy when skies are gray,
You'll never know, dear, how much I love you,
Please don't take my sunshine away..."
"You Are My Sunshine"

~by Norman Blake

N ow that we were dating, Bill's surprises were more romantic. He would pick me up, casually mention we were going to the park, and then produce a picnic basket filled with goodies he knew I'd love.

February, 1986 was our first Valentine's Day as sweethearts. I had become a cheerleader by then, and, wouldn't you know it—that night of all nights, I had a game.

Bill had already graduated high school, but he showed up at every cheerleading event to support me. On that particular night, he made an appearance at the beginning of the game, but while I was busy rooting for the home team, he quietly snuck away, and raced home to collect some Valentine's surprises he had hidden there for me. Then, according to a plan he had made in advance with my mom, he ran over to my house.

There I was cheerleading, with no idea Bill was even gone, and he was busy making sure I would never forget our first Valentine's Day. He decorated my room with dozens of pink and white helium balloons, and laid out three dozen roses all over my bed. When he finished, he raced back to the game. When he saw me, he acted very nonchalant, as if he had been there all along.

By the time the game was over, it was late, so we didn't have much time to spend together. We visited for awhile, and he dropped me off at home. As we said goodnight, I figured that was the extent of our holiday celebration. I was grateful that he had chosen to spend Valentine's Day watching me cheer, and that was good enough for me. I went down the hall to my room, opened my door, and entered an ocean of pink, white, and red. I gasped—and tears sprang to my eyes.

I thought, oh, my God! Who is this guy, anyway? And, how did he always seem to know just the right thing to say and do?

The days where everyone walks around with a cell phone were not yet upon us, so I had to wait until Bill got home to call him on his home phone. I could hardly wait. I wanted to throw my arms around his neck, kiss him a hundred times, and tell him how much I loved him. When I finally got him on the phone, I thanked him over and over, and told him how much I appreciated his thoughtfulness.

"I have to take pictures," I said, "because no one is going to believe this!"

He laughed, clearly happy to have bowled me over.

I went to bed with tears of gratitude in my eyes and a smile on my face. Bill had touched me deeply.

Another moment that stands out in my memory occurred when I was a senior in high school. The cheerleaders were having their last home game, and we all walked onto the basketball court with our parents. It was one of those moments where life suddenly goes into slow motion. I looked up at the clock on the wall of the gym, and realized that somehow, hours, days, and years had passed, and there I was—about to graduate.

Listening to the applause of the crowd, so many memories filled my mind—games won and lost, the camaraderie among the cheerleaders, the supportive relationship between the cheerleaders and our team. My heart was full, and I was fighting back the tears.

Afterwards, all the girls and I filed out into the hallway together, hugging each other. And there was Bill, waiting for me. He was the only boyfriend there—and he was holding a bouquet of flowers and a dozen helium balloons.

"I love you," he whispered to me, "and I'm so proud of you!"

My friends all looked at him standing there with balloons and flowers, and shook their heads in disbelief. "Does he really have to do that?" they asked me. He was always making the other girls' boyfriends look bad.

When they were handing out the playbook on how to win a girl's heart, the other guys must have been too busy admiring themselves in the mirror to pay attention. Bill was the only one that seemed to have read it, cover to cover. And, with that instinctive understanding of what made me tick, and what touched my heart, he would spend the next twenty-something years making me fall in love with him, over and over again.

~1989~
The Wedding(s)

"You're here, there's nothing I fear,
And I know that my heart will go on,
We'll stay forever this way,
You are safe in my heart,
And my heart will go on and on…"
"My Heart Will Go On"

~by Horner/Jennings (Celine Dion)

I f someone had taken me aside that day in the parking lot of Seven-Eleven, and said, "You may want to be nicer to this stranger because you're going to marry him one day," I would have told them they were out of their mind. And yet, looking back, I can see that the road carrying us along was always leading to the altar.

One day, when I was all of twenty years old and Bill was twenty-one, that's exactly where we ended up.

By January of 1989, Bill had served his first six months in the Navy. As for me, I was still living at home in St. Louis, preparing for our wedding day, which was set for April. One day, I went out to the mailbox, tore open a letter from him, and walked back inside, shaking and in shock. The letter read, "I'm not sure I want to get married after all…"

Granted, it had been four months since we'd even gotten a chance to talk, and six months since we'd seen each other, and the letters were just not cutting it anymore. And sure, the months apart stretched like the sea between us, creating this vast distance where everything seemed surreal—*but call off the wedding?*

I had already bought my wedding dress, and my bridesmaids had their dresses, as well. I couldn't imagine anything more mortifying than having to

20

call them and tell them the wedding was off. Sure, they would be totally sympathetic toward me, but they would be furious with Bill! This was the same Bill that had set the bar so high that none of their boyfriends could reach it.

As for me, my emotions were all twisted up. I was confused, hurt, angry, mortified.

"...Maybe," the letter continued, "we should get to know each other again before we get married. After all, we have been apart for so long..."

I was devastated. How could he have forgotten the note he left me when he took off for boot camp? It said, in so many words, "I know our love will see us through this difficult time..."

My dad was home at the time I got the "Dear Jane" letter.

He tried to play negotiator. "Well," he said, "better for him to be up front and tell you now. What if he went through with the wedding, you two moved away, and *then* you found out he didn't really want to be married?"

I was totally frantic, repeating over and over, "But, how could he do this to me?"

Dad could see that logic wasn't really helping the matter, and decided he'd better call my mom at work. "You had better come home. Your daughter is very upset..."

I was in a daze over the next week as I cancelled all the wedding plans. I called the church and the hall. One by one, I called the wedding party and told them there wasn't going to be a wedding. In my twenty years on the planet, it was easily the most humiliating thing I'd ever had to endure.

Invitations, matchbooks, napkins—all bearing the names of the bride and groom—were finished and waiting to be picked up at the place where I'd ordered the wedding cake. When I walked in, I tried not to let my voice crack. "My wedding has been cancelled."

The shop owner took it in stride. I'm sure he had heard the same story a million times. And he got paid for the work he did on our behalf whether there was an actual wedding or not.

I had to return my wedding gown. Since I hadn't yet had it fitted, I would still be able to take it back. As I carried it in to the store, I was so upset. Meanwhile, my mom, God bless her, felt badly for my bridesmaids, and reimbursed them for the dresses they had bought with their own money.

Bill's letter to me had cost everyone so much, in so many ways—financially and emotionally.

A couple of days after the last of the wedding arrangements had been cancelled, the phone rang. It was Bill. I picked up the phone, adrenaline and anger rushing through me. I couldn't wait to hear this!

He quickly blurted out, "Please tell me you did not get the letter I wrote…"

I said, "Are you kidding me? Of course I got the letter! And I've been busy canceling everything!"

"Oh, no," he said, "I was hoping it hadn't gotten there yet, and I could explain. I freaked myself out, but I'm over it now…"

"You're over it now?!" I was so upset and confused, I couldn't even think straight, much less speak. "What the hell does that mean?"

He said, "I've been at sea too long, with too much time on my hands. It was messing with my mind and making me question everything. But, I really do love you!"

Have you ever been really worried about someone you love, on pins and needles, thinking maybe something terrible has happened to them? Well, you know that feeling you get when you find out they are actually okay? First you want to hug them and never let them go. And, then you want to smack them for making you lose your mind with worry. That's exactly how I felt in that moment.

We decided then and there that if we were ever going to survive as a couple, we had to be together as much as possible during his enlistment. So, that March, I joined him on Whidbey Island in Washington. We moved in together with the sole intention of "getting to know each other again" before tying the knot.

Coming from the suburbs in the Midwest, I never thought I would end up living on a secluded island, populated mostly by Navy families and retirees. Living so far from home, there were plenty of days I wondered what I'd gotten myself into. But, in retrospect, I can see that it was meant to be. When you're separated from everyone and everything familiar, your relationship is really tested. Either you fall apart under the stress and part ways, or your bond grows even stronger.

Almost thirty days from the date of our would-be April wedding, Bill woke up, turned to me, and said, "Let's get married! I don't know what got into me before…" The apologies never stopped.

I said, "Listen, if you're sure you want to marry me, you know I will. But I've already planned one wedding. There's no way I am planning another! So, I guess we'll be going down to the courthouse for a civil ceremony."

"Listen," he said, "I don't pretend to know about girls and their dreams of the perfect wedding. But there is no way I am letting you get married at the courthouse!"

"Well, that's sweet of you," I said, willing to forgive, but not forgetting for one second what he had put me through. "But, if you don't want to get married in a courthouse, you can damn well plan this wedding. I'm not going to."

"All right, I will," he said, smiling at me.

I didn't doubt him. After all, this was the same guy who filled my room with balloons and flowers for Valentine's Day, and did a thousand other thoughtful things during our courtship.

He was really going to have to pull a rabbit out of a hat this time, because we were not getting married in our hometown, surrounded by all our loved ones. In fact, I had only made three friends since I'd arrived—Linda, a co-worker I didn't yet know well enough to invite to my wedding, and two wives of Bill's friends. I knew them only slightly better than I knew Linda.

Now, where could a twenty-year-old have her bachelorette party? We put our heads together, and came up with the idea of Canada, where the drinking age was only eighteen years old. Luckily, we were very close to the border.

As for the ceremony itself, once again Life had her own ideas. My actual wedding bore no resemblance whatsoever to the original plans I had so carefully arranged. The perfect wedding dress? Gone—along with my hand-selected bridesmaids in matching dresses, the dream wedding cake, and all the other little details I had planned out so perfectly.

In place of my dream wedding was a simple ceremony that took place on May 20th, 1989, at the top of Mount Erie, presided over by a justice of the peace. It was as if a divine hand had swept away all that was not essential, reminding us that when everything is said and done, what makes a wedding magical is the love between two people, and the promises spoken out loud and sealed forever.

Whidbey Island has perfect weather for three months of the year—June, July, and August. During the other nine months, it is a rare day that does not see some sort of rainfall.

The day dawned crisp and clear. As we looked down from the mountaintop, we could see all the way to Puget Sound. It was easy to imagine a future as expansive and endless as the sea and sky. Spring had not yet given way to summer, so there was the last hint of a chill in the air.

For a wedding dress, I wore the dress I had originally purchased for the rehearsal. It was a crème-colored satin dress that hit right above the knee. Instead of our closest friends from back home witnessing our celebration, our witness was a local friend of Bill's (who also filled in as our wedding photographer) and my two new girlfriends, one of whom was kind enough to offer to open up her home for the party afterwards.

A world away, our families were totally unaware that we were about to exchange our vows. Of course, my parents would have wanted to be there to witness the wedding of their only daughter, and I knew Bill's parents would have also wanted to be there. Everyone was going to be heartsick when they found out they had not been there to share in such a momentous time in our lives.

During the ceremony, I was so caught up in the moment, I didn't feel the pain of their absence. It was not until I woke up on the first day of my married life that I felt a pit in my stomach, and regretted that our families had not been with us at the wedding.

I picked up the phone and called my mom. "Guess what?" I said.

Right away, she said, "You got married, didn't you?"

I just about dropped the phone. That motherly instinct at work!

"Mom!" I said. "How on earth did you know?"

"I don't know," she said. "I just knew."

Naturally, Mom was very disappointed and hurt that she and my dad had not been a part of my big day.

But, what could I have done? After Bill had canceled the first wedding, I was not about to plan wedding number two. What if, at the last minute, he freaked out again and decided to leave me at the altar? Or, what if he did go through with the wedding, but my loved ones were still furious with him for his cold feet the first time around? It would have made for a very unpleasant wedding day either way.

It had just seemed safer to elope—but that didn't change the sadness my parents and I felt over their absence at the wedding.

Someone else who missed my wedding was my soon-to-be-lifelong friend, Linda, who I'd met at work. As I mentioned, we had not yet known each other long enough for it to make sense for her to come to the wedding. But, our meeting was one of those acts of Fate. She was the wife of a doctor, and she worked in his office. One day, I walked in looking for a job. Luckily for me, they had just returned from a conference to discover that they were missing one office administrator. She walked out—and I walked in, and got hired on the spot.

I had really just been looking for something to fill my time, but within a year, Linda stepped down from her position and I became the office manager.

She ended up getting divorced, but later remarried. Bill and I were very close to her and her daughter, Mandy. They were originally from Missouri, so we had that connection right away. We watched Mandy grow up, and today, she is a mother of three children.

We left the island a year after Linda did. Over the years, we have maintained our friendship, and been there for each other in so many ways.

Anyway, after the wedding, Bill and I were trying to figure out how we could afford to go on a honeymoon. At twenty and twenty-one years old, we hadn't yet had much time to save. So, a couple of weeks after the wedding, we went to Las Vegas for a little four-day getaway. I could hardly believe that this guy who had been my rock and best friend for so long had now become my husband.

I was officially a "Mrs!"

We both agreed that since we were beginning our marriage so far from St. Louis, we should hold off on having children. Eloping to a mountaintop was one thing, but we weren't about to start a family without having our loved ones around us for the pregnancies and the births.

My enthusiasm for having children while Bill was still in the Navy was also dampened by watching other Navy wives with their children. I had witnessed enough heartbreaking scenes of crying children clutching at fathers who were leaving for sea duty. I couldn't watch my own children go through that kind of turmoil. And, I definitely didn't welcome the idea of essentially being a single parent while Bill was away.

So, we agreed—children were not going to happen until Bill was a civilian.

~1989~
Married with Dog(s)

"Enjoy the little things in life
for one day you may look back and realize
they were the big things."

~by Antonio Smith

When Bill was out on the ship, I wandered around our apartment, trying to find ways to stave off the loneliness. As I've mentioned, I had a few friends, but friendship only went so far. At night, when my new husband was away at sea, my friendships weren't enough to warm my home and heart.

What I needed was a dog!

Given the size of our apartment, Bill and I agreed that any dog we got had to be on the small side. I had grown up with a Pomeranian, and loved his temperament, and it just so happened that there was a Pomeranian breeder on the island. So, it was decided. A Pomeranian would be the perfect small dog for us. Somehow we would find a way to afford the Beverly Hills price tag for the breed.

After all, I had to do something about my feelings of isolation. I couldn't very well allow my Navy husband to return one day from the ship only to find that his poor wife had expired from loneliness.

One day, when Bill was home on leave, we went to the Pomeranian farm. We picked out our first baby—a loving ball of fluff—and named her Sonia. Bill seemed completely oblivious to the fact that Sonia was not a huge German Shepard, and treated her like the big dog she was at heart. He ran her on the beach and up and down the rocks, until her fur was wet and matted with sand, she was panting and yipping with excitement, and her tail was wagging furiously.

When Sonia was about six months old, I began to realize that there were certain things she needed that only another dog could give her. It was time to find her a companion of the nonhuman variety. So, when Bill was home on leave, we once again planned a visit to the Pomeranian farm.

As we were leaving to go get our new baby, I took Sonia's little face in my hands, let her give me a doggie kiss, and said, "You stay right here, Sweetie, and when we get home, Mommy will have a new little brother or sister for you, okay?"

I know, I know. But, we didn't yet have any kids, and I had to do something with my maternal instincts.

Sonia was a typical rust-colored Pomeranian. I wanted to be able, at a glance, to tell which dog was running through the neighbor's yard, chasing their cat, and eating their flowers, so I decided we needed one that was a different color.

"We have our hearts set on either an all-white or all-black one," we told the breeder.

"Oh, I'm so sorry," she told us. "I don't have any black or white ones."

Bill and I exchanged a look of disappointment.

"But," she said, "I do know of a breeder in Oregon with a litter of black pups."

So, off we went, on a drive that seemed to take forever, to pick up a puppy we had never seen. I couldn't even tell you what part of Oregon we visited. All I knew was that I felt like a typical little kid in the car, asking every five minutes, "Are we there yet?"

By the end of our visit, our dog had a darker little sister. They were my two French ladies—Sonia and Sheba.

When we weren't playing with the dogs, we tried to find other ways to entertain ourselves. We loved to drive around northern Washington. It was so beautiful, it inspired a lot of intimate moments between us. I'll never forget the tulip festival at a farm in Mt. Vernon. There were rows and rows of tulips in various colors, like rainbows painted in the fields. The scenery truly took my breath away, and Bill and I shared some tender moments.

He was always so good at making me feel special. He didn't mind public displays of affection, and when we were together, we would either be holding hands, or he would have his arm around me. He had a way of looking at me that made me feel like I was the only one around. Even in the midst of a breathtaking scene like the tulip festival, he only had eyes for me. One look from him, and I'd forget that fifteen minutes earlier we were bickering over something inconsequential.

Whenever I was annoyed with him for some reason, he'd pipe up and say, "You know what? I know of this beautiful place… let's go!" I loved those qualities in him.

Being at the festival was incredible—walking through huge fields with rows of tulips as far as the eye could see. We went to the festival both years that we lived in Washington, and we both loved it.

Of course, duty called, and our free time always took a backseat to Bill's responsibilities in the Navy. He was on a nuclear ship that was based out of Bremerton, Washington, and he would have to be flown from Whidbey Island to Bremerton to board his ship. Because he was aboard a nuclear vessel rather than just a battleship, everything was very specialized and secretive. When I think back on those days, I don't know how I dealt with it. I have so much admiration for military families today.

Eventually, Bill's time in the service began to wind down, and civilian life was just around the corner. So, what would the next chapter of our lives look like?

On the one hand, Bill really loved Washington. Had there been an opening in his rank in Washington—and had I been on board with the idea—he would have reenlisted. But, as far as I was concerned, Washington was just too far away. We needed to be closer to our loved ones if we were ever going to start a family.

What about Guam?

Guam?! Washington was already too far from St. Louis.

Needless to say, I said absolutely not—and the other Navy wives agreed with me. "Over there," they said, "the tarantula is considered a house spider!"

The Navy said, "Okay, fine. No Guam. How about Hawaii?"

There are plenty of people that would love to live in Hawaii—but not us. We had no intentions of being the typical Navy family, living on base. The military was Bill's job, but we wanted outside lives—and if we lived in Hawaii, the cost of living would have been so high that we would have had no choice but to live on base. Living on base would also have meant a six-month quarantine for our two dogs—who were more like our babies. That was not going to happen.

Looking at our options, Bill and I agreed that it was time for him to get out of the Navy and find something else to do. We made a plan—I would stay in Washington until Bill's discharge from the service. Then we would drive back to St. Louis together.

Before Bill could get out of the Navy, Desert Storm began.

We were constantly on pins and needles because we knew that if Bill didn't get released before the war really got underway, they might not let him out.

When his release date arrived, we packed up, anxious to return home and begin our new lives. Bill went and said his goodbyes to everyone. Then, just two hours shy of our departure time, he got a call, telling him he needed to report for duty. This was exactly what we had feared—but we took deep breaths and accepted it.

Off he went to the ship. The next day, he called me. "It was a test run. I'll be back tomorrow."

That kept happening, off and on, for two weeks. I found myself on an emotional roller coaster, courtesy of the United States Navy. Desert Storm got a lot of news coverage, and I could hardly turn on the TV without being reminded that my husband was in the middle of it all.

Every time I'd begin to hope that this was really it—we were finally going back home—he'd get called back again. I just about lost my mind.

What if we'd had children? What would we have said to them? "Listen, honey, Daddy's leaving. Oh, wait, Daddy's back now. Oh, sorry, honey, I was wrong. Daddy's leaving."

I was struggling emotionally, and it was hard on Bill to see me going through all that, so, finally, we decided to put me out of my misery. I would head home, and Bill would join me when he was released.

I was so happy to be going back to St. Louis. Washington had been wonderful in many ways, but as the saying goes…

~1993~
There's No Place Like Home

"Sometimes," said Pooh, "the smallest things
take up the most room in your heart."
"Winnie the Pooh"

~by A.A. Milne

W e were about three years into our marriage, living back in the St. Louis area, when we discovered that our first little bundle of joy was on the way. When we found out we were pregnant, we were awestruck and excited beyond words, but I was also terrified of the labor. It wasn't so much the agonizing pain that frightened me—it was the needle they would be using to give me the epidural. I felt faint every time I thought about it.

Before dawn on May 18th, well before the baby's due date, I woke up and didn't feel right. I thought I might be having contractions, and called my mom.

"Well," she said, "since the due date is still three and a half weeks away, you're probably just having Braxton-Hicks contractions. You might as well go on in to work. That will help keep your mind occupied. Believe me, if it's the real thing, you will be in labor forever. There will be plenty of time to get to the hospital."

Sounded good to me! The last thing I wanted to believe was that I was actually in labor. That was just too scary. So, Bill and I discussed it, and decided we'd both go to work.

Around eleven o'clock in the morning, I was sitting at my desk, and I started to feel damp. Luckily, I had been traveling with a bag of extra clothes, so I went into the bathroom at work to change.

The whole office was up in arms. "Oh, my God! Your water broke!"

30

"I don't think so," I said, still in denial, "I probably just wet myself a little bit from the baby pressing on my bladder."

When the contractions started getting worse, I decided maybe I'd better drive myself home. When I got there, I called Bill. "Don't get nervous, but… I think I'm in labor. People are telling me my water broke. But you don't have to leave work just yet."

By the time he walked in the door around three-thirty or four o'clock, I was anxious to get the show on the road. "Come on! Let's go!"

He started frantically searching the house.

"What are you doing?" I said. "We have to get going!"

He said, "But, we need the car seat! We can't leave without the car seat!"

"Why the hell not?" I asked.

He said, "Because we'll have no way to bring the baby home."

"Look," I said, "I'm going to be in the hospital for a few days. You can always bring the car seat later!"

He calmed down. "Oh, right" he said, laughing. "Good point."

We arrived at the hospital around four-thirty in the afternoon, and for over twelve hours, I was in excruciating pain.

My best friend, Randa, came to visit me. We had been friends since the fourth grade, when my family moved down the street from her grandmother. From the moment we first met, I found her fascinating. For one thing, she was one of my first friends to come from divorced parents. Not only that, she was raised by her dad instead of her mom. I could not get over the fact that she did not live with her mother. I had never heard of such a thing.

Randa's father, Larry, was a very sweet man, but a little bit over-protective when it came to his three girls, and especially his baby girl, Randa. So, any time we ever wanted to go to a concert, or do anything her dad might object to, Randa would say she was sleeping over at my house—but leave out the rest of the details. Then, we would run and beg my mom to keep our secret.

Now, you would not think that a man that objected to his daughter attending a concert would allow her to fly to Arkansas or Kentucky for the weekend, but he did—with him piloting the plane! By day, he was a typical businessman, a single father of three girls. But, every so often, he would slip into his superhero uniform and become this jetsetter, taking young Randa and me on amazing airplane adventures.

My mom never forbade me to go—but each time we returned safe and sound, she would get a cold shiver down her spine, and think to herself, "I don't know what in the world I am doing, letting my daughter go up in a tiny plane!"

Anyway, that's my Randa—best friend extraordinaire and honorary member of my family.

On that day, while I was in labor, she listened to me screaming in agony for so long, she finally left my room in tears, saying, "I am never, ever going to have children!"

When I was told I needed to be sitting up in order to get the epidural, I got myself into an Indian-style sitting position quicker than I'd managed to do anything in nine months, and looked pleadingly at the anesthesiologist, my new best friend (no offense, Randa).

Once he gave me the epidural, I was fine.

Bill managed to stay in the room during the entire labor and birth. Not only did he make it through the whole ordeal without fainting, he watched the baby emerge. Even I had not been able to watch what was going on below my waist.

It was a boy! When they placed the baby on my chest, Bill and I both started to cry. Thank God the baby was healthy. And, thank God the pregnancy and labor were finally over—and our little guy was finally with us.

Bill was overjoyed to be a father. He had a son! He was so proud and excited over his little boy. He couldn't get over how perfect he was—ten fingers, ten toes.

As for me, I was ecstatic. I couldn't take my eyes off our firstborn.

From the moment Bill and I first agreed that the time was right to begin our family, we knew that we wanted one of each—a boy and a girl. But, we also knew that we would love our babies regardless of the gender, and so we decided to let the gender be a surprise.

Because we didn't know the sex of the baby in advance, we had two names picked out. Had our little baby boy been a baby girl instead, her name would have been Chelsea. For a boy's name, both Bill and I liked the name Dylan. I think we got the idea from different TV characters, but it sealed the deal for me when I found out that the name means "sea of love." I thought that was so beautiful. For a middle name, we chose James—the middle name of Bill's father.

Bill was initially scared to death of fatherhood. As I've said, his own biological father was not there for him when he was young. Not having experienced that father-son relationship as a child, Bill was nervous about what kind of father he would be to his own son. He had no role model.

I assured Bill that he would do just fine as a father, and encouraged him to take it one day at a time.

Just when we were congratulating ourselves and thanking our lucky stars for a healthy baby, we had a big scare. Dylan's blood count was off. They had to do so many tests on our poor little baby, they ended up sending me home without him!

I cried hysterically as I was leaving the hospital without my child. I was holding balloons but no baby. I felt like everyone was looking at me, wondering what happened to my baby. When we got to the car, there was the car seat—but no baby to put in it.

I rested at home for exactly three hours, and then I wanted to get back to the hospital. Bill needed to go to work so he could save as much of his vacation time as possible for when the baby came home. So, he dropped me at the hospital, where I stayed all night, anxious about the results of the tests.

Whatever had worried the doctors turned out to be nothing, after all. The very next day, Bill and I were able to bring our baby home with us.

As much as we had enjoyed our years as a twosome, there were no words to describe how right it felt to finally have a child. It seemed like parenthood had been a lifetime in coming.

I was so excited to be a mother, it turned me into a nervous wreck. My baby was everything to me, and I would have done anything for him. I wanted so badly to do everything right—but I had never changed a diaper in my entire life. Even at the hospital, the nurses were the ones to change Dylan.

I was very thankful for Bill—a man who had experience babysitting his cousins. He took over, saying, "Don't worry! He's not going to break. But watch out! He is going to pee on you!"

Luckily for me, in those diaper-half-on-half-off moments, Dylan always aimed for his dad.

I seemed to have the opposite of post-partum depression. I was completely overjoyed with motherhood. And unlike mothers who wish their babies could stay little forever, I couldn't wait for Dylan to become a little person. "He's a cute baby," I would say, "but I'm ready for him to walk and talk!"

I looked forward to watching him develop his own personality, and I was anxious to get the whole process going. The idea that Bill and I were going to have an effect on the kind of person our son would become was thrilling to me.

While Dylan was our firstborn, he was really our fourth child—and I wasn't the only one to think so. Along with Sonia and Sheba, by this time we also had our Rottweiler, Nadia. All three of the dogs welcomed the new baby like he was literally the fourth member of the litter—who just happened to be a little late in joining the pack.

Before Dylan was born, people that didn't know Nadia were absolutely horrified to hear that I was planning on bringing a child home to a house with a Rottweiler in it. They would say to me, "You *are* planning to get rid of that dog, aren't you? Rottweilers are notoriously bad with kids!"

They may have been right, generally speaking, but they couldn't have been more wrong when it came to Nadia. The minute she set eyes on Dylan, she assigned herself as his protector, and it was a role she took as seriously as life and death. I could lay the baby down on a blanket, and she would position all ninety-five pounds of herself by his side. And, come hell or high water, she would not budge from her post.

In all fairness to my worried friends, I too, was somewhat worried about Nadia and the baby at the beginning. But, right away, she went into Dylan's room and lay down by his crib. If he moaned or cried out when he rolled over, she would jump up. Bill and I used to joke that she was the reincarnation of Nana from *Peter Pan*. We loved all Disney movies, especially *Peter Pan*, and we always had a soft spot for Nana—the canine housekeeper/nanny for the Darlings.

I slept very well, knowing that if (God forbid) anything happened to Dylan while he was sleeping, Nadia would be right by my side, waking me up to tell me.

I feel it's important to say that I am *in no way* recommending that you assign your Rottweiler to protect your child. I am not even suggesting that you should let your dog anywhere near your baby. We just happened to get lucky. But, I know that there have been plenty of truly tragic stories on the news of various breeds of dogs mauling small children.

Over time, Nadia would become Bill's dog. She came from a Rottweiler owned by his parents, and she seemed to sense a special family connection with Bill. When she was five, she would get a bad case of hip dysplasia. Our veterinarian told us that eventually, she would probably need surgery, but since the surgery would have to be performed out of town, we could treat it in the meantime with anti-inflammatory drugs. That's exactly what we did.

Any time it got cold outside, or there was an extreme weather change, her hip would act up, and we'd have to give her the medication. At one point, her condition started to quickly deteriorate until she could hardly walk. She lost a bunch of weight.

One day, Bill called me at work—sobbing.

He said he was home with Nadia and she could barely walk. She needed to see the vet. Bill knew the outcome was not going to be good, and he was broken up over it.

It touched my heart so deeply to hear a man crying hysterically over his dog. We had that in common—we really loved our dogs. But, many men would not let themselves be that vulnerable.

As for Nadia, the vet did end up having to put her down that day. Afterwards, Bill called me from the parking lot, crying. He told me that the doctor asked him if he wanted to be in the room while they gave her the injection, and he said "Absolutely not!"

The vet also wanted to know if he wanted her ashes. "No," Bill said, "just get her out of pain."

The kids came home from school, and the dog was gone. It was so hard for us to tell them that Nadia had been put to sleep. That was the first death they had ever experienced.

After her death, I kept hearing the jangling sound of her choker chain. What the heck was going on? I thought I was losing my mind. I knew full well that she was gone, and yet I could hear her, loud and clear.

Finally, one day, I asked Bill, "Do you hear Nadia's chain? I must be losing my mind because I keep hearing it!"

He gave me a sad, little boy look, and pulled her chain out of his pocket. "I've been carrying it around with me. I'm not ready to give her up."

That was such a sad memory because it involved losing Nadia, but it would live on inside my heart and become one of my favorite memories of Bill.

Anyway, between Bill, who was a natural born father, Nadia, who was a natural born protector, and I, who went instantly into the mother-protector mode before Dylan was ever born, we had the bases very well covered at home.

Four years later, we found out that our little boy was getting a sibling. This time, we asked the gender of the baby, so we knew we were having a girl. Our wish came true—one of each!

Unlike her brother who was born early, our little girl came late. It's just like a female to take her time getting ready, while the guys are rushing out the door before they've even finished putting on their shoes.

I was secretly pleased that she was overdue, because that put her into the month of April, and I liked the idea of her being a "diamond" baby. That was my favorite birthstone. The ob-gyn, however, wasn't thinking of birthstones, and decided it was time to induce labor.

I was a little bit crampy, but I hardly had any contractions—the opposite of my labor with Dylan.

I was in the same hospital room as I had been the first time. Randa couldn't be there that time, but she kept checking on me by phone. One of her phone calls happened to come in at the very moment the anesthesiologist was ready to insert the needle into my spine. When he heard the phone ring, he kicked the side table where the phone was sitting, and sent it flying. He yelled at the nurse, "That phone is supposed to be off the hook!"

When the phone fell to the floor, the receiver came off the hook. Randa could hear the scuffle, but she couldn't figure out what was going on, and hung up. I had to call her back later and explain what had happened.

Having an angry man poised to stick a needle in my spine totally freaked me out—and I was already freaked out over the idea of the needle. I had visions of ending up paralyzed. Thankfully, the injection worked out fine.

It was now a little bit before midnight, about four hours since I'd gotten the epi-pump, and for some reason, I was not dilating very quickly.

The doctor told Bill and my parents, "You may as well all go home. It looks like this is going to take awhile."

When the baby was finally ready to meet us, she became impatient. Again, it was just like a girl. She keeps you waiting, and then bursts into the room and takes your breath away with her loveliness.

Now I was madly dialing Bill and my parents. "Quick! Get back to the hospital! The baby is coming—now!"

Some mothers-to-be have their whole family in the delivery room with them. That's not my style. I'm very modest. But, she came so quickly, Mom didn't have time to join my dad in the waiting room. She was thrilled to death she got to be in the delivery room with Bill and me when the baby came.

As the baby emerged, the nurse caught her, took one look at her, and quickly whisked her away from me. The baby was silent.

"Wait!" I yelled. "Where is she going with my baby? I didn't even get to hold her!"

Bill took my hand and said, "It will be okay, Shell. It's not like the first time. The baby is blue. They have to take her away for a little while..."

Blue? What did that mean?

"She's not getting the oxygen she needs," Bill explained. "The cord is wrapped around her neck."

As the nurses cleaned me up, Bill and my mom went down to the nursery. Our little girl was in an incubator with an I.V. and an oxygen dome.

Everyone reassured me, "She will be fine. She just needs oxygen. They will bring her to you in the morning so you can feed her."

The next thing I knew, I was waking up in a sweat. It was the middle of the night. Through the fog of half-sleep, I heard the sound of industrial fans humming in the hallway. I rubbed my eyes, thinking, "What the hell...?"

Why was it so stuffy in the hospital? And where was my baby? I still had not even set eyes on her.

I was hot. I was sweaty. I was sick and tired of waiting to see my baby. I decided right then that I'd had just about enough of the whole situation. I got up and slowly made my way to the nursery. When I got there, the nurse told me that the air conditioning had gone out in the hospital. That explained the fans—but what had they done to my poor baby? She was hooked up to an I.V. with a splint on her tiny wrist, and she had an oxygen tube in her little nose!

Why hadn't someone told me my baby was this sick?

Suddenly I felt like I was going to faint—which was not surprising, considering that I wasn't even supposed to be out of bed. The pediatric nurses could see that I was sweating and dizzy, and they did their best to look after me while I had an emotional breakdown in the nursery.

Forty-eight hours later, on day three, our daughter came home with us.

As I said, from the moment we decided to have kids, we were dreaming of one of each. Once we'd had Dylan, Bill would often say, "Now I want a little girl just like you."

We couldn't believe she was finally here! Our perfect family—one boy, one girl—was now complete.

From the day she was born, she was Daddy's little princess. Had our little princess been a little prince instead, his name would have been Dalton. We would have had our two little outlaw boys—Dylan and Dalton.

When we found out we were having a girl, we knew her middle name would be Michelle, after me. We were tossed about a first name. For some reason, giving her the name we'd picked out for the first baby—Chelsea—didn't feel right. So, off I went to the grocery store to buy one of those baby name books you find at the checkout line.

I was sitting on the couch, flipping through it, and got to the letter "P." And there it was—Payton!

We both liked the fact that it wasn't a common name. Little did we know that within a few years, thanks to football great Peyton Manning, the name would become popular for both girls and boys. That's okay. Our Payton is one of a kind.

"You know," I said to Bill, as we sat at home, gazing at our beautiful little angel, "now that you have two girls in the house, you're going to have double the trouble!"

Bill laughed and said, "Don't I know it!" He was over the moon with his little girl. And she made it easy to adore her.

There is an old wives' tale that if you have one easy baby, the next baby will be difficult. Not in our case. Dylan was an easy baby—and so was his little sister.

Right off the bat, Payton adored her big brother. Within one week of coming home, she began to light up at the sound of his voice.

He loved her every bit as much, and had no problem at all adapting to the fact that he was no longer the only child in the house. He was so attentive, jumping up to run and get a clean diaper, grab her binky, or get her swing going again. Anything to keep her happy.

Just like I did, Bill loved every second of parenthood. He was so proud of his family. Whenever he talked to anyone, he bragged about his healthy, perfect children. We were now a foursome, with our new home, and the white-picket-fence life we had dreamed about for so long.

~1999 to 2003~
Happiness on Wheels

"Don't look back,
A new day is breakin'
It's been too long since I felt this way,
I don't mind where I get taken,
The road is callin'
Today is the day…"
"Don't Look Back"

~by Tom Scholz (Boston)

Y ou might think it would be hard to look back upon the life we shared as a family and single out the most precious among all the memories we made day in and day out, year after year, for twenty years. But, the four of us agreed that the happiest time of our lives was when we were involved in BMX racing.

BMX racing is like motorcycle racing—except on bicycles.

Bill grew up riding both dirt bikes and street bikes. Street bikes scare me, and I have always been very timid around them. But, motorcycles were his passion, and once we were together, he often talked about wanting to buy one.

"I'll tell you what," I said one day. "I'll make you a deal. When you turn forty, we'll get you a Harley."

"Forty?" he said. "Why forty?"

"Because by then," I said, "I'll feel a little more relaxed about it."

In other words, I figured that by the time a person hit forty, they would have reached the height of their maturity, and be totally responsible—which meant there would be less chance of an accident.

Of course, I didn't say any of that. Instead, I said, "And by then, we will probably have more money!"

Bill went along with the plan, contenting himself in the meantime with his dirt bikes. Even though we initially agreed that Bill would get his Harley when he turned forty, he would end up getting it a couple of years early. When Bill was thirty-eight, his father happened to be selling his own Harley for a reasonable price. Since it was his dad's bike, we both felt good about the purchase. I relented, not insisting that Bill wait for the big four-o.

I knew he was a great rider, and I trusted him one hundred percent to be responsible and safe. I wasn't at all concerned about him being reckless. It was the other drivers that worried me—the ones on the road who don't respect people on motorcycles. That's why I never liked to ride with him on the highway. I was too scared. There were only so many places you could go without getting on the highway, so over the years, I didn't get asked to go on many of his rides.

Anyway, one day he came to me and said, "I'm thinking I'd like to get Dylan involved in motocross."

My response was something along the lines of, "Are you kidding me? We can't put our six-year-old on a dirt bike!"

"Well…" he said, thinking on his feet. "If you don't like the idea of a dirt bike, how about a *regular* bike? You know—BMX racing!"

With BMX, they still race around a dirt track and do jumps, only there are no motors involved.

A bicycle sounded much more appropriate for a young boy. It also seemed like a better fit with our environment. We lived in the suburbs, not out in the country, where a kid had room to ride a dirt bike.

BMX sounded great—simple and easy. Most things do in theory. It's only when you get right into the middle of something that you see what you've really gotten yourself into. Not that it was a bad thing—not at all. It became the most fulfilling and engrossing thing we ever did as a family. But, we could not have imagined the extent to which the sport would take over our lives when we walked into our local bicycle shop, intending to buy our six-year-old boy his first racing bike.

As his two-year-old little sister looked on in amazement, Dylan checked out all the different bikes, getting more excited by the minute. Bill was already amped up, imagining all the father-son fun they were going to have.

The shop owner must have seen us coming a mile away. "You know," he said, "we have been wanting to organize a BMX team of local boys to represent and promote the shop…"

Bill didn't even pretend to stop and think about it. He loved the idea right off the bat. Why not? He had experience racing cycles, which gave him the technical expertise to really support his son in the sport. He would be able to work on Dylan's bike with him, fix it when it broke, and engage in intelligent conversations with bike shop owners. He and Dylan would have a blast, and it would be easy for me to bring Payton with us to watch the races.

I thought it had all the makings of a good family sport, and I wasn't disappointed. Families from all over the region came to St. Peters to race at our track. I had no idea it was so popular.

Bill became the team coach. I became the organizer/manager. And, BMX became the center of our lives.

We saw how profoundly racing touched the lives of the kids involved, and we wanted to offer that opportunity to a few kids who didn't have the financial means to participate in the sport. Within a few months, thanks to an infusion of our own cash flow to keep it afloat, we had our own team.

Dylan caught on to the sport quickly, and started making friends at the track. The team began to travel a little bit, and soon, we had become more than just a neighborhood team, racing locally. As we traveled more, word got around, and soon Bill was making connections and meeting BMX people all over the country.

One of those meetings was a game-changer. We were at a race in Texas when Bill met Norm, who was revered inside the BMX community for his team, the Outlaws, and occasionally recognized for a cameo in the popular movie, *Urban Cowboy.*

"Listen," Norm said to Bill, "here's how I see it. You've got yourself a great little team there. I've got connections, and a team name that really means something to people, especially here in Texas and Oklahoma. If you want to take things to the next level, the Outlaws name can only help. If you'll assemble a team called the Outlaws and help me get recognized in the Midwest, we can join forces to our mutual benefit."

It sounded like a win-win to Bill. Norm had the experience, the reputation, and the team name—and was offering great discounts on parts. Now, all Bill had to do was up the ante and start recruiting kids with the skill, the commitment, and the kinds of parents that would be willing to let them travel all over the country. We were often away on weekends, but even when we weren't out of town, we were at the local track practically every day.

We became the Outlaws, and Bill continued working with the kids. Things picked up steam very quickly. The team kept getting better, and the better they got, the more notoriety they received. All the members of our team received very good rankings, both at the district and the national level.

Many local kids wanted to be part of our team, but we could only take so many. At one point, we had seven members on the team, and went out and bought a conversion minivan with built-in TV.

Because Payton was only three years old around the time we began traveling heavily, we couldn't always take her along to out-of-town races. The days were long, weather and lodging conditions were sometimes less than ideal, and being on the road was hard on a toddler. Sometimes, it just made more sense to let her spend some time with my parents until we returned from the road. Nanny and Papa were always happy to have her with them.

Since we didn't always have our little princess with us, it was nice to have Jodi along. She was the only girl on our team, and the daughter of a single dad named Steve, who helped Bill manage the team. I was the team mother, keeping everyone in line, and making sure we didn't get kicked out of hotels and restaurants. And Payton was the team mascot, our little miss sunshine. Everyone loved her.

On our team were kids of all different ages, racing in different classes. Of course, we could only accommodate so many kids on our particular team, but we helped attract many kids to the organization. It made our local track very happy to see hundreds of kids getting involved in the sport.

Bill and I were in agreement that we wanted to do more than teach kids about BMX, and help fund the sport. We wanted to teach kids what it really meant to be a team. Just as we were devoted to family life at home, we carried those same values to the track. Many of the kids had uninvolved, unsupportive parents—the type that would say, "Fine, here's the money you need. Now go away."

So, a big part of our mission was to foster character building and self-esteem in the riders.

We tried to really give them a good foundation for their lives, and to teach them good habits and coping skills. I was the positive one, always trying to boost them up. Whenever they were struggling, I would just pull out one of my many little aphorisms, like "practice makes perfect." In the moment, they may have found it annoying, but years later, I would find out that we had really made a difference in their lives.

We also taught the kids that it wasn't enough to practice; they had to also take pride in their local track. The whole sport was a nonprofit endeavor, and it relied entirely on volunteers. "This is not just a joy ride," we told the riders. "You're out there doing your dirt jumps, and it takes its toll on the track. If we don't maintain the track ourselves, it's not going to get done."

As the kids were out on the track, grumbling under their breath, they were learning values and skills that would serve them throughout their lives.

As for Jodi, our only female on the team, she was treated like one of the boys—for better and for worse!

Year-round for four incredible years, we were lucky enough to live and breathe BMX motocross as a family. It was so bonding to all have the same interests, and to each have our roles to play. It was the first activity that we did consistently as a family, and over the years, it was easy to see how it brought us closer, and how much we grew from it.

The Grand Nationals—the BMX equivalent of the Olympics or the Superbowl—was held every year in Tulsa, Oklahoma. Dylan's first big race took place there during the first year we were involved in the sport.

In BMX, the riders race around a track in a circle, as the parents scream and yell encouraging instructions to their children, like, "Pedal! Pedal!" As if they couldn't figure that out without our help. There was Dylan, still such a young tyke, racing his heart out, his little legs pedaling as fast as they could possibly go.

Up in the stands, I was thrilled, watching him pass all these other riders. I was screaming so loudly, I'm sure people thought I had lost my mind. Bill, meanwhile, was down on the track, waiting for Dylan to cross the finish line.

He came in third!

I ran down to meet them, balancing my video camera against my shoulder. Bill and I were trying to explain to Dylan that he had won third place. He was only six years old at the time, and just glad that he had finished the race and won something. He couldn't believe his eyes when he saw the enormous trophy.

"You see?" I said. "All your hard work paid off!"

It was a good thing we had the trailer with us. The trophy was so big, we wouldn't have been able to transport it home in the car.

Bill and I were grinning from ear to ear. Our six-year-old had won third place. We were probably more excited than he was—until he found out he could take the trophy to school with him.

"Can I really, Mom? Really?" He was practically jumping up and down.

"Sure, honey," I said, "you can take it to school. We just have to figure out how you're going to carry it."

In that moment, I was so delirious with happiness, I probably would have agreed to anything.

Bill was proud to see his son do so well in his first big race—and I was proud to see that side of Bill. He was the one who had brought everyone together, and it was heartwarming to see him have his moment of glory with his own son.

Jodi also did very well in that race. So did Johnny, who would end up coming to live with us for a year, and figure prominently in our lives years later.

I knew that as long as Dylan wanted to keep racing, our family would stay involved in the sport. BMX was the central thing that tied us all together, and the togetherness it brought to our family was priceless. We created a close bond, and became the strongest we'd ever been as a family.

I'm sure the fact that Bill came from a broken family helped him understand the struggle the BMX kids went through. And, it drove him to put ten times more love and energy into helping them than someone else might have under different circumstances. It made me proud and happy to see him making a difference.

Dylan may have only been six at that time, but Johnny was sixteen, so, before we knew it, he was all grown up. When Jodi and Johnny came back into our lives as adults, it was an amazing moment. But I don't want to get ahead of myself here.

In 2004, Dylan decided to stop doing BMX. We all agreed that it was time for him to try something different, so he chose football—and hated it.

We knew that he didn't like it, but we wanted him to finish the season. "Dyl," we said, "you can't quit in the middle of something!"

Even though we encouraged him to see it through, every day, we half expected him to walk in and tell us he'd quit.

One night after practice, he came home very upset, and started telling us how much he hated playing in the hot summer sun while wearing all that football padding.

Bill went upstairs to talk to him. Here's how Dylan remembered the moment: "Dad was trying to give me a life lesson. When I got up my nerve to tell him I didn't want to play football anymore, he went into a speech about how I was old enough to make my own decisions and let people know what I liked and didn't like. Then, he told me that he was happy I was not being a follower because I would be better off with my life and my dreams if I could think for myself. He also told me that if I did the right things, good things would follow. Maybe in the moment I wouldn't know what they were, but I needed to trust. And he reminded me to learn from my mistakes."

I thought they were upstairs talking about football. I had no idea Bill had gone into his whole philosophy of life with Dylan. It made quite an impression on Dylan, who would treasure it as one of his favorite memories of his dad.

~1993 through 2008~
The Holiday Spirit

"O' holy night,
The stars are brightly shining...
A thrill of hope
The weary world rejoices,
For yonder breaks a new and glorious morn..."
"O' Holy Night"

~by Placide Clappeau (Celine Dion)

Christmases were always a very special holiday in our family. Traditionally, we put up our tree the weekend after Thanksgiving. By Christmas Eve, the tree would be surrounded by so many presents for the kids, it looked like something out of a children's book illustration.

At first, Bill was overwhelmed by my approach to Christmas. He had come from an entirely different family environment, and the holidays evoked sadness for him.

I explained to him that in my family, everyone loves to give, so there have always been a lot of gifts at Christmas—and a lot of family around. I helped him understand how important it was to me to have our children grow up feeling the true holiday spirit of love, family, togetherness, and the joy of giving.

Over time, Bill became comfortable with my family's way of celebrating Christmas. He even came to accept and enjoy my family's birthday tradition where my mother cooks the birthday person's favorite meal—no matter how old they are. The only thing Bill insisted on was that I never, ever throw him a surprise party. I knew he wasn't kidding, either, so I had to honor his wishes.

As the financial planner in the family, I was the one who knew how much money it was safe to spend on Christmas, so it made sense that I would do most of the shopping. But, being a big kid himself, Bill never liked to let the season pass without joining me for at least one day of shopping.

When Dylan and Payton were small, and Santa Claus was still delivering the presents, Santa always left the gifts unwrapped around the tree.

"Wait a minute," Bill said in the beginning. "Why aren't we wrapping the kids' presents? I don't get it."

"Well, the presents from Santa are never wrapped," I explained, as if this should have been perfectly obvious. "They just sit around the tree."

"But, why not?" he persisted.

I said, "That's just how we've always done it in my family. Haven't you ever seen a picture of an old-fashioned Christmas? Well, you notice how you can always see what the presents are—all the toys and everything? That's because the elves don't wrap presents."

He gave me a look like, you've got to be kidding me, and said, "The elves don't wrap."

I said, "Nope. The elves don't wrap."

"Okay, Shell," he said, shaking his head and laughing. "If you say so."

I wanted our kids, while they were still very young, to have the experience of coming downstairs on Christmas morning and being able to see all the gifts Santa left under the tree. Those were some of my best memories of my own childhood, and they were the times I most enjoyed with the kids—the years before they stopped believing in Santa Claus.

When Santa did disappear from our lives, the kids' wish lists magically appeared. They were not little sticky notes with one or two things written on them, either. The kids always presented us with multi-page wish lists for Christmas. Who could blame them? They took us seriously when we taught them, "It is better to give than receive." They were really just trying to make sure their parents experienced the joy of giving at the highest possible level.

No matter how much Dylan and Payton may have enjoyed opening their gifts each year, it was plain to see that Bill and I were the happiest ones of all.

Now that the unwrapped Santa gifts had vanished from the tree, we had to wrap everything. I used a color-coded wrapping system. For example, maybe one year all of Dylan's gifts were wrapped in green paper, and all of Payton's in red. That way, at a glance, they would be able to say to themselves, wow, all those gifts in red, or green, are for me! It was very magical.

As they grew, Dylan and Payton became nosy rosies, sneaking around the house, trying to figure out where we'd hidden everything. Our bedroom was off limits to them, so I hid things under the bed and in the closets. But it didn't matter how ingenious I thought I was, the kids were always one step ahead of us. I even took to hiding things in trash bins in the basement. It made no difference. Our little super-sleuths would hunt them down, open them, and then rewrap them—as if I couldn't tell the difference between their wrapping job and mine!

It was easier when they believed that all the gifts magically appeared on Christmas Eve via sleigh and reindeer. Those were the good old days, when no hiding was necessary.

Bill and I never exchanged gifts with each other; our entire Christmas budget went towards the kids. But, in 2006, Bill surprised me.

"There's one more present," he said, matter-of-factly, after the kids had finished opening all of their gifts. "Go look around the tree."

I immediately got upset, and said, "We're not supposed to buy each other gifts!"

"Go on," he insisted. "Look around."

I got up slowly, my eyes focusing on the piles of wrapping paper sitting on the floor.

"Shell," he said, "it's right in front of you!"

Then I saw it, hanging from the tree, where apparently it had been hidden in plain sight all morning. It was a diamond bracelet, and it was beautiful. I was in total shock. Tears sprang to my eyes.

Bill came and stood by my side. "I squirreled away a little bit of my overtime pay," he explained, smiling and happy to see me so touched by his gift to me. He lifted it off the tree branch and fastened it around my wrist.

I was speechless, tears rolling down my cheeks.

"You deserve this," he said, kissing me. "I love you!"

"Thank you," I said, hugging him, and getting his shirt all wet from my tears.

"Oh, Daddy," Payton exclaimed. "That is so sweet!"

Dylan looked up from playing with his toys and gave me one of his signature grins.

When Christmas of 2008 rolled around, I decided it was time we start a new tradition: My parents, the kids, Bill, and I would each write down on a card three strengths, or three things we admired, about the rest of us. My vision was that once the cards were all written, they would be placed in a box. Throughout Christmas Day, anytime someone wanted to feel the Christmas spirit, they could just wander over to the box, pull out a card, and see what each person had written about them.

The three things about Payton that Bill praised on the card were, "Her effort, stylish, and loving." And for her dad, Payton wrote, "So funny, makes me happy, and drives good on a motorcycle."

About Dylan, Bill wrote, "Willingness to try hard, thoughtful, and hard working." And for his dad, Dylan wrote, "Cool, leader, loving, always there."

And to my loving husband, who wrote that he considered me "strong-minded, loving, and giving," I wrote, "I love you for being proud of your family, being a hard worker, for our life together so far, and for all we have learned together."

My parents and Bill also wrote sweet things to each other, and all the way around, the writings were very touching. I was glad I had come up with the idea.

Bill was in his element on Christmas morning, cooking a feast fit for a king, a queen, and a little prince and princess. Eggs, bacon, sausage, hash browns, mimosas (not for the kids, of course), and chocolate chip pancakes. If it could remotely be considered a breakfast food, it was included.

And that was what our Christmas Day always looked like—the whole family hanging out, eating, drinking, laughing, talking, reminiscing, and enjoying each other.

That, for us, was the Christmas spirit. I was raised Protestant, and Bill grew up Lutheran, but neither of us really went to church, or raised the kids with any religious practice in particular. The one belief our family shared, and practiced religiously, was "family first." That was the creed we lived by.

The one exception to our secular lifestyle came every year right before Christmas, when we began to pray our hearts out that we would not have a white Christmas. That's right—we prayed we would *not* have a white Christmas. While everyone else on the block was crossing their fingers and praying for that sparkling white blanket of snow, our family had visions of bone dry streets dancing in our heads.

Why? Well, Bill was employed by the City of St. Peters as part of the snow plow crew, and the last thing we wanted was for him to be called in to work on Christmas Eve or Christmas morning.

For most of our years together, we got lucky. Only once or twice did Bill end up showing up a little bit late for our Christmas celebration because he had to work. When Bill did have to work on Christmas, we woke the kids up at three o'clock in the morning, so we could have Christmas morning with them before he had to go into work. There Bill would be, yawning but happy, perfectly willing to go into work half-asleep, as long as it meant he could share Christmas morning with his family.

~July 1st, 2009~
The End of an Era

"...You may ask yourself, what is that beautiful house?
You may ask yourself, where does that highway lead to?
You may ask yourself, am I right, am I wrong?
You may say to yourself, my God, what have I done?
Letting the days go by..."
"Once in a Lifetime"

~by Eno/Harrison/Byrne/Weymouth/Frantz (Talking Heads)

S o, there you have it—a glimpse of the twenty years of marriage that led up to that fateful night on July 1st, 2009, when I returned from work to find that my husband wanted a divorce.

You're driving down the road with someone, sitting in the passenger seat beside them for two decades, and suddenly they drive the car up to the edge of a cliff. And, only *they* can flip the gear shift in reverse and back up the car. Only *they* can keep the car from going over a cliff.

All *you* can do is close your eyes, say a prayer, and hope for the best. But, upstairs in my room, rehashing everything, and trying to make sense of it all, I had little hope that Bill would change his mind. He was as serious as a heart attack about wanting a divorce.

What had happened? What was I missing here?

Saturday, Bill didn't want to drive the RV full of girls to gymnastics camp. Then, Sunday, he went for his Harley ride and didn't bother to check in with me. Then, I left town, and when I returned, he told me that our marriage was completely over for him.

All of it felt out of the blue to me—and that was the thing that stuck like an arrow in my heart. I kept asking myself, *how in the world could I have missed this?*

We had always talked about how lucky we were to be married. We would often kid around, saying, "You are stuck with me forever, you know. I'm not going to get out there and play the singles game."

It was almost a pact between us—whatever struggles we had to weather, we would get through them together. "I am stuck with you, and you are stuck with me." That was the sentiment. We planned to retire, sell everything, buy an RV, and travel across the United States.

What happened to the guy that wanted to live out his days behind the wheel of a giant RV, with me as his co-pilot? Where did he go?

And how could he just disregard the effect our divorce was going to have on our kids? The mere idea of their parents traveling around without them in an RV at some far off point in the future caused them to get anxious. "But, what about our Christmases? How will we celebrate if you're on the road? And what if we need you and we can't find you?"

We always reassured them in those moments, saying, "Don't be silly! Of course, you will be able to reach us—and we will always come back!"

Bill seemed to turn so quickly. Yet, if I really thought about it, maybe it had happened more gradually than I realized. I started to remember various incidents over the previous two years, where he had become more selfish, and less family-oriented. He was no longer as inclined to ignore his own personal needs.

If he had a bike weekend planned, for example, and we had a family lake weekend planned, he went motorcycle riding. In those cases, I didn't even know about his personal plans until the last minute.

Whenever those occasions arose, we would bicker—me, with my strong family background, and him, with his divorced family background.

I would say, "No! Your family has to come first," but in the end, I backed down.

We also had a friend named Chris, who raced stock cars. Bill was his pit crew. During the week, Bill often went to Chris's shop and helped Chris work on the race car. Every Friday night, they went somewhere to race. It was a hobby for Bill, and Chris always appreciated the help.

I went to watch Chris race—but only twice. I sat there the entire time with my stomach in my throat, and my heart racing as fast as the cars. It was too much for me to watch someone I knew race around a track, knowing they could wreck at any second. The minute the race started, I instantly went into panic attack mode. I never understood until I went, myself, why Chris's own wife had trouble watching him race.

Bill would have loved to have his own race car, but I would not stand for it, and he finally accepted that it was never going to happen. At least he could enjoy helping Chris with his car. Working with cars was also something Bill could share with Dylan. It was great father-son time for them, and I encouraged it.

The first time Bill took Dylan along with him to Chris's shop to work on the race car, Dylan was in heaven. He thought it was the coolest thing ever, to have his dad including him in his race car world. Dylan would always remember that first time with his dad at Chris's shop as one of the highlights of his life. And, he would make a pact with himself to try to one-up his dad and learn more about cars than his dad ever knew. Funny enough, he would succeed!

I didn't begrudge Bill his car racing hobby any more than I resented his motorcycle time—until the past few years when his hobbies began to interfere with family time. By the last year, even the kids were speaking up when Bill would decide to go riding or to a race with Chris, instead of coming with us to the lake. They would say, "Oh…Dad's not coming *again?* He is going riding again? Or racing with Chris?"

As I remembered more of those kinds of incidents, I started wondering whether I should have taken a stronger stand when Bill claimed the right to his personal time. I wondered if my willingness to be flexible at those times had sent the wrong message. Maybe I had set a precedent where he came to expect that ninety-eight percent of the time, I would acquiesce, and he would get to do whatever he wanted to do.

What else could I have done but relent? If I insisted he join us on a particular family outing, he pouted the whole time—which ruined it for the rest of us. So, the next time, I would say, "Fine. Go do your own thing."

I wondered what would have happened if I'd put my foot down and said, "Look, as you know, I believe that family comes first. If you no longer share those values, maybe we need to take a look at this situation." Maybe we would have had a knock-down-drag-out fight, gotten some things out in the open, and cleared the air before it was too late.

Playing Monday morning quarterback was not getting me anywhere. The fact was, my marriage was broken, and I had no idea how to fix it. I was so lost, confused, and heartbroken, it was almost unbearable. I was drained of emotion and I felt limp.

That night—July 1st—Bill slept downstairs.

Dylan happened to be at a friend's house, and Payton was still away at gymnastics camp.

As for me, I barricaded myself in my room. I must have eventually fallen asleep due to emotional exhaustion. When I woke up, I was still in my clothes from the night before.

The morning of July 2nd, we were both miserable. We could not even look at each other. I could barely function. I had to give myself a pep talk, reminding myself that I had no other choice—I had to go to work; I had to pay the bills.

We said a perfunctory goodbye to each other, and went our separate ways. As I got in the car, I was in a daze, still trying to figure out what had happened. In my state of mind, I absolutely could not deal with anybody's questions, so I decided to wait to tell everyone until after Bill and I talked that night. I would have a better sense of the big picture by then.

I only had a fifteen minute drive to work, but even that amount of time alone in the car was hard to take. I felt so alone. Bill had been my best friend for twenty-four years. Sure, I still had Randa, and other girlfriends I could count on, but it wasn't the same thing. The heartbreak was so heavy—and then the anger set in.

For so many years, I devoted my life to building a strong family. I did everything in my power to make sure my children knew that family was everything. Our entire marriage, I had worked really hard. Everything I earned went towards the family. I sacrificed all the time, rarely doing anything for myself. I earned more than Bill did, but since he worked for the city, he got great benefits. We used to joke that I brought home the bacon, and he brought home the grease.

When I arrived at work, I had to really struggle to pull myself together. I had just started the job in January, so I was still relatively new, and I didn't want to jeopardize my position. Now, more than ever, I was going to need the paycheck. I couldn't believe I was about to be a single mom.

As the Accounts Receivables Manager, I have my own office. I had never been more grateful for the ability to seclude myself. Since everyone at work knew it was my habit to keep to myself, no one was likely to think it strange if I didn't interact too much that day.

Sitting there at work, I was struck by the fact that everything happens for a reason. For seventeen years straight, I had been employed as the Director of Operations of another company. Had I not left that high-stress job in January, I would have had to manage all the stress related to my old job, and the trauma of a divorce, all at the same time. Clearly a divine hand was at work.

I forced myself to focus on work. Every time a thought intruded, I ignored it. Over the years, I had mastered the art of turning a blind eye to things.

Did I really want Bill to get a motorcycle? No, probably not. Did I agree to it and accept it, anyway? Yes. How did I deal with him having the bike? It worried me—so I ignored it.

That is just one example of my ability to compartmentalize. There were many things I blocked out during our years together. Sometimes, it was just easier to ignore something than deal with it. That's exactly what I decided to do that day. I didn't really have any choice. I had to keep it together in order to get my work done.

Bill did not make his usual call to me that day. It was fine with me. He was ignoring me, and I didn't particularly want to talk to him either.

Somehow, I made it through the work day. As I was leaving work, I started to feel like I couldn't breathe. What was going to happen when I got home and saw Bill? And how were we going to talk with Dylan in the house? Thank God, Payton was still away at gymnastics camp.

We absolutely had to face this and talk about it again. I couldn't imagine how we were going to have that conversation with Dylan in the house. In their entire lives, the kids had only seen us argue once or twice.

I had a breakdown on the way home, and sobbed all the way to our driveway. I knew I would, and took a different route home so I could avoid the neighbors.

When I arrived home, Bill was already there, sitting at the computer. During the past year, he had spent a lot of time playing computer games and visiting chat rooms. By some miracle, Dylan—who was starting his summer job the following week—decided to go hang out with his friends while he still had the chance. So, we lucked out, and didn't have to put up a front for him.

I took a seat in the family room, where I could see Bill, who was at the computer, but not be right in his face.

While I was still terribly hurt and confused, I managed a much calmer tone than I had the night before. I said, "We've got to talk some more. I still don't really understand, and I have lots of questions."

Thankfully, Bill was willing to talk.

I started the ball rolling by asking him, "How do you tell someone you love them but not as a wife? What does that mean?"

"Well," he said, taking a deep breath, "I will always care for you, and take care of you whenever you need me. But I love you more as a friend—not in the way a husband should love his wife."

My heart crumbled when he said that, and I started to cry. "Being told you're not loved like a wife anymore and not sexually attractive to your husband… I don't even have words to describe the way that makes me feel. I don't understand how you can feel that way. My feelings are nothing like that…"

He shrugged his shoulders, clearly at a loss as to what to say.

I went on. "And, what did you mean, anyway, when you said we didn't really have anything in common, anymore? Do you mean because I was scared to go on highway rides on the Harley?"

Riding on the highway on the back of Bill's Harley *did* scare me half to death, but any time he invited me, I swallowed my fears and went anyway. I figured, he was inviting me into his world, and I should go. Apparently, when I did join Bill on those rides, both he and his friends could tell I was frightened and uncomfortable. A couple of times, a friend of his commented that I didn't seem to be having a very good time.

I said, "Is that why you hardly ever asked me—because you and your friends could tell that I was scared and uncomfortable? I would have come with you more often if you had asked more often!"

That is when Bill admitted that he didn't really *want* me along when he went on his rides. The Harley was his world, and I was never going to be able to join him there.

"Oh," I said, frustrated, "so that was a no-win situation for me. Even if I hadn't been scared of the highway, you would have found another reason not to invite me."

"You're right," he said. "I'm sorry for making it seem like it was your fault that we didn't have that in common…"

The truth was, he didn't really want us to have that in common.

"Those are small things," I said. "None of that seems like enough of a reason to throw away twenty years of marriage and family without trying counseling first. I still can't understand why you are calling it quits so abruptly."

He looked down at the floor, then back at me. "I just don't want the responsibility of a family anymore."

How long had he been feeling that way?

"I don't get it," I said. "How can you turn off and on like that? It is beyond my comprehension."

"I can't do anything on my own, and it's making me feel suffocated," he explained. "I don't want the family responsibility anymore."

I was speechless. I could not believe the words coming out of his mouth. He had to have lost his mind.

"Bill," I said, "how can you say such a thing? You signed up to get married and have kids. This is all part of it! Less than three weeks ago, we were daydreaming about how we would spend our golden years after the kids are off on their own. Now, suddenly, your switch is turned off? What happened to you?"

It was clear that he was becoming more aggravated by the minute. "You will never understand," he said, getting up and walking away.

I was every bit as frustrated as he was—and maybe more so because I didn't have any idea what was going on inside of him. "Wait!" I said. "I need to ask you one more question. You are telling me for sure there's not another woman, right?"

He assured me that there was no other woman—and I had no reason to doubt him. We had always promised each other that if either one of us was ever tempted, we would let the other one know before things went too far. I knew something was not right with Bill, but I believed him when he told me there was not another woman.

I had never had a trust issue with him—except for one period of time fourteen years earlier. We had gone through a big crisis because he had gotten involved with cocaine use.

I didn't have a clue that he was in trouble. How could I? I had never been around hard drugs in my life, and wouldn't have recognized the warning signs. I might never have been the wiser had I not started receiving strange phone calls from bill collectors and banks, calling to tell me that checks were bouncing all over town.

Being the meticulous bookkeeper I was, I started yelling at the bank representative. "Look," I said, "I keep very detailed records, and I am telling you that you are crazy—you have to have made a mistake related to our account!"

They swore up and down that the discrepancy was not their fault, so I confronted Bill. When I did, it came to light that he'd used one entire paycheck to buy cocaine. Dylan was just a toddler at the time and we lived on a tight budget. We couldn't afford for him to be spending his money on drugs.

I was beside myself. I told Bill to get the f*** out of the house. Then I called my parents and borrowed enough money to help cover the outstanding checks I had written.

Things went from bad to worse for Bill. He had to move in with his mother for awhile, and ended up losing his job. (It was only later that he went to work for the City of St. Peters.) Bill's parents—his mother, stepmother, and father—interceded, letting him know that he had better get his act together.

He stayed with his mother for about a month. Then we realized we had to try to work it out. "I will never forget this," I told him. "But I will learn to forgive you and trust you again."

It was not a simple matter for Bill to regain my trust once he broke it, but I was committed to working things out. We were a family, and I wasn't going to give up on us. It took years, but he really did regain my trust. The fact that he never touched drugs again helped me feel like I was on solid ground with him once more—that and the fact that, once he started working for the City of St. Peters, he was subjected to random drug testing. I found that to be very reassuring.

We moved on from that incident, and had another child—our little angel, Payton—a couple of years later. Everything went back to normal.

Now, there I was again, questioning him about something that just did not add up for me. I was fairly sure—again, thanks to the City of St. Peter's practice of randomly drug-testing its employees—that drugs were not involved this time. After all, Bill was often the guy who was chosen for random testing.

So, if drugs were not behind his bizarre change of heart, then what?

"You are sure," I repeated, one more time, "there is no other woman."

"No!" he said. "You know we have an agreement that we would never do that to each other."

The conversation ended with us agreeing that we needed to tell the kids, and not that we were merely separating, either. Bill was dead set on divorce. What in the world were we going to say to them?

We decided that before we told the kids, we needed to take some time to figure out what we were going to do. Bill had no plan—and for the first time in our lives, I was not going to give him his plan. He wanted freedom without responsibility. Well, fine. Then he could figure it out.

My only suggestion was, "Just remember that the kids are going to need to know that you have some kind of a plan. You don't want them to see you panicked or they will panic."

We also had to take into consideration the fact that Dylan had a trip planned for the weekend following the Fourth of July. He and some buddies were planning to go to my parents' house at the Lake of the Ozarks (where we all usually spent the Fourth of July), and spend the weekend there. Dylan had just recently turned sixteen, which meant he was finally of legal age to do the driving. I remembered what it was like when I was sixteen years old and finally able to drive, and I didn't want to ruin that for him by dropping a bombshell right before they left.

It was decided—we would tell the kids after Dylan returned from the lake. That gave us time to plan how we were going to handle things, but it also meant we had to put up a front for a week.

We would just have to find things to do to keep ourselves busy in the evenings so the kids wouldn't notice that anything was up. I would do anything for my children, and waiting was what I had to do, so I resigned myself to it.

Neither Bill nor I wanted to go to battle over our assets or our children. We wanted a standard, no-contest divorce. There wasn't a lot for us to divide up, anyway. My uncle, Denny, is an attorney, and we decided that we would ask him to handle it for us.

Bill and I agreed that I would stay in the house with the kids, and he would figure out what to do in terms of housing. Hopefully, the other things we needed to sort out would become clear in the upcoming week.

It was important that everything was clarified, and we had something concrete to tell the kids before we talked to them. If we were going to tell them that our family was shipwrecked, it was our responsibility to make sure they felt like we had a really strong life raft to offer them. Making them feel like they were drifting at sea was not an option.

~July 4th Weekend~
Independence

"…Say it ain't so
I will not go
Turn the lights off
Carry me home…"
"All the Small Things"

~by De Longe/Hoppus (Blink 182)

The Fourth of July weekend was upon us, and the irony of "Independence Day" was not lost on me.

Friday, July 3rd was a work holiday. Dylan was home, getting ready for a barbeque at the neighbor's house later that afternoon, followed by fireworks in the evening. Payton was due home from gymnastics camp between 9:00 and midnight. And Bill and I were clearly avoiding each other. We circled each other, as far apart as two remote planets circling the sun.

I was in a hyper-focused mindset. I was planning everything out, doing mental calculations, imagining how we would split our finances, how and when to tell the kids we were divorcing, how I was going to tell my friends and family. And, even as I was performing all these mental gymnastics, in the back of my mind was the nagging question: *Isn't there anything I can do to fix this?*

With Payton away at camp, it was the first Fourth of July in many years that we were not down at the Lake of the Ozarks celebrating with my family. So, Dylan wanted to have a few friends over to join us for the neighborhood festivities. The two of us went and bought a bunch of fireworks. Even though I was moving through a strange mental fog all day, I did my best to keep him from sensing that anything was up. Looking back, it must have been clear that there was something terribly wrong between Bill and me. We would pass in the hallway and not even look at each other.

At one point, Bill was mowing the grass, and I was sitting in the backyard with my notebook, trying to gather my thoughts.

The time came for us to join the neighbor's day-before-the-Fourth-of-July barbeque. There we all were, with our lawn chairs and pot luck dishes—me, at one end of the yard with one set of neighbors, and Bill at the other end with a different group. I'm sure everyone picked up on the fact that we were arguing.

Bill drank more than usual that day and became playful—to the point of recklessness—with the fireworks. He was acting like a kid. It annoyed me at the time, but looking back on it, I'm sure he had no better idea than I did as to how to deal with our situation, and was just trying to distract himself. I know that's exactly what I was doing—ignoring the situation, and trying to lose myself in the festive atmosphere.

My cell phone rang, and it was Payton calling to let me know that they were about thirty minutes away. Now I had no choice but to talk to Bill.

I turned and told him what was going on, and asked him, "Do you want to go or do you want me to go?"

He said, "What are you talking about? We are both going!"

The gym where we needed to pick her up was only ten minutes away. Even so, the ten minutes in the car together stretched on and on, with the two of us staring straight ahead at the road, not saying a word. That awkward car ride dispelled any doubts I might have had about whether or not Bill was really done with the marriage. He went out of his way to avoid talking about anything with me. He even put the windows down in the car, rather than turning on the air conditioning. That way, it was extra noisy, and especially difficult to start a conversation.

I used the car ride to mentally prepare myself for seeing Payton. I wanted to make sure I put up a good front until we were ready to tell the kids. Every time I imagined having that conversation, I remembered different occasions when they had each told us how thankful they were that their family was still together. They had told us they knew that one out of every two families goes through a divorce, and they were happy they didn't have to deal with that kind of pain. Their words were weighing heavily on my mind.

Payton was Daddy's little girl, and she was going to be devastated when she found out. I didn't know how on earth she was going to handle it. I could barely stand to think about it. For the moment, I had to banish those thoughts from my mind, or she was going to see right through my façade.

The bus carrying the girls from gymnastics camp pulled up, and Bill and I instantly transformed into two different people. It was like a director had called "action" and we immediately assumed the roles we were assigned.

·

When Payton got off the bus, we made sure she knew we were happy to see her. While we waited for her luggage to be unloaded, we did an excellent job of pretending that everything was normal. She seemed to be happy to be home, and unaware that anything was off between Bill and me.

It was hard to believe that in the one week she had been away, the entire world had changed—not just Bill's world and mine, but hers and Dylan's. I felt terrible knowing I was keeping from her and her brother the fact that their whole world was about to crumble. But, I had no choice. The timing was critical.

It was around eleven o'clock at night when we got home. Payton wasn't in the mood to hang out with the neighbors, so I stayed in the house, visiting with her, while Bill went back over to the neighbors to hang out with Dylan and his buddies.

Payton wanted to sleep in my room with me. I couldn't have planned it any better. She made it so that I didn't have to dream up an explanation for why Bill wasn't sharing my bed that night. Before we went to sleep, she told me she'd been invited to the home of a gymnastics girlfriend the following day, but had been afraid to mention it after being gone a week. I told her we were supposed to go over to Bill's friend Kenny's house on Sunday, but we'd discuss it in the morning.

Bill and Kenny grew up together, and had been friends since they were teens. They lived a few streets over from each other, and shared their love of cars. They each had an older Camaro, and loved nothing more than working on them, washing and polishing them, and showing them off when they went cruising on Friday and Saturday nights. They were always at each other's house, which was how I got to know Kenny. No matter how much time went by, their connection stayed strong. They always had each other's back.

Meanwhile, Dylan had friends sleeping over. It was perfect. There was so much going on in the house that neither Dylan nor Payton seemed to notice the strangeness between Bill and me.

With Payton lying in bed beside me, I started asking myself how Bill could go through with this divorce without any apparent regret, remorse, or grief. I didn't know what "normal" looked like in a case like this, but his behavior sure didn't seem to fit any idea of normal I had. Why was I so broken up, while he seemed so unmoved?

I spent the night tossing and turning, and dragged myself out of bed early in the morning. I couldn't sleep anyway, so I figured I might as well do something productive. I wandered downstairs and turned on the computer. I didn't have anything specific in mind when I logged on. All I knew was that the computer had been Bill's territory for six months, and he had been spending a lot of time in chat rooms, talking with people from his past. Had he talked to them about leaving me? It seemed like any normal person contemplating divorce had to be talking to someone about it.

It was about six o'clock in the morning when I sat down at the computer. Maybe I'd find some answers—a clue as to how Bill could act like the last two decades of our life meant nothing to him.

Even though I am not computer savvy, I was confident that I could get into Bill's personal accounts. I don't know how I knew it, but I knew he would stay logged in, so I wouldn't need his password.

I felt like someone standing at the head of a trail, completely unprepared for what might lie ahead. There was nothing to do but put one foot in front of the other. I knew he had spent a lot of time on Facebook lately. I was unfamiliar with the site, but Randa liked the site so much that I took to calling her the Facebook Queen. "I can see why people like it for reconnecting," I would tease, "but do you really have to be on it every day?"

Randa had mentioned to me that some of Bill's Facebook posts seemed bizarre and out of character for him. He had been posting about how much he was looking forward to a weekend motorcycle ride, and how he couldn't wait to have the throttle going on the bike, and the wind blowing in his face.

I logged onto Facebook. Being unfamiliar with it, I really had no idea where to start. It took me several minutes to figure out what I was even looking at. I clicked on "Messages." I started reading emails from a woman named Lisa who was forty-one years old. The emails dated back to the beginning of May.

I understand how you are feeling, one email read, *and if you need to be free, you should. You shouldn't remain unhappy. Nobody deserves that...*

What the hell?!

Who was this Lisa? I looked back at her profile picture. I could see that she and I resembled each other, and she and Bill were the exact same age. That didn't tell me anything. I still had no idea who this woman was, or why she was telling my husband that he needed to move on rather than be unhappy in his life.

I dug a little deeper, and was able to figure out how Facebook email worked with the conversations going back and forth. Bill had deleted some of his emails, but he didn't delete his deleted emails, so they were in the "deleted" file. That meant I had a way to see everything.

I was getting very nervous and sweaty. He was upstairs sleeping in the spare bedroom, while I was downstairs, trying to make sense of why my marriage had fallen apart overnight.

I was shaking, angry, confused. What was the difference between emailing someone and posting something on their wall, anyway? Did I even understand how to tell who was emailing him? Surely, I couldn't have been reading the emails right.

I agree one hundred percent with your text, another email read. *And I can't wait to be with you.*

Another read, *Sweet dreams… wish I was there to tuck you in…*

I could see that the email stream dated back to the beginning of May.

What the hell was I looking at? Was there really another woman, after all?   I remembered the many times Bill and I had promised each other throughout the years that we would never do that to each other. I was so angry, I was vibrating. How could he do this to me? Didn't he remember what I had gone through in learning to trust him again after his substance abuse problem?

There had to be some mistake. I felt so turned around and disoriented, my brain would not accept what I was seeing.

As I was reading through the emails, I heard the shower turn on upstairs. Uh-oh! That meant I had only a little bit more time before Bill came downstairs. As I read on, I came to a message to Bill from Lisa dated June 24th—the same day we returned from our family vacation.

The message read, *I can't wait until Sunday. Rain or shine, we can ride together all day…*

Sweet dreams, Bill writes back. *Wish I was there.*

I was beside myself, my brain quickly trying to assemble all the pieces of the puzzle. They couldn't wait to go riding together on Sunday? Wait…what date was Sunday? June 28th. So, that was why he had to go on his motorcycle ride instead of taking his daughter to gymnastics camp!

How could this be the same man who was such a wonderful father, who would have given up all he had for his children and lived in a cardboard box? How could he be acting this way?

My mind swung back and forth like a pendulum. One moment I thought, this can't possibly be Bill. I must be misunderstanding something. The next instant, another missing link would fall into place. June 30th—the day I returned from Kentucky to a cold reception from Bill—he was sitting, chatting on the computer. Even when I came in the house, he did not get up.

A message from Lisa dated that same night said something to the effect of, *I just want you to know I'm here to go through this whole process with you. You have to do what you need to do. We will be together forever. I know it's easier said than done. I can't wait to be with you again. Lots of hugs and kisses to you. Love you, baby…*

There was an email from her dated July 1st, in which she clearly knew he had told me he wanted a divorce, and she asked how he was doing. There were emails discussing them getting together, and others where it was obvious they had already seen each other. *I wish I hadn't had to leave you...*

By then, I'd finished my coffee and was drinking iced tea. I was shaking so badly, the tea was sloshing out of the top of the glass. My brain was swimming as I printed out the emails and flew upstairs. I was completely out of control.

I stormed into our bathroom, where Bill was taking a shower. Payton was still asleep in our bed, but I was so furious, I didn't think before I flung open the bathroom door and started screaming and yelling loudly enough to wake her. I hurled the emails into the air, screaming, "Who the fuck is Lisa?!"

Payton woke up, and still groggy, tried to figure out why I was throwing a fit.

I lowered my voice and shut the bathroom door.

Bill got out of the shower. The expression on his face told me he knew that I knew the truth, but he thought he might still have a chance of getting out of it.

I headed him off at the pass, saying, "You can't fucking get out of this! I have the emails right here!"

"Alright," he said, "but you need to calm down. The kids are here. Let's go talk about this away from the house."

I said, "FINE!" and marched downstairs. I decided to wait for him outside where I could breathe. Payton stayed in bed. Dylan and his friends were still in their room.

Bill came outside, we got in the truck, and drove to the parking lot of the nearby Target.

"We went to grade school and middle school together," he confessed. "And then we reconnected on Facebook. We developed a connection. I didn't mean for it to happen... it just happened."

I went limp. I felt dead inside. I was in complete and total shock. Divorce was bad enough. I could not believe Bill had been having an affair! Worst of all, he still wanted to be with the other woman.

I sobbed. I felt thoroughly lost, having no idea where to go from there. There was one thing I did seem to know for sure—*now I wanted a divorce.* There was no way I would ever be able to get past what had happened. Some couples can get past infidelity, but as for me, I knew I would never again trust him to even walk to the mailbox alone. I was not going to live my life like that. And, he was not going to live his life knowing I was constantly suspicious.

I couldn't help but wonder—did he allow the affair to happen because he knew it would kill the marriage? Did he see Lisa as a way out?

Whatever might have led Bill to get involved with her, the facts were the facts. He had been having an affair, and now I was the one who wanted a divorce. And, there was no way I could deal with him living under the same roof with me in the meantime!

Knowing what I now knew, I couldn't pull off a whole week of faking it before we could tell the kids, but we decided to go through with the Fourth of July as planned. My Fourth was now ruined—and in fact, I knew that every Fourth of July for the foreseeable future would also be ruined for me. But, I didn't want that day to forever be ruined for the kids. The following morning, July 5th, we would have the big talk with the kids.

In the meantime, I was going to be taking Payton to a friend's house to go swimming, and picking her up later that evening. Bill and I were supposed to go to his friend Kenny's house for a big Fourth of July party. As I've mentioned, Kenny and Bill had grown up together, and Kenny had recently come back into our lives. There was no way I could act my way through the party, so Bill was going to take Dylan and his friend with him to the party.

When Bill and I returned home from our two-hour talk in the Target parking lot, the kids could tell that something was up. "We did have an argument," we admitted to them, "but let's just enjoy the Fourth, and we'll talk about everything later."

Bill and the boys went off to Kenny's house. It was a shame that I couldn't join them because I was looking forward to seeing more of Kenny, and rethinking my opinion of him. I had known him in high school, but as time went on, and he never got married or had a family, he began to seem too self-obsessed to form true relationships or have children.

Bill also told me that Kenny had contributed to his drug problem.

When I heard that, I suggested to Bill that he needed to steer clear of him. "I know you are an adult," I said, "and you make your own decisions, but I don't care to be around him."

Many years had passed since Bill's involvement with drugs, and I was willing to take another look at my opinion of Kenny. I figured, well, he has a steady girlfriend, and she has been with him for many years now; maybe he is a changed person. So, Kenny was making a reappearance in our lives.

Going to the party was out of the question for me now. Being around Kenny again after so long would have been awkward enough without the added trauma of what Bill and I were going through.

I took Payton to her friend's house, and then came home. I slumped down on the kitchen floor, and sobbed while the dogs crawled on me, trying to comfort me. That was my Fourth of July—me, sitting on the floor, crying, while outside the windows of my house, fireworks were shooting across the sky.

I felt so alone. Four horrible days had gone by since Bill told me he wanted out, and I hadn't talked to a soul. I felt like my life was over. I had to do something to fight off the hopelessness. It was bad enough knowing that my husband wanted a divorce. The fact that he was also having an affair was the straw that broke the camel's back.

I forced myself to get up. I went back to the computer, logged back into Facebook. There were all these strangers—Lisa and her friends—who considered themselves my husband's new best friends. I had known Bill since he was seventeen years old. Who *were* these people? And who was this guy posing as my husband? This was not Bill!

I saw all these pictures of people in their early to mid-forties, drunk and having a good time. Of course, everyone has a little bit too much to drink sometimes, and gets a little bit wild. But why would they post those pictures on Facebook? And more importantly, why would Bill want to be part of that kind of thing?

I couldn't take it for one more second.

I went to the phone. Who could I call? I couldn't call Randa and ruin her Fourth of July. We were so close that she would remember that phone call every year when the Fourth rolled around.

I wasn't ready to tell Maggie.

I decided to call my mom. I knew my parents would be at their house at the lake, celebrating the Fourth of July, as we always did together.

"Mom, it's me," I said. "Can you go into the garage for a few minutes so no one can hear us?"

When I told my mom that we were getting divorced, she started to cry. She couldn't believe it, either.

"But, you just got back from your family vacation," she said. "I thought you all had a great time…"

I said, "I know, Mom, I know." We were both crying now.

"There's more," I said. "He's been having an affair. Some woman named Lisa that he knew in grade school."

I gave her whatever gruesome details I knew about the affair, and asked her if she could talk to Denny—the attorney—for me. I explained that I wasn't up to talking to him at the moment, but I would need his input as to what my next step should be.

Mom, God love her, felt absolutely horrible for me. "If I didn't live two and a half hours away…" she said.

I said, "I know, Mom. I know you'd be here if you could."

We said a tearful goodbye. Then, I decided I would call my friend Maggie, after all. She was pregnant, so I figured she wouldn't be doing much heavy celebrating. I gave her the bare-bones version of the story, telling her about the divorce, and briefly mentioning the affair.

We had worked side by side for a few years at my previous seventeen-year job, so she was someone I saw every day until we both changed jobs.

Bill and I represented something for her in terms of what was possible between a married couple. And, just the previous October, we had gone to her wedding in Jamaica, and Bill had walked her down the aisle. So, when I told her about the divorce, she went through every imaginable emotion—she was in shock, angry, sad. Naturally, being pregnant magnified all of her feelings.

Once I'd spoken to my mom and Maggie, I felt somewhat better. At least now I wasn't the only one who knew.

I still couldn't bear to tell Randa. I knew she would take it really hard. I could wait one more day—until after the Fourth—to tell her.

I remembered I had a pack of cigarettes I'd bought when Bill told me he wanted a divorce. I am the kind of person who can smoke a few cigarettes, and not touch them again for ten years. I took my cigarettes and a glass of wine out to the back yard and sat down to think…Where should I go from here? What should my next move be?

I had the printed Facebook emails with me. I read through them again, my analytical mind in full swing. What kind of a woman was this Lisa? Reading through her emails, it was easy to see how she was comforting Bill, and drawing him close. It may have been my state of mind, but it felt like she had staged the whole thing—like she knew exactly what to say and do in order to keep pulling him closer to her.

A friend of mine who lived through an affair with her husband once told me, "You can't believe your husband could do what he did, but you can learn to accept it. What is harder to accept is that a woman would do that to another woman."

What she said rang so true to me. Women have come so far in society, and we are supposed to stick together.

Lisa obviously knew that Bill was married with children, and yet that didn't stop her. True, I didn't know what he might have told her. But, even if he'd told her that our marriage was over and it was just a matter of time before he let me know, she should have told him, "Look, you need to do the right thing concerning your wife and family. As long as you're still married, I can't get involved with you."

I was struggling with deep resentment towards her. I didn't know anyone with low enough morals to get involved with a married man.

Wait a minute—where were Bill's morals in all this? What had happened to the guy who would never had done this in a million years?

I knew I was driving myself crazy, but my poor brain would not rest.

This was the man I had trusted for so many years, and my mind did not want to accept that he had undergone a complete personality change. Yet, the reality was staring me in the face. My marriage was over. My perfect family of four was gone. My children were now going to be from a divorced family, and there was nothing I could do to stop any of it from happening.

If Lisa had not been part of the equation, would things have still played out the same way? It was hard to say, but I believed from the bottom of my heart that her presence in the middle of my family had changed everything.

Before long, it was time to pick up Payton. I took a deep inhale off a cigarette and went inside to get my purse. I thought of my little girl's sweet face, and how her expression would dissolve into tears when we told her and Dylan the news the following morning. I tried to shake off the thought of it.

For the moment, my only job was to get the kids through the night. There would be time enough to deal with tomorrow when tomorrow came.

~July 4th, Part Two~

Breaking the News

"...When you looked into my eyes
And you said goodbye, could you see my tears
When I turned the other way
Did you hear me say
I'd wait for all the dark clouds bursting in a perfect sky..."
"Rain"

~by Pettibone/Ciccone (Madonna)

When Bill was going into the Navy, he wrote me a letter saying, in essence, that even though things were going to be different for awhile, our love would see us through. In that same letter, he said that he loved me and would never leave me. Two words continued to haunt me as I drove to pick up Payton—*what happened?*

You are driving down the road of your life, and suddenly, as you glance into the rearview mirror, you realize that you are on a road with no signposts. You have no map. And, the familiar landscape behind you is growing more and more distant with each mile you travel.

I was looking out on an unfamiliar landscape. The world in which Bill loved me, and our family was in tact, was now somewhere in the past.

When I got to the home of Payton's friend, I didn't go in. I didn't want to see anyone. I called Payton and told her I was out front. She came outside and wanted me to go in and visit with everybody, but obviously, it was out of the question.

She got in the car, and I collected myself, trying my best to appear calm. We got home, and she went in to take a shower. When she came out, she was sobbing and hyperventilating.

68

"Honey, what's wrong?" I asked, putting my arm around her.

"You need to tell me!" she cried. "I know something bad is going to happen when you talk to us tomorrow…"

Then, looking me straight in the eye, she said, "You can't tell me you and Dad are getting divorced. I couldn't deal with that!"

I panicked. What was I going to do now? When Bill and I talked in the Target parking lot, we agreed that *he* would do the talking. "This is your decision," I had said. "You need to step up and start explaining all of this to the kids."

I couldn't be the one to broach the subject, and yet, I didn't want to lie to her. We sat on the floor of her bedroom, and I hugged her and told her that she was right—this was not good, but everything was going to be okay. Then I told her I would call her dad and tell him that he and Dylan needed to come home right away. "We won't make you wait until the morning, honey. You finish getting ready for bed, and I'll go call your dad."

When I got Bill on the phone, he was having a great time, and was not happy that I demanded he come home right away. He had told Dylan and his friend that they might be able to stay all night at Kenny's house.

"That's too bad," I said. "You've got to get home. I'm sorry but it is no longer about you. It is about our children, and Payton is very upset. Come home now."

Bill hung up with me and went to round up Dylan and his friend. Dylan later shared with me that Kenny looked at him and said, "Sorry you have to leave. Your dad has done something really bad."

Dylan knew that whatever was going on, it had to be serious for Kenny to say such a thing to him. I never have had the nerve to ask Kenny what possessed him to say that to Dylan.

Bill and Dylan dropped off Dylan's friend, and then came straight home. When the boys arrived, Payton was sitting on the loveseat on one side of the family room. Dylan took the recliner chair. I sat closest to Dylan on one end of the couch, and Bill was at the complete other end. It was clear that we didn't want to be anywhere near each other.

It was past midnight by this time.

There was no way in hell I was going to start the conversation, and since Bill didn't seem to be in any hurry to say anything, we all sat there, looking at each other. Payton was still crying. Dylan was sitting there with a look that said, "Okay, what's going on?"

The longer Bill delayed the conversation, the angrier I got.

I gestured at Bill as if to say, "Come on, already! We all know what you're going to say."

He gave me a blank look.

I was furious. This was on him, not me! It was not my place to get the ball rolling. When I couldn't stand the silence anymore, I spoke, trying not to cry. I felt horrible—like Bill and I were letting them down as parents. "I'm sorry…I'm sorry…" If I said it once, I said it five hundred times.

I started by saying that I knew how they felt about divorce. I tried to explain to them that their dad did not love me anymore as a husband loves a wife. I explained that we were going right into divorce rather than having a separation period.

By then, everyone was in tears.

Bill was hunched forward. He could barely look at the kids.

Dylan and Payton had so many questions, but they were hard to answer, because Bill and I had agreed not to mention his girlfriend. The kids didn't need to hear that. They were going to have enough on their plates just dealing with their parents' divorce. I did say, "There are contributing factors, but they are grownup issues."

They wanted to know, "But, where are we going to stay? Where is Dad going to go?"

Looking at their beautiful faces filled with pain and fear, I was so torn up inside—and so angry with Bill. How could he put them through this horrible suffering?

"Well," I said, "you will stay right here at home with me! As to your dad, we are still working all that out. The main thing you need to know is that we love you more than anything, and we will always put you first. And your dad and I will remain friends."

Friends! Ha! Even as I said it, I felt like I was lying because I knew that in the eyes of the kids, "friends" meant that we would be buddy-buddy. Sure, we would remain civil for the sake of the kids. But, friends? How could we ever go back to where we once were—those best friends from long ago?

All of us were in tears, but Dylan was the first one to articulate how he was feeling. He views the world like someone much older and wiser than his actual years. Even when he was younger, he was always a beautiful combination of a young kid and an old sage.

He looked at me and said, "As long as you're both happy, that's all that matters. We will make this work."

I was already beside myself, but when Dylan said that, I lost it.

The bravery and grace Dylan showed in that statement broke my heart even more deeply—and made me that much more upset with Bill. I wanted to shake him and say, "Was being with me really so bad that you had to do something that would put your children in a position like this? Can you not see what you are doing to them?"

I did my best to assure the kids that we would work it out, everything would be okay, and their dad would still be part of their lives.

Once I had broken the ice, Bill finally started chiming in, also reassuring them that he wasn't going anywhere, and would still be involved in their lives.

Payton had always been Daddy's little girl. Now she was in shock, overcome with questions and fears about how her life was going to change.

I was shaking, and felt like I might vomit.

Bill was crying as well, but he seemed calmer than I was—relieved, even. Maybe he was grateful to know that everything was out in the open. But, it was hard on me to see him so calm in that moment. Why didn't he seem to be experiencing the same distress that I was feeling?

Of course, I had no idea what he was going through on the inside. Coming from a split family, he knew from personal experience how hard it was going to be for Dylan and Payton. I'm sure he couldn't have felt good about that. I remembered back to when we first had children, and how scared he was that his own broken family would lead him to become a disconnected father. Now he was becoming the part-time dad he had feared turning into.

At least Bill had Lisa to comfort him through this ordeal. I, on the other hand, was responsible for making sure the kids came through the divorce in tact. I was the one who was going to have to live with the fallout, twenty-four/seven, while he got to escape into the world he wanted, with little responsibility. He would have his freedom, and be able to come and go as he pleased.

Around two in the morning, we were finally all talked out. Everyone was exhausted. The kids went upstairs to bed, and Bill and I talked a little bit more about where he would go. He still had no plan, and no idea where to go. His relationship with his mom—who lived in the area—had gone downhill, so he wasn't going there. Despite my anger, I still loved the man, and knew the struggles he had gone through with his mother. So I said, "I agree. That's not the best place for you to go."

He said, "Maybe I'll call my friend Vinnie in the morning and see if he'll let me crash there until I can figure out what I'm going to do next. He's got that finished basement at his house."

Vinnie was a divorced dad that lived nearby, and that plan made sense to me.

Totally drained, we both turned in for the night—my husband of twenty years on the couch, and me, alone in our bed upstairs. I doubt that any of us slept a wink that night.

~July 5th~
Split

"A room is still a room
Even when there's nothing there but gloom;
But a room is not a house
And a house is not a home
When the two of us are far apart
And one of us has a broken heart…"
"A House is Not a Home"

~by Bacharach/David (Dionne Warwick)

At the beginning of 2009, when I was anticipating all these upcoming milestones, they all seemed like great events that were coming to pass. Now, in light of the fact that Bill had left me, each milestone took on a different tone.

Bill and I had celebrated our twentieth wedding anniversary, and I dreamed of us, twenty years down the line, celebrating our fortieth. That was never going to happen now.

And thinking I had a strong marriage, I had been excited about turning forty, and looked forward to growing old with Bill. Now, I was forty, and about to be divorced.

I had been excited to see Dylan turning sixteen. Now, I thought, oh, my God—my son is at such a pivotal age in his development, and he's not going to have his father under the same roof to help him get through it. How could I be both mother and father to my kids?

I had to sit myself down and give myself a serious talking-to. I told myself, okay, you have to look at the upside here. Things could be worse. You and the kids are still here, and you are healthy. One out of two families goes through a divorce, so there has to be a way through this. Whatever it is, you'll find it.

The morning after we told the kids, it was very somber around our house. Nobody was really talking to anybody. Everyone was avoiding eye contact.

Bill got Vinnie on the phone, who said, "Of course. You can stay as long as you need to."

Then, the house phone rang and Bill picked it up. It was Randa, who was in a mood. Everyone was on her last nerve, and she launched right into a rant. It took about a minute before she picked up on Bill's awkwardness and realized that something was wrong.

She said, "Let me talk to Shelly."

Bill said, "She can't talk right now, but she really does need to talk to you. I'll have her call you back in a little while."

Once Bill left to go see Vinnie, I called Randa—but I didn't have much time to talk at that moment. I had planned to take the kids to the movies to allow Bill time to pack a suitcase, and get out of the house without the kids having to watch.

I knew this was going to hit her hard. Not only had Bill and I been friends since high school, but so had Bill and Randa. I took a deep breath, and told her everything—or almost everything. I didn't mention anything about Bill having a girlfriend, figuring there would be time enough later to give her all the details.

Randa immediately started sobbing, and I cried with her. She absolutely could not believe that Bill and I were splitting up. To her, we had always been "Shelly and Bill, the couple that would make it through thick and thin, and be together forever."

She could sense that there was more to the story than I was telling her. We were so close, and she knew damned well I wouldn't just say, "Oh, well, I guess my husband doesn't love me anymore." I'd never roll over that easily. But, she also knew I didn't have time to go into anything right then, so she didn't press me.

I promised Randa I would tell her everything she needed to know later. Then I took the kids to the movies. It seemed like such a strange thing to be doing at the moment—just going to the movies like everything was normal— but we had to find some way to get out of the house, and it seemed like a good way to distract ourselves. We saw *Transformers 2*, and it did manage to take our minds off the situation for a little while, on a surface level anyway. But, even as I was getting lost in the story, another part of my mind knew perfectly well that, as the three of us sat in the dark, staring at the movie screen, Bill was at home, packing a suitcase.

When we came home, he was gone. His absence in the house was deafening. It was one of the saddest days of my life.

If I had not been forced to stay positive and upbeat for the kids, I'm sure I would have had a total meltdown. But, I had to stay strong for them. No child—especially when they are already suffering—wants to see their parents unhappy. The last thing I wanted was for Dylan and Payton to take on my sorrow, and begin to feel like any of this was their fault.

"We are going to be just fine" became my new mantra.

Rose-colored glasses aside, I was very aware that our family had changed forever, and I needed to prepare myself for whatever lay ahead. My own parents have enjoyed a long, happy marriage, so I knew nothing about divorce. It was time to read everything I could about the subject. I wanted to make things as easy on the kids as possible.

The next day was a Monday. I went in to work, and Payton went to gymnastics, where she would share what was happening with friends. The gymnastics girls were such a tight-knit group, spending at least twenty hours a week together during the school year, and even more during summers. It was really good for her to reach out for support, and I was happy to see her doing that. It reassured me that she would be okay in the end.

Dylan had a close friend, Sean, who was from a divorced family, and he took comfort in talking to him.

But, as much as it did my heart good to see the kids reaching out to their friends for support, I knew how important it was that they kept talking to me, as well. I was worried that they might be afraid to talk to me because they didn't want me to see them upset—or upset me by asking questions.

I was right, for the most part.   Payton was deeply wounded, and didn't like to talk about what had happened. I continually had to draw her out, asking her, "How are you doing? How was your day?" It would take a long time for her to open up with me.

Dylan talked to me more than Payton, but even when he did, he was very tempered, and I always got the impression he wanted to say more.

They preferred to confide in each other—a fact which Dylan shared with me only later. Even now, they avoid talking about their dad around me, and prefer to talk between themselves—especially Payton. When she does want to ask me something, she will run it by Dylan first.

With the kids' well-being weighing heavily on my mind, I arrived at work. One look at me and it was obvious that I had been crying. I decided to go in and talk to the owners so they would know what was going on.

One of the owners had gone through a very messy divorce, and I knew she would understand. She turned out to be the perfect person for me to talk to. I felt like she could really relate to my feelings.

The other owner was also very caring in his response to my news. He is a registered nurse, and has that warm bedside manner the best nurses have. He sat and listened without judging me, and I so appreciated that. He picked up a pen and drew a chart of a bell curve. "This is what the next several months of your life are going to look like—up and down." I still have the note containing the chart on the bulletin board next to my desk. Whenever I am having a blue day, I look at the sketch and say to myself, okay this may be a down day, but it has to go up from here.

I felt like I'd won the jackpot in terms of having the perfect bosses during the long, hard journey of divorce I was facing. It was great knowing that one of them could sit and bitch with me, and the other could listen and offer a shoulder. And, they were both great about letting me take time off to handle divorce matters. They allowed me the flexibility I needed for an occasional long lunch or early departure from work.

I also met with Denny that Monday. I told him that Bill and I wanted to get the divorce done as quickly as possible, and were hoping he could represent us both.

He explained to me that a family law attorney can only represent one party in a divorce, but I could act as a liaison between them. That way, Denny could answer any questions Bill might have through me. Bill and I knew that even though Denny was my uncle, he would look out for the best interests of us both.

Denny and I went over everything, and he gave me a list of all the paperwork I needed to gather. I am very organized by nature, and I already had pretty much everything I would need. We made an appointment for the next day to give him time to prepare. He also told me that, in the State of Missouri, there is a thirty-day waiting period for a divorce. Even though that length of time is considerably shorter than in some states, it seemed ridiculous. I wanted it to go as quickly as possible, and thirty days was an eternity to me at that point in time.

Why couldn't I get divorced in a week? I got married in a week!

He explained that the quickest Missouri divorce he had ever handled was done in thirty-one days.

I said, "Okay, then, let's make sure mine doesn't go any longer than that, and in fact, let's get it done in thirty days!" The quicker this nightmare was over, the quicker I could move on, and regain control over my life.

I also knew that Bill's girlfriend had been twice divorced, and might try to sway his decisions related to our divorce. It made me both scared and angry to think she would be privy to the intimate details of our lives, and I told Bill he had better not share our financial information with her. We had always been very private people.

I made more money than Bill did, and I didn't want anybody saying to him, "If you're going to walk away from a woman who earns more than you do, why should you have to pay any child support at all?" I didn't imagine that Bill would go down that road with me, but then again, I never imagined that another woman could influence him enough to have an affair, either.

Those were my reasons for wanting the divorce over with as quickly as possible.

As for Bill, he wanted it done just as quickly because he wanted to move on. In his eyes, he had found a wonderful new girlfriend. The whole spiel he had given me on July 1st was a lie. He said he was leaving me to become independent, but if you have a girlfriend, you are not independent.

As we got the ball rolling for the divorce, there were many things to consider in terms of who was going to be financially responsible for what bills, and the amount of child support Bill would pay—which turned out to be a surprisingly small amount.

I was the person in charge of our finances, so it made sense that I would break down our budget. Naturally, he would take his truck, and I'd take my car. Since I earned more money, and would be the one staying in the house with the kids, I would assume all financial responsibility for the mortgage, taxes, and upkeep on the house.

Speaking of the house, even though we were staying there for the time being, I was really hoping the kids would want to move. But, as I started reading about the effects of divorce upon children, I learned that children generally prefer to stay in familiar surroundings. It gives them some sense of stability.

So, what was the answer? There was no way I could come home to a house that looked exactly the same as it did before. Every time I walked in the door, I'd be reminded that our lives were not remotely the same. I was going to have to knock down walls and totally refurbish the house if the kids really wanted to stay there.

As it turned out, I didn't have to worry. Both kids decided they wanted to sell the house for the same reasons I did. They said it would be too weird to come home to the same house and the same routine, when their lives had been turned upside down. They wanted a fresh start. I was surprised—and incredibly relieved.

Payton only had one stipulation: wherever we moved to, she did not want to switch schools. She was in middle school (seventh grade), and it was an important time of life for her.

Bill said he intended to stay in the area, as well, so he could be there for the kids. His plan was to find an apartment or condo in the same school district, to make it easy on everyone.

It was time for Bill to review and sign the divorce paperwork. Naturally, he didn't want to be served at work. It would have been humiliating. And he didn't want the sheriff showing up where he was living, either. I was fine with that. As I said, we were very private people. So, Bill went by my uncle's office and picked up the papers.

Bill and I were supposed to individually review everything, discuss what we could by phone, and eventually get together to discuss any questions or concerns we had. I had already highlighted sections that I knew would raise concerns. For example, with Bill's job working for the city, he had great benefits and a robust retirement package. I felt that, after twenty years of marriage, I deserved to reap some of those benefits, as well.

Then I found out that the retirement benefits of city employees—police officers, firefighters, teachers, etc.—were protected. Once they were divorced, their spouses couldn't touch those benefits.

Bill did agree to give me a percentage of his 401K, but by law, I couldn't touch his pension. That was the nest egg I had been counting on my entire life. In all the years we both worked, we had always planned on living on Bill's retirement from the city. Now, here we were, at a point in our lives where it was time to start considering how we were going to handle retirement—even though it was still many years down the line—and I could potentially be left high and dry because of an unexpected divorce!

It was a devastating thought.

Even though Bill was out of the house and staying with his friend, we agreed that for the time being, we would leave things more or less the same in terms of the way the household finances were handled. His check would still be deposited into our joint checking account, I would still pay the bills, and he would still withdraw money for living expenses.

For our cell phones, we had all the phones on a family plan. Bill naturally wanted his phone off the family plan, but he was worried about the penalties we might be charged. When I called Sprint and explained the situation, they were actually very nice. Because I still had three phone numbers on the family plan, they agreed that they wouldn't charge any penalties for Bill to remove his number and go get his own account.

In the meantime, I was still getting copies of all the phone bills.

Wait a minute! *I was still getting copies of all the phone bills.* That meant I could go online and look at the call history. I still had so many questions, and so few answers, and I couldn't stop myself.

There it was in black and white. Bill had been talking to Lisa on a regular basis—even once while we were on our family vacation. How could that have happened right under my nose, without me having any inkling?

I thought back several months, and remembered an instance sometime between May and July (before our vacation) when Bill's phone was sitting on the kitchen counter, vibrating. I could see he had a missed call from someone named Lisa, but figuring it was his friend Lisa from work, I didn't think twice about it. Now I kicked myself. Why didn't I pick up the phone?

I was being so hard on myself, second guessing everything. I couldn't shake the sense that the whole divorce disaster was somehow my fault, and if I'd only been paying attention, I could have prevented it. Logic told me that just wasn't so, but the feeling dogged me. It would be some time—and a bit of counseling—before I awoke to the fact that none of it was my fault.

Bill and I continued to sort out our divorce by phone. In our situation, everything was pretty basic. Bill still didn't have his own place to live. So, he decided he would take the kids every other weekend instead of shuffling them back and forth between us, half the week here and half the week there. That way, the kids could keep their normal routine. If Dylan and Payton had been smaller, we would have felt compelled to split the time with the kids more evenly. As it was, Dylan would soon be getting an after-school job, and Payton also had plenty of her own things going on.

Coming from a divorced family where the custody arrangement was such that he only saw his own father occasionally, Bill probably felt it was best that way. Plus, he wanted his freedom.

It was fine with me. If that was the level of visitation he was available for, I certainly wasn't going to force him to do anything that would make him miserable.

~July 10th~
Filing for Divorce

"...We told Uncle Walter that he should be good,
And do all the things that we said he should,
But I know that he'd rather be out in the wood,
I'm afraid we might lose Uncle Walter for good!
We begged and we pleaded, 'Oh, please won't you stay!'
We managed to keep him at home for a day,
But the bears all barged in and they took him away!
Now, he's waltzing with pandas, and he can't understand us,
And the bears all demand at least one dance a day.
There's nothing on earth Uncle Walter won't do
So he can go waltzing with bears..."
"Waltzing with Bears"

~by Seamus Kennedy

We filed the signed divorce papers with the courts on July 10th. We still had some final negotiations to sort out, but we would have the thirty-day waiting period to get all of that in order.

One of the first things we needed to figure out was what we were going to do during the times when I was in Kentucky for work. I was gone every other week, and there was no way out of it. Who was going to take care of the kids while I was away?

Bill had stayed at the house with the kids for one night—July 8th. It was terribly awkward for all concerned. They didn't hang out or talk that evening. When bedtime came, it was bizarre for the kids, having their dad sleep in the same house where he used to live with us. And, then in the morning, everyone was so uncomfortable, no one really talked to each other. Bill just went off to work, and the kids went off to school. It was an unmitigated disaster.

When I returned from Kentucky, we unanimously agreed that it wasn't going to be a workable option for the future.

Bill had already expressed to me that the place where he was staying wasn't really suitable for the kids. I had never been to Vinnie's, but I took Bill's word for it. So, if I couldn't get out of my bi-weekly trips to Kentucky, and Bill couldn't sleep at our house or see his children at Vinnie's, how was this all going to work?

I said to Bill, "Look, you really have to work on getting your own place to stay. The kids need stability!"

I was completely panicked. I had been hired with the understanding that it was no problem for me to travel; I had a husband to look after the kids while I was away. Now the equation had changed.

Not only did I have a trip coming up in a couple of weeks, but there were various family appointments I no longer knew how to cover. Every aspect of our lives as a family was built upon the fact that there were two adults—not one!—to look after our two children. The kids needed to go to the orthodontist, and get their annual physicals to prepare for going back to school in the fall. Payton needed to get to and from gymnastics. Our beagle was seeing a chiropractor. I know, I know.

Naturally, the orthodontist appointments never fell after hours—only during work hours. Doctor's appointments, whether they were for the kids or the dogs, were the same way.

Bill had totally checked out, which left everything on my shoulders, and I was really feeling the weight of it all. I now had to go to work, manage every appointment related to the kids and the dogs, try to be normal for my children, and try to steal a moment here and there to ask myself what the hell had become of my life.

I was totally losing my mind—and it was giving me newfound respect for single parents. How in the world did they do it, day in and day out?

My own parents felt horrible about all of this. They helped in every way they could, but they were already retired and living at their lake house, which was a few hours away, so they couldn't help cover the daily appointments.

On July 13th, I left work early so I could take Dylan to a doctor's appointment. We were sitting on one side of the waiting room, and other patients were sitting directly across from us, no more than five yards away. Dylan turned to me and said, "Dad has a girlfriend, doesn't he?"

I was speechless. I couldn't believe he was doing this in a quiet doctor's office where other people were within earshot. Even though the waiting room was freezing cold, I started sweating. My thoughts started racing. How was I supposed to respond to that statement? I had no idea what to say.

Suddenly, the research I'd been doing on children going through divorce kicked in. I remembered that the experts agreed on one thing—make sure you are honest with your children but don't indulge any negative feelings you might have about your spouse or go into great details about things with your children. It is detrimental to them to have one spouse painting a bad picture of the other.

After a thirty-second delay, I said simply, "You're right. He does. But, why don't we talk about this when we have a little more privacy?"

Two agonizing minutes passed, and then Dylan's name was called. As we got up to go in to see the doctor, I felt the anger rising inside of me. I couldn't believe my sixteen-year-old son had this weighing so heavily on his mind that he felt he had to bring it up to me in the doctor's office! I was furious with Bill.

We sat in the treatment room, waiting for the doctor to come in, and talked a little bit more.

"Yes, he does have a girlfriend," I repeated. "If you have any questions, I will do my best to answer them, but I don't know her, and I don't know much about her. You need to talk to your dad."

"I knew it," Dylan said. "I just knew he did."

"I'm so sorry, honey," I said. It pissed me off to have to apologize for Bill, but it seemed like the right thing to do.

Dylan said, "Whatever you do, Mom, please don't tell Dad that I know. I want him to face me and tell me, himself."

I promised I wouldn't say anything. Outwardly, I remained calm. Inside, I was seething. I wanted to call Bill and say, "Look, you f***ing ass! Your kid figured it out, and now he has to deal with this crap. He wants you to man up and come talk to him about it."

But, a promise is a promise, and as hard as it was going to be, I had promised Dylan I wouldn't say anything.

When the doctor came in, I was so disoriented, I almost forgot the problem that had brought us into the doctor—Dylan's metal allergy.

As we left the doctor's office, I talked to Dylan about the importance of not telling Payton about Lisa. We would tell her eventually, but for the time being, she had enough to deal with. Dylan agreed with me one hundred and ten percent. He wanted to protect his little sister.

Before I knew it, my next trip to Kentucky was upon us. I had not yet come up with a workable solution, so we had no choice but to have Bill stay with the kids again. This time, Payton refused to stay at the house with him. She slept at a friend's house instead.

I said to Bill, "Look, you have got to get a stable place so the kids can come see you!"

He said, "I'm looking! But everything is more expensive than I thought it would be, so I'm trying to save up for the move."

I reiterated, "You just have to find a place! The kids feel weird having you sleep here, and we have to figure something out. You know I have to travel every other week."

By this point, he was irritated with me. "Let's just drop it. I'll find a place."

What a sad comment—Bill's daughter was so uncomfortable under the same roof with him that she would rather sleep at a friend's house. Why hadn't he made more of an effort with the kids when he stayed there on July 8th? How could Bill—the proudest and happiest father I knew—cut off his relationship with his kids?

The day came that Bill and I were supposed to get together to go over the notes and questions each one of us had for the other concerning the finalizing of the divorce papers. After that session, I was to take each of our concerns back to my uncle and let him know what adjustments needed to be made in the documents.

As I mentioned, I was not eligible for any part of his pension, but I would get a portion of his 401K.

We had taken out a loan, and he was going to need to make a monthly payment for his share of the loan payment. Considering that he had written maybe five checks in his entire life—because I handled all the bills—the thought of having to rely on him to pay his share of our debt drove me insane.

Then we had to consider the subject of Payton's gymnastics. Between the monthly tuition, the cost of leotards, travel expenses, and coaches' fees, it was a very expensive sport.

I was being as fair as I could be. Some of my loved ones felt I was being too fair, considering the circumstances. Because Bill was not accustomed to paying the bills, he needed a strict regimen. So, I told him that if he would pay the gym tuition that was due at the first of every month, I would take care of the payments that came up three times a year. My share was much higher, so I felt I was being very generous.

Even so, he wasn't happy with it. He said that his budget was very tight, and he didn't have the income to pay for things like gymnastics. I think Bill had hoped that, when he told me he wanted a divorce, he was going to be able to walk away from all family responsibilities.

Nope! Sorry! He still had bills to pay, and responsibilities to his children.

Happy or not, he agreed to the gymnastics payment, and that was the last of the details we needed to discuss. It was all pretty civil. The next move would be for me to take the few minor changes in the paperwork to Denny.

Everything was settled—until two hours later when the phone rang.

"You know," said Bill, "I'm not happy with the split on gymnastics. You make more money than I do, so you should pay more than me."

"I am going to end up paying more than you!" I said. "The three payments throughout the year are going to come to a lot more than the monthly tuition."

He also objected to the fact that I was planning to sell the house, and buy something smaller. In his mind, if I was going to end up with a smaller house payment, he should end up with fewer bills to pay on his end. I had already been more than fair, but what he failed to understand was that, no matter *how* we split our bills, I would always be better off than him because I earned more money than he did.

I was so aggravated. After thirty minutes of screaming and yelling on the phone, we ended up with the same financial agreement we'd had before he called. I had walked outside to talk to him, because the kids were home, and now I stayed outside so I could calm down before going back inside. I looked around, feeling like I needed to apologize to my poor neighbors for my public outburst.

I couldn't believe he was questioning paying for Payton's gymnastics. The man I knew would have worked ten jobs to make sure his kids got what they needed and wanted. I couldn't help but wonder who he had been talking to. Two hours earlier, he was fine with the split on gymnastics, and then, suddenly, he turned on a dime.

Maybe the legally mandated parenting classes we were required to take would give him a new perspective. Pregnant women don't have to take a class prior to having a baby, but once you've already become a mother, and decide to get divorced, *then* you have to take parenting classes. It made no sense to me.

Like it or not, the classes were required, and since we were on the fast track for our divorce, we needed to schedule them as soon as possible. We couldn't both enroll in the same class, either; we had to go separately. That meant we both had to enroll, attend, and complete our classes before the divorce was final.

I went first. I was in a class with about twenty-five other single parents who had been separated for various lengths of time. We were taught the basics of responsible post-divorce parenting—how and when to introduce a girlfriend or boyfriend to the kids, the importance of not baiting the other parent, and not fighting in front of the kids.

I got my classes over with, and then Bill scheduled and took his.

Too bad the classes couldn't make my feelings over the divorce magically disappear. Now, that would have been a worthwhile use of my time.

~Mid-July~
Countdown

"Prince Charming: You! You can't lie. Where is Shrek?
Pinocchio: Well, uh, I don't know where he's not.
Prince Charming: You don't know where Shrek is?
Pinocchio: On the contrary.
Prince Charming: So you do know where he is!
Pinocchio: I'm possibly more or less not definitely
rejecting the idea that I undeniably...
Prince Charming: Stop it!
Pinocchio: ...do or do not know where he shouldn't probably be.
If that indeed wasn't where he isn't!"

~from "Shrek III"

Before everything fell apart between us, Bill and I had planned to take the kids to my parents' lake house on the weekend of July 18th. After we separated, we decided that I would take the kids to the lake house, and the following weekend would be his turn to be with them. Since he was no longer able to offer the kids the stability of being under the same roof, we agreed that he had to get into an every-other-weekend visitation pattern as soon as possible. That way, the kids could relax into some kind of a routine.

Our weekends at the lake had always been relaxed and easy, but this was the first time we had been there without Bill. Everyone was off their game and we were all walking on eggshells. We took the boat out on the lake. We water-skied. We engaged in all our usual activities, enjoyed being with my parents, and appreciated the beautiful surroundings. Still, everything that wasn't being said hung in the air.

The following weekend was Bill's weekend to take the kids—and he still didn't have a place to take them. Vinnie's place wasn't going to work, and his mother's house wasn't a good option because he had a strained relationship with her.

As I've mentioned, his dad and stepmother lived in Cuba, a little town in the country in southwest Missouri. The kids loved going there. They could ride dirt bikes and four-wheelers. Bill decided to take them there. Bill, Sr. and Judy are great people, and I love them dearly, so I liked the plan. Since it was still summer, Bill was supposed to pick up the kids on Friday and return them on Sunday. He told me he had plans for Friday night, and would come for the kids on Saturday morning.

Ever since the kids were born, Bill had spent every single day of their lives with them. Now that he no longer lived with them, he was missing one day after another. He finally had a chance for three whole days with them, *but he had plans?* What was so important that he would let it interfere with his time with them?

I was really starting to understand the extent to which he did not want any responsibilities.

In advance of their visit, I called Bill's stepmother, Judy, to tell her how sorry I was that she had to deal with the fallout from our divorce, and to let her know how much I appreciated her welcoming the kids. I knew it was going to be a bit awkward for them all.

Judy was beside herself over the divorce.

I thought to myself, well, you don't know the half of it. You would be really upset if you knew about the affair!

Bill also had a half-brother, Michael, and half-sister, Jeri Ann—Bill, Sr. and Judy's kids—and they were also deeply hurt by our divorce. They looked up to Bill as a man with a wonderful family and a great life. They were disillusioned and disappointed when they heard the news.

Bill hadn't told his parents the full story, so they were naturally confused. But, even though Judy and Bill, Sr. didn't have the full story, Judy is very grounded, with good intuition and street sense, and she picked up on the fact that there was more to the story than Bill was sharing with them.

She asked me, "Is there more to this, Shelly? Is there another woman?"

It was not my place to go into that with her. So I said, "You will need to talk to Bill about that."

That was all I had to say. She knew right away.

"My God!" she said. "What on earth is he doing?"

She then told me that Bill, Sr. was going to have a father-son talk with Bill, to ask him if he'd lost his mind, and to make sure he really knew what he was doing. I appreciated the sentiment, but I'd been witnessing Bill's change of heart for several weeks and I knew that nothing—and no one—was going to change his mind.

Despite a certain level of awkwardness, the kids and Bill still managed to enjoy their time in Cuba.

In mid-July, Payton decided she wanted a Facebook page. Considering that it was on Facebook that I discovered Bill's affair with Lisa, I had strong feelings on the subject.

Because MySpace preceded Facebook, and Dylan was older than Payton, he was into his MySpace page and hadn't really mentioned Facebook yet. But, all of Payton's friends had Facebook pages, and she wanted one.

How was I going to handle this? I couldn't very well risk her "friending" her dad, and seeing his Facebook page.

Randa had warned me that Bill had already changed his relationship status. When I saw it with my own eyes, my stomach hurt. We were not even divorced yet.

I said to him, "You are going to have to be the one to have this Facebook conversation with your daughter, and explain why she can't have a Facebook account. This is your doing, not mine."

He didn't understand at first why Payton couldn't be his Facebook friend.

"Look at your page!" I said. "You are not exactly posting family-friendly comments on there. Being 'lost in your ride on your motorcycle' is not something she needs to see right now. Plus, with your relationship status changed…"

He seemed genuinely startled. "What?! Are you kidding me?"

He realized it was something Lisa had done on her own.

Oh, great, I thought, now Lisa is playing games with his Facebook page.

"I will take care of that right away," he said.

"Well, in any case," I said, "you can see why we can't let Payton have a Facebook page."

Part of Bill understood—and part of him didn't.

I wanted to shake him and say, "Why can't you see what you are doing?! Don't you see what's wrong with this picture?"

"Listen," I said, "I will talk to her and tell her she can have a Facebook page, but she can't be Facebook friends with you."

When I talked to her, she didn't understand. I tried to explain without telling her why. "Dad is just going through a time where there are things on his Facebook page that are inappropriate for kids. It won't be this way forever." It was a hard thing to say to her.

I knew Payton was upset about it, and she told Randa as much.

It seemed like every day, some new challenge of divorcehood presented itself. I really needed someone to talk to, and I was anxious to start therapy.

I had my two friends, Ann and Maggie. They were the ones who kept me grounded in reality.

I had my mother and my best friend, Randa, who—God love them—were so close to me that my heartbreak was their heartbreak. I ended up consoling them as much as they were consoling me. There were times I wanted to say, "Listen, why don't you two just call each other?"

I still needed another kind of support—professional. I was counting down the days until my appointment. I couldn't wait.

The kids, unfortunately, did not share my enthusiasm over seeing a counselor. In fact, they were adamant—they definitely did not want to go. I knew it would be good for them, but it didn't feel right to force them. I decided to let it go. It was only a month into the separation, and I didn't want to push them over the edge. I thought that maybe once I started going, I could go back and tell them how much it was helping me, and suggest that maybe they would also feel better if they went.

So, that was the plan—or as much of a plan as I could seem to muster at the time.

Meanwhile, I asked Bill about how little time he'd spent with the kids in July, and he said, "I feel they need space to get used to me not being there."

That made no sense to me. "How can you even say that to me? This is not normal! Before the separation, the kids never went a single day without seeing you, unless you were out of town. How are they supposed to deal with this?"

He said, "Like I said, they need to get used to me not being there."

I knew that what Bill was doing wasn't good for the kids. But there wasn't a single thing I could do about it. I felt angry, hurt, sad, and overwhelmed by the awareness that I was essentially going to have to be the kids' only parent.

I wondered if I was overreacting, and making too much of things. I questioned whether someone else would have been as upset as I was over Bill wanting to get his own children used to his absence. I was second-guessing everything I was thinking, feeling, and saying.

Then, I remembered what Denny had said to me.

"Divorce is a grieving process you go through," he explained. "It is just like losing a loved one."

Suddenly, my anger and hurt made sense. I was definitely grieving. I felt like I had lost Bill emotionally. And, physically, he was hardly around anymore.

On top of my fury over Bill pulling away from the kids, I had great anxiety over finding myself suddenly single after a twenty-year marriage. I couldn't fathom starting over at forty years old.

Even the act of going to bed alone at night in the house became problematic. For one thing, I was sleeping alone for the first time in over two
decades. That was a very strange and lonely feeling. Added to that were
thoughts I was now having about safety and security.

For that first month, I couldn't sleep to save my life. My mind was going
a mile a minute, my emotions were all over the map, and I was filled with anxiety. I was lonely, and slept with one eye open. It was so troubling to realize I
was suddenly the sentry in the house. I was so accustomed to having the man
of the house there to protect us.

Bill was always there for me. He was our protector. When he occasionally went out for the evening, I still slept well, because I knew that he would
be coming home at some point. I never had to think twice about security.
Now, when I went to bed at night, all I had to keep me safe was the burglar
alarm. Setting the alarm at night made me aware of his absence.

For the first time in twenty-four years, I felt alone and unsafe. I did not
like the feeling of being the only adult in the house.

At the end of July, Bill announced that he was getting a storage unit to
house some of his personal belongings. We also discussed what furniture he
wanted to take.

The fact that he was getting a storage unit told me that he wasn't going
to be getting his own place any time soon.

"I don't want to take anything that will disrupt the kids," he said. So,
that meant he wouldn't touch the living room furniture or TV. Over the years,
we had collected enough furniture to fill two houses, so he decided to take
some of the older pieces. I was fine with that.

He told me he was bringing a couple of friends to the house to pick up
some things.

The night before he was due to arrive, Randa and I packed up some of
his things. I insisted on doing it without him because frankly, I knew he was
being heavily influenced by his girlfriend.

He said, "Fine with me. You're the one who knows where everything is,
anyway."

It was tough going for Randa and me.

The entire process was painful, but there were two things I simply could
not bear to do. I did not want to go through any photo albums. And, I could
not go through any holiday decorations. Halloween and Christmas were my
favorite times of the year—they had been Bill's too—and I went overboard
with decorations. I promised Bill that when we got closer to the holidays, I
would go through those things, but I couldn't do it now. Same thing with the
photos—only when I was ready.

He completely understood.

When the time came for Bill to pick up his things, I asked my neighbors to keep an eye out, and let me know who was arriving at my house before they were actually on the porch and knocking at the door. I wanted to make sure you-know-who wasn't with Bill. I told him in advance he had better not bring her, and he promised he wouldn't, but I felt I needed someone to stand watch, in case he had a lapse in judgment. The events surrounding the separation—and the fact that it hit me like an eighteen-wheeler, out of the blue—made it so that I no longer trusted anyone, and certainly not Bill.

He kept his word. Lisa did not show up.

Bill brought a couple of guys with him, and they took some furniture and boxes. I was left with a profound feeling of emptiness.

The kids probably didn't even notice the things were missing, but I knew.

~August~
Seeing the Doctors

"All is fair in love
Love's a crazy game
Two people vow to stay
In love as one they say
But all is changed with time
The future no one can see
The road you leave behind
Ahead lies mystery…"
"All in Love is Fair"

~by Stevie Wonder

T hank God, it was finally here—my first appointment with the coun-selor. I had never been to therapy before, and I had no idea what to expect. I was a little intimidated walking into her office for the first time.

As I entered the small waiting room, I tried not to make eye contact with the others who were also waiting. There was a man sitting by himself. What was he there for? What about that other woman who was by herself? Wait a minute. What about the father with two children by his side? Was that what I should have done—had Bill take the kids to a counselor?

I also wondered about the protocol for counseling sessions. What was going to happen when she called me in there? Was I going to have to lie down on a couch? All I knew of therapy was what I had seen on TV shows—some-one asking questions and writing down notes on a pad of paper.

Questions about the unknown were vibrating between my ears as I sat in the waiting room. The fact that it was so quiet in there didn't help the matter.

The counselor called me in, and I immediately felt better. As soon as I saw her, I was reminded that we'd had a really good connection during the initial meeting by phone.

I took a seat, and when she didn't suggest I lie down, I was relieved.

She explained how the process was going to work, and assured me that our discussions would be kept entirely confidential. The only time she was mandated by law to disclose anything I told her was if she felt that I was either a danger to myself or others. Or, if my records were subpoenaed for a court case.

So, how was I feeling? Depressed? I hadn't been having any suicidal thoughts, had I?

No, I wasn't depressed, and I definitely was not suicidal. Before, I had been geared towards my children and my husband. Now, more than ever, I knew that I had to be there for my kids. Suicide never crossed my mind.

Okay, what about medication? Was I taking any anti-depressants?

I wanted to say, "No, not yet. What do you have in mind?"

I had been walking around feeling like everything was my fault, and torturing myself with questions about what I could have done to prevent the divorce. I felt like my poor kids were going to have to live with the pain of divorce because their mother could not figure out how to fix the problems in her marriage, and wasn't observant enough to notice that their father had been having an affair.

Why hadn't I figured it out? I am a very intuitive person. I should have known. I had begun to lose respect for myself because I felt I should have seen it coming.

Worst of all, I felt like I had let everyone down—my kids, my husband, and myself. The feeling that I had failed everyone was the hardest thing of all for me to take, because that's not how I roll. I have always lived for my family.

Within the first thirty minutes of our session, my counselor had already turned me around. I could have gotten up, shaken her hand, and walked out feeling like a whole new person.

She told me, "This is NOT your fault, Shelly! Bill is his own person. His actions and choices were his own. You have no way of knowing the exact moment he made his decision, but I do know this—there is nothing you could have done to stop him."

She told me that, from what she observed, I was a very strong woman. She assured me that while it was going to take some time, everything really would be okay.

"From everything you have told me so far," she said, "Bill seems to be going through a severe midlife crisis. Sometimes, they are caused by a chemical imbalance, which is why he seems to you like a different person now."

I made a mental note to read more on midlife crises, and I put "buy a journal" on my shopping list because she suggested I begin writing down my thoughts.

I felt an overwhelming trust in her that went beyond a doctor/patient dynamic. She had a very compassionate, nurturing, and down-to-earth demeanor. I could tell that, woman to woman, she genuinely understood my feelings.

I think the fact that she was around my own age made me especially comfortable. If she had been elderly, I would have felt like she was giving me advice.

Telling myself I could not have changed things had not been effective. Hearing it from a trained professional was so validating. Bill had made his own choices! It wasn't my fault! I wasn't crazy!

Before I left her office, she told me, "You don't have to do it right away, but it will be important to get your children in to see someone at some point."

As I said goodbye, I felt so grateful to her. I had been questioning my very sanity. Because Bill was acting so bizarrely, but refusing to acknowledge that his behavior was crazy, I kept asking myself, okay, then, am I the crazy one?

Having my friends and family tell me what I wanted to hear was com-forting—but not necessarily reassuring. Of course, they were going to be sup-portive of me. Hearing from a professional that there was nothing wrong with me, and that none of this was my fault, made me feel lighter than I'd felt in weeks.

I committed to memory three things she'd said:

It was not my fault.

There was nothing I could have done.

And, I was not crazy.

I knew I would need to remind myself of those things later when I started feeling discouraged again.

Now that I had seen a professional for my mental and emotional health, I knew there was something else I needed to get checked out. I was trying to ignore it, but this nagging question kept returning: *What if Lisa wasn't the only one?*

The thought that there may have been others over the years was troubling to me on so many levels. Even if Lisa *was* the only one, I was nervous. I had seen photos of her on Facebook, and it was easy to see that she was a very out-going girl. I had no idea of her sexual history before Bill.

I could not believe I was actually going to have to pick up the phone, call my doctor's office, and ask for a test for STD's. I cringed at the thought of it. It was so humiliating—and infuriating!

Luckily, it was time to make the appointment for my annual pap exam anyway, so I didn't have to call and make a special appointment for the STD test. I just requested the first appointment with the doctor I could get, and figured I'd ask for the additional tests when I arrived.

"Oh, I'm sorry," the receptionist said. "We are setting those appointments about four months out."

So much for my plan. I now had no choice but to tell her why I needed to get in more quickly than that.

"I really can't wait that long," I explained. "I'm breaking up with my husband, and…"

Normally, the doctor would look in my chart, see that I had been married for twenty years, and skip any extra testing.

During my doctor's visit, I felt like he would never look at me the same way again. I even worried that there might be a permanent mark on my chart. The HIPAA laws probably prevent such things from happening, but nothing could prevent me from feeling permanently marked on a personal level.

The few days I had to wait for the results were agonizing. I went over all possible outcomes, and tried to imagine how I'd handle the worst case scenarios. Meanwhile, I told my mom and Randa about my appointment, and they were also furious with Bill for putting me through that.

I was so relieved when all the tests came back negative.

During the entire month of August, I was losing sleep, as the computer system in my brain tried to grapple with my divorce and come up with a forecast for the future that did not look bleak.

How was I going to make ends meet financially?

Going forward, how were things going to play out for Dylan and Payton?

I could not believe, for example, that Payton's eventual prom and wedding would find Dylan and me in attendance without Bill by our side. Daddy's little girl would not have her Daddy there when she needed him most. Or, if he was there, he would be sitting off by himself, either alone or with another woman.

I couldn't stop thinking about all those milestones in life that I'd looked forward to experiencing as a family. Bill and I had worked so hard to be a tight family unit for our kids, and now it was all being taken away by something I didn't even understand. It was beyond me that Bill could throw away so casually the same marriage vows I took so seriously. Over the years, opportunities had presented themselves for me to have an affair, but I never did—and never would have—pursued them. It wasn't even hard for me to resist because I was so deeply devoted to our family.

How did someone go from being married and having a family to beginning an affair, and slowly getting up more and more nerve, until they treated the affair like it was the normal relationship, instead of the marriage and family? How does that happen? Who makes the first move?

I tried a few times to ask Bill about it, but he always said in so many words that it was none of my business; it was between him and Lisa; and I would never understand.

I would say, "Fine, but can't you give me some clue as to how it happened so I can understand how my life turned upside down?"

Nope. He would not engage in any conversation along those lines whatsoever.

Since he wouldn't fill in the blanks for me, my poor brain—awake or asleep—worked overtime to try to produce the answer to a million unanswered questions. How did the affair start? He did try to kiss her? Did she try to kiss him? Wasn't that awkward for Bill? What did they talk about? And how did he live with himself afterwards, knowing he had betrayed so many people, including himself?

Bill was such a strong-willed person, I couldn't imagine how he could allow that to happen to himself—or live with the guilt over even a one-night-stand. Obviously, he couldn't live with himself afterwards, because he began to wear the guilt on his face. When I returned from that trip to Louisville in early July, it was clear that something was wrong with him. And, if I hadn't asked him about it, I believe he would have eventually broken down and told me. There was no doubt that it was weighing on him.

He started seeing her in May, and I didn't ask him about his change in demeanor until July, so that was a long time for him to live with that.

I tossed and turned at night. I slept in increments, then startled awake. I would wake up, go downstairs to the kitchen, and mop the floor, or do the laundry at three o'clock in the morning. Then, I'd sit on the mopped floor and cry, feeling like I'd lost my mind.

I was trying to be as strong as I could, and keep wearing my Positive Polly hat for the kids. At least by the beginning of August, the kids were getting back to a normal routine, which was more than I could say for myself. They were both starting back to school, which was a saving grace. After school, Payton was only home for one hour before she went to gymnastics for four hours. After gymnastics, she came home, showered, and went to bed.

I began to realize that I really needed to handle my insomnia problems. The owners of my company could see the toll everything was taking on me. I had dark circles under my eyes from not sleeping, and I generally did not look well. I couldn't very well take sleeping pills, being the only adult in the house now. I couldn't afford to be drugged up in case, God forbid, there was some kind of emergency.

Friends told me that Xanax would help take the edge off enough for me to fall asleep, and stay asleep, without having the effect on me of a full-blown sleeping pill. I saw the doctor, who gave me the lowest possible dose. It did help. I took it about an hour before bed. I was finally able to sleep in four-hour blocks without losing sleep over feeling like my life was falling apart.

The one thing the Xanax could not help me with was the fact that, whether I slept for fifteen minutes or four hours at a time, I woke up crying. I would awaken, feel the tears on my face, realize I had been crying in my sleep, and then be so saddened by that fact, that I would start crying all over again.

It was really wearing on me.

Teary-eyed or not, I got up every morning and play-acted the role of a functioning parent. I used the old "act as if" routine. I had no choice. Bill had stepped down from his parenting role, and that left only me. He had been with the kids a total of three or four times in the entire month of July—two or three times on the weekend, and one night when I went to Kentucky.

Dylan had taken over Bill's job of driving Payton to gymnastics. After school, he made sure he was home in time to take her to gymnastics, and then he had time after that to do his homework and hang out with his friends. I went and picked Payton up in the evenings.

It galled me that Bill was only ten minutes away at Vinnie's, and yet he couldn't pick up his daughter from gymnastics. Every single night, I was the one to go get her. Each time I thought about the promises he made about staying involved in the kids' lives, I got upset all over again. He had promised those things the night we told the kids the news, but it had taken only about one week for everything to fall apart. Now, instead of being committed to staying involved, he was making a concerted effort to stay out of the picture so the kids could get used to him being gone.

Get used to him being gone? Seriously? That was his goal for our children? The sadness was almost more than I could bear.

~August 13th~
The Divorce is Final

"Take the way home that leads back to Sullivan Street
Cross the water and home through the town
Past the shadows that fall down whenever we meet
Pretty soon I won't come around…"
"Sullivan Street"
~by Malley/Gillingham/Bowman/Immergluck/

Duritz/Bryson (Counting Crows)

On August 13th, I found out that our divorce had become final on the 11th—exactly thirty-one days after July 10th, the date we had filed. I was in Kentucky when I found out. For that trip, I had arranged for my parents to stay with the kids because Bill still did not have a place of his own.

Anyway, I was in Kentucky when I called my uncle to find out if the divorce was final. After he told me that it had become final on August 11th, he told me that the original copy of the divorce decree would be sent to me in the mail, and I would then have sixty days to start getting my name off everything.

I was officially divorced. The emotional realization that my marriage was over took the wind out of me. I was in my Kentucky office at the time, and I started hyperventilating. I had to sit back in my chair and try to catch my breath.

Twenty-four years of my life was gone—twenty years of marriage, and the four years we'd known each other beforehand.

Forty days ago, I found out my husband was having an affair, and wanted a divorce.

Thirty days ago, I filed for divorce.

Now, it was finished. How could that be? How could twenty-four years just wash down the river like a leaf?

I started to panic. Had I filed for divorce too fast?

I had to talk myself down. I'd done what I had to do in the time frame that made sense to me. Everything was going to be fine in time. I truly believed that a year from then, whatever changes Bill had been going through would have passed, and we would be the typical divorced family. He would want to do everything with the kids, just like he had all their lives.

And, at least now that everything was final, Bill could not challenge me on either our financial agreement or our custody arrangement.

I called him. "Well," I said, "our divorce is final. Denny will be mailing me the paperwork, and you will need to come get your copy."

He was supposed to take the kids that weekend—August 15th. He said, "I am having a hard time figuring out a place to take them. Dad's got something going on at the house this weekend…"

"Look, Bill, I'm not an idiot," I said. "I know you are living with Lisa!"

He let out a big sigh. "You're right. Yes, I am living with her."

All my urgings for him to get his own place where the kids could go visit him had fallen on deaf ears. I had told him several times that I didn't want my children around someone who would be engaged in an affair—and certainly not this quickly. Everything I read about divorce stressed the importance of introducing your children to the new boyfriend or girlfriend in stages. I reminded him that during our divorce negotiations, we had agreed that we would decide together when it was time for Lisa to be introduced to the kids.

"Shelly," he said, "there is nothing you can do about the fact that I'm with her. You're just going to have to deal with it! But, sure, I'll just take the kids to a hotel. But, I can't do it for the whole weekend. It will have to be for one night. The kids can hang out at the hotel and go swimming in the pool."

Payton still knew nothing about Lisa, but when she found out her dad still didn't have his own place, she said she didn't want to be him at all that weekend.

"But, honey," I said. "It's only going to be for one night. Are you sure?"

"I just don't want to," she said. "Staying at a hotel is too weird. I would rather just sleep over at a friend's house."

That meant whatever Bill had in mind, it would just be him and Dylan. When Dylan heard about the hotel idea, he was not happy either.

He said, "Dad told me he doesn't really have the money to spend on a hotel."

I didn't know whether to scream or cry. The weekend before, Bill was on a weekend trip with his girlfriend. Now, he was telling his children he didn't have any money? He had the money; he just chose to spend it on something else.

I was dying to say to Dylan, "Let me tell you what's really going on. The reason your dad has no place to take you kids is because he is shacking up with his girlfriend instead of renting his own place!"

Dylan knew his Dad had a girlfriend, but he didn't know he was living with her.

Dylan said, "I'm going to tell Dad not to spend the money on a hotel. We can just hang out for the day, and then he can bring me back home."

The twenty-four hours that Bill was scheduled to be with the kids was my meltdown time. It was time that I didn't need to pretend that everything was okay, and I needed that so badly.

During the entire day that Bill and Dylan spent together, I kept wondering if Bill would get a hotel room for them, after all, or just bring Dylan home. I tried so hard to resist calling to ask Bill what his plans were. I finally called that evening, but Bill let my call go into voicemail and left it at that.

I thought, okay, well, I guess they stayed in a hotel, after all.

When I finally reached Bill on Sunday, he told me that he, Dylan, and Dylan's friend Sean had all stayed at Lisa's apartment!

I was so angry, I was speechless. I simply hung up the phone. I had just reminded Bill that the timing of the kids meeting Lisa was something we had to figure out together. It was one thing for him to tell me there was nothing I could do about him being with Lisa, but it was another thing entirely to shut me out of the decision as to when it was appropriate for the kids to meet her—much less sleep at her apartment!

I called him right back, ranting and raving. "Don't you understand what you've done? By telling Dylan you didn't want to spend money on a hotel, and suggesting he just go stay with you at your girlfriend's house, you put him on the spot. You didn't give him the option to do it when he was ready."

"Shelly," he said, "calm down. Dylan was fine with it, believe me!"

"That's what you're not getting," I said. "He's a sixteen-year-old boy who wants to please his father. Of course he's going to say yes! This child just found out forty days ago that his parents were getting divorced. Now, he's already being asked to sleep over at his dad's girlfriend's house? Have you lost your f***ing mind? This will NEVER happen again!"

~Mid-August~
More is Revealed

"Yesterday a child came out to wonder
Caught a dragonfly inside a jar
Fearful when the sky was full of thunder
And tearful at the falling of a star,
And the seasons they go round and round
And the painted ponies go up and down
We're captive on the carousel of time
We can't return, we can only look
Behind from where we came
And go round and round and round
In the circle game."
"The Circle Game"

~by Joni Mitchell

I tried to calm myself down before Sean drove Dylan home. It was important to talk to my son without going into attack mode.

When Dylan got home, he went up to his bedroom, and I followed him up. "Were you really okay going to Lisa's apartment?" Dylan had high enough morals to know that it wasn't right to be sleeping at his dad's girlfriend's house so soon.

He said, "Yeah, it was fine. Actually, they were having a party, and Sean and I were at the swimming pool the whole time. Dad came down from time to time to check in and hang out with us."

I couldn't believe my ears. They were having a *party* on Bill's weekend with the kids? My blood started boiling again.

I said, "Don't you see how wrong this is? Your dad made a bad choice in taking you over there. He should never have put you in that position."

I tried to give Dylan a moral perspective on the situation.

He tried to reassure me, telling me that he and his friend Sean slept on the couch and floor in the living room, while Bill and Lisa slept in their room.

There was so much wrong with that picture, I didn't even know where to begin. I could feel myself becoming a hawk with its claws out, as I aggressively tried to get Dylan to understand what I was saying. I figured I'd better leave well enough alone for the moment, and I left his room.

A few minutes later, I went back into his room, crying.

He looked at me and said, "Mom, I don't get why you're so upset."

I said, "I just don't understand, Dyl. How can you say you're okay staying with your dad and the woman he had an affair with?"

He whipped his head around. *"What did you say?"*

In that instant, it hit me—when Dylan told me at the doctor's office that he knew his dad had a girlfriend, he assumed she was a *new* girlfriend! He had no idea before that moment that his dad had been having an affair. Now, I was really panicked. What was I going to do?

I didn't have any choice. The cat was already out of the bag.

So, I reminded Dylan of the night that Bill and I had talked to him and Payton about the divorce. "Remember, honey, when we said there were other issues in play? Things you kids didn't need to hear about right then? Well, that's what we were referring to…"

Now that he understood that Lisa was "the other woman," he was freaked out. In some strange way, I found that terribly reassuring. I just knew that my son should have been reacting differently than he had been, and now it all made sense.

"I'm so sorry," I said. "When you said you thought your dad had a girlfriend, I just assumed you knew he'd been having an affair. Now I realize you thought he had a *new* girlfriend."

Dylan didn't say much. In typical guy fashion, he was quiet while he processed what he was feeling. I had just crushed his image of his father—his Superman. He looked so disappointed and hurt, my heart went out to him, but I knew I had to honor his need to be alone with his thoughts. He stayed in his room alone—probably texting his friends—and eventually fell asleep.

I went downstairs, called my mom, and told her what happened. We both sobbed. Dylan's dad was his idol, and without meaning to, I had just stepped all over that.

Later, Dylan and I had another conversation in which I reiterated to him how important it was that Payton not know anything just yet. As much as he hated keeping a secret from his sister, he knew it was for the best. She was not ready. She had enough hurt and anger to work through without having to hear about her dad's affair.

I was one hundred percent sure I needed to wait to tell Payton—but then on August 19th, I had one of those mother's-intuition feelings, and decided I'd better pay attention to it. My daughter has a dog's acute hearing and a cat's soft footsteps, which meant she could accidentally happen upon a conversation between Dylan and me, without us knowing she was there. I needed to make sure she didn't hear the wrong thing at the wrong time.

I also didn't want Bill giving her some explanation in which he was trying to rationalize everything.

Payton had an orthodontist appointment that day. My plan was to tell her after her appointment. My heart was beating hard as we both got into the car and I pulled to the back of the parking lot.

"Honey," I said. "We need to talk."

She was fidgeting in her seat and avoiding my eyes. After the bomb Bill and I dropped on the kids the night we told them about the divorce, she had to know it wasn't good news.

"I am really sorry to have to tell you this," I said, "but your dad has a girlfriend." I decided that was the best strategy—to tell her the truth in pieces. She didn't need to know about the affair right at that moment.

I was trying not to cry. But, when she looked at me, my tears started flowing.

"So," she said, "my dad is a cheater."

So much for my plan to tell her about the girlfriend first, and the affair later. Now what was I supposed to do? Well, I wasn't going to lie.

"He did have an affair," I explained. "That's what you call it when you're married."

She asked if I knew the woman and I said no, and explained about Bill and Lisa being old school friends and reconnecting on Facebook. I said I didn't know much more than that. I also told her that her brother already knew.

She was clearly heartbroken—sad for me, and disillusioned over her dad. While she never said it in so many words, the questions she was asking me made it clear she was grappling with how her father could have left us for another woman. I couldn't really help her there. I had the same questions and no answers.

She asked, "Does he live with her?"

I said that he did, but that I'd just found that out.

"Well," she said, "I want nothing to do with her."

I said, "I'm going to let your dad know that you know."

"You can," she said, "but I don't want to talk about it. And, I don't want either Dad or Dylan to talk to me about it until I'm ready."

I said, "I'm so sorry, Sweetie. I never thought this would happen to me or to us. But we will be fine. We'll get through it. And, I'll make sure Dylan and your dad know you don't want to discuss Lisa or meet her until you are ready—whether that is next month or next year."

The two of us cried together.

My heart was torn in two for her. For me to watch Daddy's little princess having to deal with this new information on top of the hurt she was already feeling was almost too much to bear. It was insult on top of injury.

From then on, Payton wanted the security of sleeping in the spare bedroom, right next to my room. Normally, she slept at the other end of the hallway. There was a lot of memorabilia of Bill's in that room, and she wanted it all taken out. Then she started scouting the house for other photos and items she wanted removed.

That was hard for me. I wasn't ready yet.

Every photo of Bill with the family had to come down—anything that reminded her of him. She had been hurt all along, but now her hurt was tinged with anger over the affair. She was outraged. Being twelve years old, with the hormones just beginning to surge, didn't help the matter any.

I figured I'd better let Bill know the state that his daughter was in, so I called him that evening and told him that she knew. He was furious that I told her. That was interesting to me. He wanted Dylan to meet Lisa, and even stay at their place. But he didn't want Payton to know anything. I'm sure he cherished the way his daughter had looked up to him.

I explained that I'd had to tell her before she overheard Dylan and me talking. Then I explained how I'd thought Dylan already knew about the affair because of what he'd said about his dad having a girlfriend.

When Bill found out that Payton not only knew that Lisa was his girlfriend, but that they'd been having an affair, he almost lost his mind.

He said, "How dare you tell her I had an affair!"

"I didn't tell her," I said. "She asked me if her daddy was a cheater, and I wasn't going to lie. I didn't call you a cheater. She did. I just explained the word 'affair' to her."

When he started scolding me, I put a quick end to it, reminding him that he had no place to be scolding me. "You have made this bed, now you will lie in it."

Bill was also upset over Dylan's reaction to the affair. But, after the initial shock of what I was saying wore off, he calmed down. Deep down in his heart, he knew that what he was doing was wrong.

We ended the conversation with me telling him that, under no circumstances did Payton care to discuss the matter before she was ready. I reassured him that we didn't need to let it go on for too long, but we needed to respect her wishes and give her some time to adjust.

"By the way," I said, "you know how I had an intuition that I'd better tell Payton before she overheard something? Well, she told me that she'd overheard bits and pieces of the conversation I had with Dylan the night it came out that he knew about Lisa, but not the affair. She couldn't put it all together, but she knew something was really wrong."

Now that the secret was out, I started confirming the suspicions of my friends who had been asking me all along, "Is there someone else?"

I wished I could be a fly on the wall when Bill told people why we got divorced. I was dying to know what he was saying. The friends he and I had together were more his friends than mine, and none of them were picking up the phone and talking to me about the divorce. I wasn't reaching out to them, either. I felt too awkward. Having no idea what Bill had told them about us made me feel anxious and uncomfortable.

I envisioned him saying bad things about me to make himself feel better about what he'd done. Otherwise, what would he say? "Shelly and I were really happy together, but I impulsively decided to leave her for this other woman."

When Payton went on the rampage, taking down photos and memorabilia around the house, I felt validated. Even my daughter was angry over what was happening. I also felt liberated. She was doing what I hadn't been able to bring myself to do.

As for Dylan, his mission in life was to make sure his sister was okay. Whatever she needed to do to feel better was okay with him. He was ever the protective big brother.

Around this same time, I realized that the only way I was going to survive the divorce was by instituting a policy where Bill and I talked only when necessary. As it was, we were talking several times a week, and it was too hard to move on when I was talking to him that much.

It also bugged me to no end to think that while Bill was talking on the phone to me, Lisa might be sitting right there, listening to every word we said.

Strangely, I wasn't plagued by curiosity about Lisa. The only thing I really wanted to know was where she lived, in case Bill took the kids there again. Everything else about her was right there on Facebook—which had its upside and its downside.

On the downside, the daily updates on everything she and Bill were planning in their new social life together were painful. On the upside, I knew things before Bill told me. That was how I knew that he had gone camping the weekend before he told Dylan he had no money. Facebook was definitely turning out to be a double-edged sword. It broke up my marriage, but it also allowed me to track the aftermath.

Thanks to a friend of Bill's who had an open Facebook wall, I had even been able to see photos of Lisa, and photos of her with Bill. I looked at them on the morning of July 4th when my snooping led me to the discovery of their affair. Not surprisingly, we resembled one another (as I've mentioned), right down to our body type. Sure, her dishwater blonde hair was long, and my strawberry blonde hair was short—but Bill preferred it long. There were definite similarities.

Seeing photos of them together tore me apart. Looking at those photos, I could see that he cared for her. My sense of it was that he had a different kind of feeling for her than he did for me. She seemed to symbolize that responsibility-free life he was craving.

~Late August~
Acceptance

"Today you are you,
That is truer than true,
There is no one alive who is youer than you."

-by Dr. Seuss

Anxiety over what Bill might be saying about me, and what his friends might be thinking, was contributing to my growing feeling of insecurity. I was still young, and not about to become the old woman who lives in the shoe. So, that meant I was going to have to eventually start a relationship with someone new. And, that meant somebody new was going to see me naked!

I had never felt pretty enough or thin enough in the first place, and the thought of going through the early stages of dating with a stranger was enough to make me start biting my nails. It was time to take matters into my own hands and call a personal trainer. It was one of the only times in my adult life when I spent any money on myself. I considered it an investment.

I had worked out at a gym off and on throughout my life, so I knew how much better I felt when I was working out. I was aware of the endorphins that were released during a workout, and that seemed like a much healthier coping strategy than smoking cigarettes or overeating.

Having an appointment to meet the personal trainer at the gym would get me out of the house. The exercise-induced endorphins would improve my mood. The reshaping of my body and the inevitable weight loss would boost my self-confidence. There was no downside.

I got lucky with Spencer, the trainer I chose. I really liked him. I'm a bit of a whiner when it comes to having someone push me during a workout, but he had a great attitude, and could easily handle my personality. He had, no doubt, seen it all in the course of being a personal trainer.

August was coming to a close, and I had another Kentucky trip on my work calendar. Of course, Bill did not inquire as to what I was planning to do for childcare. This time, I had Randa stay at my house to look after the kids. It was fun for her because it was like a hotel stay—it got her out of her own house, for a change. And the kids adore her. Payton, especially, was excited that Randa—a great cook—would be staying with them.

She asked me,   "What do you mean Bill doesn't know I'm going to be staying with the kids? Didn't he even ask you what you were planning to do for childcare coverage?"

I said, "Nope! He didn't even ask."

As I've said, Randa had known Bill for as long as I had, and she was deeply saddened to know that their friendship was never going to be the same again. How could it be? She'd watched him destroy our family. She was furious with him, and itching to give him a piece of her mind. There was much she needed to get off her chest, but she had not spoken to him since he left me. She didn't want any potential backlash from their conversation to affect the kids or me.

"There will be a time," I said to her at the beginning of the separation, "but for now, please just hold off."

The weekend after my Kentucky trip, Bill was supposed to take the kids. Now that his living arrangements were common knowledge, we all dispensed with the charade that he was going to take the kids anywhere but their apartment. That meant he would only be able to pick up the kids for lunch, and then return them before dark. Payton was fine with that, as long as he didn't bring Lisa, or talk about her.

It was bad enough that he was going to have so little time with the kids. Then he told me that there was a possibility he'd end up with "the beeper" for the weekend, which meant there was a chance he'd actually have to work, and not be able to see the kids at all. He had always managed to get rid of the beeper on the weekends when we were married, but what could I do?

I had made some kind of peace with the whole situation. If he was going to act like a crazy ass, I just needed to let it happen. I figured the quicker it ran its course, the quicker it would be over. My job was to maintain some kind of calm in the midst of the storm.

The serenity prayer became my new M.O. I tried to accept the things I could not change, change the things I could, and learn to pause long enough to know the difference.

I focused on making positive changes wherever I could. I worked out. I saw my counselor, who continued to help me see that everything was going to be okay, told me that the step I took in limiting contact with Bill was a good sign of my instincts towards self-preservation, and even suggested a book on divorce, which I read. I borrowed a tip from the book—scheduled phone calls between the spouses, with an agenda of what would be discussed during those calls. The idea of having an agenda to help keep those phone calls on track appealed to me as a business person.

I told Bill that, from then on, we were going to have scheduled phone calls only, unless some kind of emergency arose. I suggested he make a list of what he wanted to discuss with me, and I told him I would have my list ready, too. Our first scheduled conversation was at the end of August. I really worked hard at sticking to my agenda, and tried to avoid the impulse to throw daggers—which is not to say I was fully successful. He made some comments that I had retorts for, but it was one of the first generally civil conversations we had been able to pull off since our separation.

One day, Bill's mom, Jan, called to let me know she had met Lisa, who was with Bill when he went to his mom's to collect his mail. Jan told me that Lisa walked into the house and said, "Hi, I'm Lisa, the party girl! Nice to meet you." Jan was very upset by this.

She said, "What was that supposed to mean, Shelly? What kind of woman walks into your house and says that? Especially not one that is forty-two years old! Doesn't she realize how inappropriate that is? Bill is not the only one going through these things. The rest of us are, too."

As much as I agreed with everything that Jan was saying, it seemed odd for me to be having this conversation with her. Was it normal to be getting a call from my ex-mother-in-law, telling me she had met her son's girlfriend?

She then went on to express to me how strongly she felt that Bill had made the wrong decision, and again, while I shared her feelings, the whole idea of having that conversation with her somehow threw me.

She asked me, "Why can't he see that, Shelly? Why is he doing this to you and the kids?"

I had the exact same questions, and I didn't need to be reminded by her. What could I say in response? "Yeah, it sucks alright."

I knew she didn't mean to add salt to the wound, but that's what she was inadvertently doing.

As the season began to slowly change, and the approach of September heralded the time for the kids to return to school, I found myself in a deep period of reflection. We had all innocently begun the summer with the highest of hopes, and now we were ending it with our lives unrecognizable.

I was no longer someone who naturally trusted people. I questioned everything. I constantly thought about, and fretted over, the future. For twenty-four years, the wheel of life had turned in a wonderful and predictable cycle, and now the spokes had fallen off.

I did not want to spend the rest of my life alone. As someone who loved companionship, I would wake up in the morning, unable to believe that I was without a mate with whom to share my life.

How would I find a new mate? By dating! But, how the hell was I supposed to date? I didn't even know what that meant. I hadn't been on a date in over two decades. My few single friends had told me enough horror stories that I was definitely not looking forward to that particular adventure.

I was someone who had built a life around marriage and family, and suddenly I found myself thrust into a world of singles. I'll never forget a woman I met at a friend's party. Like me, she had gotten divorced after several years of marriage. "One of the hardest things for me," she said, "was to get myself out of my comfort zone. That meant that instead of spending all my time with my married friends like I'd done before, I had to get out, join groups, and meet other singles."

I thought, oh, my God! How was I going to do that?

As I tried to picture my life as a single woman, Bill was rushing headlong into his new life. The kids got one or two texts or phone calls from him each week. It is hard to articulate how angry and hurt I was, seeing him intentionally disconnecting from them, supposedly "for their own good, so they could get used to him being gone."

I couldn't very well tell the kids how I was feeling. It wasn't the sort of thing you want to share with your children. They already had their emotional hands full with the devastation over the divorce and the affair. And, as angry as I was with Bill, I didn't want to make him look any worse in the eyes of his children.

But, he wasn't making things easy for me. Every time I turned around, he was doing something else that made it hard for me to hold my tongue.

~September 14th~
Birth Days

"May you grow up to be righteous,
May you grow up to be true,
May you always know the truth,
And see the lights surrounding you.
May you always be courageous,
Stand upright, and be strong,
May you stay forever young..."
"Forever Young"

-by Bob Dylan

B ill's birthday was September 14ᵗʰ—a Monday.

He could have cared less about birthdays. As I've mentioned before, he loved making others the center of the attention, but hated being the center of attention, himself. To him, birthdays were just another day. He always said, "You are only as old as you feel," and he always felt like a kid.

For twenty-four years, I'd made a big deal over his birthday, anyway, but what was I supposed to do now? Buy him a gift? After going back and forth in my mind, I finally picked out a card for him and decided the kids could give that to him. I had good reasons—finances, the divorce, the knowledge that he wouldn't have bought me anything if the tables were turned. But, that didn't stop my heart from breaking over the fact that it was the first time in years I wasn't doing anything for Bill's birthday.

The weekend before his birthday was his weekend with the kids, but Dylan was talking about having other plans. Bill was good about being flexible. He figured the kids were old enough to have lives of their own, and he didn't want to force them to give up time they spent with their friends, or involved in their favorite activities.

The thing was, Payton would not be alone with Bill. I think she was afraid that he would start talking about Lisa and the divorce. "Well, if Dylan's not going with Dad," she announced, "I'm not either!"

Dylan changed his plans, and both kids spent time with their dad.

When Bill dropped off the kids after their time together, I fully expected him to say, "By the way, my birthday is Monday, and I'd like the kids to go out to dinner with me."

He did not say a single word about it. And, neither did I. As a rule, I tried not to quiz the kids about time spent with their dad. But, in that instance, I needed to ask them if Bill had said anything about them spending his birthday with him. They said no.

I found out belatedly from Jan that Bill had spent his birthday with Lisa. Then, on Wednesday, Jan, her boyfriend, Bill, and Lisa all went out to dinner together. Afterwards, Jan once again felt the need to call me and give me the play-by-play on the evening. She shared with me the fact that she didn't care for Lisa, that Bill was making a mistake, and that he had a new group of friends—no doubt because they were the only ones that would give him the approval he was seeking.

They didn't know him before, so why would they object to his new lifestyle? Everyone else—his family and the friends he'd known all his life—was totally horrified by his choices.

As I hung up with Jan, I kept thinking to myself, all of this insanity related to Bill's midlife crisis will pass. It's just a chemical imbalance. He will get it out of his system, and a year from now, we will be the normal divorced family.

On September 17th, I had to do another of my bimonthly trips to Kentucky.

Again, no acknowledgment from Bill that I needed childcare coverage for that trip, so this time, my brother stayed with the kids. Mitch came over with my sister-in-law, Theresa, and my niece, Reagan, and they had dinner with Dylan and Payton. Before bedtime, Theresa took Reagan home to put her to bed, and Mitch stayed over.

I'm not sure my brother knew what he was signing up for when he offered to watch his niece and nephew. His only child was six years old, and in preschool. I'm sure he thought, well, Dylan and Payton are older. They can take care of themselves. That is definitely true, but he failed to take into consideration that he was dealing with a very emotional twelve-year-old.

I knew that whatever came up, Mitch would be able to deal with it.

Meanwhile, in my hotel room, my plan was to take a sleeping pill and go to bed. I told myself, if the hotel catches fire, I am going down with it! I am so exhausted, I have to sleep.

There were no fires, thank God, but as I was getting ready for bed, my cell phone rang. It was Payton, crying hysterically. She missed her dad, and she was really struggling. I'm sure the fact that I was away at the time made the absence of her dad seem that much more real. But, the thing that was weighing on her most heavily was the fact that she had never confronted her dad, and told him how she felt. And she had made Dylan and me promise that, not only would we not bring anything up to her, we'd make sure that Bill didn't, either.

I said, "You know, Sweetie, you've really got to talk to your dad. You can't let things keep going like this."

Payton was upstairs in her room, calling me, and my brother was apparently downstairs, with no idea that she was having a meltdown.

I told her, "Just take a shower, and go to bed. Tomorrow is a new day, and I'll be home tomorrow night."

The minute I hung up with her, I dialed Mitch on his cell phone. When I told him what was going on with Payton upstairs, he was stunned. He had no idea. I asked him to check in on Payton later. She needed a pat on the shoulder and reassurances that everything would be okay.

I took comfort in knowing that Mitch was there for the kids, and was willing to stay with them any time I needed him.

During that same overnight trip to Kentucky, I got some good news.

Before I left town, I'd told my very pregnant friend Maggie, "I just know you are going to have the baby while I'm gone." Sure enough, as soon as I left, she went right into labor.

So, when I returned from Kentucky, I wanted to fly in and drive straight to the hospital. There was only one problem—Payton was still going to need to be picked up from gymnastics. I had given up on expecting Bill to help out. So, for the first time ever, I asked Dylan to pick up his sister. He had been driving her to gymnastics, but since the separation, I was the one who had been picking her up.

It was the first time I was relying on Dylan to do something for me. Thanks to my son, I was able to go see Maggie and her wonderful new baby boy.

For so long, Maggie had been unhappily married, with no plans to have children. Then she got divorced, remarried, and pregnant.

For so long, I had been a happily married woman with a husband, two children, and dogs. Now, I was the one who was divorced.

"You're the woman who was never going to have a baby," I said to her. "Now look at you! You can't imagine your life without this baby."

Seeing Maggie and her baby brought up a lot of mixed feelings for me. It stirred happy memories of having Dylan, my firstborn child. It also gave me hope. If Maggie was able to find somebody else, maybe I would, too. It was also bittersweet for me to realize how my life had done a complete one-eighty.

When I got home from the hospital, I was folding laundry in the laundry room, and I suddenly had an overwhelming feeling of guilt. Why did I have to ask Dylan to pick up his sister, when Bill was perfectly capable of doing it?

Dylan heard me, and came in. "Mom, what's wrong?"

Before the divorce, the only time the kids ever saw me cry was when I was watching a touching movie. Now, I was fighting back tears. Between sniffles, I said, "I'm sorry, Dillie, that I had to ask you to go get your sister. You can't be an adult yet. You're still a child."

Dylan—God bless him—was so great with the way he handled the situation. "Don't worry, Mom, it's okay. We'll get through this fine. I'll do whatever I can to help you."

Why was I having to rely on my son to pick up his sister when she had a perfectly capable father? It was in that moment that it really hit me—Bill was not in his right mind.

One after another, the dominoes kept falling.

Meanwhile, the kids had been back in school for a little over a month. Resuming their routine was very helpful.

Payton was again in the habit of coming home from school and going straight to gymnastics. She was very busy.

Dylan was going to school, dropping off his sister at gymnastics, and then hanging out with friends. Every month, I was giving him some extra walking-around money as thanks for being Payton's chauffeur. Not only was he helping me out a lot, but it was making me feel good to know that he and his sister had at least seven minutes in the car together every day. They needed each other right now.

Dylan and Payton had returned to their usual routines, but it was definitely not business as usual at school, as I discovered when I went online to check their grades. I was shocked to see that—even though they had only been back at school for a month or so—Dylan already had some "F" grades on tests and homework. I had no patience for failing grades. It was completely uncalled for.

If someone studies for a test, they are not going to get a failing grade, so an "F" told me he wasn't bothering to study. Of course, both kids had been deeply affected by the divorce, so it was understandable—but that didn't mean it was acceptable.

Over the years, Dylan typically got "A" and "B" grades. When he did get the occasional bad test grade, Bill and I would bring it to his attention. With a little bit of study and extra-credit work, he would bring up his grades. Now that Bill and I were apart, I needed to put it on the agenda for our next phone call.

When Bill and I did talk, I said, "I went online and looked at the kids' grades, and Dylan's got a few 'F's' on homework and tests."

Bill's response blew me away. "You do whatever you need to do to help him improve."

Whatever I needed to do to help him? What about him? He wasn't planning to have a talk with his son? I couldn't believe I was on the hook for all the twenty-four/seven parenting, while Bill played part-time dad.

Clearly, Bill was having major issues. I no longer had the energy to question him or fight him on anything. All I could do was hope that one day, he'd come back to his senses.

I talked to my son, who has never been able to lie to me for two seconds. In the end, he always blurts out the truth. "You're right! I didn't study! I need to buckle down."

He did buckle down and study. Later, he said to me, "Hey, when you study, tests are easy!"

Being able to keep up with your kids' grades online is a great tool for parents, and it's one I don't think we should feel ashamed of using. These days, we hardly talk to teachers anymore, so the online posting of grades is a great way to keep up on how your kids are doing in school.

~Late September~
Clearing the Air

"I can't make you love me if you don't
You can't make your heart feel something it won't
Here in the dark, in these final hours
I will lay down my heart and feel the power
But you won't, no, you won't
I can't make you love me if you don't..."
"I Can't Make You Love Me"

~by Shamblin/Reid (Bonnie Raitt)

September turned out to be a time for everyone to speak their mind and clear the air.

First it was Randa. Her impulse to speak out ended up dispelling the mystery of what Bill might be telling people about our split. I had been feeling very anxious about that, and the suspense was killing me. I got a little taste of an answer when Randa had to attend the funeral of a friends' grandmother. She saw our mutual friend Kenny there, and snuck a call in to me.

"Kenny is here!" she whispered. "I'm trying to avoid him. I really don't want to talk to him..."

Randa had been upset with Kenny ever since we found out he'd had a hand in getting Bill involved in drugs—according to Bill, anyway.

Randa was a walking time bomb. She'd been carrying all this anger over Bill and the divorce, and Kenny was a sitting duck. All it took was him saying to her, "Randa? Are you ignoring me?" She completely went off on him, letting him know exactly what she thought of Bill—how irresponsibly he was acting, how he wasn't living up to his duties as a father, how hurtful it was for all concerned. Then, just for good measure, she threw in how disgusted she was at Kenny for helping to contribute to Bill's downfall with drugs.

114

Kenny denied it. "I don't know why you're bringing me into that! I had nothing to do with it. Anyway, I just talked to Bill the other day. He said that he and Shelly had been unhappy for years."

That did it. Randa let an avalanche of four-letter words rain down on Kenny's head. She ended by saying, "Anyway, you saw Bill and Shelly together! Did they *look* unhappy to you? Did they *look* like they had been having problems for years?"

Hearing this exchange from Randa confirmed my biggest fear—that Bill had been telling people things about me that weren't true. We definitely didn't have the perfect marriage, but we also didn't suffer through years of unhappiness, and we certainly were not on the brink of divorce.

I was so hurt. I had trusted Bill with every single thing in my life. To hear that he was saying such things made me sick to my stomach. Maybe Bill had to spin it that way to get people to be more accepting of Lisa, but whatever the reason, it stung.

The next person to speak out was Payton.

My daughter finally felt comfortable enough to talk to her dad about her discomfort over Lisa—as long as she could talk to him over the phone.

I don't know what they said, word for word. I do know the general gist of it: Payton was unhappy and hurt, and she did not want her father forcing her to meet Lisa until she was ready.

I was so proud of Payton for sticking to her guns, letting Bill know he had hurt her, and telling him she didn't want him pushing her into anything.

After Payton talked to her dad, Dylan became a little more vocal as well, saying, "I don't want to hang out with Dad if Lisa is going to be there." Dylan was always the one protecting Payton, so it was sweet to see that, in this one instance, Payton was able to clear the way for Dylan.

The very last weekend of September was Bill's weekend with the kids. He still didn't have anywhere other than Lisa's to keep them, so he was just going to be taking them out to lunch. After lunch, he was going to drop off Payton at a friend's house, and take Dylan to Rampriders to ride BMX bikes indoors.

When Bill came to pick up the kids, he pulled up in a new truck—which was not a total surprise to me. He took the kids to lunch, dropped off Payton at a friend's house, and brought Dylan back home.

I went outside to meet them, trying to put on a good face for Dylan's sake. Bill didn't know that, courtesy of Facebook, I already knew that Lisa had helped him get the truck. "Yeah," he said, "I got a new truck. Lisa got me the friends and family discount."

An actual slap across the face would have been easier to take. The *friends and family* discount?

"Now," he continued, "your name is off it. It's just in my name. So that's all worked out."

The new truck was Bill's way of getting my name off his truck. I had my bills I was responsible for, and he had his, and as part of our divorce agreement, we had sixty days to remove the other person's name from everything that wasn't their responsibility. For me and my Ford, I simply had the company send papers for Bill and me to sign, and it was done. For Bill and his Chevy truck, it was more complicated.

I was now free of any worries over him falling behind on payments on a truck we owned together.

As if we were not having enough fun already with all the talk about his new truck, he chose that moment to share more news with me.

"Lisa and I have been looking at new apartments," he said. "On October 24th, we're moving into a two-bedroom. That way, the kids will have some place to stay when they are with me."

Bill showed no hesitation or remorse as he told me about the new place he was planning to move into with his girlfriend. It was heartbreaking on so many levels for me to hear about his new apartment. Beyond the obvious hurt it caused me as his ex-wife, I couldn't believe this man I'd lived with for so long in a nice two-story, four-bedroom home was going to live in a little apartment. It seemed like such a step backwards to me. But I know that, to him, it was one step closer to freedom.

I reminded him that he would need to work it out so that Lisa wasn't there when the kids came over, because they didn't want to be around her. He may have been placating me so he could get out of there, but he said that the children had already told him about their feelings, and he understood. He assured me that we would work something out in terms of the visiting arrangements.

I was beside myself. On the Fourth of July, the kids found out their family was splitting apart. Now, only a couple of months later, they were going to find out their dad planned to get an apartment with another woman? You don't do that to your children.

Sure, the kids knew that their dad was *staying* with Lisa, but knowing he was getting a new apartment with her was a whole different story.

It was mind boggling to think that Bill could move forward with getting an apartment with Lisa so soon, considering that his kids already told him they weren't ready to interact with her. I tried to picture him sitting in an apartment, watching TV with Lisa. I couldn't even place that image in my head.

I had been slowly making peace with the fact that Bill had lost his mind, and I felt like I knew what was wrong with him—but, what was wrong with *her*? How could this woman be doing this? I tried to put myself in her shoes, but I wouldn't have been able to live with myself. It defied imagination.

Why not live next door to her for a year or so? Bill was street smart. He had been around the block. He was an intelligent man. So, why could he not see that this sort of thing was unlikely to work? In every movie, TV show, or book I've ever read, rebound relationships never last. Throw kids into the mix, and the odds of the relationship failing go way up.

Before that summer, whenever we saw a special on TV about deadbeat dads, Bill would always say, "Look at that man! How could you do that to your own children?"

In advance of that weekend, my mother and some girlfriends had planned a night out for me. "Shelly needs to get out and live again" was the general sentiment. It wasn't a divorce party, just a girls' night out. They figured it was safe to make plans, knowing that it was a weekend that Bill had the kids. In light of the new truck, and the news about Bill and Lisa moving in together, I was definitely ready for some girl time.

As I said, Bill didn't end up taking the kids overnight, but both Payton and Dylan stayed overnight at friends' houses. Dylan was in charge of coming home and taking the dogs out.

That left us girls free to visit a local casino on the Mississippi River. We had a fun night out. So we wouldn't have to worry about choosing a designated driver, we had a shuttle take us back to a hotel. It was great—my mom, my aunt, my sister-in-law Theresa, and several of my girlfriends had decorated a hotel room with balloons and a banner saying, "You will survive. Divorce isn't the worst thing in the world."

I was able to relax, knowing that the kids and dogs were being looked after.

On Monday, Bill called and offered to take both kids to their orthodontist appointment on Wednesday, September 30th. I thought, wait a minute! Was this a turning point for Bill? It may have been a small gesture, but it was the first one since the Fourth of July, and I was thrilled.

"Absolutely!" I said. "That would be wonderful. I'd love for you to take them."

"Great," he said. "I only got to see them for an hour on Saturday, so I will take them to dinner afterwards."

I couldn't believe my ears, and said, "I know they'd love that!"

He did exactly that—picked them up, took them to the orthodontist, took them out to dinner, and dropped them off at home. They all had a nice time. And I was over the moon. It gave me the first shred of hope that maybe, just maybe, he was beginning to see the light, and return to the Bill the kids and I knew and loved. I knew he and I would never get back together. But, I was seeing a glimpse of the so-called normal divorced family I was hoping we'd become after Bill got through to the other side of his midlife crisis.

I was so happy.

Part Two

FINAL DRIVE

~October 2nd~
The Beginning of the End

"It's my life,
It's now or never,
I ain't gonna live forever,
I just want to live while I'm alive,
It's my life,
My heart is like an open highway,
Like Frankie said, "I did it my way,"
I just wanna live while I'm alive
'Cause it's my life..."
"It's My Life"

~by Bon Jovi/Martin/Sambora (Bon Jovi)

T hings are looking up. You see the light at the end of the tunnel, and you begin to believe that at last, better days are on the way. Then, on a day that dawns with such promise, the phone rings.

The first phone call came on Friday, October 2nd.

I was at work. It was the school nurse, telling me that Payton was sick and needed to be picked up from school. That was the period of time when people first became worried about the H1N1 (swine) flu, so there were many children out of school, and entire schools shutting down over fears of an epidemic. Parents were taking their kids' stuffy noses and sniffles more seriously than usual. And, it sounded like Payton had more than a case of the sniffles.

As soon as she got into the car, I knew she had strep throat. Dylan had suffered through more than one case of strep throat the year before, and even had his tonsils out as a result. So, I had become an expert on its peculiar signs—and smells. Knowing it was nothing to mess around with, I drove straight to an urgent care facility. They did a rapid test on Payton, and declared, "Sure enough, she's got strep!"

On the way home, we picked up antibiotics, cough medicine with codeine in it, and some soda. Then I texted Bill to let him know Payton was sick, but that there was nothing to worry about. When I didn't get a text back from him, I figured, whatever—I've done my part.

When Payton and I got home, Dylan was already home from school, and several of his friends were outside with him. They were working on Dylan's bike in preparation for a Rampriders event the following night—Saturday.

Dylan was getting very frustrated. He and his friends could not quite get his bike in the shape it needed to be for Rampriders. Dylan came in the house and said, "I want to call Dad, and see if he can come over and help me with my bike."

I glanced over at Payton, who was lying on the couch, sick, and then back at Dylan, whose face was filled with frustration. My heart bled for both of my kids, trying to get through life without the full participation of their dad.

"Okay, Dyl," I said, "but just remember, it's Friday night. Your dad may be out doing something. So, you might want to give him the option of coming over in the morning instead."

I was trying so hard to be the peacemaker between the kids and Bill, so they could get on a good footing again.

Dylan made the call. "Dad said he'll be over in about thirty minutes."

An overwhelming feeling of relief hit me. I thought, oh, my gosh, he's really coming by! I was so afraid Bill would tell Dylan he was too busy to help him, and I knew that would have crushed Dylan. Before our divorce, Bill had always been there to help our son with his bike.

Three months earlier, Bill and I would have both been home with the kids. I would have been watching TV with Payton, who was sick, and Bill would have been outside, helping Dylan with his bike.

Quit it, I said to myself. That's not the way it is now, and it is never going to be that way again. At least Bill is coming over to work on Dylan's bike with him. That's a good step forward.

The next thing I knew, Bill was on the porch, asking to come inside. It was so strange to hear him asking permission to come into the house.

I said, "Hi! Come on in."

Bill walked straight over to Payton, "You're not feeling well, Princess?"

She said, "My throat hurts, Daddy."

"Well, since you're sick," he said, stroking her hair, "I'm not going to kiss you, but I love you and I will see you later."

Then, Bill went outside to check out Dylan's bike. A few minutes later, he came back inside.

"We are going to run out for a few minutes and pick up something for Dylan's bike," Bill said. "I'll have the boys back before you know it."

"Okay," I said, "well, thank you! I know it's Friday night and all. Thank you for coming and helping him."

"Don't worry about it," Bill said, and took off with the boys.

There it is! I thought to myself. Another little baby step. Maybe Bill is finally seeing how important it is for him to be involved in the kids' lives. I couldn't remember him showing any real parental responsibility or involvement since before the Fourth of July. Bill was now the party guy. He lived for the weekends.

I had been so certain he would refuse Dylan's request, but I was wrong. I had a deep sense that Bill had somehow awakened from whatever state of mind had kept him from his children. And, the feeling of relief and comfort that overcame me was something I hadn't felt since our separation.

I was so grateful.

Bill even gave our dogs an extra helping of attention that evening. Mia, our beautiful beagle, was Bill's dog, and he loved her to death. That evening, he didn't stop at a perfunctory hello and pat on the head. He really showered Mia with love, petting her and cooing to her. He also took the time to pay some attention to Izzy, the toy Pomeranian he had given to Payton and me as a Christmas gift the year before. He picked up Izzy in his arms and was baby-talking to her.

My parents happened to be in town for Theresa's birthday party. Whenever my parents came to visit, they alternated between staying with me and staying with Mitch, and it was Mitch's turn to host them.

The party was set for Saturday. Since Payton was down with strep throat, she and I had to stay away from the party. We spent the day relaxing. She was on her antibiotics and cough medicine with codeine, so she was perfectly happy to lie on the couch all day.

When the afternoon rolled around, Dylan took off for his friend's house. Later that evening, Dylan and his friends would all go to Rampriders, and not be home until very late at night.

Around seven o'clock that evening, I started feeling like I might be coming down with something, myself, so I decided to take a shower and turn in early. Payton was already zonked out on her medication, and I decided the best thing I could do was to call it an early night.

As I was rinsing off in the shower, it hit me—I couldn't get sick! What would I do if I got really sick? For all practical purposes, I was the kids' only parent now—the only one consistently showing up for them, anyway. I no longer had Bill there to pinch-hit for me when I was sick. The thought made me uneasy.

On the other hand, maybe a miracle was still possible. After all, Bill had managed to tear himself away from whatever he would normally be doing with Lisa on a Friday night, so he could come over and help Dylan with his bike.

Payton was already snoring away in the other room. So, I knew it was safe to totally knock myself out, and let the combination of Nyquil and an extra good night's sleep start to cure me. And with that, I downed more than the recommended dosage of Nyquil and climbed into bed, vaguely aware that Dylan should be calling at any moment, to let me know he'd gotten safely to his destination.

The Rampriders events were held in a sketchy neighborhood in southern St. Louis, so we had a standing agreement that Dylan would always call or text me when he arrived, and again when he left.

At a quarter 'til eight in the evening on October 3rd, I fell into a deep, medication-induced sleep, having no idea on earth that as my eyes shut, I was forever leaving behind life as I knew it.

~October 3rd~
The Accident

"Oh, I ran so far through a broken land
I was following that drummer
Beating in a different band
And somewhere on the highway
I let go of her hand
Now she's gone forever
Like her footprints in the sand…"
"My Baby Needs a Shepherd"

~by Emmy Lou Harris

A round nine o'clock, I was startled awake. Was I dreaming, or was the phone ringing? I was in a daze from sleeping so heavily. Then, it hit me—it was Dylan calling to let me know he'd made it safely to Rampriders.

I rolled over and reached for the phone. "Hello? Dylan?" I said.

"Shelly," the voice said, "you don't know me, but…"

Through the haze of cold medicine, I was having trouble focusing. I said, "Dylan? Honey, is that you?"

"You don't know me," the voice repeated, "but I'm Jan's friend."

"Who?" I asked. "*Who* is this?"

"You don't know me, Shelly," he said, one more time. "I'm John, Jan's friend…you know, Bill's mom, Jan. I don't know how to tell you this, but, there's been an accident."

As he was talking, I was looking around my room, trying to decide whether or not I was dreaming. What was happening here?

He said, "Shelly? Shelly, are you there?"

I said, "*Who* is this, and *what* did you just say?"

124

"I'm so sorry," he said, "but, there's been an accident. Billy is gone."

Bill's mother always called him Billy.

Gone? Bill? *My Bill?*

I sat up further in bed, struggling to shake off the effects of the Nyquil I had taken only two hours earlier.

"We were going to be leaving on a cruise tomorrow," he continued, "and Jan suddenly felt like she had to talk to Billy. She didn't want to leave town without letting him know we'd be gone for awhile."

That was a first. In the past several years, there had been only a couple of Jan's trips that we knew about in advance. We usually didn't even find out she had been traveling until months after she'd been home.

"Anyway," he went on, "she had this overwhelming need to call Billy. When she called his phone, somebody answered—but it wasn't him. Jan hung up, thinking she had the wrong number, and then called right back. The same strange voice answered, and said, 'May I ask who is calling?' And Jan, thinking it was Lisa, who is not exactly her favorite person, got defensive, and said, 'Well, who is *this?*' Then the woman identified herself as a nurse…"

A nurse? Why was a nurse answering Bill's cell phone? My eyes were moving back and forth over the room. I looked down at my body, and hardly recognized it. I could hear the words coming through the phone, but they did not compute.

John was saying, "And then the nurse said, 'I need to know who I am speaking to.' And Jan said, 'I am his MOTHER!'"

As the story came out, each fragment ricocheted around in my brain.

John said, "She was a nurse from St. Joseph's Hospital in Madison County, Illinois…"

Madison County, Illinois? Why would a nurse in Illinois have Bill's cell phone? I looked at the phone receiver, unable to speak. My mouth no longer seemed to be working. I could not move.

"Shelly," he said, "the nurse said that there had been an accident. Billy did not make it."

What did he mean, Billy did not make it? The words seemed to be hanging like a cloud in front of me, making it impossible to breathe or think.

"He's gone, Shelly," John said. "I'm so sorry."

What did that even mean, "gone?" How could Bill be gone? It was impossible. We just saw him last night, at the house! There was obviously some mistake.

With tears flowing down my cheeks, I found my voice. "Do you mean to tell me," I said, "that Bill is *dead?*"

"Yes, honey," John said. "I'm so sorry a stranger had to be the one to tell you."

He explained that Bill had been on his motorcycle. There was another motorcycle and a truck involved in the accident.

"But, are you sure?" I said. "Are you sure it was Bill's motorcycle?"

It was only then that I heard a terrible wailing in the background—it was Jan, screaming in agony. It sounded like there were words mixed in with her cries, but I couldn't make out what she was saying.

The news this man had just delivered to me was trying to settle into some kind of order in my mind. But every time I started to feel like I could make sense of it, everything became confused again. It was as if someone had a remote control, and kept shuffling my thoughts from one channel to another.

"Jan and I are going to come get you," he said. "We will take you to the hospital."

Okay, I'm thinking, focus, focus. Jan had spoken to a nurse in Madison County. There was an accident. Bill had been in an accident.

Oh, my God! Bill had been in an accident! It must have been a horrible accident for a nurse to have Bill's cell phone. I had better do something—but, what? Call my mom. Yes! I needed to call my parents.

"No, no," I said to John. "My mom and dad happen to be in town, and I will call them. We will meet you at the hospital. Give me the phone number and address."

My parents were staying at Mitch and Theresa's, but what was Mitch's number? How could I have forgotten his number? I simply could not recall it, and had to get up and go downstairs to find the phone book.

Theresa answered the phone.

I blurted out, "Theresa! I need to talk to my mom."

She could hear in my voice that something was terribly wrong.

"Jeanne! Quick," she yelled. "You need to get over here. It's Shelly. And she's crying."

"Honey?" my mom said. "What's wrong?"

My words were all scrambled, and I couldn't get them out fast enough. All I could manage to say was, "There was an accident."

"Michelle!" Mom said, trying to shock me out of it. "What happened to Dylan?"

I said, "No, mom, it's not... it's not Dylan, Mom."

"It's not Dylan?" she repeated.

"No, it's Bill," I explained. "He was in a motorcycle accident. And he's dead."

Silence. Then, "What did you just say?"

I said, "Mom, I have to get to the hospital right away! Bill needs me."

Mom asked, "Where did the accident happen?"

I said, "Illinois. Madison County, Illinois. It's about an hour away, I think."

"Shell…" My mother's voice was suddenly very stern. "Listen to me. You are not driving. Do you hear me? Do NOT get behind the wheel. We're coming over right now. Stay put until we get there."

Right. Stay put. They would come get me.

I noticed I was still in my pajamas.

My God! I had better hurry. I ran upstairs and started tearing around my room, looking for some kind of clothes I could quickly throw on. Okay, good. I was dressed. Now, what?

I had to get to the hospital right away. Bill had been in an accident, and he would need me. We had a situation here, and I needed to fix it—immediately. That's what I do. I'm the fixer.

I flew downstairs. My family room and kitchen are connected, and I wore out the floor, pacing back and forth between them. Time had taken on a surreal quality.

There is a sliding glass door from the kitchen into the back yard. There it was—the same yard where just one day before, Bill had been helping Dylan with his bike. I felt weak. I slid down the sliding glass door, and let myself crumple on the floor. Why did everything now look so strange? It was as if someone had torn down the movie set that was our home, and erected a new one in its place.

This cannot be happening to me…this cannot be happening to me. These words kept repeating in my mind.

Then it hit me—oh, my God! What would I tell the children? How could I tell them their father had been in a horrible accident? How could I tell them he was terribly hurt? The kids would be so upset.

Another voice said, hurt? No, not hurt—dead.

He can't be dead…he can't be dead…that is just not an option. I heard myself screaming out in a hysterical voice.

I hushed myself. Shh… you can't wake up Payton.

As I sat slumped on the floor, the dogs climbed all over me, sensing my agitation and grief, and trying to soothe me. I shooed them off of me.

I sat there on the kitchen floor, looking around at the walls, the cabinets, the appliances. Nothing had moved, but everything seemed foreign, out of place. I thought, well, at least Payton is sleeping through this, thanks to the codeine in her cough medicine. Good thing I took her to the doctor right away. Bill's going to be fine, too. The nurse obviously made some kind of mistake.

Then, I thought, it's taking Mom and Dad forever to get here—or is it? When did I talk to Mom, anyway? It could have been an hour before, or it could have been five minutes. I couldn't tell.

I grabbed my glasses instead of putting in my contacts, didn't bother to brush my hair, and walked outside to wait for them. I must have been a real sight. Right as I closed the front door, my mom, dad, and uncle pulled in. Vickie was driving separately.

It was nine-thirty at night when the car pulled into the driveway. Only thirty minutes before, I had been sleeping in bed. Half an hour—that's all it took for the universe to disassemble my entire life.

My mom put her arm around my shoulder and said, "Shell, are you sure you want to go to the hospital?"

I gave her a look that said, "Are you kidding me? Mom, please!"

Mom could see the desperate plea in my eyes. "Never mind, Honey. I know the answer."

I had the address of the hospital, but no idea how to get there. Mom and Dad, God bless them, had already pulled out a map on the way over, and were trying to figure out where we were going.

Here was the plan—Mom, Dad, and I were going to the hospital. Denny and Vickie were staying at my house. Someone had to be there for Payton in case she woke up—which was unlikely, but possible. Dylan was expected home around midnight, and someone had to be home when he got there.

I couldn't get us in the car fast enough. "Let's go!" I said. I had this all-encompassing need to get to Bill as fast as I could. Everything Bill and I had been through in the last ninety days faded away like a child's handprint on a frosty windowpane.

As we were figuring out our game plan, Vickie pulled in. She took one look at me, and said, "You guys just get in the car and go. We will figure out the kids, and you can call us from the road."

Dad drove, and I sat behind him in the back seat. Mom was in the passenger seat. We knew the general vicinity of Madison County—that it was in a rural area of Illinois, but that was about it. Mom said, "Why don't I call the hospital and find out exactly where we're going? I will also double-check everything…"

When she reached the hospital by phone, I heard her say, "I'm checking on a patient brought in from a motorcycle accident—William… Can you tell me his status?"

A motorcycle accident. I flashed on an incident that occurred while Bill was in the Navy. He had gotten a dirt bike before I went up to Washington to join him. There was a racetrack on base, and since Bill had been around motorcycles his whole life, it made sense that he would want to get a bike.

He told me before I got to Washington that he'd gotten a dirt bike, and I wasn't surprised. I didn't mind dirt bikes at all. It was street bikes that scared me. Bill would ride with his friends while I sat out in the sun. We didn't have a lot of money at the time, and going for a ride was a great way for him to enjoy himself, with only the expense of gas to worry about.

One particular day, Bill and some buddies went out riding, and as he was returning home, I could see him coming up over a hill, holding his shoulder.

"I wrecked," he said. "We need to go to the hospital."

His arm did not appear to be broken, but I was very concerned about the fact that he was vomiting. Since he had military health insurance, I needed to get him to the military hospital. In order to get there, we had to drive over a big hill with a steep incline—in his little red Toyota truck, *with the manual transmission.*

Wait a minute! There was something wrong with his arm, after all, and his collarbone was sticking out. The vomiting was an indication that he probably had a concussion.

I was totally panicked. I did not know how to drive a stick-shift.

What could I do? I got behind the wheel, and tried to wing it. I did know when to shift, at least, and Bill was trying to talk me through it. When we reached the base of the steep hill, he said, "Now, you've really got to give it gas…"

So, there I was, trying to get us up the hill, as my poor husband—who was clearly in a lot of pain—kept having to open the car door to vomit. When we got halfway up the hill, I stalled the car. We started rolling backwards; I started crying, worried that he had some sort of brain injury; and in between spasms of agony, he was yelling at me, "You can't drive this car!"

Before long, the truck had rolled all the way back down to the bottom of the hill. At that point, I threw on the emergency brake, flung open my door, crossed my arms, and announced, "Either we are walking to the hospital or you are going to have to drive!"

I'll never know how he did it, but somehow, Bill managed to drive us to the hospital with one arm. What else could he do? He had no choice, and somehow his adrenaline must have kicked in. Thank God, the hospital was no more than five minutes away.

Once we got him examined, we discovered that he had a concussion and a broken collarbone—but no brain injury.

That was a relief. We still had to find a way to get Bill's truck back to our apartment. Luckily, we were able to get a friend to come and drive us home.

I snapped back to the reality of the present moment when I saw my mom's expression change, and her tears begin to flow. The nurse had said the word, "deceased." Mom had now heard it from an official source. In that moment, it became concrete. She went into a daze. She couldn't believe it, either.

"I'm bringing in my daughter," she said to the nurse. "She is Bill's ex-wife, but they've only been legally divorced for fifty-two days, so she is still family. Bill's mother will be meeting us there. Also, can you tell us the best way to get there?"

The Ford Escape SUV rolled along, and I stared, unseeing, out the window. Every mile was carrying us closer to a destination I couldn't reach fast enough—but wanted to avoid at all costs. I kept thinking that maybe if I blinked, the entire scene would change, and I would still be lying in my bed, groggy from the Nyquil, grateful that it had all been just a terrible nightmare.

"Randa," I would say on the phone, "you wouldn't believe this horrible dream I had last night…"

But, no… We were on a road that was leading us to Bill—and I could neither turn back nor face where we were going. I was stuck in some horrible purgatory.

Mom asked me to repeat back to her what John had told me, and I did, in remembered fragments of conversation. There was so much I still didn't know, so many answers we still didn't have.

"Honey?" Mom said. "Would you like me to call Bill's dad for you?"

"Oh, my gosh!" I said. "That's right—Bill and Judy. Yes, you have to call for me, Mom. There's no way I can do it. Thank you."

I was so thankful to have my mom and dad with me. I felt as if my mind, my heart, my soul, were all suddenly burdened with an unbearable weight—a weight too heavy for one person to carry. I felt like I was a breath away from crumbling.

Even on that darkest of nights, as the SUV rolled towards the hospital, I had the sense that everything happens for a reason. Payton just happened to get sick, and ended up with a prescription for cold medicine that knocked her out so she slept through the terrible phone call when it came in; and Dylan just happened to be at Rampriders that night, so he missed the initial horror and chaos.

The night before, Dylan just happened to be having trouble with his bike, and had to call his dad, who came to the house—one last time—to help his son; to sit beside his sick daughter on the couch and show her some love; to say goodbye to his dogs; and to have one last pleasant exchange with me.

And my parents just happened to be in town because it was Theresa's birthday.

You are driving down this road, I think to myself, because everything happens for a reason. Everyone has a destiny. What was happening now was Bill's destiny—and mine.

I knew when Bill and I got divorced that there was a reason why it had happened. At the time, I couldn't imagine what the reason might be, but I firmly believed the day would come when I would understand. Looking out the window as we got closer to the hospital where Bill lay, it struck me. *If we had not gotten divorced when we did, I might have been the one on the back of Bill's motorcycle, and my kids could have lost both of their parents in one day.*

As it was, Bill's strange behavior since the divorce had caused him to pull away from both the kids and me. I now saw how merciful it was that life had allowed us a little bit of distance from him before losing him completely. If he had still been my husband, and the kids' steadfast dad who was always there for them, this all would have been even more devastating.

We could have been living together as a family, and gotten a phone call out of the blue. Bill could have been ripped away from us suddenly—instead of the incremental way we'd been losing him since the beginning of the divorce in July. It would have felt like someone tearing our hearts out of our chests.

This pain, this knowing that Bill was lying in a hospital after a terrible crash, this awareness that at some point, I was going to have to tell the children that their father was gone—was almost more than I could bear. I was so grateful that we'd been given a little bit of time in advance to begin to grieve Bill's presence in our lives.

So, had every bit of this tragedy—the divorce, the affair, and the accident—happened for a reason?

~Late Night~
The Hospital

"...Since their wings have got rusted
You know the angels wanna wear my red shoes
But when they told me 'bout their side of the bargain
That's when I knew I could not refuse
And I won't get any older
Now the angels wanna wear my red shoes..."
"The Angels Wanna Wear My Red Shoes"

~by Elvis Costello

The nurse had said that Bill was deceased.

I wouldn't believe it until I saw it with my own eyes. And, if it really was true—if Bill was not only terribly hurt, but *gone,* how in the world was I going to tell my kids? Almost ninety days earlier to the day, they found out their family was destroyed. Now, I had to face them to tell them their dad was gone forever?

What kind of higher power would do this to my kids, to Bill, to me?

If everything happens for a reason, what could possibly be the reason for something so unfair?

"Mom?" I said. "Maybe you'd better call the house. Dylan will be coming home, and there's always a crazy chance that Payton might wake up."

She said, "Okay, honey. What do you want me to have Denny and Mitch tell the kids?"

Vickie had already returned home to care for their son, Matt. When she left, Mitch came to my house to keep Denny company.

I didn't really think Payton would wake up, but I knew for sure that Dylan was going to be home soon, and I had to make sure that my brother and my uncle knew what to tell him.

I said, "I don't know… maybe they should just say there's been an accident. Until we get to the hospital, we won't know what's really going on."

We were almost to the hospital when my phone rang. I looked down at the phone and said, "Oh, no! It's Dylan calling! Mom… Mom… what do I do? Do I answer the phone? I can't tell him this over the phone!"

Mom quickly said, "Well, you've got to answer it!"

I kept repeating, "Oh, my gosh…oh, my gosh…" Finally, I answered the phone. "Dylan," I said, "we're on our way to the hospital."

"Mom," he said, "I know. I just need to know one thing."

My brain was screaming, Baby, no—don't ask me that! I can't bear to tell you…

"I just want to know," he said, "was the accident in Dad's truck or on his motorcycle?"

I said, "It was on his motorcycle, Dillie."

"Okay," he said. "That's all I need to know. I know you're on your way and you're in a hurry. I love you, Mom."

"Love you too, Dillie," I said.

Leave it to my firstborn. He is such a wise child. He knew just the right question to ask to get the answer that would tell him just how serious the accident had been, without having to ask me the one question I couldn't bear to answer. He also knew that asking me that particular question, rather than the question of whether Bill was dead or alive, would give him a fuller sense of what had actually occurred.

I was so thankful for the way he had handled the phone call—but, my heart also hurt for him. I couldn't imagine what he must have been feeling.

As we drew closer to the hospital in the small town in Illinois, some confusion arose as to exactly where we were going. The address and directions we were given seemed to correspond to a little strip mall. That couldn't be right. We pulled into the parking lot, and looked at the building.

"This is it?" I said. "This can't possibly be it."

The hospital was smaller than my house. In my previous job, I had traveled a lot to small rural hospitals like this one. I would always joke to my assistant, "If, God forbid, anything ever happens to me when I'm traveling, and I end up in one of those tiny rural hospitals, you have to promise to get me out of there right away."

Now, here we were, parked in front of one of those very hospitals. And inside, was Bill.

We looked around for Jan and John. "I don't understand why they're not here yet," I said. "They were ready to walk out the door when they called me, so they should have beaten us here!"

There were maybe twenty cars in the whole parking lot, none with Missouri license plates on them. They were all from Illinois.

The urge to go inside was so strong, and yet, I also felt strongly that I should wait for Bill's mom. But, where were they, anyway? We sat in the car for an excruciating length of time. In actuality, it was probably no more than twenty minutes. In the entire time we sat there, we saw no activity at all. Not a single person entered or exited the hospital. After awhile, I wondered aloud, "Are they even open?"

I was anxious to get inside, and frustrated over having to wait. This was made all the more intense by my awareness—thanks to the fact that I work in the medical field—that I might run into resistance from the medical personnel. Since I was now, technically, Bill's ex-wife, I was afraid that the HIPAA laws would prevent the doctors and nurses from telling me anything.

I desperately needed to know what had happened, and I began to imagine the worst case scenario. I started getting angry over the prospect of being stonewalled. It seemed so unfair. I spent twenty years as Bill's wife, and for the past fifty-two days, we'd been divorced, and suddenly I had no rights because technically I was no longer his wife?

After waiting an interminable length of time for Jan and John to show up, we finally gave up.

"I can't wait for them any longer," I said. "We have to go in now."

We got out of the car, and began to walk towards the doors of the tiny rural hospital. The night was unseasonably chilly—too cold for a motorcycle ride. I moved as if through a cloudbank, my spirit hovering above me. My body felt leaden, weighted down by sorrow, confusion, and anger. Struggling to put one foot in front of another, my mind kept repeating, this can't be true…this cannot be my life. My children can't be forced to deal with such a terrible loss. It is just not fair.

I had never in my entire life felt so hopeless and lost.

The next minute, my mind said, wait, I bet none of this is real, anyway. It is probably all just some horrible dream. Walking, floating, I thought, yes, this must be one long bad dream—*all of it.*

Maybe there was never any midlife crisis for Bill. Maybe we didn't get divorced. The thought that I was dreaming would explain everything, because Bill was not the type to have had a completely personality change. He was too good a husband and dad to suddenly start pushing the kids and me away. And Bill wasn't the type to get into a horrible motorcycle accident. He was too good a driver.

The second I walked through those doors, I would probably snap awake and be back in my old life again—the life where Bill was my same old Bill—

my best friend and husband—and we were married and happy; just a typical Midwestern family.

We reached the emergency room doors, the kind that slide open as you approach. Not only did the doors not slide open—they were locked! It was like I had been thrust into a strange film.

A security officer came to the door to let us in, and with him was a nun. I thought, are you kidding me? I am being greeted by a policeman and a nun? This *has* to be some kind of surreal movie!

I passed through the doors and did not awaken. If anything, the dream only became more bizarre.

The nun reached out and took both of my hands in hers. "Hello, dear," she said. "I am Sister Marilyn." I recognized her name right away. She was the one my mother had spoken to on the phone when she called to get directions and verify everything.

I have worked in the medical field for twenty years, and I know the distinctive smell of hospitals—that nauseating blend of sickness and cleaning agents. This wasn't the busy emergency room you find in the city, but that smell told me it was definitely a hospital. As my nose was assaulted by the familiar odor, reality hit me like a cement wall. Suddenly, I couldn't put my next foot forward. I could not believe what was happening.

I glanced to the right, where I saw a desk, a small room, and doors leading back to the emergency room. To the left I saw a bigger waiting room, restrooms, and a tiny gift shop, which was closed.

"I need to use the restroom," I announced, needing to buy some time to pull myself together.

Standing before the mirror in the restroom, I splashed water on my face, and then looked at my reflection. I looked exhausted. Beyond that, I looked like a stranger. The shock I was experiencing was so complete, I felt disconnected and removed from the woman looking back at me.

Being greeted by a nun and a security officer began a fissure in my wall of denial, and the crack was quickly growing larger. Bill must really be gone, I thought. Either that, or this was the strangest movie ever.

"Okay, Shelly," I said to myself, "you've got to get yourself together. You can do this. You *have* to do this. You need to really pay attention, and listen very carefully to everything they are going to tell you, because the details will be important later. You'll need to remember every word that they say. So, focus."

While I was in the restroom, my mom was filling in the details for the nun: Bill and I had been together for twenty-four years, married for twenty, divorced for fifty-two days, and had two children.

"We will do everything we can," she assured my mother. "Don't worry about the divorce. We will treat Shelly as family."

When I came out of the bathroom, Sister Marilyn said, "We are going to walk down here now, to a smaller, private waiting room. We can wait there for Bill's mother to arrive."

When we got there, I sat down, and Sister Marilyn took a seat next to me, and put her hands on mine.

She said, "I am so sorry, dear. I can't imagine how you must be feeling."

After expressing her condolences again, she went on to give me the details of the accident:

There had been Bill's motorcycle and one other motorcycle. A total of four people involved in the accident—all badly injured. Bill was the most seriously hurt—deceased. The other three had been airlifted to St. Louis. To her knowledge, they were all in critical condition.

Four people. From the moment I heard about the accident, I figured Lisa had been riding with Bill. Over the last few months, they had been riding together quite a bit. I imagined that, since the accident had occurred in Illinois, they must have been on some kind of all-day ride.

Four people in the accident—but Bill was the most seriously hurt of all. Deceased. A nun was telling me this. A holy person. My entire body was shaking, trembling from deep inside my soul. I had often heard the term "brokenhearted," but not until that moment did I truly understand what it felt like to have your heart fractured. It skipped and jumped in an abnormal rhythm, and there was nothing I could do to stop it.

My heart knew what my mind could not accept.

What was I going to tell the kids? Payton lay sleeping in her bed at home, having no idea that her entire world had been shattered. Dylan was home grappling with the terrible knowledge that his father had been in a motorcycle accident. What *was* I going to tell them? This thought kept intruding on my awareness, and each time, I had to push it away, block it out.

I kept saying to myself, focus, focus. Don't zone out. You have to pay attention. You can't miss anything these people are telling you. You'll need to remember every detail years from now, to make sure the kids really understand.

I started to feel itchy again for Jan and John to show up so we could hear the rest of the details about the accident.

I said to my parents, "Let's try calling Jan. It's been forever, and they should have beaten us here."

I dialed her cell phone and the call went straight to voicemail. I didn't know John's cell phone number, or whether he even had a cell phone, for that matter.

"Let's wait just a little while longer," said Sister Marilyn, "and then the E.R. doctor and state trooper will come in and talk to you."

She stepped away, leaving me sitting in the small, sterile waiting room with my mom and dad, the walls closing in on me. Night was heavy and dark, a thick blanket draped against the windows that ran along one wall of the room.

Where in the world were Jan and John? I felt like if I had to wait one more minute to find out exactly what had happened, I would crawl out of my skin.

Scattered words passed between the three of us, like dark birds flying past.

About fifteen minutes later, Sister Marilyn returned.

"Your mother-in-law is not here yet?" she asked.

I said, "No, I tried calling, but she's not answering. I know they're on their way, but maybe they got lost. I know we had some trouble finding the place."

"You're probably right," she said. "Well, would you like to go ahead and speak to the E.R. doctor?"

I couldn't wait one more second. I had to know. I said, "Yes, please. That would be great."

She left and returned with a small Asian doctor.

So, I'd met a nun, a security guard, and an Asian E.R. doctor out in the middle of rural Illinois—a rare sight. The doctor took the seat next to me, and placed his hand gently on my knee. I felt his sincerity as he told me how sorry he was for my loss.

"We worked on your husband for a little over an hour," he explained. "We did everything we could, but it was too late. I want to assure you, and I really mean this, he felt hardly any pain. He lost consciousness almost instantly. I know you are in shock, so this may not mean anything to you right now, but it will be important later. He really experienced very little pain."

The compassion coming from the doctor was such a gift, and suddenly, I realized that in some strange way, I was lucky that Bill's accident had taken place in this rural area. If it had been closer to Chicago or St. Louis, I wouldn't have gotten the personal touch they were giving me. Had we been in downtown St. Louis at one of the hospitals there, the HIPAA rules would have undoubtedly come into play, and they would have said, "Oh, she's just the ex-wife. We have to wait for the next of kin to arrive."

I was so thankful. For so many years, I had made fun of those rural hospitals, and now I was thanking the Lord that Bill was in that place. I truly felt their sincerity.

The doctor looked into my eyes and said, "Let me explain to you what I know from what the state trooper told me about the accident. That way, you will be able to understand some of your husband's injuries."

He had used the term "husband" several times in our conversation, and I finally felt compelled to say, "Well, I'm actually the ex-wife..."

He nodded, and went on.

"There were two bikes," he explained, "riding together, side by side. One was leading, and the other was hanging back a little bit. The one in the lead was the closest to the inside of the two-lane country road. Your husband's bike was on the outside, closest to the shoulder. Based on the internal injuries he sustained, we believe he was probably traveling about seventy miles per hour—without a helmet."

This last bit of news did not surprise me. In the State of Illinois, there was no helmet law. And, any time Bill was riding in a state without a helmet law, he always removed his helmet. The minute I'd heard that the accident happened in Illinois, I knew that Bill's helmet was off.

"It was about seven o'clock in the evening," the doctor continued. "Not quite dark yet..."

~October 4th, Early, Early Morning~
The Theories

"...Sometimes all it takes
is facing the night alone
And that's when you know
A man ain't made of stone..."
"A Man Ain't Made of Stone"

~Burr/Lerner/Golde (Randy Travis)

As the doctor spoke, I could almost see the two bikes as the sun was beginning to set, riding side by side in that murky half-light that causes your eyes to play tricks on you.

"Here's what we think happened," he said. "In front of the two bikes, there was a car, and immediately in front of the car was a pick-up truck. The bikes must have come up on the two vehicles very quickly, not realizing they were actually stopped. They decided to pull out and pass them, which would have been fine if the other vehicles had been moving—but they were not."

The doctor proceeded to tell me that the man on the lead bike, who was carrying a passenger, pulled out to pass the car and the truck.

Bill was letting another bike lead? That did not make any sense to me. Bill was never one to hang back and let another rider take the lead position.

"What they didn't realize," the doctor explained, "was that the truck was making a left turn."

Oh, my God! I gasped.

"Both bikes managed to get around the car which was stopped—but they hit the truck," he said, his hand gently on my knee to steady me. "Being unfamiliar with the area, I'm sure they had no way of knowing there was even a road there where someone might want to turn..."

I could see it all in my mind... Bill and the other driver, zipping along at seventy miles per hour, shapes and forms becoming hazy in the changing light of dusk.

"The other rider," the doctor continued, "was maybe one motorcycle distance ahead of your husband..."

I kept repeating, "I am just the ex-wife."

"Oh, right. Anyway," he continued, "his motorcycle hit the front of the truck, and both he and his passenger flew over the truck and landed on the grassy side of the road."

Then he told me that Bill probably had a few seconds after he realized what was happening—just a moment of time to decide what to do. It was believed, based on his injuries and the skid marks on the road, that Bill decided to lay down the bike on its side to avoid hitting the truck. I knew how heavy that bike was; I could barely hold it up by myself.

Before Bill's bike hit the back of the truck, they slid quite a ways on the asphalt. When the doctor told me that Bill had decided to drop the bike down on its side, I knew right away that his injuries had to be very bad. According to the doctor, that is what caused Bill to become unconscious right away—his extensive injuries.

So, with the entire weight of his Harley Road King motorcycle pressing down on him, the man I spent twenty-four years of my life with—my former best friend and husband, the father of my children—slid along the asphalt of a country road. Ultimately, he still ended up hitting the back of the truck, despite his best efforts to maneuver out of the way.

I pictured Bill, lying in the road, very badly injured. I imagined his passenger, too, with serious injuries.

As the doctor spoke, I sobbed quietly, tears flowing down my face. I don't know if I've ever cried that way before or since. It was a completely involuntary outpouring of tears.

The skid marks on the road, and the positions of the bodies as they finally came to rest, gave the state trooper a picture of the likely accident scenario.

As for the man in the pick-up truck, he was already into his left turn when the two bikes collided with his truck. He remembered feeling the impact, and hearing a boom-boom sound. He had no idea what had hit him until afterwards when he saw the devastation surrounding him. After he finished his left turn, he pulled over to the side of the road to try to determine the cause of the sound.

The truck carried three small children, all under the age of ten. Their father was in his thirties, and told his kids, "Stay in the car." I could picture them kneeling on the seats of their daddy's truck, peering out the windows, as he faced the injured bodies and tangled motorcycles scattered on the road. I could only imagine what must have gone through their young minds—or their father's—as the police arrived, and the medevac helicopters hovered overhead.

The driver of the car that was between the motorcycles and the truck, and the driver of a car coming in the other direction, also got out of their vehicles to help. Someone called 9-1-1, and the others tried to assist at the scene.

Between 7:05 and 7:15 p.m., the accident occurred. At 7:33, the ambulance arrived on the scene.

"Your husband had a compound fracture in his leg, and lacerations on the back of his head, but his injuries were primarily internal," the doctor continued. "He had a lot of blood in his lungs."

As he was speaking, I kept waiting for that reassuring phrase, "But he's going to be okay." I so desperately needed him to say those words. I had already been told that Bill didn't make it, and yet...and yet, that sliver of hope, or disbelief, kept emerging inside me, whispering, "This is not what really happened...it can't be."

I had to be able to make this better. There was always something I could do, some mountain I could climb, some force of will I could summon to make everything better, to make everyone okay.

The doctor told me that the other three people involved—the two passengers and the other driver—were very critical. The passenger of the other bike was airlifted from the accident site straight to a hospital in St. Louis. The driver of the other bike and Bill's passenger were both brought to the same hospital as Bill, and then immediately airlifted from there to a hospital in St. Louis. Bill was already too far gone. (A medevac only takes passengers when there is a possibility of them living. Bill was already in cardiac arrest when the ambulance arrived.)

"Was there drinking involved?" I asked the doctor.

"The likelihood is yes," he said. "When they were brought in, we could smell the alcohol."

That was one more thing that did not add up in this new upside-down universe. Bill *always* watched his alcohol intake when he was driving his motorcycle. I thought back to times when we would go on all-day rides, and he'd make sure that we both watched how much we drank. Not even the passenger can be drunk on a motorcycle. Driving with a drunken passenger is difficult and precarious, and could cause you to have an accident.

It was hard for me to believe that Bill would let the other driver lead, and it was impossible for me to believe that Bill had been drinking and then got on his bike. I told the doctor as much.

I knew that Bill had lost his ever-loving mind, from the dawning of his midlife crisis through all the days that followed, but certain things I knew to be true about him: His bike was his world before our divorce, and even more so afterwards. He respected his bike and the rules of the road. *And, he would not get on his bike if he were drunk.*

Had Lisa's influence caused Bill to abandon not only his family, but the foundational principles by which he once lived?

I just didn't buy it.

~October 4~
Final Drive

"...And as we wind on down the road
Our shadows taller than our souls
There walks a lady we all know
Who shines white light and wants to show
How everything still turns to gold
And if you listen very hard the tune will come to you at last
When all are one and one is all, yeah, to be a rock and not to roll,
And she's buying a stairway to heaven."
"Stairway to Heaven"

~by Jimmy Page and Robert Plant (Led Zeppelin)

I had now expressed my disbelief to the doctor over his statements that Bill had been drinking, and had let the other bike lead. When I became vocal, and started questioning him, the doctor seemed uncomfortable, and pulled out his iPhone to show me a map of the road where the accident occurred.

The doctor and I were both leaning over his cell phone. He said, "You can see how this road kind of curves. That two-lane highway is Interstate-40. And right here is where the driver of the truck was making his turn. That is Final Drive."

I just looked at the doctor, stunned. "Did you just say, *Final Drive?*"

My mother's eyes met mine, and she shook her head and looked away.

"What kind of ironic world is this?" I said.

"Yes, I know," the doctor agreed.

The state trooper came in. He was on the young side, not terribly arrogant, but with plenty of swagger. He asked me who I was and I identified myself, and then introduced my mom and dad.

He began describing how the accident had happened. The doctor had already told me some of the story, but the state trooper filled in more details. "In addition to your ex-husband, ma'am, there were two other motorcycle passengers, and one other driver, involved."

I spoke up. "Who were the other people?"

"I'm sorry," he explained, "but I can't divulge that information."

Why not? It wasn't like I was some disinterested observer. "Well," I said, trying to keep an irritated tone out of my voice, "if I give you a first name, can you at least acknowledge whether or not that person was involved?"

He agreed.

So, I asked, "Was one of the three people named Lisa?"

"Yes," he confirmed. "She was the passenger on the other bike."

"No," I said, "you must be mistaken. She would have been the passenger on Bill's bike. She was his new girlfriend."

"No, ma'am," he said. "She was definitely on the other motorcycle."

I said to the state trooper. "I'm sorry, but you must have this wrong."

And then to my parents, I said, "I would never ride on the back of another man's bike. Lisa had to be riding with Bill."

I only knew one other couple Bill was in the habit of riding with, and I wondered if they were the other two people in the accident. When I asked the state trooper if the other two victims were named Jim and Sandy, he said no.

"Apparently," the state trooper said, "according to some eyewitnesses, the four of them were on a poker run."

In a poker run, which is a common riding game, you ride your motorcycles from bar to bar. At every bar, you pick up one more playing card. Once you've hit the last bar, everyone looks to see who has the best poker hand, and that is the winner.

"So," he concluded, "most likely, drinking was continuing all day long."

I had just been through this with the E.R. doctor. I was not about to keep my mouth shut while he told me that my ex-husband died from drinking alcohol while riding his motorcycle. I knew Bill too well to believe it.

Again, I spoke up, and said, "I can't believe you just said that. You don't know that for sure. This man would not do that."

He replied, "Excuse me, ma'am, but you could smell the alcohol on his breath. There was definitely alcohol involved."

I dropped it, and asked the state trooper how the man in the truck and his three children were doing.

He told me they were all fine—and had turned out to be great eyewitnesses, in terms of filling in the blanks about what happened. Then the state trooper excused himself, saying he was heading to St. Louis to start his official report, submit his statement, and see what was going on with the other three passengers.

As he was leaving the room, Jan and John finally arrived.

Looking at Jan's face, I saw the blankness of shock, and recognized my own expression. Sister Marilyn immediately went over to comfort her.

I thought, I can't imagine how she must feel. Bill was her only son. And, she can't really know how I feel, either.

I knew I was going to have to be the stronger person, the one to keep focused, and keep it together. I could see that she was not capable of handling anything. She was a delicate woman to begin with—not that I felt like a pillar of strength in that moment, either. But, I knew that somewhere inside me was some kind of fortitude I could draw upon.

Together, the E.R. doctor and I explained to Jan a little bit more about what had happened.

Before long, a young man walked in and introduced himself as Shane, the county coroner. I looked at this kid, thinking, oh my gosh—you're the coroner? The investigator on this case?

I couldn't believe a young man in his twenties would be drawn to that line of work. I wondered what kind of person he was on the inside, to be able to deal with such things, day in and day out. Was he caring and compassionate? Or, did he have some strange mental twist or sickness in his soul?

Within a few minutes of talking with him, it was obvious that he had a big heart. Even in my distress, I couldn't help but marvel over all the special people who had attended to us that day.

He gave us a more detailed description of Bill's injuries, explaining, "They tried to do a tracheotomy, putting in chest tubes to drain the blood from his lungs, but his internal injuries were so great, his esophagus moved over, so it didn't help."

It gave me a weird sense of comfort, knowing that this little rural hospital had done everything they could; and knowing that Bill had such wonderful, compassionate people looking after him. I truly believed they had done everything possible on his behalf, and I didn't feel he could have gotten any better care if he'd been in a big city.

The coroner said, "You will need to decide what kind of arrangements you want to make."

As he spoke, I saw his lips moving, and heard the words, but it was hard to get a grip on what he was saying. The world slowed way down.

Arrangements?

Until that moment, I had been to only five funerals in my entire life, and never had a member of my immediate family die. How was I supposed to know how to make arrangements? Yet, it was true—I was the only one who did know what Bill would have wanted. There was no way around it. I was going to have to be involved.

The fact that I was going to have to begin making funeral arrangements for Bill had the effect of someone slapping me across the face with reality. I began to sweat—and my eyes teared up again. At the same time, the fact that I had been assigned a serious task was just what I needed. I would now be able to drive some of my energy in a direction other than the endless, exhausting loop of questions that was occupying my mind.

Maybe if I concentrated on the decisions before me, I could quiet the unsettling feeling that nothing about this was adding up. And, maybe I could channel some of my anger at the state trooper, who I was convinced was wrong: Bill occasionally did poker runs, but he did not drink and drive his motorcycle!

"I'd like Bill's services to be at Baue," Jan said.

Mom said, "Jan, isn't that where your father's service was held?"

I was already prepared for the fact that Jan would likely want Bill at Baue, a funeral home near our house. I knew it would mean a lot to her to have him there. I did not fight her on that. I was too busy trying to catch my breath for the bomb I was about to drop.

"Jan," I said, sighing, "I need you to know that Bill's wish was to be cremated."

Then I waited for her to object. I was surprised when she did not. Maybe she sensed that I was firm in my resolve. I knew this man, and I knew what he wanted, and that was simply the way it was going to be.

The coroner spoke to us in very precise detail, but with a mellow, calming tone. Even though the things he was telling us were piercing my heart and numbing my mind, I couldn't help but think, wow, this is an amazing young man. By the time he had finished talking with us about the arrangements, he had completely won me over. He had so much sincerity and compassion for someone so young.

"Now, keep in mind," Shane said, "that it will take several weeks or even months for the toxicology report to be done. The State of Illinois is really behind, and we can't get you a death certificate until the toxicology report is in."

At the time, I didn't understand the significance of what he was saying. I just knew he had a lot of experience with how such things worked. This was his job, his life, his calling. As for me, I had never dealt with a death certificate before, and I didn't understand what I would need it for.

When the coroner finished talking with us about the arrangements, he asked us, "Would you like to see the body now?"

Again, I had the feeling of being on one side of a curtain as someone on the other side was speaking—removed, distant, muted. "The body?"

Bill—my Bill—had now become "the body."

~Pre-Dawn~
The Body

"There's a place for us
Somewhere a place for us
Peace and quiet and open air
Wait for us
Somewhere
There's a time for us
Someday a time for us
Time together with time to spare
Time to learn, time to care..."
"Somewhere"

~by Bernstein/Sondheim

On Friday night, Bill had been Dylan's dad again, helping him with his bike. He had been Payton's dad again, comforting her because she was sick. And he had been the man I'd spent most of my life with, standing in my house again, managing a pleasant conversation with me.

"Someone," Shane explained, "has to visually verify the identity of the body."

"Yes," Jan said, "I would like to see him."

I wasn't at all sure how I felt about seeing him in that shape. The sum total of the funerals I'd been to at that point in my life amounted to services for the parents of friends. And, in none of those instances had I been able to make myself walk up to the casket. Nobody likes funerals, but I am especially anxious about them.

When I was a senior in high school, working at Dairy Queen, one of our regular customers was the director of a funeral home right down the street.

One day, he came into Dairy Queen, and I said to him, "You know, my mom would love to watch you do what you do."

My mother has always had a fascination with surgeries. Our local hospital had a policy where the public could add their names to a waiting list, in hopes of observing a surgery. Mom was on that list, but had never been called. Knowing how my mom felt about surgeries, I figured it wasn't a giant leap to imagine she might enjoy watching a body being prepared for viewing at a mortuary.

"Really?" he said. "You really think she'd be interested?"

"I know she would," I said. "Weird, but true!"

"Well," he said, "if you really think so, the next time I get a John Doe in who has no family members, I could let you know, and she'd be welcome to come in and watch me do the embalming and preparation of the body. Here's my phone number."

My mom was excited when she heard what I'd done, and talked me into going with her if the funeral director ever did end up calling her to observe.

She said, "How interesting would that be, Honey?"

I definitely did not share her enthusiasm, but I figured it was safe to agree, because the funeral director would probably forget about the whole thing. No such luck. One night Bill and I were at my parents' house, and we had all just finished watching the ten o'clock news. The phone rang. I picked it up, and it was Dan—the funeral director.

"Shelly," he said, "I have a body!"

I looked at the phone, made a funny face, and said, "What? A body?"

My mom was blow-drying her hair, getting ready for bed.

"Well, Shell?" she said to me. "Are we really going to do this?"

Bill wanted nothing to do with the idea, and thought we were totally insane for even considering it.

On the way there, I had some serious second thoughts. I was afraid to go in, but, what could I do? It was late at night, and I couldn't very well stay in the car in the dark cemetery by myself. I was only seventeen years old.

We went inside, and Mom got up close and personal with the entire procedure, while I cowered in the corner, wishing that Mom would decide it was time to get out of there, already.

There were so many disturbing aspects to watching the preparation of the dead body, it would be hard to say what freaked me out the most, but it might have been the corpse's eyes. That day, I found out that the way they keep the eyes from popping open during the viewing is by either sewing the eyelids closed or using contact lenses with hooks on them. I definitely did not need to know this. I was also haunted afterwards by the smell of blood, and memories of the dead man's leg twitching.

Mom, on the other hand, was right in the mix, sewing up the man's leg where they had cut the main groin artery as part of preparing the body. Watching her stitch him up put me over the edge. I kept backing up until I couldn't go any further without becoming part of the wall. That experience ruined me forever, in terms of my ability to tolerate viewing dead bodies.

"Ma'am?" The coroner was talking to me. "Would you like to see the body?"

"I...I...I...I don't know," I admitted. Then, it was like a bell went off, and a voice inside of me said, "You know, you really need this for closure. You hear of so many people who are missing family members and never get any closure."

I knew it was true. For my own peace, I needed to see Bill.

They told us it would be just a little while longer. "The nurses are getting him all cleaned up, so there will be no blood and he will look as good as he can, considering... And, by the way, from the neck down, he will be covered."

"Okay," I said, inhaling deeply. "I can do this. Let's go."

When they were ready for us, all five of us went through the double doors and into the quiet emergency room.

Jan went in first. I went in behind her. Bill was lying there, covered in a sheet. I wanted to shake him, and say, "Wake up, Bill! Get up!"

I was on high alert, scanning him for any traces of blood. When I didn't see any blood, I thought, okay, maybe this is not going to be so bad—but then I started crying hysterically.

I asked, "What in the world is wrong with his mouth?" I could see his teeth, and they were all messed up. The tracheotomy they put down his throat to drain the blood apparently messed up his teeth. I could also see that his gums were much darker than normal, due to the bleeding.

On the left side of his forehead was a square of gauze. Remarkably enough, there was not another scratch on his face. Considering how far he had skidded on the bike, it was incredible to me that his face didn't sustain any other injuries. Maybe the accident hadn't really been as bad as everyone thought. Obviously, if his face looked so normal—except for his mouth—I might be able to get him to wake up.

As I was fighting the urge to try to awaken Bill by shaking him, Sister Marilyn asked Jan if she would like to be alone with her son.

The rest of us walked out into the hallway. A little while later, Jan came back out into the hallway, a strange expression on her face. "Now," she said to me, "you get to go in by yourself, too."

I felt like I was wearing lead shoes. I couldn't move. I had already seen what I needed to see. Did I really need to go in again?

I'm not sure what Sister Marilyn said to me in that moment, but she let me know that regardless of how I was feeling, I was going in there.

There we were, alone together for the last time. I put my hand on his shoulder, and said, "I'm so sorry this all had to end like this, Bud… but, I know you are safe now."

Over the past ninety days, I had worried about him so much, and wondered what would become of him. Between the partying he was doing with Lisa, disconnecting from the kids and me, and his general recklessness, I definitely felt uneasy about his future. Now the suspense was over.

"I hope you found some peace," I said. "And please know I will do my best to take care of our kids."

My chest was heaving, and tears were getting all over the sheet covering Bill's body. "I never stopped loving you," I said, as I kissed his cheek, "and I hope you really did find your peace."

Then, I turned and walked out of the room. I was grateful to Sister Marilyn. She had been adamant that I spend that time alone with Bill, and she had been right. Because we were alone together in the room, I was able to release all the feelings I would have otherwise held inside. The outpouring of emotion freed me to think about taking care of business.

I had a new resolve. This was as real as it gets. Bill was never going to wake up, and I had to deal with it—I had to be a good mom to my children, make sure Bill's wishes were honored, and make sure everything went the way it was supposed to. Having allowed myself my moment of grief, and the chance to say goodbye, I reverted back to my true nature. All my motherly instincts kicked in, and I was ready to take on whatever I needed to in order to get everything handled properly.

I wasn't exactly in my body at this point in time, but some sort of automatic cruise control seemed to take over, steering me through the actions I needed to take. When I felt my emotions rising up again and threatening to take over, I just focused on the state trooper, and how angry I was at him.

There was a group of us discussing the final arrangements—including two nurses, Sister Marilyn, my parents, and Jan and John. The fact that the accident had occurred in the State of Illinois turned out to be problematic. The body had to be released first to a funeral home in Illinois, and then they would release him to Baue Mortuary in Missouri. So, the hospital got in touch with a local funeral home, and we were instructed to contact Baue the next day.

The worst night of our entire lives had somehow, minute by excruciating minute, become morning. We were all standing in the hallway in the darkness of early morning, looking at each other, lost. What did we do now?

The hospital staff gave Bill's belongings to Jan—other than the clothing they had to cut off his body. Jan didn't know what was in the bundle, exactly, but she promised that the following day, she would give me his wallet and anything else he had on him that I might need.

"Well," I said, "we've got to get home… and I've got to decide how to handle he kids."

I then invited Jan and John to follow us back to my house. They agreed, and we all walked outside. I couldn't believe that I was walking away, leaving Bill in the hands of strangers. It felt wrong.

~Pre-Dawn II~
Breaking the Terrible News

"What are little boys made of?
Frogs and snails and puppy dogs' tails,
That's what little boys are made of.
What are little girls made of?
Sugar and spice and everything nice,
That's what little girls are made of."

~Nineteenth Century nursery rhyme~

We got in our cars. As I buckled my seatbelt, I realized I had a completely different sense leaving the hospital than I did when I arrived. I thought to myself, I am so fortunate that Bill was taken to this tiny hospital, where he received such good care, and where we, his loved ones, received such personal attention and care. Thank God I was able to be here, in this particular place, to say my goodbyes to him.

Now, what was I going to do? A sense of dread and panic came over me. I had exactly the length of time it would take to drive home to decide how I was going to tell my children the most devastating news of their lives.

What could I say? Ninety days ago, I had to tell them their parents were getting a divorce, and now I had to tell them their dad was gone forever?

"Mom," I said, "how am I going to tell the kids? What am I going to say?" I must have asked my mom this ten times.

Mom kept reminding me that *whatever* I decided to tell Dylan and Payton, it needed to be said right away.

Wait a minute. Once I did tell the kids, how were we going to live? How was I going to pay all our expenses by myself? The reality of our situation started hitting me.

At least the kids had me. It had to be destiny—this whole mess. If we had not divorced, I would have surely been the one on the back of Bill's motorcycle when it crashed.

I suddenly remembered that we had to call Bill, Sr. and Judy again—who lived too far away to join us at the hospital—to update them on what we'd learned.

After we called Bill, Sr. and Judy, Randa popped into my head.

I remembered how upset she had been with me that I didn't call her right away to tell her about the divorce. After all, she was my closest friend in the world. It didn't matter that I waited a few days to tell everyone else. As far as she was concerned, I should have told her the second it happened. She was right. I was trying to save her future Fourth of July holidays from being ruined, but she was right. I should have called.

But, did I want to wake her up with this tragic news in the middle of the night? Would she want me calling her so late—or early, depending on your vantage point?

Yes. Yes, she would. I knew Randa, and I didn't want to think about what she might do to me if I waited to call. I dialed her number, knowing that the late hour of the phone call would signal to her that something was wrong. First I called the house. No answer. I called her cell. Again, no answer. I dialed the home number a second time.

Randa lost her father seven years ago, and she still struggles with the issue of death, reading the obituaries in the newspaper every single day, like an elderly woman who is facing her own mortality.

She answered the home phone, and I broke the news.

"Oh, my God," she said, crying. "I'll be over first thing in the morning, so I can be there when the kids get up. I'll do whatever you need me to do."

"If you could start networking for me," I said, "letting people know what happened, that would be great. I definitely can't handle talking to anyone right now."

I knew that Randa either personally knew everyone who needed to be notified, or knew someone who knew them. As soon as I got on the phone with her, I knew I'd made the right decision not to wait to call her. Just knowing she was there to support and help me brought instant relief.

After I hung up with Randa, I fell quiet again, and the silence in the car was like a thick fog, covering us all. Over and over, my mind circled around how I was going to handle everything—what I would say to the kids, and how we would manage living our lives with Bill completely gone from the picture.

I had entered a dark tunnel in my mind, and kept drifting deeper and deeper inside my own thoughts. Bill had sixty days from the date of our divorce to get my name off the bills he was responsible for, and because there were still several weeks before that sixty day mark, he had not yet done that. Now that he was gone, was I was going to be responsible for all of our debt, not just the portion I was responsible for according to our divorce decree? How was I ever going to manage it all?

Also, it hit me that the small amount of child support I was receiving from him was out the window now. How was one parent expected to handle everything on their own? Sure, logically I understood that single parents all over America somehow managed to pull it off, but that was cold comfort in that moment.

The house had been on the market since July. Now, I was going to have to take the quickest offer on the house I could get, even if it meant taking a loss. How else would I ever be able to take care of our debt, and support all of us? I certainly didn't want to add to the grief the kids would be feeling by yanking them out of their home and putting them into some tiny apartment somewhere.

My brain ached from the weight of it all, and it was hard to breathe. I didn't know how I was going to do it. My parents, God bless them, were very reassuring, saying, "Don't worry about that, Shell. Of course, we are here for you."

To which my pragmatic mind replied, I appreciate that, but that is only going to get me through *temporarily.* How was I going to handle everything, long-term? What kind of situation was I going to find myself in several months down the line?

House payment. Debts. Telling the kids. House payment, debts, telling the kids. Everywhere I turned, there was another set of frightening thoughts, waiting to ambush me.

When we pulled into my driveway between 1:30 and 2:00 in the morning, the one thing we were all very clear about was this: I absolutely had to wake the kids to tell them. I could not let them wake up to this news in the morning. It was life-changing news, and it could not wait. I knew I would be angry if my father passed away while I was sleeping, and my mother waited until I was awake to tell me.

I knew I couldn't wait. But, I also knew the emotional rollercoaster I had been on since I heard about the accident, and I couldn't imagine how a twelve-year-old and a sixteen-year-old were going to handle it. In the past ninety days, their lives had been turned upside down, and their father had been disconnecting from them. Now, I had to tell them he was completely beyond their reach? How could I tell them that? My heart was breaking for them, and just thinking about it made me start sobbing.

We walked into the house—the very same house that had seemed so open and full of light on Saturday afternoon. I asked my parents to stay downstairs. This was something I needed to do by myself. Tears were pouring down my face, and I had to will my legs to climb the stairs, they were shaking so badly. I was a dead man walking.

I had no idea of the wrong or right way to say what I needed to say to them, and I knew that ultimately, whatever I said was going to devastate them. They would remember this moment for the rest of their lives, and I didn't want to screw it up.

My poor kids.

The kids' rooms are right across from each other. With my entire body trembling badly, I walked first into Dylan's room and shook him. "Dylan, Honey," I said, "I need you to wake up and come into Payton's room." Then I quickly walked out before he could ask me any questions. He, at least, already knew there had been an accident. Payton, on the other hand, had innocently slept through all of it.

Then, I woke up my twelve-year-old, who went to bed sick. "Payton, Honey, wake up…" I turned on her lamp.

She was very disoriented to begin with—and then she saw the look on my face. "Mom?" she said. "What's wrong?"

She could easily see that something was horribly wrong. Tears were flowing down my face and I was a wreck.

Dylan was in Payton's room now, as well. It was time.

The words were right there, waiting for me, but for a minute that seemed to stretch on forever, I could not bring myself to say anything. All I could do was sit there, my head bent over.

Then it hit me—I couldn't let them see me like this! I was the only parent they had left. I had to be strong. If they saw that I was not together, they were not going to be able to handle this. It was as if I had been in a trance, and suddenly someone snapped their fingers.

I took a deep breath and said, "There has been a terrible accident with Dad on his motorcycle, and he didn't make it."

Dylan knew right away what I meant, and he started crying. He had been kneeling on the floor, and now he put his head in his hands, with his arms bent at the elbows on the bed, and cried.

Payton gave me a look like she wondered if she was dreaming. She immediately started crying, and said, "He's dead?"

I was crying harder, now. "Yes. I'm sorry. He's gone."

Payton let out a scream, "NO! He can't be!"

The protector instinct in me kicked in, and I took her hand in mine. "The doctor told me we have to look at one thing to help us get through this—Dad was not in any pain. We have to be very thankful for that."

Payton was in shock, looking at me with a blank stare. Our little princess, devastated.

Dylan was on his knees, his head bent over the bed.

I kept repeating, "I'm so sorry. I'm so sorry... I can't believe we're having to deal with this, but we're going to be fine."

By now, they were both crying hysterically, and I desperately wished my words could be of some comfort to them. But, in that moment, my words rang hollow.

Up until then, I truly believed that the worst experience I would ever have in my life had already occurred the day I'd had to tell the kids that their father and I were getting divorced. I couldn't imagine that life could possibly present me with anything more terrible. Even finding out that my husband was having an affair, and then having to read all about it on the computer wasn't as bad as having to tell my children about the divorce. I wouldn't wish that upon anyone.

Now, I'd had to tell them that their father had departed this earth—in the most shocking, final way imaginable. He was forever beyond their reach.

In addition to the feelings of grief and loss flooding them both, I could tell that Payton was also struggling with tremendous feelings of guilt. Over the past several weeks, she had been very vocal with her dad about her anger over the divorce, his girlfriend, and the way he had been acting towards us all.

She was beside herself, saying, "Now, I'll never be able to talk to him again. How will my dad be able to be there for me?"

"He will always be there," I said. "He is an angel now. He will always watch over us."

As we all sat on the bed together, crying and hugging, I kept trying to reassure them. "We'll be fine, you'll see. We will get through this. Remember, everything happens for a reason. We don't know at the time why horrible things happen to us, but someday we will know."

"Mom?" Dylan asked me. "Was drinking involved in the accident?"

I was taken aback by the question. "Well, Dillie," I said. "The hospital and the state trooper said that alcohol was involved, but they had to send away for blood tests, and we won't know the whole story until the tests come back."

Leave it to Dylan—my sensitive, insightful firstborn. The question probably arose in his mind because of Bill's erratic behavior in the weeks before the accident.

Payton had a question of her own. "Was Dad's girlfriend there, Mom?"

I wondered if one of them would bring up Lisa. "Yes," I said. "There were four people in the accident, and one of them was Lisa. The other three were flown to a hospital in St. Louis. We don't know any more than that right now."

Other than Jan, Dylan was the only one of us that had ever met Lisa.

The conversation reached a natural lull, and I told the kids that Nanny and Papa (my parents), and Grandma Jan were all downstairs. They left Payton's room at that point, and went downstairs.

I stayed behind, sitting on Payton's bed, sobbing. When would I wake up from this horrible nightmare? But, it wasn't a dream—the sobs coming from downstairs told me that.

How could this be happening? It was so unfair. I was the kids' only parent now. How was I going to do this? I was a strong person but I wasn't sure I could pull this off. Sure, I'd had a dose of being the only parent when Bill checked out after the divorce. But, all along, I was counting on having a so-called normal divorced family once Bill's midlife crisis passed.

Now, I was never going to get my friend back. The kids were never going to get their dad back. And somehow, I was going to have to carry the entire responsibility of their well-being on my shoulders. I prayed I didn't fail them.

My body felt anchored to the bed, but I knew I needed to force myself to get up, go downstairs, and join everyone. When I got downstairs, there was a heavy silence, a pall in the air, and it was easy to tell that everyone had been crying. Mom took me aside and told me that they had been able to hear the kids' cries all the way downstairs.

I could feel my legs walk across the room, hear words come out of my mouth, watch myself pick up a cup or a glass, and yet it was as if I was watching someone else do all these things. I'd had a similar feeling of shock and disconnection since Bill told me he was leaving me. Now that he had really left me—and all of us—for good, the feeling was only that much more intense.

My parents returned to my brother's house at 2:30 in the morning, because all their belongings were there. They told me they would bring everything back to my house on Sunday morning, and stay with me. Jan and John must have gone home, but I can't remember them leaving.

I don't recall falling asleep. I don't know if I slept or how much.

~Dawn~
First Steps

"If you should lose your place
This world should hide its face
And go where you can't follow to
I will come and look for you
And you can just hold on to me
Strangers in another country..."
"Another Country"

~Tift Merritt

I had no idea what happened after John, Jan, and my parents left. I had told the kids they needed to try to sleep. Unbeknownst to me, they apparently stayed awake, texting people, which explains why, when I woke up on Sunday, I had a house full of the kids' friends. It couldn't have been more than a few hours since the kids supposedly went to sleep—yet these people had all somehow materialized in my house.

What happened? When had I fallen asleep?

Randa told me that she was the first one at my house on Sunday morning. When she got there between 6:30 and 7:00, she said I was awake. She had already started making phone calls and networking. Apparently, some of Lisa's friends were posting comments like "Rest in peace" on Bill's Facebook page.

I had not even had twenty-four hours to digest the news, and already, my neighbors were coming over to tell me how sorry they were. When I asked, "How in the world do you know this news already?" They told me they'd seen it on Facebook.

My hell began with Facebook during my divorce, and it just kept going. The internet buzz was unbelievable. Between Lisa reconnecting with my husband after so many years, and all the online chatter following Bill's death, there

159

seemed to be an important lesson: Sure, the internet can be a great tool, but it can also be the most harmful thing ever, if people are not careful, thoughtful, and considerate.

At one point, I looked around the house and realized that nearly all of Payton's gymnastic friends were there, along with many of their parents, who had brought over baskets of food—and it wasn't even noon, yet!

I couldn't even begin to thank everyone. I was so amazed by their generosity. True, my daughter and theirs spent twenty hours a week in gymnastics together, but it wasn't like we, as parents, were close.

Dylan's three closest friends—Sean, Mike, and Jake—also came over. Sean, especially, understood what Dylan was going through. His family had gone through a divorce, and he had recently lost his own father to a tragic death. Jake and Dylan had been friends since they were four years old, and Jake was very close to Bill. I could see that he was taking the news really hard, and I hoped it wouldn't affect him in later relationships. Even the divorce had been hard on Jake. "I can't believe this," he said to me when he heard we were getting divorced. "You two are everything!"

You don't realize that other people may look at your marriage and say, "Now there is a couple that will never get divorced." You don't know how your life affects other people.

Dylan's friend, Mike, also stuck right by Dylan's side.

My parents returned to my house, as they promised they would. Uncle Denny and Aunt Vickie came back, as well, and so did Jan and John. Everyone was there before noon.

It was so heartwarming—and sad—to see tragedy bringing everyone together in such an outpouring of generosity. I could see how good it was for the kids, in particular, to have everyone there. It would have been fine with me if a million people had shown up, if that's what they needed to get them through. It didn't matter what I needed. Knowing that the children had the support of their friends and their friends' families was all that mattered to me.

So, I had an open door, and all day long, people came and went.

Arrangements had been made for us to go to Baue Funeral Home at 10:00 on Monday morning, so Sunday was just a sit-and-wait kind of day, with everyone sharing stories about Bill. I was in complete amazement that, in that moment, everyone seemed to have completely forgotten that Bill had ever divorced me, or had an affair. Everything the kids and I had gone through after he left was erased.

As angry as I still was about all of that, I also knew that in that moment, it wasn't important. I needed to let that all go, and deal with the reality—and the finality—of Bill's death. He was never coming back.

Whenever that anger came rising up, I tried to remember the sense I had, even at the hospital, that everything had happened for a reason—even my divorce. I was not involved in the accident because I was no longer Bill's wife. And because of that, my kids still had one parent.

That knowledge did ground me, and gave me some kind of crazy comfort. It gave the divorce and the affair *meaning*—at last.

I also couldn't shake the sense that the affair was necessary to seal the deal, so to speak. It was the one thing that Bill knew I would never be able to get past. He knew that if he had an affair, that would be it for me. There would be no turning back.

Now, with Bill's death, it was as if people had a shared language for all that had been lost. Death was black and white. It didn't have the awkwardness of a divorce and affair. It is so much easier for people to say, "I'm so sorry for your loss" when someone passes away.

As grateful as I was to have some meaning for everything that happened in the divorce, and as much as I needed to set aside the divorce and affair for the time being, I didn't want to forget what happened—ever. I was hurt beyond any kind of pain I've ever experienced from a man I trusted. I didn't want to forget.

I felt like if I let my guard down, I would be traveling in unknown waters. I was completely blindsided by the divorce and Bill's affair. If I started trusting now, what could happen to me next? If you are on a lake in the morning, and dawn is just coming up, and the fog is rolling in, there is no way to know what is hidden beneath the fog. It gave me an uneasy feeling—like the ominous calm before a storm.

If I were to forget, I might be susceptible to having it happen to me again.

And so I lived between those two zones—the comfort zone of, well, thank God I am starting to make some sense of this, and the guarded zone of, I want to make sure I never forget what Bill did to me and the kids.

The fact was that, yes, we were all grieving Bill's death, and rightly so, but in some very real way, the kids and I had been grieving for ninety days. Bill's death was a continuation and an escalation of that grief.

All day long on Sunday, friends of Payton's and Dylan's from school and gymnastics were coming in and out of the house, and other people started finding out about Bill's death in the paper. Dylan went online to look at the newspaper clippings.

One of the articles that appeared in the paper on Sunday, October 4th (the accident had occurred on Saturday night) was from Madison County, where the accident had occurred. The article misprinted Bill's name as

"William… from O'Fallon, Illinois" instead of O'Fallon, Missouri, and stated something to the effect that two people were killed, and two others severely injured. Then it listed the names of the other two passengers and the other driver.

That was how we found out that Lisa had also died in the accident. She was the other fatality.

The same article specified where the accident occurred, stating that two motorcycles were riding side by side down Route 143 at Final Drive, and two people were killed.

Bill was listed as one of the drivers. It listed the name of the driver of the motorcycle upon which Lisa was the passenger (whom I will call Driver X). It also listed the name of the twenty-one-year-old female passenger on Bill's bike (whom I will call Passenger X). It gave the full names of the passengers, and the towns where they lived. Now that we had their names, and knew where they lived, it was easy to start inquiring as to how they had fared in the accident.

The article also reported that the state trooper said that "alcohol may be a factor in the crash."

That really upset me. The fact was that nothing had yet been confirmed about alcohol being involved in the accident. Simply inserting the phrase "may be" didn't take away the impact of that phrase. Didn't the writer take into consideration the two people who had died, and their families and children? This forever changed my opinion of the media.

Dylan ended up seeing not only the newspaper articles, but bloggers' comments. He became very upset seeing phrases like "fatal motorcycle accident" and comments like, "another drunken motorcycle rider bites the dust."

What kind of crazy world was this where people did not think before posting comments like that? They may have thought they were just giving their opinions, but people had just died, and their loved ones might be reading the insensitive things that were posted online.

Dylan found all of it terribly upsetting, and suddenly announced that he'd like to visit the crash site.

Visit the crash site? Seriously? I was definitely in no state to do that.

So, my dad offered to drive Dylan and his friends over there. It was a nice, sunny day, and they would have good weather for the drive. Before they took off, everyone chimed in with their opinions as to whether or not they thought it was a good idea for Dylan to go. They could keep their opinions to themselves. This was my kid, and this was what he felt he needed to do, and my father was willing to help him do it. That was good enough for me.

Dad, Dylan, and his friends took off.

When Jan had returned to my house that morning, she brought with her Bill's wallet, keys, cell phone, and other belongings she thought I might need. We were all sitting around after Dylan and my dad left, and suddenly, a cell phone started ringing. Thinking it was her phone that was ringing, Jan reached for her purse.

Randa looked at me and said, "Don't you remember that ringtone? I remember it! It's Bill's!"

Jan pulled Bill's phone out of her purse and handed it to me.

I recoiled from it, my hand shaking, and said, "I am not answering that phone! I don't even want to see who is calling!"

Randa took the phone and went outside to answer it. It was a new friend of Bill's who had heard what happened, didn't have Bill's home phone number, and instinctively called his cell phone. Randa had very strong feelings about the divorce and was not happy about talking to any of Bill's "new friends," but she managed to be pleasant and civil, and confirmed that yes, there had been an accident. She finished the conversation with the person outside, out of my earshot.

Hearing Bill's phone ringing, and having to field that call, was a traumatic moment for Randa, one that has stayed with her over time.

I turned off Bill's phone right away. I didn't want to hear it ring again. But, before I turned it off, I called it, needing to hear his voice on his voicemail one last time. Several other people told me later that they had done the same thing. The phone had hardly any life in it, and completely died the next day. I was glad for that, and did not re-charge it to call any of the contacts in his contact list.

It was early afternoon, and Dylan and his friends were still with my dad at the crash site. As for me, I felt no more anchored in my body than I had the night before. I was still floating through the day, utterly disconnected from myself. Payton was congregating with all her friends from gymnastics, who decided in the afternoon that they wanted to stay the night with her. They were a tight little group of girls, and wanted to do everything they could to comfort her.

"Stay all night," I said. "It's fine with me."

One of Payton's coaches who was there with the girls piped up and said, "Listen, Shelly, you have enough to deal with. I'm going to let all the girls stay at my house."

At her house? She had little children at home, and she was willing to take on twelve girls? What an act of kindness! In a related act of kindness, the parents of all these girls let their daughters take off school the following day—Monday—to be Payton's zone of support. It was unbelievably kind and generous, and it worked out very well because Monday morning, I would be going to the funeral home. It was a great relief knowing Payton would be in such good hands while I was dealing with that stressful experience.

So, Coach Lisa and all the girls left for her house.

The rest of the afternoon, condolence phone calls were coming in, and people were coming and going. I called my boss, Penny, who was devastated on my behalf. She had watched me going through all the day to day challenges of the divorce, Bill's change of personality, and his affair—and now this?

She could not believe everything I had on my plate. She told me to take whatever time I needed, and not to worry about anything.

~October 4th and 5th~
The Media

"Lord won't you tell us,
Tell us, what does it mean,
Still, at the end of every hard earned day
People find some reason to believe..."
"Reason to Believe"

~by Bruce Springsteen

S

ix months prior, I had decided to leave my job of seventeen years, where I was director of operations. If I had still been in that position while having to go through all of this, I would have ended up in the loony bin. I simply could not have dealt with the level of stress I'd been managing from the time of the divorce through Bill's death, if I had not left my old job and started the new one.

Something or someone was definitely watching over me. During the worst possible economic times, I found a new job, working for great people. Even though I was going through the worst time of my life, I still felt lucky and thankful.

After I talked to Penny, I called some friends of Bill's and mine—friends I had not talked to since the divorce. I told them I'd let them know as soon as I had information about the arrangements.

They had already heard through the grapevine and the newspaper. I was completely amazed. There it was, Sunday afternoon—not even a full twenty-four hours after Bill's death—and everybody already knew what had happened. I had never experienced anything like it.

My mom and Randa were fielding calls on my cell phone for me, so I wouldn't have to talk to a lot of people. People from Bill's work were calling. The whole network had been alerted within hours. When you added in everyone who was chiming in on Facebook, it was almost more than I could handle.

I was trying to keep calm, but my stress level was so high. Vickie had brought me over some strong Xanax. I took one of those, and it helped me stay calm. It took the edge off things, and allowed me to chill out without knocking me out. I'm glad I took it.

I needed to keep myself together so my children could have the security of knowing I was okay, but letting myself be looked after a little bit allowed me to gather my strength. It was strange, allowing people to take charge. I was usually the one in control, but just for that one day, I let go.

It had gotten dark outside, but my dad and the boys were still not back. They finally checked in with us, and told us they had gotten lost. Their directions had taken them the wrong way out of town, and they'd gotten all turned around. Eventually they did find the accident site.

When they arrived back home, Dylan seemed to have a new calm. He said, "I'm really glad I went. Oh, and I found this on the side of the road, and brought it home with me." He held up the brake lever from Bill's motorcycle.

When Dylan left the room, Dad filled us in on the details. Dylan had been trying to get a picture in his mind of how the accident could have happened. The intersection where the highway met Final Drive was on a slight curve in the road. So, it was easy to understand why, if they were going too fast, they might not have seen what was in front of them in time to be able to stop. Dad also told us that there was still blood on the road, and some scattered bits of motorcycle debris, so small that they were off the radar of whatever forensics crew had cleaned up the site.

Dylan and his friends walked all the way down the road, and stopped and surveyed the scene, asking themselves, where had Bill's motorcycle been? Where was the other bike? How far over had Dylan's dad been leaning to try to avoid hitting the back of the truck? Where was the point of impact? What had gone wrong? They replayed the whole scene in their minds, going over the potential scenarios over and over again.

While they were at the accident site, a car stopped and the passengers talked to my dad. "There was a horrible motorcycle accident here last night."

"I know," my dad said. "My son-in-law was on one of the bikes. And this is my grandson here…"

The car's occupants expressed how sorry they were, and went on their way.

I had been a little uneasy when Dylan announced he wanted to go to the crash site, but seeing him return with a new level of peace made me feel good about his decision to go. I could never have gone to see the site, but everyone has their own way of dealing with things, and that was what he needed.

"I also had reservations about Dylan going," my dad admitted. "But after seeing him there with his friends, I realized it was the best thing for Dylan and those boys. Dylan honed right in on that brake lever, by the way. He recognized it as Bill's and was determined to bring it back home."

Dylan is the type of person that needs to get a grasp on something, so he can visualize it. That's just the way he is wired. If it's within his control to change a situation, he will, but if he can't, then seeing the story behind it in his mind, and understanding the rationale, is the next best thing. It helps him deal with the reality. My son was handling everything in a way that was typically male—keeping his feelings inside, looking for the logical reality behind what happened, trying to understand it.

Even knowing that's the way Dylan is wired, it shocked me. I kept thinking, *he shouldn't be acting this way. He's handling this too well.* It was as if he had the maturity of a forty-year-old man, but in actuality, he was only sixteen years old. Sure, he was upset and crying, but he wasn't fully expressing his grief. Of course, I had faith that when his feelings were ready to come out naturally, they would. But, I decided right then and there that both kids were going to see a counselor.

I advised Dylan to stay off the computer so he wouldn't have to be exposed to what people were saying. There were too many people posting things about the accident, with no regard for people's feelings.

"What a great lesson there is for us to learn here," I told the kids. "Before you say or write anything, think about what your words might do to somebody else."

He followed my suggestion, and stayed off the computer, but the damage had already been done. My children, my family, and our friends had already been exposed to so much that had been written about the accident, and it infuriated me. I was so riled up over it, I ended up contacting one of the writers of one of the articles that appeared in the newspaper. I couldn't drop the subject without making my feelings known.

That particular article confirmed that Lisa had passed away. Another part of the article stated that Passenger X—the rider on the back of Bill's bike—was alive, and in critical condition. We were getting conflicting reports about Driver X, the driver of the bike upon which Lisa was the passenger. Through the grapevine, we heard that he was in critical condition. The other article had said that he'd died.

All we knew for sure was that Bill and Lisa had died, and Passenger X was in critical condition. I was tempted to call the hospitals, which were located forty minutes away in downtown St. Louis, but I knew they wouldn't tell me anything because I wasn't family.

The section of the article that had me aggravated enough to contact the writer stated, in effect: Lisa worked for the auto dealership where Bill bought his new truck; Bill worked for the City of St. Peters; relatives of Lisa and Bill could not immediately be reached for comment; some guy that Lisa and Bill had known in high school reconnected with them through Facebook, spent time with the couple over the summer, thought they were a great match, and thought Lisa was a really amazing, fun person to be around, the kind of person who enlightened everyone.

I was fuming while reading this.

I tracked down the writer and gave him a piece of my mind. Not surprisingly, he thought I was a nut. Why was I contacting him? He'd done nothing wrong!

I was less than satisfied with his response, so I contacted his main editor and filed a complaint with him. I eventually got an apology—no retraction, just an apology. I was able to reach another journalist. When I explained my situation to her, she told me that the journalist's behavior could only be considered lazy reporting, pure and simple.

I was on a crusade. I sent emails to people I knew, saying, "Look, my kids are seeing this. They don't need to read that Bill and Lisa were 'a great match.' Just sixty days ago, their lives were destroyed by the divorce." Then, I suggested that they also contact the paper to complain.

After doing all that, I felt a little bit better. But, as Sunday night wound down, I was acutely aware of all that still lay ahead of us. Monday morning, I was expected at the funeral home.

Thanks to all of the support of family, friends, and generous, open-hearted loved ones, we survived the worst of it. I was reminded of the phrase, "It takes a village." That's exactly what we had—a whole village of people surrounding and supporting us through our tragedy.

~October 5th~
Arrangements

*"To live, to die... it's all about letting go.
The death of a loved one is rebirth for the living."*

~by Bob Lancer

onday arrived as if the world as I knew it had not completely shifted over the weekend. Time just went about her business, as usual. I could hear car doors opening and closing as people drove away to work. Kids in the neighborhood left for school. It was startling to see everyone functioning in a normal way—everyone but us, anyway.

In my world, all usual activity was altered. Saturday night and Sunday were all about processing our grief and shock, hunkering down with family and loved ones, and gathering all the love and support we were going to need to get through this nightmare. By Monday morning, I was in full blown taking-care-of-business mode.

I did not go in to work. The kids did not go off to school. Payton was still with her girlfriends at the home of her gymnastics coach, and Dylan and his three buddies had slept at our house. My parents also stayed over at my house to continue to offer support.

"Okay," I said to them, "help me figure out everything I need to do this morning."

The one thing I needed *them* to do was the one thing they could not do for me— snap their fingers and make my appointment at Baue Funeral Home magically disappear. I'd never had to visit a funeral home to make arrangements, and I was scared. I was also haunted by my childhood experiences of watching the embalming.

I simply could not bear the thought that I had an appointment with a funeral home to discuss the disposition of Bill's body—Bill! The man I had known my entire life. My children's father. Never in a million years did I think I would have to do such a thing.

Yet, there it was—waiting for me, my 10:00 appointment at the house of death. Everything about the idea freaked me out. So, I kept busy.

First, I had to call both schools and let them know what was going on. Those were not phone calls I was looking forward to, so I made sure I got up extra early. That way, when I called in, I would reach the school voicemail instead of a live person. I definitely did not want to talk to anyone. I couldn't bear the thought of explaining things one more time, or fielding questions. I didn't even have the energy to listen to expressions of sympathy, as well meaning as they would be.

Sure enough, at both schools, my calls went straight to voicemail. Perfect. I left messages saying that the kids' father had passed on Saturday, and they would not be at school. Then, I promised I would check back with the schools later on in the week to let them know when the kids would be returning to classes.

I was also kept busy with friends who were stopping by on Monday, everyone bringing something to make our lives easier—baskets of food, drinks, gift cards to restaurants we visited frequently.

I then had to call Marcy, the counselor who had seen me through my divorce. I had an appointment with her for October 7th, and needed to cancel that for the time being. There would be time enough later for processing my feelings in therapy. "You're not going to believe this," I said in my voicemail message for the counselor, "but here is what I'm going through. And, very soon, we will *all* be coming in to see you!"

I didn't even discuss it with the kids, because not going wasn't an option. They were going to see somebody, and that was that.

At a few minutes before 10:00, my mom and I headed over to the funeral home. Bill, Sr. and Judy had arrived in town, and would be meeting us there. Just like Sunday, Monday was a beautiful day. The weather in no way matched the reality of our lives. The skies were cloudless and blue. If you didn't know better, you might have believed that everything was right with the world.

We had been to the same funeral home when Jan's father passed away, so I knew it was located in an historic, beautiful part of St. Charles, close to our home. But, I didn't *want* Bill, who had died so young, to be buried in an historic district—however architecturally beautiful. It didn't match him. Some place more modern would have felt less creepy, and more appropriate for a man of Bill's age.

It was a different story when we'd gone to Baue for the funeral of Jan's father, an elderly person. Not that there was anything I could do about it now. We had already acquiesced to Jan's request to deal with the same funeral home that handled her father's arrangements.

Bill, Sr., Judy, Jan, John, and Joanne—Jan's older sister—were meeting us there.

We were greeted by our coordinator, Niva, and the exaggeratedly sweet, suffocating smell of flowers. From the moment I first saw Niva, she reminded me of a doting aunt. You just had to look at her to see what a caring person she was, and I thought, wow, she really found a job that was well-suited for her. It was the same sense I had gotten from Sister Marilyn, the E.R. doctor, and the young coroner at the hospital.

Niva wanted to know more about what had happened to Bill, and we were standing in the lobby, talking with her. Jan, John, and Joanne were already there, but Jan was completely withdrawn. She was not on medication, but she was clearly in shock, and could not function. I understood on the one hand that everybody handles things differently, but why did I always have to be the strong one? I couldn't imagine what it was like to lose your only child, but I needed her to step up and be an active participant in making Bill's arrangements. It was too much for me to be expected to carry alone.

When Bill, Sr. and Judy arrived, it was our first time seeing them since we'd gotten the news, and it was a very emotional moment. I knew that Jan still held onto some feelings over the past, and was uncomfortable around (her ex-husband) Bill, Sr. and his wife, Judy.

But, I was so happy to see them. Judy has the most wonderful, straightforward, bubbly, personality, and I really needed that. She fills up a room with good cheer. And it was so comforting to see Bill's dad.

We all hugged and cried together.

Now that we were all there, Niva gathered us together and told us it was time to go downstairs to the arrangement room. Downstairs—into the basement? Why not stay upstairs, in the sunny part of the mortuary? I vowed in that moment, if I ever won the lottery, I would buy a funeral home and make sure it was a sunny place for people to go, full of windows and light.

I went first, leading us down into the dungeon. Jan and her family followed behind me, and Bill, Sr. and Judy brought up the rear. On the way downstairs, Jan collapsed on the steps and would not get up.

No! It was not fair for her to say she couldn't walk down the steps. I needed her to rally and deal with the situation so we could get it behind us.

I didn't want to deal with it either, but it had to be done.

She sat there on the steps, crying hysterically, and would not get back up.

I was so frustrated. We all had those feelings, but we managed to walk down the stairs. I was at a loss as to what to do, and thankfully, that is where Niva's experience came into play. She sat down next to Jan, put her arms around her, and comforted her, telling her everything was going to be okay. Then, she helped her get up, and walked her downstairs into the arrangement room.

Part of my irritation with Jan stemmed from the fact that over the last several years, she and Bill did not have a good relationship. Bill held a lot of sadness, hurt, and resentment from his childhood, and the two were rarely in contact. I was always the one to say, "Call your mom," or "Let your mom know this or that."

He would always say, "Look, it takes two to make a relationship. If she doesn't make the effort, why should I?"

To which I'd always reply, "Because you need to be the bigger person!"

He also harbored a lot of hurt over the fact that his mother missed many of the children's events, and I was angry on his behalf. She couldn't show up for her grandchildren's events unless her son called her? Why couldn't she have picked up the phone and called him?

In that moment when she was collapsed on the stairs, her inertia reminded me of all the times she had been unable to show up for Dylan and Payton. It may not have been fair of me, but I was annoyed at her for two decades of what I saw as inconsiderate behavior.

When we finally got into the room, we were presented with various options. Niva had all the paperwork ready, and laid everything out before us as if we were shopping for carpeting. Would we prefer this option or that option? How about a photography package?

I was horrified. It all felt inappropriate and wrong—not that there was any other way for them to go about it. They were perfectly sensitive and compassionate, but the whole situation seemed surreal and completely overwhelming.

We also discussed the finances of the situation, and that day, I found out that funerals cost quite a bit of money. About ten minutes into the discussion, Jan spoke up, saying, "I don't have any money. I can't pay for this."

I was sitting at the head of the table, with Jan to my left, and my mom to my right. I turned and looked at Jan in disbelief. Had she really just brought up the division of costs—now, in this moment? I had naturally assumed we would all chip in to pay for it. I wasn't imagining that she would pay for the whole thing, or that I would. But, sorting all that out during the discussion with Niva was the last thing I expected to do.

After a very awkward silence during which the cat definitely seemed to have gotten my tongue, Judy looked at me and said, "Don't worry. We are paying for everything. You and the kids have been through enough. Don't worry about a thing."

I got tears in my eyes. I was so touched and grateful to Judy.

Then, Bill, Sr. looked at Niva, and referring to me, said, "That woman right there will make all the decisions and I will be responsible for the bill."

So, I was in charge of making funeral arrangements for Bill.

That realization suddenly caused the last wall of denial to crumble inside me, and I started to cry hysterically. Not even seeing Bill's dead body in the hospital hit me as hard. Never in my life had I imagined planning Bill's funeral. The fact that I was now doing exactly that drove home to me the full force of him being gone. It was so final.

He once said to me, "When the time comes, I want to be cremated." We both knew, as he spoke those words, that the time to worry about such things was far in the distant future. The idea that it would become a reality any time soon seemed like science fiction.

Yet, here I was—in charge of the one thing in the world for which I was utterly and completely unprepared.

It was hard to think straight with the waves of emotion washing over me. I knew what Bill wanted—but I also wanted everyone else to feel good about my decisions, as well.

Because a person's next of kin is their mother, that meant that Jan now had to sign over her rights to all decision-making, and her financial responsibility, to Bill, Sr. and Judy, who would be footing the bill. She was perturbed that she had to do that—and I was annoyed that she was hesitating. I wanted to say, "Look, you're not having to pay, so sign the damned papers!"

While everyone was signing paperwork, I was able to take five minutes to pull myself together. After taking a break, I felt a little more under control, emotionally.

Everything we needed to decide upon was laid out on a checklist. We got down to the nuts and bolts. For starters, I knew for sure that I wanted to have the service and the other arrangements done as quickly as possible. I didn't want to drag it out. The accident happened on Saturday. It was already Monday—and rumors were flying. The best way to put those to rest was to get on with the service.

Niva was looking over their calendar. "Let's see," she said, "with someone younger passing, there are bound to be lots of people showing up, so you will need the big room... Well, we have space available tomorrow, Tuesday, October 6th. How does that sound?"

I immediately said, "Great. Let's do that, then."

"If you want to do it tomorrow," she said, "I'll need to get the notice turned in to the newspaper before noon. Now, Shelly… what arrangements would you like for the body?"

My eyes welled up again, and my heart was heavy. There was something so final about referring to Bill's dead body.

I managed to say, "Bill definitely wanted to be cremated. And, he wanted his ashes scattered over the Black Hills of South Dakota. He was very connected to the Black Hills."

I'd already told Jan at the hospital that it was Bill's wish to be cremated, so I knew she wouldn't be shocked hearing it again.

Now, was there going to be an open casket or closed?

Having never gone through the death of a family member or really close friend, this was a first for me—having to consider such things as whether or not to have an open casket. Now that I was thinking about it, I knew that Bill would be absolutely beside himself up in Heaven if I allowed an open casket for visitation. He would not want people to see his dead body.

At the same time, I realized that my kids needed closure. They needed to see their dad. When Sister Marilyn insisted I see Bill's body Saturday night at the hospital, I wasn't sure I could go through with it, but now, I was so thankful I had made the decision to see him. Now I had a good picture in my mind of the condition he was in. This was important to me in terms of thinking about the viewing. I knew that his face wasn't scratched up and, in fact, he had only one gauze patch on his forehead.

I said, "Bill wanted a celebration. He did not want everyone coming up to the casket and saying how wonderful he looked."

This was the plan: The visitation—or "services"—where everyone is included, would be on Tuesday at the funeral home. The viewing—where only family could view the body—would be earlier in the day, also at the funeral home.

Bill was in the Navy for four years, and as a member of the armed services, he was eligible to be buried with honors at Jefferson Barracks National Cemetery. In order for that to occur, I needed to track down Bill's separation paperwork from the Navy. Finding it was going to be a challenge, because I had returned all his paperwork to him after our divorce. We would proceed with the funeral plans, on the assumption that I'd be able to get my hands on that paperwork in time.

Next, Niva had to figure out what to put in the paper. Since deciding such matters was a routine part of her job, she had some good suggestions. The same notice would appear on the Baue Funeral Home site, where the obituaries were posted.

As we were discussing amongst ourselves what to put in the paper, I was shocked to hear that everyone thought I should be called "the wife of Bill..." This opinion was shared between them as if I were not in the room!

That made me uneasy, and I said so. "I can't be listed as the wife."

In the midst of my feelings of grief, all those hurt and angry feelings were still with me, as well. Bill had put the kids and me through hell for the last ninety days, and I couldn't just sweep that under the rug. The reality was, I was no longer his wife.

I explained to Niva, "We had been legally divorced less than two months before the accident. We were together for twenty-four years, and married for twenty. But, to call me the current wife doesn't feel right."

"I understand," she said. "I think the best way to put this is to call you, 'the wife of twenty years.'"

I liked that compromise. It was an acknowledgment of our long marriage, but it wasn't a rewriting of history.

"That's classy," I said. "I love that." I was relieved to have gotten out of the way what seemed like a big obstacle to my peace of mind. We had all really struggled over the right way to handle that.

Once that was decided, Niva's assistant came in. She needed to get the notice to the paper right away.

"How does this all work, exactly, in terms of the timing of everything?" I asked Niva, hoping she understood my question, so I would not have to spell it out.

"After the viewing, Bill's body will be cremated," Niva explained, knowing exactly what I meant by my question. "Then the urn containing his ashes will go to Jefferson Barracks. You can either have them in the crematorium, or have them buried."

The grounds at Jefferson Barracks Cemetery are beautiful, and I said that I wanted Bill's remains outside, not kept in some cold building. I also expressed that I would like some of Bill's ashes to go to each child, as well as his parents.

"I'm hoping," I said to Bill, Sr. "that you can scatter the ashes when you go up to Sturgis in August."

That was a hard thing for me to say out loud, but everybody agreed that it was perfect.

Then, Niva informed us that since there was going to be a viewing, we needed to get some clothes for Bill.

We all looked at each other, and I said, "How are we supposed to do that?"

Jan said, "Actually, some of Lisa's friends called me, and offered to bring over Bill's clothes."

So, Jan would be getting the clothes from friends of Lisa's.

Meanwhile, Lisa's mother lived near Bill, Sr. and Judy, and managed to find their name in the local phone book. She called and told them she would arrange to get the rest of the things from Lisa and Bill's apartment to them— but she was clear that she would deal only with them.

In light of the fact that Bill had just died, I was put off by the conditions Lisa's mom had put on the hand-off of Bill's things. There was no way around the fact that we all found ourselves in an odd situation, but my priority was that we all get past the weirdness, and take care of business. I wanted Bill's belongings for my children, and wanted to make sure they did not stay in the hands of Lisa's family.

So, everything was all set.

After they left the funeral home, Judy and Bill, Sr. would call Lisa's mother again so they could get whatever Bill had at the apartment.

Friends of Lisa's would bring Bill's belongings to Jan's house.

I would deal with Bill's storage unit later in the afternoon.

I told Jan, "When you do get the clothes, keep in mind that this viewing is mainly for my children, so I want Bill to be in his normal clothes—blue jeans and a motorcycle t-shirt or car racing t-shirt."

Bill had a shaved head, and always wore a baseball cap or golf hat. He always wore his hat backwards, so I had to instruct Baue to turn the hat around on his head.

At this point, Niva grabbed a remote control, turned on the TV, and a video began to play. It was a presentation of the various types of caskets—as well as thank you cards, urns, and other merchandise.

I couldn't believe my eyes. The fact that they were showing us what could only be called an infomercial about caskets seemed incredibly inappropriate and insensitive. Of course, the funeral business is a business like any others, but it was truly bizarre.

Niva explained that we would rent a casket for the viewing and the funeral. Obviously, since Bill was being cremated, we wouldn't need a permanent casket.

We had to *rent* a casket? Who was in it before? I couldn't take another minute of this process. First, I had to watch an infomercial, as if I were in the market for bridesmaid's dresses and a wedding cake. Then, I had to imagine the poor soul that might have occupied whatever casket we had to "rent" for Bill?

Suddenly, I was feeling extremely claustrophobic in the basement room of the funeral home.

Jan and John are smokers, and chose that same moment for a cigarette break. I figured they were going outside to smoke, and it seemed like the perfect opportunity for me to step out for a few minutes. So, I followed them outside. I should have just excused myself and gone to the restroom or something, but fresh air sounded really appealing.

Once we got outside, Jan and Joanne took a seat on a bench, John stood a little ways away, out of earshot, and I stood in front of the bench, feeling completely overwhelmed. Jan chose that moment to go on a rant about Bill, Sr. and Judy, expressing all the anger and resentment she had apparently been keeping inside.

She said, "How dare Bill make a decision to pay for my son's funeral! He didn't pay for him to have shoes when he was a baby."

I said, "But you were only sixteen and seventeen years old! He couldn't even pay for his *own* shoes."

She ignored my comment, and went on about the past, saying how upset she was that Bill, Sr. had saved the day.

I couldn't understand her outrage, considering the fact that she had already stated that she was in no position to pay for anything.

"We need to let go of the past," I said. "This memorial is about Bill and the children. We have to stick together. I understand that all of this is very painful for you, but I am not about to let my children see us fighting over crazy things from the past. If we can't stick together as a unit and show strength, then I am going to have to make sure my kids don't see us in the same room together, because I can't have them exposed to that kind of thing right now!"

She was taken aback, and looked at me with an expression of shock.

"By the way," I continued. "Did you remember to talk to your doctor? You'll need to get some meds to help you through everything that's coming up this week. I highly recommend Xanax. It will really help you relax."

Her sister, Joanne, spoke up, saying that they had contacted the doctor, but were told that she couldn't get an appointment until Wednesday or Thursday.

I was at the end of my rope at that point, and said flatly to Joanne, "Wednesday or Thursday is not going to work. She's going to need something to get her through tomorrow night. I have some Xanax. Let me give you some. Give it to her to keep her relaxed."

Once Jan saw that I was not going to put up with any unnecessary drama, she put out her cigarette, and went back inside. I was irritated at having to take over and play mother to her, but I had no choice. It needed to be done.

Our break from the arrangements room had been good. Not only did my verbal slap in the face seem to snap Jan out of her emotional state, but while we were gone, Bill, Sr., Judy, and my mom picked out everything. Perfect. I was sick of looking at that ridiculous infomercial screen.

When they asked me what I thought of the selections they had made, I said, "Fine! Great. Let's finalize everything."

"A lot of families," Niva said, "like to do a poster board of photos, especially when there is a closed casket, as there will be for the visitation. It gives more of a celebratory air, and reminds everyone of happier times."

~Afternoon~
Snapshots

"Time it was,
And what a time it was
It was...
A time of innocence
A time of confidences
Long ago... it must be...
I have a photograph
Preserve your memories
They're all that's left you."
"Bookends Theme"

~by Simon and Garfunkel

There were a couple of other details, and then we were finished. Thank God.

Each of us—Jan, Judy and Bill, Sr., and I—was to take a poster board home with us. We would bring them back the next day. I knew it would be good for the kids to do it, but I couldn't even go through photos after my divorce, so I knew there was no way I'd be able to do it now that Bill had actually died.

My assignment was to handle the flowers for the casket. I was happy to have anything to focus on to keep from losing my mind.

We discussed the fact that we needed to get engraved plates to go on the urns for my kids and Jan. The urn for Bill's father would be a breakable urn, so it wouldn't need an engraved plate.

Bill, Sr., also had something to talk to us about. He worked for Wallis Oil, and mentioned that the family of the late owner of the company had established a scholarship fund for his employees and their children. He

179

suggested—and we all wholeheartedly agreed—that, in lieu of flowers, we would accept donations to the Wallis Oil scholarship fund in Bill's name. Winners of the scholarship would be chosen by members of a committee, who would judge essays submitted by the children of Wallis Oil employees.

It seemed like a great way to honor Bill—nice and simple, since the scholarship fund had already been established by Bill, Sr.'s employer.

I also knew that it would make my children feel good, and be a great alternative to well-intended gifts of plants and flowers. This way, people could contribute to the scholarship fund instead. Inevitably, some people would still send flowers and plants.

I was excited about the scholarship fund idea, and Judy said that she would be in charge of it.

It had been hell getting through it, but at last, all the arrangements had been put in place to memorialize Bill the following night—October 6th.

We all said our goodbyes. We would meet up again on Tuesday at the funeral home.

Bill, Sr. and Judy went off to meet Lisa's mother.

Jan went home, took some Xanax, and waited for Bill's clothes to arrive.

Meanwhile, Mom and I had to find a current photo of Bill.

From the moment Niva mentioned that I was going to need a current picture of Bill for the obituary and the reception table at the funeral home, I knew exactly which photo I wanted to use. When Mom and I returned home, I went right to the photo. It was a picture of Bill from our family vacation on Whidbey Island in Washington State in June—right before the divorce. He was standing by himself on a beach.

I hadn't even looked at the rest of the photos from our vacation because, not long after we returned home, Bill told me he wanted a divorce. When I picked up the envelope containing the photos, I had a moment where I thought, wow, these are the pictures of our last family vacation. Then, I focused myself on the task at hand.

We also needed to get Bill's separation papers from the military, and get them to the funeral home. When we divorced, I gave Bill an organized file box containing all his financial information, and even a monthly budget. I was sure that the separation papers from the Navy would be in there, and I had high hopes that they would turn up among the things that Lisa's mother was going to turn over to Bill, Sr. and Judy.

I also needed more information about Bill's storage unit, because whatever personal effects of Bill's were not at the apartment he shared with Lisa would be in the storage unit.

I knew that Bill usually kept a lot of paperwork in his truck, so I figured there might be something of importance in there. He kept his motorcycle at his friend, Vinnie's house, so I imagined that his truck would be there, too. I needed to get to Bill's truck before the dealership repossessed it.

As Mom and I drove to Vinnie's to find Bill's truck, I felt like a soldier on assignment, going through the motions of taking care of business without engaging any of my overwhelming emotions. I figured there would be time enough for feelings later. The fact that the world I was moving through had taken on a completely surreal and bizarre quality helped me stay in automaton mode. Nothing seemed real, anyway.

We hit the mother lode when we found Bill's truck. He had his motorcycle papers in there, as well as extra copies of his insurance papers—things we were definitely going to need. We even found the number of his storage shed.

The truck itself held no memories for me. It was Bill's new truck, and I'd only seen it twice. There was only one thing inside that really got to me. Every day for as long as I had known Bill, he played the lottery, and sure enough, there they were—lottery tickets for the day of his death, October 3rd. I let out a big sigh when I saw them, and tucked them away in my purse as a keepsake. I never even looked at the tickets again, but I felt good knowing I had them squirreled away.

Next, I called Bill, Sr. and Judy, and left a message letting them know I now had the storage shed information. All I needed was the key to unlock the unit.

As my mom and I were trying to figure out how we could get into the storage unit, my cell phone rang. I assumed it was Bill, Sr. and Judy, calling me back.

It was the car dealership, calling to tell me that I needed to return the truck. I had no idea how they got my cell phone number, how they knew that I would know where Bill kept his truck, or why they figured I had keys to it. Thankfully, Jan had given me the truck keys when she gave me Bill's wallet and cell phone.

Here's what the dealership told me: I needed to return Bill's new truck, because his loan application hadn't go through—the loan application on the truck he had been driving! Then they told me I was welcome to take back the old truck, which Bill had traded in for the new one.

Up until that moment, whenever my mind drifted to fears over how I was going to provide for my family without Bill's help, the one comforting thought about money was the fact that, since we were divorced, I had no responsibility for the truck payment on Bill's new truck. That was the whole reason he bought the new truck—so my name wouldn't be on the vehicle he was driving.

Now, they were telling me that they needed me to return the new truck, which I was not responsible for, and they'd give me back the old one, which I was responsible for, financially, because my name was on it.

It seemed out of the realm of possibility that they even had my phone number. In fact, the whole thing seemed like a prank phone call. How did they find me?

"Are you telling me," I said, "that Bill has been driving around in this truck for ten days, and now, suddenly, you decide that you're not approving his loan application? Are you kidding? I don't know of one car lot anywhere that would give you a car for ten days without loan approval! There's something fishy about all of this, and I'm going to get to the bottom of it. I want to talk to your manager. Have him call me back."

Now, I was angry. They were trying to take away the one little thing I thought I had going for me, financially—the fact that, thank God, I wouldn't have to make a truck payment!

If I couldn't get it sorted out, I would have to think about selling our old truck to get out from under the payments. But, how was that going to work? I couldn't even sell my house, which had been on the market since July.

Mom was trying to calm me down, saying, "Don't worry, Shell, it will all work out. Your father and I will help you. Try to forget about finances right now, and concentrate on other things."

Bill, Sr. and Judy had gotten my message, and called back to say that when they got Bill's things from Lisa's mom, the separation papers we needed for Jefferson Barracks weren't in there. They offered to go to the storage unit for me to see if they could find the papers in there.

I was relieved that they were taking care of that for me—until they called back a little while later to say that they had gone to the storage facility and were told that Bill and Lisa were the only ones authorized to get into the storage unit. I would have to wait to get into the unit until I got the legal documents stating that I was the executrix of the estate.

"But, if we don't have the separation paperwork," I said, "Bill can't be buried at Jefferson Barracks!"

At this point, I was on overload. I couldn't take any more. Tears were flowing down my cheeks, and I didn't feel like I could keep it together one more second. I had endured enough over the past ninety days to last me a lifetime. What else could go wrong?

Sitting in Mom's car with her, crying my eyes out, I suddenly had a lightbulb moment. Why hadn't I thought of it before? I was an organization freak, so surely I would have a *copy* of Bill's separation paper in the files related to the first home we bought.

I told my mom that we had to go home right away so I could look for the file.

Mom just stared at me in disbelief. "Really? You have files from that long ago?"

The question didn't even require an answer. My mom knows me well enough to know how organized I am. So we went back home and, sure enough, I found the file, and there it was—a copy of Bill's separation paper from the Navy, sitting in the file for the home we bought on a V.A. loan.

What made me remember, in the middle of a full-blown meltdown, that I would have a copy of that paper in an old file was beyond me. Something or someone put a little bug in my ear. Once we found the paperwork, Mom and I drove back to the funeral home and gave it to Niva along with the photo.

"Okay," Niva said. "We're good to go. I will get in touch with Jefferson Barracks, and when I see you tomorrow for the services, I'll let you know what has been arranged."

On the way home from the funeral home, Mom and I were trying to figure out what to do about the truck situation when my phone rang. It was the manager of the car dealership. I repeated my spiel, telling him I felt something fishy was going on, and saying that I couldn't believe that they would withhold loan approval after letting a buyer drive around in their truck for ten days.

The manager said, "Well, ma'am, there was some information missing on his loan application, and now that he is deceased…forgive me for saying so… but now that he's deceased, the deal is null and void."

"This is unacceptable!" I said. "You don't give someone a truck for ten days, and then pop up and say something like this. Something is not right, and I will get to the bottom of it. Meanwhile, I want the title to my old truck."

"Here's the thing," he said. "We can't find your title. The file is missing."

"Are you kidding me?" I exclaimed. "You give a truck to the friend of an employee, and let him keep it for ten days. Then you say the loan application was denied? Now, you're telling me you can't find my file, so I don't get my title   back?"

"I promise you," he said, "we are looking for the file."

"You know what?" I said. "I'm done. You are not getting the truck back from me. It's not going to happen. This is an outrage, and you will be hearing from my attorney."

My poor mother had to listen to my obscenities the rest of the way home.

When my blood pressure began to normalize, I looked out the car window and up at the sky, wondering about the saying that God doesn't give you more than you can handle. Did God honestly think I was a person that could handle all this?

When we got home again, I knew I needed to keep moving so I didn't collapse. I dialed Randa's number. "Okay," I said. "All the arrangements are set for tomorrow night, and it's in the paper. You can get the network going again."

She was very quiet. "Okay," she said. "What time?"

I told her that the visitation for the public started at four o'clock. I could hear in her voice that something was wrong.

"What is it?" I asked.

"Remember I went to the doctor, and my mammogram came back bad? Well, I have to have my biopsy tomorrow morning."

She'd had biopsies before, and they all came back fine. "It will all be fine," she said. "Don't worry. I'll just stuff some icepacks in my bra, and we'll be good to go."

Now, my second in command was having to deal with a breast biopsy on the same morning as the funeral for Bill. Perfect.

What was happening here, really? Sure, terrible things happen to people; much more terrible than what I was going through. But, to go through what I've gone through in such a short span of time? How is that fair? And how did a higher power possibly expect me to be able to handle all this?

My best friend needed my support and I needed to be there for her—and I wasn't going to be able to.

"God," I said, "how can you do this to me?"

People had been asking me for the past forty-eight hours how I was managing to get through Bill's tragic accident. The answer was, I didn't have a choice. I couldn't very well curl up in a corner.

My children needed to see me as a rock. But, I was starting to feel like a *falling* rock. And, I honestly didn't know if I could hang on much longer.

I had to get some time to myself—immediately. But it was too early in the afternoon for that to happen. My family was still there, and friends were popping by. Payton was still at her coach's house and Dylan was still out with friends, but I had a full house.

The only thing to do was get busy. I didn't have enough solitude to really get myself sorted out, so sitting around wasn't going to cut it. I jumped up and started cleaning. I wiped down tables, washed dishes, and sorted through the food that people had been kind enough to bring over.

Then, out of the blue, a little surprise arrived on my doorstep. Maybe God had heard my prayers, after all.

~Afternoon~
A Surprise Visitor

"Amazing grace, how sweet the sound
That saved a wretch like me
I once was lost but now I'm found
Was blind but now I see…"
"Amazing Grace"

~by John Newton

I t was Johnny—from the BMX days!

He had lived with us as a young man, at a time in his life when he was headed down the wrong path. We tried to steer him in the right direction, but he ended up in prison for three years—and we hadn't seen him since he'd been out. He was a young adult now, in his twenties, and he had arrived at my house with Michelle and Terry, friends I hadn't seen since the BMX days. That was the happiest time in my life, and to have them show up at the saddest time of my life seemed like a full-blown miracle.

The three of them found out that Bill and I had gotten a divorce, and then they found out that Bill had died.

"I am so sorry to hear about everything," Johnny said, giving me a bear hug. "I can't even believe this is all happening."

We both had tears in our eyes. "I know," I said, "I know…"

He said, "And I'm so sorry for the way I messed up my life. I know you and Bill really tried to help me. You're the strongest woman I've ever known, and if I had only listened, things could have turned out so differently. "

Michelle and Terry are much younger than I am. They got married young, and looked up to Bill and me. We were their roles models for marriage. They expressed to me that they couldn't believe that Bill and I had gotten a divorce, or that Bill had a girlfriend.

Then, Johnny spoke again, "I'm so proud of my little girl. And I'm determined to stay on the right track for her. I want to be able to be there for her, and be a good role model—like you and Bill were for me."

He had been out of prison for a year. His daughter had been born right before he went in. So, he missed some important first milestones in her life. Hearing him talk about her made me feel so good.

It was great to see him as an adult. There was so much more at stake for him than when he was a sixteen-year-old, smart-ass kid. I wished things would have turned out differently for him, but it wasn't too late to turn it around. He was still young.

And, while Bill and I might not have been able to change the course of his life when he was younger, the choices he was making now concerning his daughter and his life told me that he really had learned from us. I felt so proud knowing that Bill and I did do what we wanted to do, after all. We did make a difference. We just didn't get to see the results at the time.

I hated that it took what it took for Johnny to learn, but everything happens for a reason. And I hated that Bill did not live to see Johnny turn his life around.

Terry and Michelle and I caught up on each other's lives, and shared memories. I was transported back to happier times, and it was very grounding; just what I needed.

Then, I told them about the funeral arrangements, talked about Bill being buried at Jefferson Barracks, and said that Dylan would be presented with a flag.

"Oh," Johnny said, "you will get a flag? You have to let me get the flag box. Can I do that for you?"

I was touched that he wanted to do that, and said, "Wow, that would be so great. I'd love that!"

Before they left, they told me that they had been trying to reach Jody, and finally got a hold of her to tell her the news. She was my little tomboy, the only girl BMX-er who had traveled with us. They told me they were very worried about how she had taken the news about Bill's death. Her own father was not there for her very much, and she and Bill had become very close. Johnny, Michelle, and Terry were going to come to the visitation the following night, and they said that they'd keep an eye out for Jody, who promised to show up.

Seeing all of them was so heartwarming. It allowed me to go back in time, and reminded me that we used to be a happy, normal family—people who touched other people's lives in a positive way. I felt so proud of Johnny, and so refreshed by their visit, I completely forgot about everything for awhile.

About the time they were leaving and promising to see us the following night at the visitation, Randa arrived, and the kids came back. They each had two friends with them for support.

I was nervous talking to Dylan and Payton about making poster boards, knowing my own feelings about looking at pictures of Bill. My fears were unfounded. Before I knew it, they had photos spread out all over the family room. Pictures were everywhere, and they were cracking up, looking through them.

I stayed back, out of the way. There was no way I could look at pictures. If it wasn't for Niva, I wouldn't have even suggested my kids do it, but it turned out to be a great moment for them.

Mom, Randa, and I just observed them. There they were, all six kids—Dylan, Payton, and their friends—looking at old photos of Bill and me that went all the way back to the high school prom.

Every now and then, one of the kids would shout out something like, "Oh, my God, look at that one!" Or, looking at a photo of me with my crazy 1980's hair, someone would say, "Mom, look at your hair in this one!"

Dylan and Payton each had their own poster board to do. For his board, Dylan chose pictures from the past, from BMX days. For Payton's board, she picked out more current pictures—from our recent family vacation, and from a recent Christmas.

In that moment, I wished I could be a psychologist, and get into their heads so I could better understood what their choices signified. But, all that mattered was that they were having a great time doing it.

By the time evening fell, all my visitors were gone. It was just my parents, the kids and their friends, and me.

Suddenly, I remembered that one of my assignments for the following day was to get the flowers! I got completely sidetracked with my visitors. What was I supposed to do now? I needed the flowers the following day! And not just any flowers, but the most important ones, the ones that would go on Bill's casket.

Randa had already gone home, but I called her, in a total panic. I explained everything, and asked her what she thought I should do.

"Don't worry about it," she said. "Let's just call Kenny. Remember, his mom owns a flower shop. The flowers were wonderful for Rhonda's grandmother's funeral."

That was the same funeral where Randa had a meltdown when she saw Kenny. It was ironic that she was suggesting we now call him for flowers.

"Have you even heard back from him?" I asked, knowing Randa had been leaving him messages.

"Nope," she said. "I've left messages, but I haven't heard a word."

I was trying to forget the past, but it wasn't easy, and I still was not real sure about Kenny.

I said, "Well, give me his number. I'll try calling him myself."

We also talked about my fears that the "new friends of Bill's" were going to show up at the visitation. The thought terrified me. I didn't have the faintest idea how I was supposed to act around them, and I didn't want my kids having to deal with them, either.

These new friends were friends of both of both Bill and Lisa, and they thought of them as a couple. Even though Bill and I spent twenty-four years together, his new friends never knew us as a couple. They were people who reconnected with Bill on Facebook, who went to junior high school with him and Lisa, and claimed they had known Bill their whole life.

That made me so angry. No, they did not! They knew him the last ninety days of his life, but before that, they hadn't spoken since they were children.

The rational side of me knew that, of course, these people needed to come and say their goodbyes, but the emotional side of me simply did not want them there. I fantasized about confronting them, and saying, "You should not be here. This is about my children and their father. How dare you think you could come here? You did not even know this man! You claim you knew him your whole life? Well, I did know him for twenty-four years, and I know for a fact that you were not around during any of that time!"

I felt that, in some way, they had taken Bill from us. I knew it didn't make any sense, but feelings are just feelings, and that's how I felt. Everything was fine with Bill and the kids and me until these people started popping up out of Bill's past on Facebook.

It didn't seem fair, and just imagining all these people showing up at Bill's visitation made me so uncomfortable, and pissed off. Having them show up would feel as if they were throwing in my face the fact that before Bill died, he was a couple with Lisa, not me. I just didn't think I could handle it, and I was afraid of making a spectacle of myself.

Randa told me, "If the worst happens and they show up, I'll take care of it."

"That's comforting," I said, "but really, what can you do?"

She said, "Well, I know what a lot of them look like from Facebook. I can keep an eye out for them."

Randa wanted me to know she had my back.

After Randa and I talked, I called Kenny and left a message. Before long, he called me back. He sounded so calm—strangely soothing, even.

"Don't worry about a thing, Shelly," he said. "I already heard about what happened to Bill, and I don't want you worrying. I will take care of everything."

I had a big lump in my throat as he told me that he would always be there for the kids and me, no matter what.

"I don't even know what to say," I said.

"Well, you better not even think of not calling me," he said, "if you or the kids need anything at all."

I had been in such a tizzy, and not even my mom had been able to calm me down. And yet oddly, here was Kenny, the last person on earth I would expect to have such a calming effect on me, soothing me, and helping me relax. It was a very bizarre moment.

We were wrapping up our conversation when he suddenly asked me, "Wait! What's your favorite color?"

"My favorite color?" I said.

"Yes," he said. "What is it?"

I said, "Um, it's yellow."

"Okay," he said. "That's all I needed. Don't worry about tomorrow. I'll be there early."

We hung up.

What was I supposed to make of all that? The guy on the phone, the guy who was willing to do anything to help me, just did not match up with the freewheeling lifestyle I thought he led.

I couldn't make heads or tails of it. I only knew he had somehow managed to accomplish the impossible—giving me a sense of peace when I so desperately needed it. And for that I was grateful.

Before turning in for the night, we found out that Lisa's visitation was going to be on Thursday. For reasons I didn't really understand, I was glad that her services would not be on the same day as Bill's.

Another day was over, and it was time to take my evening shower and go to bed. As soon as I turned on the hot water and stepped into the shower, the tears came. The shower, the kitchen, and the laundry room had all become havens for me—places where I could break down in private.

How was I going to prepare myself for the services on Tuesday? People would be coming out of the woodwork, some of whom I was close to, and others whom I hadn't seen in ages. I knew there would also be the unexpected guests. How was I supposed to know how to act in front of everyone?

Everything had happened so fast. In the past forty-eight hours, I had become completely confused as to who I was supposed to be in this scenario. Was I the wife, the ex-wife, the widow? The answer depended on who you asked.

Once Bill's accident occurred, everyone—other than the "new friends"—seemed to forget that our divorce had ever happened.

Not me. Over the past few months, I'd had my life turned completely upside down. And a huge part of what I'd been wrestling with since the divorce was the idea that I might be alone for the rest of my life. Now, Bill was dead, and it gave whole new meaning to the word "alone."

I didn't want to be alone for the rest of my life. I didn't want the children to be without their dad for the rest of their lives.

And, how was I going to pay for Bill's truck—and handle all the bills by myself, with no child support?

What about Randa? What if things turned out badly with her, and it ended up being cancer? What was I going to do?

My mind zoomed from one fear to another in a sort of frantic prayer. Was God even listening? How could he do this to me? How could he expect one person to handle all this?

In between feeling exhausted and overwhelmed, I had moments of gratitude that things had played out the way they had.

Again, I thought how grateful I was that the kids and I had been allowed to let go of Bill a little bit at a time. If losing Bill had happened completely out of the blue, if the police had one day showed up, knocking on our door to tell us he had been in an accident, and everywhere I looked around the house, I saw Bill's things, I don't think I could have handled it.

That was saying a lot. I'm one of the strongest people I know, and I still don't think I could have handled it. Dealing with Bill's storage unit and Lisa's mother was not something I wanted to do, but it was a hell of a lot better than having everything he owned still under my roof where it would haunt me at every turn.

Everything really did happen for a reason.

Maybe I was losing my mind, but I was beginning to believe that Bill had left the kids and me *before* he died, so that none of us would have to deal with that knock on the door. Maybe somewhere deep inside his soul or his subconscious mind, he felt his own end coming, and wanted to spare us from having to deal with the shock of it all at once.

Could that really be true? Could he have left us because it was ultimately what was best for us?

I thought, if so, then thank you, God, for that. Thank you—but I need a little more. We need a little more.

Before long, the weight of the world had literally pushed me down onto the bottom of the shower, where I sat, with the water pouring down on me. I must have blacked out with the water pouring over me. When I came to, the hot water had become freezing cold.

~October 6th~
The Visitation

"You touched my heart
You touched my soul
You changed my life and all my goals...
I've kissed your lips and held your hand
Shared your dreams and shared your bed.
I know you well, I know your smell...
Goodbye my lover
Goodbye my friend
You have been the one
You have been the one for me..."
"Goodbye My Lover"

~by James Blunt

This was becoming a habit—waking up in the morning to discover I had no recollection of falling asleep or even going to bed.

I woke up in mother-bear mode, ready to protect my children from whatever the day might bring. The kids were my focus, and that was a good thing; it took my mind off my personal anxieties about the day. Right away, the phone started ringing off the hook, with friends and family calling to confirm the details of the visitation. I was grateful to have Mom fielding the calls.

Dylan's school called, wanting to know where he was—which was very upsetting to me. I had already called and left a message with the school the previous day, and I didn't appreciate their insensitivity in calling the house. I was already terribly on edge, so everything was irritating to me. Again, I had to explain to the school why Dylan would not be coming in, and to remind them that I didn't know exactly when he would return.

I also got a mysterious phone call from the car dealership, telling me that if I brought back the new truck, that would be the end of that. My truck payments on the old truck would go away, and I would have no truck payment. In terms of the effect on my finances, it would be as if Bill's application had been approved after all, and the deal had gone through.

I wouldn't have either truck, but I had my own vehicle, so I didn't care about that. I just didn't want to owe them any money. I lucked out. I'll never know what happened, exactly. I just know that the whole financial nightmare went away.

One of the gymnastics families called to tell me that they had all gotten together and decided to provide the food for the visitation, so I wouldn't have to worry about ordering food.

I was so grateful to know they were handling that because, frankly, the concept of feeding people had never occurred to me. The private viewing was from 1:00 to 4:00 p.m., and then, at 4:00, we were opening up the visitation to everyone else, and that would last until 9:00 p.m. So, that really was going to be a long day. And we would definitely get hungry along the way.

I was also able to reach Linda (Dylan's godmother) and Mandy. You will remember that I worked for Linda when Bill and I lived in Washington. She and Mandy both lived outside of Kansas City and couldn't get off work for the visitation. They would be coming in on Friday for the funeral at the cemetery. I was so happy I had been able to reach them.

After the phone calls slowed down, the house grew very quiet. It was a gloomy day, not quite raining, but overcast. What did we do now? We were all in limbo, waiting for the viewing, and having no idea what to do with ourselves in the meantime. We all focused on what we were going to wear.

"You don't have to wear black," I told Dylan and Payton. "That's an old wives' tale. But you don't want to wear flowers, either."

Dylan chose brown khakis and a cream colored sweater.

Payton wore black gauchos and a white shirt.

And I wore all black—blouse, skirt, and shoes.

Was it ever going to be time to go? Time was creeping along at a snail's pace, and I couldn't take it. I had high anxiety over how I was going to handle myself, and how the kids were going to respond to the services and to everyone that would be attending. None of us had ever had a close family member pass away before—and now it was their father. It was horrible.

I just needed it to be over with, already.

At last, it was time to go. The kids gathered their photo boards, and we all got in my parents car. I was still not allowed behind the wheel, which, in retrospect, was probably wise. I couldn't even remember going to bed at night, so I had no business driving.

On the way to Baue Funeral Home, there wasn't much talking. Everyone was grappling with their own set of anxieties, and lost in their own thoughts. I hate the unknown, and the next several hours were completely unknown to me. I didn't know what—or who—to expect. I was out of my comfort zone and it made me feel out of control.

The viewing was private—for family only. It was going to be me and my family, Jan and her family, and Bill, Sr. and his family. Jan and most of her family were already there when we arrived, as was Kenny, who had arrived early to make sure the flower delivery went well. That meant we were just waiting on Bill, Sr. and Judy, and whoever was coming with them.

We gathered in the lobby area, waiting for them to arrive. Niva came in, got the poster boards from the kids, and took me aside.

"I don't know how to act or what to do," I told her.

"Well, don't worry about anything on our end," she said. "Everything went fine. Bill is already in the room. I was very thankful, by the way, that you decided to put his hat on him, because of some of his head injuries."

I knew she was trying to reassure me that he looked okay for the kids, but what she said totally freaked me out. I now had a visual in my mind of Bill's injuries, and I already had enough going on in my head without having to picture that. And anyway, I didn't understand. I had seen him the night of his accident at the hospital, and I didn't see a scratch on his face. There must have been more damage to the back of his head than I had seen, and the hat was keeping everything in place.

I just shook my head in agreement.

I asked her, "Does he at least look a little natural, for the kids' sake?"

I hoped she wouldn't tell me how beautiful he looked. The fact is that no one looks beautiful lying in a coffin, embalmed.

"Yes," she said, "he looks absolutely fine."

While we were talking, several flower arrangements and plants started arriving. These were not the ones from Kenny's family's floral shop. These were from well-wishers.

"Well," she said. "When you're ready, let me know. You and the children will go in first."

My mouth fell open. What? We were not all going in at the same time? I just stood there, looking at her with my mouth half open. I started to panic. Could I really do this? I wasn't sure. It all seemed so unreal. How was I supposed to cross my foot over into that room? The three of us were just supposed to walk in there like it was the most natural thing in the world?

Dylan and Payton, meanwhile, were very melancholy. I could also see that they shared my discomfort, in terms of not knowing how or where to stand, what to say or do. They didn't know what to expect, or how to respond when people came up and hugged them, saying how sorry they were for their loss.

They did seem to instinctively sense that the body in the other room was not really their dad. He was already gone.

When Kenny arrived earlier, he'd said that, if we didn't mind, he'd like to go in and see Bill after the family was done. After the kindness he showed us with the flowers, and all the comfort he'd given me, I was fine with it—still confused about him, but fine. I knew that things might not go well with him, but I was willing to give him the benefit of the doubt.

We were still waiting on Bill, Sr. and Judy, who were coming from the town of Cuba, which was further away. When I got them on the line, they told us to go ahead and get started, knowing that my family was going in first.

They had opened up two funeral parlors for us, which were separated by double French doors. We entered from the back, where they had all the photos lined up. My kids had brought their poster boards, Jan had brought hers, and Bill, Sr. and Judy's kids had dropped off theirs.

As the three of us entered the room, crying, Payton, who was in front of me, started leaning back into me with all her weight, trying to get away from what awaited her. She did not want to walk in there. Dylan walked ahead of us. None of us knew what to do with ourselves, and my heart broke for my kids.

In the middle of the room were chairs and couches. Up front, there was the casket and two huge pictures. One was the black and white family photo we had taken in the summer of 2008, with everyone in the family but Bill cropped out of the photo. That photo had been provided by Jan's side of the family, and was right next to the casket.

On the other side was a big picture of him next to his motorcycle. Several people ended up asking me how I felt about having a photo of Bill with his motorcycle, but I didn't mind. The fact was, his motorcycle was a big part of his life. What bothered me more was seeing him wearing the black leather jacket I'd bought for him, with the patches my mom had sewn on it. The thought of him wearing that jacket while riding with Lisa was disturbing to me.

He died wearing that jacket.

Next to the photos was the reception table, with the candle and photo I had provided, of Bill standing on the beach. On the table were memory cards for people to take.

I could only imagine what my children were feeling. As for me, I was feeling a jumble of emotions—pain, sorrow, loss, and the agony of having to watch my children go through such pain. It was feeling their pain that helped me stay strong through my own emotional hell.

Dylan, God bless him, was very focused on Payton, helping me comfort her—just as he'd done all his life.

We could do this. I would see us through this ordeal. "Why don't we just look at the pictures first," I suggested, hoping that would make it easier on everyone. "Those were wonderful memories of our time together. Then, when we are ready, we can walk up to the casket."

Then, Dylan said something like, "This was our dad. We will always remember him, and these are our happy memories with him, here in these pictures."

I knew Dylan was experiencing his own sense of loss, but he was handling it more like an adult than a teenager. He was very protective over us, following my cues as to how to help Payton through everything. He was taking his role as the new man of the house very much to heart.

Dylan took Payton's hand, and we all slowly looked over the photos, lingering longer when one sparked a personal memory. Around this time, the rest of the family started coming in—my parents, Theresa and Mitch, Jan and her family, Bill, Sr. and Judy. I stayed focused on Dylan and Payton. Having everyone else in the room with us lifted some of the tension.

In those excruciating moments before everyone joined us, it was just the three of us, alone in this huge room with Bill at the front in a casket. It was so eerie, I hated every second of it. When everyone else started coming in, I let out a sigh of relief, thinking, okay, great, other people are here, now.

I took that strength and held onto it. I was determined that for the rest of the evening, I would be the strong one, the one who was there for the kids to lean on. It was important that they didn't witness me having a meltdown. I needed to show them that everything was going to be fine.

Dylan was the first one to go up to the casket.

I sat in the back of the room, holding Payton, and crying with her. As I said, I had been to a handful of funerals in my life, but I couldn't remember ever being in a room with so much sadness and sorrow.

"I think we better go up there, honey," I said to Payton. "You really need to see him. I promise you he's not scratched up or anything. He looks fine."

So, we took baby steps. One step forward, then we would stop, catch our breath, and anticipate moving forward again. With each step we took, our eyes were riveted on our destination—the wooden casket that held the lifeless body of my children's father. Finally, we were standing over Bill's body.

Our hearts were overflowing with sorrow as we stood there looking at him, tears pouring down our faces. Payton looked up at me with the eyes of a child who has just lost her father, and said, "Is it okay if I touch his hand?"

I don't know how I did it, but, needing to show my daughter that it was okay, I reached right into the coffin and squeezed his hand. "It's fine, honey. See? He's just a little cold. Now, remember, this is just Dad's shell. His soul is already an angel."

Just a shell. Already an angel. Just a little cold. I couldn't believe these words were coming out of my mouth. I couldn't believe life had led us to this moment where I would have to be saying those things about Bill.

So, she worked up her courage, inched her hand in his direction, pulled it back a couple of times, and then finally, shot her hand in there quickly and touched him one last time. Once she had touched him, her body seemed to relax a little.

I was so glad I had realized that the kids needed to see their father one last time. If they had missed the opportunity to have an open casket, I'm not sure they would have been able to say goodbye.

Payton and I returned to our chairs, and we hugged and cried. Dylan and I exchanged hugs and shed some tears together. They were wordless moments where nothing needed to be said. What *could* be said? They had had just seen their father lying in a casket.

Now that my children were settled, I remembered that Kenny was waiting in the lobby, and I asked Jan, and Bill, Sr. and Judy, if they minded if he came in. They all agreed that it would be absolutely fine, so I went out into the lobby and told him to come in. Kenny needed to see Bill, and I needed to make that happen for him.

It was time to shut the casket, in keeping with Bill's wishes. He probably wouldn't have even wanted the family to see him like that, but there was no way around it. We all needed closure. Now, we needed to honor his wishes, and shut the casket before everyone else began arriving.

We all took our seats. The pastor said a prayer of peace, a blessing over the casket as it was closing. We bowed our heads as the pastor prayed. When we lifted them, they were starting to shut the casket. In that moment, I felt like I was the only one in the room. Memories flashed before my eyes like a rapid slideshow—a phenomenon I have heard happens to people right before they die...

The day Bill and I met in the parking lot of Seven-Eleven...The day of our wedding in Washington State...Bill crying on the phone to me over Nadia having to be put down...Holding our kids for the first time...Bill rubbing my feet...Bill hiding a bracelet for me on the Christmas tree branch.

Memories from our life together projected onto the screen of my mind—and then the casket started to shut. As it began closing, my shoulders slumped down with it.

Inside I was shouting, wait! What about me? Don't leave me here! How could you do this to me? I am going to have to be the sole keeper of our children, now. How can you leave me completely? How will I be able to go on?

They were having problems shutting the lid. That was weird. Maybe he hadn't really died, and so of course, the lid wouldn't shut.

Another person from the funeral home joined in the effort to shut the lid, saying, "Sorry, we're having a little trouble."

They finally closed the coffin. And I returned back to the present—just as Kenny's family arrived with dozens of the most beautiful yellow roses. There were ten dozen roses, in four enormous arrangements, all gorgeous. In that moment, I realized why he'd asked me my favorite color. I was overwhelmed by the gesture. It was so thoughtful, and it made me feel really cared for.

There was still time before the guests were due to arrive. I returned my focus to my children, making sure they were holding up okay. We walked around the funeral parlor, reading the cards that came with the flower and plant arrangements people had sent. It was very touching, and kept our minds occupied, but the scent of flowers was overwhelming, and that smell alone made it impossible to forget for a moment that we were in a funeral parlor.

I have always loved flowers but on that day, the smell was just a nauseating reminder of where we were and what we were doing.

After some time passed, people started showing up. Randa came in with her ice-packed bra, following her biopsy. Her plan was to toss the ice pack at the point that the ice was all melted.

"So?" I asked her. "How did it go? What did the doctor say?"

"I am really sore, but I guess it went fine," she said. "The doctor told me not to worry about it."

We were both sure everything was going to turn out to be nothing. She'd had a biopsy before.

My dear friend Ann from Chicago had arrived in town, and she showed up. We had attended high school together. I was so grateful that her partners in the medical office where she was a physician agreed to cover for her so she could come. It had all been so last minute.

After Ann arrived, it was as if I blinked my eyes slowly, and opened them again to find that the funeral home was filled with people. They just materialized before me. Where did all those people come from, all of a sudden?

The appearance of the crowd suddenly made my stomach clench again. How was I supposed to carry myself in this situation? Several people did not even know that Bill and I were divorced, and they would be finding out at the funeral.

I also knew that Jan, and Bill, Sr. and Judy, really still considered me "the wife," which made me very uncomfortable.

How was I supposed to act? Why wasn't there some sort of manual for such occasions? I didn't have the faintest idea what to do with myself. And, I didn't want to do the wrong thing.

To start off the evening, I was sitting in a chair up front, near the casket. From time to time I would be introduced to someone I had never met.

"This is Bill's wife...Dylan and Payton's mom...my daughter-in-law."

I kept my chin up. Whatever anyone wanted to call me was what I was going to sit there and take. My pride had no place in that room that night, and I was at peace with that fact. I needed to be a rock for my kids, and that's what I intended to be.

Payton's friends from school and gymnastics showed up, and she started roaming around with them. I was so grateful that the children's parents had brought them to support her. It was an amazing gesture.

Jody did show up, and she was very emotional over the loss of Bill. Other old friends from the BMX days had Dylan surrounded. And, his friends Sean, Mike, and Jake never left his side. They were like the Three Musketeers, protecting him.

I watched Payton and Dylan from a distance, so thankful that they each had their group of friends for support. As comfortable as the kids were with their friends, there was no way around the fact that they were experiencing much the same thing as I was experiencing. We had to interact with all these people. Some we knew, some we didn't. People were constantly coming up to us and offering their condolences. While the kids couldn't escape their obligations to be gracious, at least having their friends there allowed them a little bit of a buffer.

It wasn't only their friends that showed up to support them. The vice-principal of Payton's school and several teachers came to support her. Her vice-principal told me the story of how he had lost his own father at a very young age, and truly understood what she was going through.

I was so touched to see her entire school, in one of the biggest school districts in Missouri, backing her. I couldn't believe that they had taken time out to come and be there for her. I was truly at a loss for words.

During the divorce and then during this tragedy, it was easy to lose faith and begin to expect the worst—from life and from people. But, seeing this whole support team show up from Payton's school reminded me that there really were good people in the world.

There were wall to wall people at the visitation. The funeral director estimated that we had six hundred guests. Thankfully, there was no other visitation going on at the same time, because we had so many people, they really had their hands full. In fact, they had to refill the pages for the guest book twice. If I turned to the right, there was someone offering their condolences. If I turned to the left, my mom would be introducing me to someone. Or, I would see someone at the back of the room and remind myself that I needed to make sure I talked to them before they left. The next thing I knew, it would be an hour later.

Suddenly, standing right in front of me was the couple I thought might have been riding with Bill on the day of the accident—Jim and Sandy. When I saw them standing before me, I burst into tears. I had only met them a handful of times, and barely knew them, but because I had thought they might be the other couple in the accident, I felt overwhelmed at the sight of them.

Bill and Jim went to high school together. They had reconnected about a year before our divorce. I figured Jim and Sandy must have gone on some rides with Bill and Lisa, but I had known them before they met Lisa.

I needed to explain to them why I was bawling. When they heard that I thought they might have been the ones in the accident, they understood my tears, and started crying, themselves.

"Oh, my God," said Sandy. "We were thinking of joining them on the ride but we decided not to because it was too cold."

Several hours into the evening, my friends, who had been checking on me all night to see how I was doing, suggested I take a break, and told me I needed to go downstairs and get something to eat. I was hot, and I had been standing in my heels for hours. I did need a break. So, I turned to leave the room, and I was shocked to see a line of people outside the foyer, still waiting to come in.

I couldn't believe my eyes.

I turned and walked right back into the room. I couldn't leave. Receiving guests was what I was there to do.

"All I really want is a Diet Pepsi," I told Randa.

"I wish you would eat something, but okay," she said. "I'll be right back with it."

The visitation was scheduled from 4:00 to 9:00, but there were so many people in attendance, it was more like 10:30 p.m. when it finally started winding down. The funeral parlor had been extremely generous with us, allowing us that extra time.

Eventually, the only ones left in the room were family and several close friends.

Randa came up to me at the end of the evening, when I was standing around with my mom, and said, "You didn't see them, did you?"

I asked, "What are you talking about?"

"They were here!" she said.

"You're kidding me!" I said. "The new friends were here?"

"Yes!" she said. "I saw them walk in. They entered through the back of the room. There were about ten of them I recognized from Facebook. They looked at the pictures and then exited out the back door, as well."

"Where was I?" I said, incredulous.

"Well, I was keeping eye contact with you from across the room, watching to see if you recognized them. You didn't flinch when they came in, so I knew you hadn't seen them. Then, I just made sure I kept you occupied so you wouldn't have a chance to notice them..."

I remembered a moment where Randa seemed to be acting strangely, and I laughed. "So, that's what you were doing?"

"Yes!" she said, laughing. "I was diverting you from seeing them. But, actually, they were very respectful, entering from the back, keeping a low profile, and then leaving through the back."

"They never even approached anyone in my family," I said.

"I know," Randa said. "But, I'll bet they noticed all the pictures of Bill with you and the kids... him, being happy with his family for the last twenty years!"

I wondered what they were thinking, whether they felt uncomfortable looking at all those photos. I'd never know. All I knew was how grateful I was that nobody approached me.

In fact, all things considered, things had gone very smoothly. The evening had been like a circular race track, and moment by moment, hello by hello, one tear at a time, we made our way around the track, and finally reached the finish line. By the time it was over, the kids were completely exhausted, and I was emotionally spent.

We began to collect plants, flowers, and other remembrances left by guests. As we prepared to go, I knew that we were leaving Bill behind and would not see him again on this earth.

For me, that gut-wrenching moment of having him torn from me had already occurred earlier in the evening—in that excruciating expanse of time when his casket slowly closed. So, it wasn't like I was shutting the door and leaving. I had already done that.

Now, I was consumed with mundane details. Who would take which plants and flowers in their car? It was agreed upon that all the plants and flowers would come to my house, and later I'd decide what to give away, and to whom.

The funeral director also gave me the memory candle, the thank you cards, and the guest book. The next day, they would deliver the floral arrangements we couldn't transport ourselves.

We said our goodbyes and expressed our appreciation to Baue Funeral Home. Then we all went and got in our vehicles. We had done it. We'd made it through the evening—somehow. My mind replayed various moments...

I'd told the story of the accident so many times that night. The first few difficult times, I fought back tears and a heaviness in my chest. But, over the evening, I told it hundreds of times, until it finally became less traumatic, and I became numb. I felt badly that as the night wore on, and I became more and more emotionally spent, I lost my capacity to really give fresh responses to people. Eventually, I couldn't bear to tell the story one more time.

There was such a wide spectrum of responses I'd heard that night:

"Oh, I'm so sorry about the divorce..."

"I can't believe this accident...what happened, anyway?"

What I told people was what we knew at that time. We knew that the motorcycles were traveling along, side by side, one slightly ahead of the other, and I told them about the truck that was stopped to make a left-hand turn. We knew that Lisa had died. We knew that the passenger on Bill's bike was still in critical condition, and that the driver of the other bike was alive.

Most of the guests had shown a lot of compassion and sensitivity, but I was amazed by the audacity of those who asked, "Was there drinking involved?"

I couldn't imagine being at a funeral and asking such a question. The first few times I was asked that question, I was completely taken aback. I knew people had seen in the paper what the state trooper said about alcohol possibly being involved.

There were only seconds within which to decide how to answer it. I decide to answer it truthfully, but with tact and respect.

"There was a suspicion about alcohol use, but a toxicology report was done, and until the results come back, no one will know for sure."

As we pulled out of the funeral home parking lot and began to make our way through the dark streets toward home, there was a sense of completion, of having successfully run the race.

My parents and I were praising the kids, "You did really well. You did exactly what you were supposed to do."

I knew that Bill had been watching over us that night. Despite all the emotions and crises we had gone through in the ninety days before the accident, he was still with us, still watching over the kids and me. And I knew he was regretting that we had to be in that situation, at his funeral. I also knew that Bill would be the first one to tell you that if it had to be one of us in the position of single parent, I'd be the one to pull it off and get the kids through it.

Knowing he was feeling that gave me some kind of peace—and I hoped he was at peace, himself, knowing we had made it through the night.

All through that day and evening, I couldn't believe what we were having to go through. Then, by the end of the night, I couldn't believe we'd actually gotten through it.

As I rinsed off in the shower and got ready for bed, it struck me as odd that Niva's last words to me were, "Now, remember, you have to be patient, waiting for the death certificate. It may take awhile because of the toxicology report."

Only later would I understand the significance of the death certificate.

At that moment, all I knew was that we had somehow entered the most difficult situation of our lives, and come out the other side. Soon, we would all be tucked into bed, exhausted and wrecked, and about to face the rest of our lives—whatever that might mean.

We just had to get through Friday. The official start of the rest of our lives wouldn't come until after the funeral at Jefferson Barracks. But, I wasn't going to think about that yet. We had made it over one major hurdle, and I needed to collapse into bed, and sleep.

~October 7th –9th~
The Jigsaw Puzzle

"Sometimes when we have been deeply wounded,
there's a time during which we have to let our souls bleed,
take the pain, and wait 'til the cycle completes itself.
You can't rush a river or a heartbreak.
Just know that 'this too shall pass.'"
Excerpted from "The Gift of Change"

–by Marianne Williamson

The next several days were filled with many logistical details. There were things to organize, sort out, finish up, and complete. It was like a jigsaw puzzle. Once it was finally all put together, we'd get a better picture of what our new lives might look like.

Wednesday when I woke up, I knew that there would be a flower delivery from Baue, and I needed to figure out what I was going to do with all the plants and flowers they would be dropping off.

I was also expecting Kenny to drop by. At the visitation, he had told me that he would drive the new truck back to the car dealership and deal with them, so I didn't have to, and he was going to stop by to pick up the keys. Once he returned the new truck, I'd be free and clear in terms of the dealership. I was so grateful that he was going to be in charge of that errand for me. I wasn't sure whether I'd be able to keep my cool if I saw those people.

It had been agreed upon that I was going to be the executrix of Bill's estate. I knew, logically, that this was the best thing for the kids, but it also meant that Bill's death would remain an ongoing fact of my life—above and beyond the usual grief and healing. I needed to make lists of things to do, and stay very organized. As you know by now, I'm super organized by nature, so that wasn't a big stretch for me.

I had to get a plan in place. I knew that was a strange blessing, because it would force me to focus on practical details, and keep me out of my own head.

The flowers started arriving, and just kept coming. It took three separate trips for the funeral home to deliver them all. Big vases of flowers were put on my kitchen counters. Plants and flowers were put in the two front rooms of my house, filling it to the point where you had to move foliage out of the way in order to walk through.

What the hell was I supposed to do with all those flowers?

Someone had told me I could donate them to a local nursing home, which would gladly accept them. The nursing home would then rearrange them, set them on dinner tables, place them at nursing stations, or give them to patients who needed cheering up but may not have family of their own to bring them flowers.

That seemed like the perfect solution to me, especially because my daughter has a special fondness for the elderly. Whenever she sees an older person, she gets teary-eyed and immediately wants to help them in any way she can. She has been that way her whole life. Many small children get shy around elderly people, but not Payton. From the time she was very little, she was always crawling up in their laps.

So, I knew the idea would be a home run with her.

"Oh, my gosh, Payton," I said. "I don't know what to do with all these flowers, and I'm thinking of donating them to a nursing home. Wouldn't that be great? We could give them to the elderly."

"No!" she said. "These flowers are my father's. You can't just give them away."

I was stunned by her reaction. I looked around at all the fresh cut flowers. What was I supposed to do with them all? First of all, we didn't have the room we would need to store them all. Secondly, we would all get allergy attacks with that amount of pollen in the house. And lastly, our house now smelled like a funeral home—and I'd had as much of that smell as I could take for one lifetime.

Then, I came up with an idea. Payton and I walked around to all the different arrangements and took flowers from each one. With those flowers, we mixed and matched until we came up with eight separate arrangements. We put one in her room, one in my room, one in the bathroom. We selected some of the plants to keep. Once we had distributed everything around our house, she felt fine about donating the rest to a nursing home.

First, we had to collect all the cards that came with the plants and flowers, because we needed to write thank you cards—and we were each planning to write out our own. And, I needed to have Dylan drop off arrangements at Jan's house.

I packed my car with flowers, and even had some on my lap as I was driving. Payton came with me to the nursing home, holding some flowers, as well. I made sure I picked a nice nursing home so she would feel comfortable when we got there. Payton was a little uneasy in the car, but once we pulled up, she saw that it was an upscale place, and well-maintained. Little old ladies were sitting in the dining room and chatting on the couch. A few were playing cards.

Seeing all this, Payton got excited.

The lady that met us at the door gushed over us, telling us how sorry she was for our loss, and letting us know she couldn't thank us enough. "There are so many people here who don't have anyone," she said. I hadn't even told her about Payton's affinity for the elderly, but she focused on Payton anyway, talking to her like I wasn't even there, probably because she was a child who had lost her father.

"By this evening," the young lady explained, "we'll have all the arrangements distributed, and every dinner table will share memories of your father."

Payton relaxed so much that she began sharing with the woman about how much she loved the elderly, and wanted to go give them hugs.

"Well," the lady said. "You could be a candy striper! How old are you."

"I'm twelve," Payton said.

"Well, when you're thirteen," she said, "you can come back here and be a candy striper, and give these people some love."

Payton and I left there with a plan for her to become a candy striper the following summer.

While Payton and I were visiting the nursing home, Dylan was dropping off several arrangements at Jan's. He was in the mindset of, "Whatever you need me to do to help, just tell me. I will do whatever." I was so proud of him.

My mom and dad, meanwhile, realized they needed to go home. They had only been planning on being here for two nights, for Theresa's birthday. That was before the entire world changed. Before they knew it, Saturday night had turned into an endless nightmare without end. Tuesday, they'd had to buy clothes to wear to Bill's services. Now it was Wednesday, and they were still here. They really needed to go home, and have at least one good night in their own bed.

So, they took off for the three hour drive back home.

That left me alone with the kids for the first time in days. The first thing I did was begin making lists of everything I was going to need to take care of Bill's affairs. At the same time, I started my own what-if file, containing everything my parents might need to know if I were to die.

I had to make an appointment with the Social Security office to find out how the kids would receive their father's Social Security benefits. I found out that if Bill and I had still been married, I would have received benefits, but because we were divorced—only fifty-two days!—I was not eligible. The woman on the phone was very sympathetic when I told her how recently I was divorced.

She then told me that the benefits to me would have amounted to fifteen hundred dollars a month. It was somewhat depressing, realizing that fifty-two days was all that stood between me and benefits which would have gone a long way toward helping me and the kids at a time when I was panicking over finances. Oh, well, it was what it was, and there was nothing I could do to change it.

Next, I started looking into our life insurance policies. I knew Bill had a policy through his work. I also had to cancel Bill's truck insurance. Somehow, I'd already thought to cancel his motorcycle insurance.

I still needed to get into Bill's storage locker, but until the papers came back stating that I was the executrix of the estate, my hands were tied.

Bill also had a 401K and veteran's benefits, and I was going to have to find my way through all that red tape.

At some point, I was going to need to go to Bill's work and turn in his work I.D. and keys. They also needed a copy of the death certificate—but what else was new? Everybody needed it. His work needed it, the insurance companies did, the Social Security office—every single entity I spoke to needed it. Then, it hit me. This was why Niva kept stressing to me that it might take awhile for me to get a hold of it. Given that this was her business, she knew I was going to need it for everything. There was hardly anything I could handle without it.

I'd been told it would probably take months to get the death certificate. I was starting to get very depressed. I needed to keep organized, but my hands were tied. What was I supposed to do?

Suddenly, out of nowhere, a terrifying thought occurred to me. I don't know why it took so long to hit me, but when it did, it totally knocked me down: *Could the surviving passenger on the back of Bill's bike sue me?*

The mental road I was traveling that led me to that thought started with the awareness that there are so many lists to make when your spouse dies. Then I started wondering if everyone goes through the same thing when someone dies. Then, I started imagining who was doing the very same activities I was doing on behalf of Lisa.

Thinking about Lisa got me to thinking about the other people involved in the accident—the two who had survived. That was how I arrived at a full blown state of panic, afraid that I might get sued by Passenger X.

Legally, what *was* going to happen to Bill's insurance money? I hadn't imagined the insurance money would amount to much, but up until that moment, I had counted on the kids having some sort of payout that they could count on. Now, I was feeling shaky, imagining that Bill's passenger could potentially pull the rug right out from under us.

I called Denny, and asked him whether I could be held legally liable for the accident. Could the surviving passenger sue me, and come after my house?

I knew that, before the accident, Bill still had two weeks left to get my name off the bills I was no longer responsible for according to our divorce decree. But, now that he was gone, what was going to happen?

Denny said, "Well, this is one upside to your divorce. Bill's passenger cannot touch your house because you are legally divorced."

He was not one hundred percent sure that she couldn't get the proceeds from Bill's life insurance policy, because if Bill hadn't changed the benefits to go to the children after our divorce, then they would go into the estate—and if they went into the estate, it would be a free-for-all.

Denny tried to keep me calm. There were still plenty of unknowns but he felt positive that everything would play out in my kids' favor. And, worst case scenario, whatever else happened, my kids would not lose their home. I took what comfort I could in that fact.

After I got off the phone with him, I got several phone calls from friends. First Randa called, just to check in and see how I was doing—and she got an earful. I was on a guerilla mission, to inform everyone that they needed a "what-if" file. Randa was the first to hear my sermon on the subject. "You've got to get this file done!" I told her.

I could hear in her voice that something was up beyond annoyance over my preaching. When I asked her what was going on, she said, "Have you been online? Have you looked at Lisa's obituary?"

I said, "No, I have not been online looking at obituaries!"

As I said, my dear friend Randa reads the obituaries every day, and I mean the obituaries of people she doesn't even know. But it doesn't hold the same fascination for me.

"Well, you need to prepare yourself," she said.

Immediately my defenses went up. "Why, what does it say?"

After hearing from Judy, who had spoken to Lisa's mother, we knew that Lisa's services would be on Thursday. I was so grateful they were not held on the same day as Bill's.

"Well," Randa went on, "Lisa's visitation is on Thursday, but she is being buried on Friday, the same day as Bill. But there's more…"

"What!?" I said.

"Lisa's obituary," she said, "refers to Lisa and her 'dearest fiancé, the late Bill…'"

I went numb. "What did you just say to me?"

"I can't believe they would put that in there," she continued.

I started ranting and raving. I was furious with Bill, furious with Lisa's family. There was so much wrong with that obituary language, I didn't even know where to start. How could they do that, knowing that Bill had children that would be affected by whatever they chose to write?

Randa tried to convince me that it couldn't be true—they couldn't have been engaged.

"Maybe it is true," I said. "After all, he lost his fucking mind. Also, that would explain why Bill kept telling me that I was going to have to learn to live with the idea of Lisa, one way or another."

"No way," she said. "He never would have gotten engaged to her. Not that fast. He knew his children would never accept it!"

I said, "Yes, but, you have to remember, he had completely lost his mind!"

Bill, Sr. and Judy had also seen the obituary, and called me. Judy was as horrified as I was, but she felt she needed to attend Lisa's visitation on Thursday. She explained that she needed to see if Lisa had a ring on her finger—that is, if there was an open casket. After all, this was a woman their child may or may not have been planning to marry—a woman Bill had only been dating a few months, and no one but Dylan and Jan had ever even met.

Judy also told me that she wasn't sure if Lisa's mother had returned all of Bill's belongings, and suggested that it was important that we all stay on her good side.

I told Judy that I agreed. Even though Lisa's mother had supposedly given back all of Bill's things, I knew for sure that there was missing paperwork, at the very least. I recognized that Lisa's family was also going through a terrible loss and were probably scattered.

Judy asked me if I would mind if they attended Lisa's visitation, and I told her I had absolutely no objection. We were both on the same page—we needed to know if she really had a ring on her finger, and we wanted to make sure we stayed on good terms with Lisa's mother.

So, it was decided. The following day—Thursday—Judy and Bill, Sr. would attend Lisa's visitation. It would turn out that when Judy went to the visitation, she did not see a ring on Lisa's finger.

I didn't yet know that, so I was left wondering…Had my husband of twenty years really gone that far? He had really gotten engaged to a woman he had only been with for a couple of months? I knew he was in a serious midlife crisis, which could make a man do crazy things. And, maybe he felt that getting engaged was something he needed or wanted to do. On the other hand, he knew his children would never accept his quick engagement to another woman, so I couldn't imagine he really would have done that.

Later that day, Kenny came by to pick up the keys to Bill's truck, so he could return it to the dealership for me. And, we got a chance to really have a heart to heart talk. It was our first one-on-one conversation where no one else was around, and we were both very emotional. We had our conversation out in my driveway, leaning up against his truck, talking about the changes that he—and other friends of Bill's—had seen in Bill since the divorce.

He said, "When I first heard that you were going to be getting a divorce, I just couldn't believe my ears. And, then when I met Lisa, I was even more blown away. She was just not his type. She had one of those big, not-afraid-to-speak-her-mind type personalities. She was a real party girl. She didn't seem to fit Bill's personality. And I tried to ask him, 'Have you lost your mind? What are you thinking? You are actually going to leave your family for this life?'"

So, it wasn't just me! I felt so validated by my conversation with Kenny. Everything that had happened with Bill since our divorce was so out of character that I'd begun to question myself. Was his behavior normal? Was I the crazy one?

It was so cleansing to hear Kenny say that he couldn't believe what Bill had been doing. I knew that Kenny was not a person who was particularly biased in my direction, and had no bias against Lisa, either, so that gave his opinions a lot of weight in my eyes.

Not only did he make me feel like I hadn't been out of my mind for thinking Bill had been acting strangely, but he shocked me by his reaction to Bill's choices. Was it possible that the two friends actually *envied* each other's lives?

Bill seemed to have been chasing Kenny's lifestyle—a life where he had no one to answer to but himself. I already knew that. But, did Kenny also envy Bill? Listening to Kenny talk that day about Bill's choices, that was the impression I got.

I was left with such certainty that Bill had been suffering from a terrible midlife crisis. Along with my newfound certainty came a profound sadness. Maybe if I'd known for sure that Bill was just going through a midlife crisis, I could have helped him through it.

Before Kenny left, he also shared with me that he had been extremely upset at Bill. He said, "Why would Bill implicate me in his drug use when it just wasn't true? I had nothing to do with any of that, whatsoever. And, I did not appreciate him making me out to be the bad guy. I said to him, 'How dare you bring me into it!' It's hard, knowing that some of my last words with Bill were angry words. We talked again after that, and made our peace, but things were never quite the same again…"

Apparently, Kenny had also been very vocal with Bill about Lisa—which upset Bill.

Kenny and Bill had been good friends for many years, and I could see that it weighed on Kenny, knowing that they had not left things on the best note between them.

As we said our goodbyes, and I thanked Kenny for handling the return of Bill's truck, he kept stressing to me, "Now, remember, I'm here for you and the kids, whatever you need. So, prepare yourself. I'll probably get on your nerves, I'll be calling to check in on you so often."

I wasn't sure how seriously to take what he was saying. I must have had hundreds of people the night before saying, "Now, if you need anything…" and I was sure I'd never hear from half of them. But, he really did sound sincere—incredibly sincere, in fact. And I couldn't figure out why he would go out on such a limb for us. He didn't owe us anything.

I felt really good after our visit. He had lifted my spirits, restored my faith a little bit, and reminded me that people can still surprise me—in a good way. I'd had enough unpleasant surprises to last me a lifetime.

~October 7th~
Old Routines and New Beginnings

"A journey of a thousand miles
Must begin with a single step."

~Lao Tzu

I t was time to start thinking about getting the kids and I back into our normal routines—the sooner, the better. It was time to call the kids' schools,
let them know that they would be returning to school on Monday, and find
out about picking up homework.

Dylan was beside himself, knowing how far he was falling behind.
Unlike Payton, none of Dylan's teachers had shown up at the memorial service, and he was feeling overwhelmed.   In particular, Dylan was upset over
missing so much of Spanish class. He was missing school during the very week
they would finally start speaking entirely in Spanish.

Payton, on the other hand, could have cared less. Her teachers had reassured her at the memorial service that she didn't have anything to worry about.
The difference in the way the two schools handled Dylan and Payton may
have just been the difference between high school and middle school—but
still. I didn't feel like Dylan got the support he needed. Payton's school was
making Dylan's school look bad.

I called Payton's school first, spoke to the vice-principal, and let him
know we would be coming by to pick up homework. I also expressed to him
how much we appreciated that he and his team of counselors and teachers
showed up for Payton at the visitation.

"Well, I've been through this, myself," he said. "And I know how hard it
is. In fact, you know what I'm thinking? Why don't you bring Payton up during lunchtime? She can eat with her friends, and I will sit with her, too, and

211

that way, when she comes back on Monday, she won't have to field all the questions. It will be a way to break the ice in advance."

My heart really went out to him. "Really?" I said. "You would do that? That would be so wonderful. I can't believe you would take time out of your day…"

He said, "It would be my pleasure."

I could not have been more thankful.

So, Dylan and I made a plan to drop off Payton at lunchtime at her school, and zip around the corner to his school to pick up his schoolwork. It would work out perfectly.

When I called Dylan's school, identified myself, and said we would be by on Thursday to pick up his homework, I was told that they were not sure they would have anything ready for me. I was apparently violating the school policy by not giving them forty-eight hours notice. A child had to be out of school for two days before they could pick up homework.

So, what was the problem? It was Wednesday—three days out of school!

I wanted to say, "You should really learn from your middle school vice-principal." Instead, I just said, "I will be by at noon tomorrow, and there had better be homework waiting for me when I get there."

She said, "I will try my best."

The kids felt good knowing we had a plan for the following day. Dylan was happy that he would have the weekend to get caught up on his homework, and Payton loved the idea of the lunchtime icebreaker.

I also spoke with the City of St. Peters, and made a plan to stop by on Thursday morning, drop off Bill's keys and I.D., and pick up a packet of paperwork for Bill's insurance and 401K.

Although Jan had given me his wallet days earlier, I had not yet looked inside it—and I was not looking forward to it.

Before I knew it, the day wound down, and Wednesday came to a close. I'd had a heart-to-heart with Kenny, and he returned the truck for me. I had taken care of business, making the various appointments I needed to make for Thursday. My parents had headed home to get a change of clothes and a good night's sleep in their own bed.

The bar was set a lot lower in this post-accident world in which we were now living, and according to those new survival standards, it was as close as we were going to get to a good day. True to my new pattern, I fell asleep that night with no memory of even having turned down the bed.

The next thing I knew, another day had dawned, and with it, everything that awaited us.

First thing on Thursday morning, I had to go to Bill's work. As I reached for his work keys, I remembered the comfort of seeing that same set of keys sitting on our kitchen counter every night during our marriage. After our divorce, it was one of those strange little thoughts that snuck up on me—I wonder where he keeps his keys these days; I always knew where they were at my house.

Then, I took a deep breath, and opened Bill's wallet—the wallet that always sat in either his front or back pocket, depending on the pants he was wearing. It smelled like him—leather mixed with perspiration. It was jammed full of business cards, just like I remembered. And right behind his debit card was his work I.D. I couldn't bear to look too closely at anything in the wallet. I just slipped out his I.D., tried to breathe deeply again, and took a moment to gaze at his picture.

He was such a hard worker, and so well liked on the job. Everyone knew him, from the administrative assistants at City Hall to the street workers.

When I got to his work, I started to get sweaty and nervous. I didn't want to go inside the building. I was dreading going through it all again—all the well-meaning expressions of "I'm sorry," some of which would feel sincere, and some of which would not. I learned such a big lesson from people who offered me their condolences: Always remember that the way you speak to people is important. So is your body language.

It was hard to walk into City Hall, the place where Bill had gone to work for thirteen years. He was respected and well-loved for being a hard worker, and really loved his job working in the utility department. Sometimes he worked in swamps, digging out pipes, even in freezing winter temperatures and one-hundred-degree summer weather. Not many people could do the kind of work Bill did, but he liked it, worked hard, and took great pride in his work. And, everyone knew it.

The human resources director was very sweet and kind to me. She had probably gone through that sort of thing many times before. She gave me an envelope of paperwork, all organized and labeled. It showed that she had taken a lot of care with it, and was sensitive to the state of mind I was in. To make sure I didn't forget anything, she went over with me which forms I needed to sign and which entities I needed to call. I was grateful. Otherwise, I know I wouldn't have gotten past the parking lot before I realized I needed to turn right around and go back in because I had a million questions.

I was more or less fine while I was meeting with the H.R. director. Her sincerity helped ease me through that difficult errand. But, once I got into the car and closed the door, I started crying. It was so hard, thinking about how well-liked Bill was by everyone who worked with him, and knowing he was never going back into work. I didn't think he ever really knew how highly people regarded him, and that made me very sad.

That got me to thinking about his memorial service on Tuesday night. I was sure Bill would have been shocked to see how many people showed up, and how many lives he had touched.

I think Bill thought of himself as a black-and-white kind of guy, in the sense that people either liked him or they didn't. But, you can never really know the effect you have on others. It made me understand the desire to give your children their inheritance while you are still alive, so you can see how they spend it, or the desire to attend your own funeral, just so you can see whose lives you've touched.

Pulling out onto the highway, I couldn't believe it was only eleven o'clock in the morning, and I already felt emotionally exhausted. At least it was another beautiful day, weather-wise.

When I got back home, I picked up the kids, and we went to Payton's school first. She was thrilled to have the chance to have lunch with all her friends before having to face everyone at school on Monday. After Dylan and I dropped off Payton, we went to his school. I was not surprised to find that some of his homework was ready for us, and some of it was not. We took what we could get, and left.

"Let's just forget it, and deal with it next week," I told Dylan. "That way, we can move on."

So, Dylan and I waited for Payton to finish with lunch. When she came out to the car, she was so much more relaxed, just knowing she'd gotten past that initial awkwardness of needing to explain to everyone what had happened. Now, she wouldn't have to dread returning to school on Monday—unlike Dylan.

While it was clear from Payton's body language that she was more at ease after the school lunch, she did not want to talk about anything related to Bill. She was very straightforward with Dylan, me, Randa, my parents, and anyone else who asked her, that she simply did not want to talk about it.

I respected her for having the strength to make her wishes known. I was aware that, along with the terrible loss of her father, she was still dealing with so much guilt over having been angry with him before his death. I didn't want to push her to talk, and wasn't sure how to handle her silence on the subject of Bill. And, we weren't seeing our counselor until the following week, so that was no help.

In the meantime, I told everyone to respect her wishes until I could figure out the best way to approach the situation.

As for Dylan, he was still in the mode of the protector and man of house, and was behaving in a very adult manner. It was obvious that he was very sad and wished that this new reality was not our life, but he seemed to be letting everything roll off his back. I knew there was more depth to his feelings than met the eye, and I figured he was just modeling Bill—trying to be the stoic provider-protector that his father had been for us.

That was totally in character for Dylan. In many areas of his life, he would watch his Dad, learn from him, then take those lessons and try to go even further with them than Bill ever had. In those areas where Bill was good at something, Dylan wanted to match his Dad's successes—and then surpass them. In those areas where Bill had faults or failings, Dylan swore to himself that he would avoid those same pitfalls. He never wanted to repeat his father's mistakes.

Dylan told me, "I'll never cheat on my wife… I'll probably drink but I will never touch drugs."

I asked him, "What are you saying? Are you using these things as positive inspiration, so you won't be tempted to do the same thing?"

He told me that was exactly what he was doing.

Dylan idolized his father, and would never say a bad word about him, or second-guess anything he did. When he heard that Bill was leaving us, in fact, Dylan simply said, "This is not something I ever thought would happen, but if it is going to happen, I just want you to be happy." Dylan's reaction was a great example of the total trust he had in his dad's decisions.

Then, as more details started coming out—about Bill's affair, his girlfriend, and eventually about his one-time drug use, he was shattered. Those flaws in his father just did not fit with the perfect image Dylan had of his dad.

The things Dylan discovered about Bill shattered not only his view of his dad as a perfect man, but everything Dylan believed to be true about his own world. It seemed that his way of adjusting to that new information was to say to himself, well, my dad may not have lived up to those ideals all the way to the very end of his life, but I still believe in them, and *I'm* going to live up to them.

And the truth was, with the exception of the last few months of Bill's life, he always exemplified the qualities of a faithful and devoted husband and father.

Dylan seemed to make a vow to hold onto those values he held dear. He had already lost so much.

Payton was struggling with something similar, only she wasn't showing it. Her image of her perfect daddy crumbled during the divorce when she found out about his affair. How could he do that to her?

She seemed to be using denial to deal with her feelings. It had to be terrible for her. She had been so upset with her dad for months over how he handled himself during the divorce. Then, her dad died. How could she be upset with him, now? It was as if she said to herself, wait a minute, my dad is dead! What kind of horrible person am I if I am still angry at him? So, her way of coping was to shut down, and avoid talking about it.

If Dylan managed to find solid ground under his feet by clinging even tighter to the values that Bill had modeled for most of his life, Payton seemed to be standing on quicksand with the world shifting beneath her. She drew closer to me, not wanting me to leave her sight. The combination of our divorce and her father's death instilled in her a terrible separation anxiety and sense of abandonment.

I was concerned about her on the one hand, and on the other hand, I was happy and proud to see her instinctively seeking support through bonding even tighter with her close circle of friends. They were like her second family.

Bill and I had always taught the kids, "It's family first. And, family is always there for each other."

Now that Bill was gone, I was becoming even more extreme in stressing to them, "Remember, family is the most important thing in your life. You have to stick together."

Come what may, that was something I didn't want them to ever forget.

~Afternoon—Evening~
The Others

"I found out what the secret to life is: friends. Best friends."

~from "Fried Green Tomatoes"

I was looking forward to seeing my friend Linda, who was driving in with her daughter Mandy, and expected to arrive that evening. While I kept half an eye on the clock to make sure I didn't lose track of the time, I went over paperwork, and tried to keep myself busy.

I started reading over one of Bill's life insurance policies. One of the clauses stated that, in the event the insured was intoxicated, or found to be under the influence of illegal drugs or alcohol, the policy would be considered null and void. In the event that the death of the insured was caused by suicide, the policy would also be nullified.

Heart in my throat, I re-read what I had just read. Did that mean that the policy was null and void if the person on the policy was intoxicated when they died? Or did it only refer to situations where the death was *caused* by intoxication or drunkenness? I had no idea that such policy exclusions and provisions even existed.

I started to panic. So, the little inheritance my children were supposed to get might be threatened if the toxicology report turned up drunkenness?

I went back over the same clause, trying to fully understand the legalese. You needed to be an attorney to accurately interpret it—and since I wasn't a lawyer, and wasn't accomplishing anything other than raising my own blood pressure, I decided I'd better stop reading. I would turn it over to Denny later. He would know how to interpret it.

In the middle of my life insurance policy crisis, Randa happened to call, and she got an earful of my ranting and raving.

"Can you believe this?" I said. "One more thing I'm having to deal with…"

"Well, I just happen to have some news of my own," Randa said, "about Bill's passenger. Her family set up a page on the Caring Bridge website. It's mainly for people with cancer, where family and friends can go and share feelings and condolences. Also, the family can post updates on a person's condition."

We knew the names of the other people involved in the accident from the newspaper. Dear, ever-resourceful Randa, had managed to uncover the information about the Caring Bridge because a friend of ours had lost her mom a few months earlier from cancer, and had a page on that site. We already had the name and age of Bill's passenger. Now I had a way to keep up with her progress.

The site was open to the public, so I was easily able to access the information. Her page stated exactly what had happened to her, and listed all her injuries. The site listed multiple injuries to the left side of her body, a broken arm, broken leg, lacerated liver. It also mentioned that she was having complications from the accident due to a preexisting case of cystic fibrosis (lung disease). Her disease was in overdrive because of the stress put on her body by the accident.

She was in ICU, struggling for her life.

It was so surreal to read about her—this stranger who somehow ended up on the back of Bill's bike. I still couldn't figure that one out. *Why had she and Lisa decided to switch places?*

It was disturbing to think about Passenger X fighting for *her* life, yet Bill had lost his. It was a strange connection they would forever share—her here on earth, him gone. It was a lot to wrap my brain around.

Who were these two people—Driver X and Passenger X? I knew they hadn't gone to school with Bill because none of our other friends—old or new—knew who they were. Yet, they would spend the rest of their lives with this profound connection to my ex-husband, a connection formed in an accident that took his life and spared theirs.

Why had it played out that way?

There were so many things going on inside of me when I thought about Passenger X. Along with all the unanswered questions, there were conflicting emotions. One side of me felt tremendous sadness and sympathy for her condition. I was very interested in her well-being, and prayed daily for her healing. I was very thankful for the Caring Bridge website, which allowed me to get daily updates on her condition.

At the same time, I couldn't ignore the fact that, depending on the state of her injuries and her health, she might very well try to sue me for payment of her medical bills, and compensation for possible ongoing, accident-related problems she might have to struggle with for the rest of her life.

Of course, I was also concerned about the well-being of Driver X, but the impact of his situation on me was different because he wasn't actually on Bill's bike with him, and therefore didn't pose the threat of litigation.

I wasn't sure that a twenty-one-year-old young lady would even have health insurance—until I saw that she had cystic fibrosis. Then, I realized she must have some kind of health insurance, and that was reassuring. But, even if she did have insurance, she was likely to incur hundreds of thousands of dollars in medical bills. So, even if she never sued me, Bill's motorcycle insurance would undoubtedly come into play.

I felt like I was in an impossible position. My heart went out to this young lady who was fighting for her life. But, I was in mother-bear mode, anxious to protect the future of my own children, and any inheritance in their names.

Finally, there were lingering questions in my mind: *What did this woman remember? Did she recall anything about the accident? Would she ever be able to tell me?*

I didn't know whether she was conscious, but the Caring Bridge website postings stated that she was getting oxygen from a ventilator, couldn't really talk, and was in really bad shape.

I was also asking myself: Does she realize what really took place—that Bill's last minute decision to lay down his bike on its side may have saved her life? That thought struck me hard. I wanted so badly to post on her web page something to the effect of, "You are in my prayers, but do you realize that he may have saved your life? He couldn't save his own, but he may have saved yours."

I wished I could see her—just show up during visiting hours at the hospital and see if she could tell me anything about the accident. Of course, I couldn't do that. It would have been totally inappropriate. To her, I would be a stranger. It was so odd to think—but it was true—that from her perspective, I had nothing to do with the whole situation. In her mind, Bill was an unmarried man.

In that respect, I was in the same boat. I had no idea who she was. She could have been anyone. She could have been Lisa's best friend from work, for all I knew.

Needless to say, I wouldn't be going anywhere near her hospital bed. I did find myself looking at her Caring Bridge page every day to see how she was coming along.

Thursday evening, Linda and Mandy arrived. I was excited to see them. Linda was my most religious friend, so I had saved up a million meaning-of-life type questions I wanted to ask her.

They were excited to see us, too, but they were also very sad. Bill and I had been role models for their family over the years.

Linda is now in her mid-fifties, and remarried. Mandy is now thirty, and has three kids of her own. But all those years ago, Linda was a young wife with a small baby. They ended up getting divorced, and while we were still living in Washington, Bill stepped in and became something of a father figure for Mandy. We spent a lot of time with Mandy, and became her babysitters—the ones that were responsible adults on the one hand, but still let her stay up late to watch movies that were a little outside of what her parents might have allowed. We used to joke that we didn't yet have kids of our own, so we needed to corrupt someone else's.

We looked after her like she was our own, and I can still see Bill teaching her to play ball. Later, when Mandy married, Bill and I, along with our kids, were all in the wedding. Mandy has a lot of good memories of Bill, and she was devastated over his death.

After Linda and Mandy arrived, we all visited until late. Mom and Dad came back that evening, and were staying in the spare room, so Linda and Mandy took Payton's room. Payton was staying with me in my bed.

Linda, Mandy, and I sat in our pajamas on Payton's bed, reminiscing about old times and good memories.

After awhile, the conversation turned deep, and Linda said, "This whole thing is so ironic, the fact that it all played out the way it did."

We agreed that everybody has their own destiny that no one can control or change.

I said, "We had our good times, and our bad times, but the kids and I are very fortunate to have had the time we had with him. Bill gave me twenty-four years of good times and bad. He gave me my children and our life together. Then, for whatever reason, he made his decision. I think on some level, he knew his destiny was coming."

Linda and Mandy were listening intently, and nodding.

And then, as heartbreaking as it was for me to admit, I said, "I believe Bill did love Lisa, or care for her deeply. And, I believe God took Bill and Lisa together so they could spend the afterlife together."

"No!" Linda said, clearly upset. "When you're in the afterlife, you are not the same as you are here on earth. In Heaven, everyone is an angel, in unison… not a couple, as we humans think of couples, not even a mom or dad. You recognize each other still, but the relationships up there are not the same as they are here on earth."

I'm sure I must have been looking at her like she was from another planet.

I said, "What are you talking about? I don't know anything about any of that…"

Mandy spoke up, "I think Mom's kind of right. That everyone is an angel up there. Together—but not like we are together."

I felt unsettled over what Linda said, unsure what to make of it. So, she promised that when they got back home, she would find the Bible verses that would give me a better understanding of what she was trying to say, and she would email them to me.

It was hard. I finally had some sense of what I wanted to believe about Bill's destiny, and here was one of my dearest friends, disputing it with me. I decided to take her suggestion, and just put it out of my mind until she could get home and send me the Bible verses. I would figure out how to make sense of it then.

Later, she sent me the Bible verses. Thankfully, she sent me the study-Bible version, which was easy to understand. Mark 12:24-25 stated, in effect, that believers that die have a perfect spiritual relationship with everybody; there are no exclusive relationships, no sexuality.

"For when they shall rise from the dead,
They neither marry, nor are given in marriage;
But are as the angels which are in heaven."
-Mark 12:25, Holy Bible

They are eternal spiritual beings that never die.

It went on to explain that it didn't mean that you wouldn't recognize loved ones or spouses in the Kingdom of Heaven, but the natural or physical rules that apply to this earthly plane no longer applied.

So, everybody was an angel, in perfect harmony with all the other angels?

That actually brought me great relief, knowing that Bill was now an angel watching over us. I also felt better picturing him somewhere, full of happiness. And if he was with other "angels"—whoever they might be—so be it. As long as he was surrounded by happiness, I could find comfort in that.

After Linda sent me the scripture, I understood why she had gotten upset when I said I thought that Bill and Lisa were a couple in Heaven. She wanted me to be at peace, knowing that Bill was an angel in a happy, harmonious place, watching over the kids and me.

~October 9th~
A Military Burial

"I am a man of constant sorrow
I've seen trouble all my day...
My face you'll never see no more
But there is one promise that is given
I'll meet you on God's golden shore
(He'll meet you on God's golden shore)."
"I Am A Man of Constant Sorrow"

~by Norman Blake

W e all awoke on Friday with the awareness that our last hurdle was before us. Bill would be buried at 10:30 that morning at Jefferson Barracks.

The burial services happen every twenty to thirty minutes. When they told us that Bill's was set for 10:30, they meant 10:30 on the dot. With a military burial, they start with or without you! They tell you that right up front: "We will perform the service even if nobody is present."

I was a total Nervous Nellie, and grateful that my parents were going to be doing the driving.

Even though we were going after rush-hour traffic, it would take us a good forty-five minutes to drive there. I wanted to be there early, and to allow enough time for anything that could go wrong.

There was going to be a lot to deal with, and a lot of commotion with all the people we would see. But, afterwards, we could finally relax. We were almost to the finish line. All we had to do was get the burial behind us, and then we could start looking to the future.

My parents, Linda and Mandy, the kids, and I were all running around, trying to get ready. I didn't feel quite the same sense of heaviness that I'd had on Tuesday, and I don't think the kids did either. But, I was shaking on the inside, like I'd had too much caffeine. I kept looking down at my hands and knees to see if they were visibly shaking.

We all got into the car. I was trying to stay positive and keep up a good front for the kids. I glued an upbeat expression on my face. All week long, I had been in a daze. But whenever I felt the teeter-totter of emotions, I made sure I was sending out the signal to the kids that everything was going to be fine. It was a hard balancing act.

I experienced so many conflicting emotions. I felt a horrible sense of loss, and missed Bill terribly—yet I'd been missing him ever since our divorce. During that week, I'd have moments of feeling the anger I'd been feeling since our divorce. Then, I'd think it wasn't appropriate to be angry with him now that he was gone—and I'd try to wish away my feelings of anger. Or, I'd just block everything out. I had become very good at that.

Driving in the car to Bill's burial services, I forced myself to be okay. I kept saying to myself, this is closure, this is it. I just have to put up a front for one more day. Everything was building up inside of me, but I only had to keep the volcano from overflowing for one more day.

I sat by the window, staring out at the cloudy, drizzly, dreary day. Payton sat in the middle, and Dylan was against the other window, also staring off into space. Every now and then, I threw out a positive, soothing thought for us all to hang onto: "We will get through this. It will all be okay."

We knew that during the burial services, Dylan would be the recipient of the formal, military presentation of the flag. None of us knew how that would work, but we were told that it would all be explained when we arrived—whenever that might be. It seemed like the drive to the cemetery took ten hours. It was the longest short drive of my life.

In reality, we were sailing along with absolutely no traffic. Yet, I kept thinking, my gosh, what is the problem? What is taking so long? This is the same drive I did every day for seventeen years, when I was on my old job, and I never remember it taking this long!

I wanted it to be over, already.

As we pulled into the cemetery, the kids felt very overwhelmed. They had only been to one funeral when Jan's father passed away—and that was a regular civilian funeral.

I'd tried to prepare them, saying, "Now, your dad's burial is going to be a lot different than a regular funeral," I said. "The military ones are very formal and uniform. Real regimented."

I told them some more of the details and tried to minimize the surprises for them.

"Where is he going to be?" Dylan asked. "Will we be able to have him buried in the ground or are they going to put him in a building?"

"I don't know yet, Dyl," I said. "We have to wait and see."

Everyone wanted Bill buried outside, but Bill, Sr. and Judy set everything up, so I was not sure how it was going to all play out.

Although Judy and Bill, Sr. had paid for the services and cremation, I was supposed to be in charge of arranging those things. But, they stepped up and offered to handle the burial to take the burden off of me. I was happy to accept their help. The burial service had to be coordinated between Baue Funeral Home and Jefferson Barracks, and it was good knowing that I didn't have to be the point person for one more thing.

As for me, I knew what was coming, and I knew I would get very emotional. Judy's mother had been a nurse in the armed services, and I had vivid memories of her military funeral. Bill, Sr.'s father—the grandfather Bill went to live with as a teen—had passed away several years earlier, and was also buried at Jefferson Barracks. I couldn't go to the funeral because Payton was sick, so Bill and my mom went.

I get all choked up even watching a military funeral on TV.

I knew that the light rain that was falling would not stop the proceedings. I didn't think they cancelled services for anything short of a natural disaster.

We drove to the main office, where everyone was to meet. When we walked in, carrying our umbrellas, we found that Bill, Sr. and Judy were already there, and Bill, Sr. was taking care of things. "They will provide a bench for you, the kids, Jan, and me," he explained. "Dylan will need to sit on the left end of the bench. The folding of the flag by the military personnel will proceed in that direction, until they finally reach the final fold, at which time they will present it to Dylan."

Customarily, the flag is presented to either the wife or the mother, but we had all agreed that Dylan should be the one receiving it.

I was surprised by the number of guests that began arriving, considering that the burial service was going to last no longer than fifteen or twenty minutes. There were about fifty people altogether, jam-packed into the small cemetery office.

They called our name, and told us that we all needed to follow the military car which would lead us to the site where the service would be held. The actual burial of the urn would be in another location.

We all filed out of the office, Bill, Sr. picked up the urn, and we headed for our cars. I started getting nervous.

We followed the military car to a little pavilion. The minute we pulled up, it stopped drizzling. The sky remained overcast, but we no longer needed our umbrellas. A small miracle.

Bill, Sr. walked up and handed the pastor the urn, which had been tied with a piece of fabric that had a Harley-Davidson emblem dangling from it. The pastor placed the urn on the table which had been set up in the middle.

Bill, Sr., Jan, the kids, and I took our place on the bench.

The urn was right in our line of vision. How could that be Bill in there? It was unbelievable. In fact, in that moment, I was having a really hard time believing it. And if I was struggling with it, how in the world were my kids dealing with it?

Payton was crying hysterically. Her brother—being a guy—was in tears, but crying more inwardly. Everyone else had gathered around the outskirts of the pavilion.

Once the movement of people arriving had subsided, and it was clear that we were all there, the chaplain spoke. "I would like to thank you all for coming..."

Bill's father stood. Bill, Sr. is a highly professional man in the oil and gas industry. By nature, he is very subdued and quiet. To look at him, you would never guess that he had tattoos under his shirt, or that he was completely devoted to his Harley. My son never even knew that Grandpa Bill had tattoos until he was ten years old.

When I saw Bill, Sr., a man definitely not inclined to show his feelings, standing there in such obvious emotional pain, I could not control my tears. It was so out of character for him to bare his soul before a crowd. Before he ever spoke a word, my heart was breaking for him.

He said something to the effect of, "I would like to thank you all for coming. Sadly, my son had such a short life. It is a shame he never got a chance to know how many people he had touched. In fact, until this tragedy, I didn't even realize how well-loved he was..." At that point, he was too choked up to go on.

It was the only time in twenty-four years that I had ever seen him cry. Judy—who was standing right behind the bench on which we were sitting—later told me that she could count on one hand the times she had seen him cry.

I slipped behind a curtain of my own tears, and although I could see his mouth moving, I was crying too hard to hear what he was saying. I knew he was struggling with the guilt of having sold his son the motorcycle he died riding. And I imagined he might have also been grappling with feeling like he had not been around as much as he would have liked when Bill was a child.

I had always wished Bill, Sr. would have had a greater presence in his son's life, but I loved the man dearly, and had an instinctive understanding of who he was at his core.

As I've mentioned, it was only when Bill was older that he got to enjoy a closer relationship with his father.

So many times, I had tried to reassure Bill, Sr. that selling his motorcycle to his son did not cause Bill's death. Naturally, my attempts to comfort him didn't really take away the question in his mind: "What if I hadn't sold him that bike?"

Bill, Sr. sat back down, and the Chaplain recited the poem, "If I Knew" by Norma Cornett Marek:

"IF I KNEW…
If I knew it would be the last time that I'd see you fall asleep,
I would tuck you in more tightly and pray the Lord your soul to keep.
If I knew it would be the last time that I'd see you walk out the door,
I would give you a hug and kiss and call you back for one more,

If I knew it would be the last time I'd hear your voice lifted up in praise,
I would videotape each action and word,
so I could play them back day after day.
If I knew it would be the last time, I could spare an extra minute
To stop and say 'I love you,' instead of assuming you would know I do.

If I knew it would be the last time I would be there to share your day,
Well, I'm sure you'll have so many more, so I can let just this one slip away.

For surely there's always tomorrow to make up for an oversight,
And we always get a second chance to make everything just right.

There will always be another day to say 'I love you,'
And certainly there's another chance to say our 'Anything I can do?'

But just in case I might be wrong, and today is all I get,
I'd like to say how much I love you and I hope we never forget.

Tomorrow is not promised to anyone, young or old alike,
And today may be the last chance you get to hold your loved one tight.

So if you're waiting for tomorrow, why not do it today?
For if tomorrow never comes, you'll surely regret the day...

That you didn't take that extra time for a smile, a hug, or a kiss
And you were too busy to grant someone,
what turned out to be their one last wish.

So hold your loved ones close today, and whisper in their ear,
Tell them how much you love them and that you'll always hold them dear

Take time to say 'I'm sorry,'
'Please forgive me,' 'Thank you,' or 'It's okay.'
And if tomorrow never comes,
You'll have no regrets about today."

It was a poem the Chaplain happened to choose for memorial services, and it took me off guard. Wow, I thought, that is so appropriate. Anyone who has lost someone could find at least a line or two in there that had meaning for them.

As he spoke, I could see that Payton was paying very close attention, as well, and was really shaken up by the sentiment expressed in the poem.

After the Chaplain finished reciting the poem, the services took on a different tone, as the military rituals began.

A lone soldier put a trumpet to his lips and began playing "Taps."

At the same time, a few uniformed troops lifted the urn, picked up the flag which had been lying beneath it, and moved off to the side of the table. Then, in a very stiff manner, they began a very precise folding of the flag.

Three or four soldiers lined up and in perfect unison, loaded, and lifted their firearms. Then, they aimed their guns heavenward, and simultaneously fired three blanks. The officiousness of the ceremony made it all the more agonizing, and drove home the gravity of the situation.

Watching my children was unbearable. I don't even have the language to articulate the sorrow and heartbreak I felt on their behalf.

Dazed, I looked around... Bill's good friend, Chris, stood directly across from me the entire time. He was a crying mess. I had never seen him like that. And, there was Randa, sobbing. And, her oldest son, Brendan. There was Payton's friend from gymnastics, Courtney, and her mom, Vicky.

Was this really happening? It felt more like a movie than reality—one where the character gets a glimpse of a possible future, and the message is, "You had better be good or this is what your future could look like!"

Why did it all have to happen this way? And why did God choose me to deal with it?

By the time the soldier had finished playing "Taps," I was better able to focus.

Two soldiers approached Dylan and saluted him. Then, in an official motion, with their hands placed on top of the flag, they handed it to Dylan, and saluted him again.

Dylan was crying and shaking his head. Payton was in tears. They were lost inside their own sorrow, with no idea what to do or say. I was crying so hard, my whole body was shaking. My babies! *Our babies!* Why was this happening to them?

The Chaplain stood again, said something to the effect that Bill was now at rest, and thanked everyone for coming.

It was over. Time to go—quickly. It was made clear that there would be no lingering around. People were approaching me, saying, "Give me a call if you need anything," and I was thanking them for coming. Bill, Sr., Judy, and Jan were also thanking everyone for coming. Jan was very emotional, but thankfully, she had the benefit of medication to help her through it all. That was also how she'd made it through the visitation.

As for my own parents, they were standing behind me throughout the services, and from time to time, put their hands on my shoulders. Mitch and Theresa were standing with them, as well as Kenny.

Mom and Dad told me that they'd made arrangements for the family to go to a restaurant for lunch, so off we went—Mitch and Theresa; Uncle Denny and Aunt Vickie; Bill, Sr., Judy, and their kids—Jeri Ann and Michael, Jeri Ann's husband, Charlie, and their baby Jackson, Michael and his girlfriend, Melissa (who would soon become his fiancé). Jan had her sisters, Judy and Joanne, with her, as well as Joanne's daughter, and her children. Jan's brother Ken might have also been there, but I was in such a fog at the time, I couldn't swear to it one way or another.

My parents, bless their hearts, had reserved and paid for a private room at a restaurant. We all met there, and unbeknownst to me, both my mom and Judy had brought pictures of Bill to share with everyone. It was still hard for me to look at pictures, and I only looked when someone made a point to show them to me.

The kids were bringing me pictures, and Bill, Sr. and Judy had pictures of Bill and me going as far back as high school, when I was seventeen. There we were as teenagers, riding dirt bikes at Bill, Sr. and Judy's place. Everyone was giggling at the sight of me on a motorcycle.

Seeing the motorcycle got me to thinking again about how Bill spent his whole life riding either dirt bikes or street bikes. I knew that he was a good rider, and smart, and I was always very comfortable with him being on a bike. What scared me was that other cars don't pay attention to motorcycles. I had been with him so long, I had many memories of driving in a car with him, and him pointing out some vehicle and saying, "You see that car up ahead? They are too close to that motorcycle."

For twenty-four years, that was drilled into my head—the fact that it's the other car that doesn't know what they are doing.

Having been told that alcohol might have been involved in Bill's accident totally threw me for a loop because I was so certain of Bill's abilities and judgment as an experienced motorcycle rider. Between the possible alcohol component and the fact that Bill had let another bike take the lead, I was having trouble coming to terms with the whole accident. Bill was not a guy who let others lead, unless he was with his father's group of older friends. Then he would defer to an older man.

On those rare occasions when he was with a group but not in the lead position, he hung back far enough to keep a good eye on what was going on up ahead.

The entire accident did not add up for me. I could not wrap my head around how it could have happened.

But, not even the questions swirling around in my head could dampen the relief I felt at having all the funeral services finally concluded. I wasn't the only one—everyone's mood at the restaurant was considerably lighter than it had been earlier in the day. It was clear that everyone had breathed a collective sigh of relief, knowing we had gotten that over with and done. And the pictures really helped—being able to have a laugh over Bill and me when we were young, and the kids when they were babies.

Bill, Sr. took a moment to pass out small urns of Bill's ashes to Dylan, Payton, and Jan. They were packaged in a thoughtful way, wrapped in tissue paper. It was a lovely, heartfelt gift from Bill, Sr.

Dylan could not even look at his. Payton did manage to look at hers—a heart-shaped urn. Jan was given an identical one.

Payton looked over at me, and I told her we'd get a metal plaque made for the urn. Dylan's was a triangle shape, about three inches taller, made of glass.

Bill, Sr.'s mother, Jeri, was not able to be there. She was the grandmother that Bill had lived with all those years ago when he ran away from home as a young boy. She was around eighty years old, a strident woman, and did not get along well with Jan. She'd brought to the burial some pictures she had at her house of when Bill, Sr. and Jan were married. At the burial services, she had slipped the pictures to Bill, Sr., who now handed those to Jan, saying that she could keep that stack of pictures.

Bill, Sr. did not bear any ill will towards Jan, and for her part, she was very gracious, offering him her sincere thanks.

Jan had spent her entire life believing that Bill Sr.'s mom had conspired to take Bill, Jr. from her. She had always felt slighted by not having any baby pictures of Bill, Jr., so it was a big moment—her simply graciously accepting photographs that had come from Grandma.

It made me feel good to see that, after so many years of acrimony, Jan finally was able to reach a peaceful truce with Bill, Sr.

Perhaps inspired by the clearing of the ill will between herself and Bill Sr., Jan then got on a roll. She and her family started talking about wanting to play a larger part in our lives, wanting to be advised when the children's activities were taking place, and hoping to attend Payton's gymnastic meets.

Other than visits at the holidays, Jan and her family had kept a very low profile with my children, and never showed any real initiative in terms of being involved in their lives. And because of her passiveness in terms of reaching out to us, Bill had stopped reaching out to her. I was always the one to initiate plans.

Now that Bill was gone, and the children and I were the only ones left, she expected me to welcome her and her family with open arms?

It was all a bit hard to take—especially her family's sudden interest in the kids' lives. I knew they were probably feeling guilty, and felt that reaching out was the proper thing to do, but it just hit me the wrong way. After the luncheon, I told my mom how irritated I was, and she said, "This is just what people say. Don't let it bother you. Let's just wait and see whether or not they give you a call."

As we left the restaurant, Denny gave me the papers I needed to sign to become the executrix of Bill's estate. On Monday, he would turn them in to the court. That meant that, at last, I would have access to the various documents I needed in order to get all of Bill's affairs in order. This was great news because in the next few weeks, there was a lot of paperwork that was going to come into play.

Lisa was also put to rest that Friday afternoon—a fact we discovered from her obituary. I never mentioned it out loud to anybody, but I had been aware of it all day. Curiously, as much as I had not wanted their visitations to be on the same day, there seemed to be some sort of symmetry in knowing their burials were on the same day. I wouldn't go so far as to say I was at peace with the situation—I was still angry—but it made a certain kind of sense to me.

My acceptance surprised me.

I did not like what I knew of Lisa, and though I did not blame her one hundred percent, I did assign a certain amount of responsibility to her for what happened to my life. Yet, I could see that Lisa and Bill had entered into some strange journey together, and now, they had left it together, on the very same day.

I have never said these words out loud, and I cannot believe I am writing them here, but that is what's in my heart. My mind is another story.

That evening at home, I had my first glimpse of life returning to normal, and a strange sense of peace.

~October 10th, 2009~
More Bad News

"...God forbid you ever had to wake up to hear the news
'Cause then you really might know what it's like to have to lose
Then you really might know what it's like
Then you really might know what it's like
Then you really might know what it's like to have to lose."
"What It's Like"

~by Erik Schrody (Everlast)

Friday night, Mom and Dad decided to go back to Mitch and Theresa's to sleep, to give Linda and Mandy some time with the kids and me before leaving to return home on Saturday. When we woke up on Saturday morning, we were busy with getting them packed and on their way back to Kansas.

Meanwhile, Payton was looking forward to an overnight birthday party with her gymnastics friends. I knew that being with her group of supportive friends would put her in good spirits, and that was just what she needed. She was always in good hands when she was with them.

Around nine or ten o'clock that morning, the phone rang. I figured it was Randa calling to do her daily check-in, and I was partially right—it was her. But, she sounded off. After a few moments of forced chitchat, she told me what was on her mind. As we were leaving the cemetery the day before, she had gotten a phone call with the results of her biopsy.

"It's not good news," she said. "I have a type of breast cancer called ductal carcinoma in situ. That means it's in the milk glands."

All I heard was the word "carcinoma." I was speechless. My best friend had breast cancer? I didn't understand how that could possibly be. Her biopsy was supposed to be nothing, just a routine test.

The news took the breath out of my lungs.

"I'm so sorry," I muttered, starting to cry. "You know I will be here for whatever you need."

She was crying now, too. "God love you, but...how can you say that?" she said. "With what you're going through?"

I said, "How can I not say that? I will find whatever strength I have left... I will be there for you."

We both forced ourselves to focus on the positive, and launched into reassurances with each other that everything was going to be fine. We did have good reason to be optimistic. She told me that the doctor had told her that if you were going to get breast cancer, the best place to get it was in the milk glands. It is very contained when it's in that area.

That made sense. They would just take out her milk glands.

Dylan was sleeping. Payton was upstairs getting ready for her party. They had no idea what was happening downstairs on the phone. I was so grateful that they were not in the room when I got the news.

There would be more doctor's appointments, and decisions to make about next steps and surgery. And, I would have to learn everything I possibly could about the type of cancer Randa had.

"Well," she said, "I have some more calls I need to make, so I guess we had better go."

I think she instinctively knew that I needed some time to absorb everything, and she needed some time, as well.

I didn't know enough about that type of cancer to tell the kids anything yet. The only people I knew who had dealt with it were acquaintances whom I hadn't known well enough to ask questions. I knew my kids would ask me questions about it, and I wanted to be ready with some answers before I told them the bad news.

Randa had been a big part of their lives ever since they were born, and she is like an aunt to them. And I knew that for children—and even with adults, for that matter—when you hear the word "cancer," you think "death." I just couldn't go there yet.

So, once again, it was time to put up my front. I went upstairs and helped Payton get ready for her overnight party. Dylan was awake and moving about.

I took Payton to her friend's house, and seeing her happy made me happy.

When I got back home, it was around three o'clock in the afternoon, and Dylan was out with friends. I went out to check the mail and picked up a letter addressed to "The parents of Dylan…" What in the world could be coming from Dylan's school?

It turned out to be a letter from the vice-principal, making sure I understood the severity of Dylan having missed a week of school, and stressing the negative effect it would have on him. Did I realize, the letter asked, that this extended absence would put him behind the other students, and could academically ruin him?

I was walking up the driveway towards the house as I was reading, and I stopped in my tracks. How could these people be so colossally insensitive? Did they have no compassion? I knew that many kids had been out of school with the H1N1 flu virus, so I could understand why the school might have been noticing a lot of absences, but even those kids had legitimate reasons for staying home. What was wrong with these people?

This letter, this little bit of insensitivity, was the last thing I needed, and it really put me over the edge. I had been successfully juggling so many stresses, burdens, and emotions, but in that moment, all the plates I had twirling in the air came crashing down at once.

The kids were away from the house. I was alone with that damned letter, the awareness that my best friend had been diagnosed with cancer, and all the grief, anger, sadness, and confusion I had been managing to keep at bay.

That did it. On Monday, I was going to contact the school. I started rehearsing my rant: "How dare you direct a letter like this to me? I just lost an ex-spouse and my children just lost their father. Even if I hadn't, how dare you question me over whether or not I understand the effect my child's absence could have on his academic baseline? What do you think I am—stupid?"

At the same time, I figured I would also take the opportunity to let them know that their school should give some serious consideration to hiring the vice-principal of Payton's school to teach them how to handle delicate situations!

I took another look at the letter to see if maybe it had been stamped and sent out among a group of other letters. Nope. It had an actual signature on it. That meant a real person actually had the audacity to compose and sign it. That made it even more personal and infuriating.

I knew I needed to pull myself together, and decided to take a shower. I turned on the hot water, got in, and started talking out loud to myself. I was going to give those people a piece of my mind. Wait until Monday—they were going to be sorry they didn't have the decency or compassion to keep that letter from going out. The water ran and ran, and I ranted and raved, and eventually, I found myself again at the bottom of the shower, sitting there, sobbing.

I screamed at God, "How could you do this to me? First, you think I can handle an affair and a divorce, and then you take my children's dad away from them? Now, on top of Bill's accident, you somehow expect me to find the strength to help my best friend deal with cancer? Seriously? I don't know why you think I'm a person who could handle this. I am having to be as strong as I can for my children—and now I get this extra weight of worrying about Randa. Well, I want to know why! I want *answers!*"

I screamed at God until I lost all my hot water. I hadn't really screamed up until that point, and it felt good. After I got done with my screaming and yelling, I felt a little bit better. I didn't have answers, but it felt good.

Suddenly, I got nervous, thinking, oh, no, I've just had a crazy-person freak-out; I sure hope I'm by myself. Otherwise, the paddy-wagon is likely to pull up outside and men in white coats are going to come take me away. I grabbed a towel, tiptoed over to the bathroom door, and stuck my head out. Thankfully, no one had witnessed my meltdown. I felt exhausted but strangely refreshed.

My state of mind shifted. This was my life now, and there was nothing I could do about that fact. My normal life was gone. All I could do was be the best I could be—the mother/father for my children. I needed to show them I was strong. Otherwise, they would feel insecure. I also needed to be strong for Randa.

I had long ago chosen to be this strong person, and I needed to remember that now.

I started reflecting back on dates... milestones. I have always had a fixation for certain dates. They have always stood out in my mind.

I knew that 2009 was going to be a really big year in terms of important dates. Now, I had new dates to keep in mind, dates I'd never be able to forget...

July 1st, Bill told me he wanted a divorce.
July 4th, I found out about his affair.
October 3rd was Bill's fatal accident.
Now, I had October 6th to add to the list—Bill's visitation and Randa's biopsy.
October 9th—the date Bill was put to rest and Randa found out she had cancer.

These dates were locked in my mind, and they were never going to go away. This was my life now, and I had no choice but to deal with it.

Actually, I did have a choice. I *chose* to be strong, to deal with things, for my children, my family, my friends, myself. That is the type of person I am—I am not going to let things get the better of me.

I knew I had to find the emotional courage to get through the hard times, and I knew I would find it. You can, too. You just have to search for it. And I know that life does go on.

In a crazy way, it was good that I got that letter. It was just the catalyst I needed in order to have my very healing, very refreshing little meltdown.

Sunday, I decided I needed to tell the kids about Randa. I wasn't really sure how to go about telling them, so I figured that a matter-of-fact approach would be the least alarming. I told them that it was in the best possible spot, that I was sure the doctors would get it all out during surgery, and that everything would be fine.

My attitude was very breezy, and the kids followed my lead. I guess they figured, well, if Mom is telling us that Randa is going to be okay, she will. I'm glad I did it that way instead of being overly-technical with them, and giving them medical definitions. That would have just scared them.

The kids did ask me, "Mom, how is Randa doing with all of this?"

I said, "She just found out she has breast cancer, so she's sad. But, she is feeling positive. And of course, we will be there for her. Together, we will her get through it... just like she has been helping us through our tragedies."

Monday came around and I was thinking about all the different opinions I'd heard about the timing of the kids and I returning to school and work. Some people couldn't believe we were going back so soon. Other people understood that, since the kids and I are creatures of habit and routine, returning to our routines was the best possible thing for us.

Life was going on, and we couldn't just sit around. All that would accomplish was to keep us out of step. The tragedy of Bill's death had forced us into an altered, surreal reality, and we needed to do everything we could to get back into the flow of life again. The best way I knew to do that was to return to our routines.

I had talked to the kids on Friday and asked them how they felt about going back to school and gymnastics. I'd also spoken with Judy and Bill, Sr. at the luncheon, and found out that Bill, Sr. was also returning to work Monday. He was overwhelmed with guilt, however unfounded, and also needed to return to his routine. Jan was not doing very well. She said she was not planning on going back to work yet, and wasn't sure how long it would be before she was ready.

As I was thinking about the kids going back to school, I was also thinking about my vow to let Dylan's school know just what I thought of their letter. I was preparing myself to go on the warpath—but I was going to do it via emails and phone calls. Dylan would have been embarrassed if I'd stormed down to his school, and both he and Payton still had years ahead of them at that school.

As much as I knew that we all needed to get back into our routines, Monday was a scary and confusing day, as well. There was going to be a lot to face for all of us. Everyone we knew—however close to us or not—was going to want to talk to us, hear an explanation of what had happened, possibly ask questions, find out how we were doing, and offer their condolences. Even though we understood that, for the most part, it would be coming from a good caring place, it was going to be hard to deal with all of it. We couldn't wait to get that first day over and done with; from there, everything would start to go more smoothly.

Payton's re-entry lunch with her friends at school had really helped her, and of the three of us, she was probably the most at ease. I had to give kudos to her vice-principal for coming up with the idea.

For me, things were stickier, because people would not know how to frame the fact that the same man who had divorced me, been having an affair, and totally traumatized me by his recent behavior, had now died in a motor-cycle accident. I knew how awkward the whole situation would be for every-one.

No one would know what the hell to say to me. I was completely fine with that.

When I walked into work, I didn't blame those who chose not to say anything beyond "Hello, and welcome back" or "Good morning" to me. What could they say? Of course, everyone was sorry, but they were very uncomfortable, and frankly, I was uncomfortable for them.

I was actually relieved that most people didn't feel the need to come into my office, sit down, and talk to me about how sorry they were. I didn't want that, and wouldn't have known what to say to them, either. I was completely at ease with the way everyone chose to handle it.

Meanwhile, I was on a mission to get every email address I could for the high school personnel, from the superintendent of the school district on down through the ranks. I couldn't wait to let them know just how upset I was over the way they had handled everything—the phone call they'd made to the house asking why Dylan wasn't in school, after I'd already called to tell them his father died; the rude way they treated me when I called the school asking to pick up Dylan's homework; and that incredibly insensitive letter.

At the same time, I planned to let them how wonderful Payton's vice-principal had been through all of it.

It wasn't long after I sent out the email that I got a call from the high school principal, apologizing for the behavior of the vice-principal.

"I'm so sorry," he said. "Those things never should have happened. We definitely have policies we need to look at and change."

I thanked him, and that was that.

I was satisfied. He did what he was supposed to do—called and apologized. We all learned something, and I was willing to leave it at that. I only hoped he would do the same thing for all those kids who took off from school because they were truly sick.

That evening, the vice-principal called me at home. I could hear from her voice that she was in tears as she was apologizing. She said she had simply signed a stack of letters, having no idea she had inadvertently sent out a letter to a kid who had just lost his father. She didn't try to make excuses. Instead, she acknowledged that she should have taken the time to read each student's name before sending out the letters, some of which legitimately did need to go out.

I felt her sincerity, and it felt good.

She knew Dylan personally, and shared with me how highly she thought of him, saying he was a rare, very mature, young man. She added that, knowing how remarkable Dylan was, she felt all the worse about causing him more pain. She ended by saying again that she was truly sorry.

She was very dear, and her phone call meant a lot to me. By the time I hung up, I was the one who felt bad for the horrible things I'd said in my email. But, she had done something wrong and she knew it, and learned from it. I truly hoped the policy would be changed, and there would be a live human being checking the letters in the future before they went out.

~Mid-October~
Finding Our Way

"I was thinking about her
Thinking about me
Thinking about us
What we gonna be
Open my eyes...
It was only just a dream.
So I travel back down that road
Wish you come back
No one knows,
I realize, it was only just a dream."
"Just a Dream"

~by Nelly/Love/Romano (Nelly)

T he kids got through their first day of school. Payton was back in gymnastics, and Dylan and I were going through our routines as best we
could. I had appointments for everyone to see Marcy, the counselor.

My appointment was set for the following week, and personally, I
couldn't wait. I had so many questions about how to approach the kids. I
didn't want to say too much or too little, and didn't have the faintest idea how
to handle things.

Even the dogs seemed to be in mourning. Every time anyone in the
neighborhood started up their motorcycle, the dogs would run over to the slat
windows next to the door, and peer out, waiting for Bill. The dogs might have
been doing this ever since Bill left when we first separated, but the kids and I
were noticing now because we were doing the exact same thing. The sound—
or sight—of a motorcycle made us jumpy.

239

Watching the dogs run over and wait so innocently for Bill tugged at my heart. I hugged and kissed them more than usual, and really empathized with them. "I know, I know," I would coo. "We miss him too."

I had always thought of my dogs as additional children, but I never realized until then that they were capable of grieving.

That same week, I began having recurring nightmares. I was experiencing a whole new level of exhaustion, and I desperately needed to sleep, but every time I would climb into bed and drift off to sleep, I was greeted by the same dream. The Xanax I was taking to rest did little to help me.

I don't remember ever having recurring dreams before then.

It was one of those dreams where I was hovering above the scene, watching it happen...

Below me were two motorcycles, cruising down a two-lane country highway. No one could see me hovering above, but I could see them. I couldn't see faces, but I knew that one of the riders was Bill. And I knew he had a passenger. On the other bike were a male and female—again, no faces, but I knew it was a man and a woman. As they rode, I floated along with them. Initially, they all rode along very relaxed. The feeling was one of complete freedom, the wind blowing through their hair.

All of a sudden I could no longer see. Everything became gray and foggy. I heard brakes screeching and tires squealing. I heard a terrible crash. Then I heard children crying. The next thing I knew, I was standing on the highway. Nobody could see me, but I saw people running around. I was asking myself, what just happened? Who were those people? And why couldn't they see me?

As I walked, I came upon a body. I didn't see the face, but I knew it was Bill, lying face down. His body was tangled. His leg was twisted. I could tell he had broken bones. I was standing over the body. People rushed up and tried to help him, but they couldn't see me.

I didn't say a word. Everywhere I looked, there was so much blood. Any which way I turned and looked—more blood. I stepped away. I was walking backwards, trying to absorb what I'd seen. I saw other bodies lying there.

Suddenly, I flashed to the hospital. It was the Saturday night of the accident, and I was in the room, looking at Bill's body. His mouth was not right. It was just me, standing next to him, saying, "What is wrong with your mouth? It doesn't move."

I was leaning against the table sideways. Then, I turned my body towards him, and blood began to seep through the sheet that covered him, totally soaking it...

Then I woke up.

I had this same dream two nights in a row. In the morning, I would wake up horribly upset, and go to the computer to look up internet sites for dream interpretation and analysis. All the sites said was, "Your mind is trying to tell you something."

Why couldn't I see the accident occurring, instead of simply hearing the crash, and seeing the aftermath? Why couldn't my dreams have given me more? And why did they start then? Why not the Sunday night right after the accident? It seemed strange that the dreams would start up nine days later, when we were trying to return to some kind of normal routine.

I walked around haunted all day after I would have one of the nightmares. I could live with the horrible visuals in the nightmare—until the very end, when I was standing there, so disturbed by the position of his mouth, and the blood seeping through the sheet. In actuality when I went to the hospital, there was no blood on the sheet, but that was the cause of death—chest trauma, and loss of blood.

By the third night, I knew I was going to have the dream again. And, for the first time since I was a child, I was afraid to go to sleep.

I wasn't the only one. Payton was struggling with the sound of sirens. It was October, and the first hint of fall was in the air, so the windows were wide open during the day and open just a sliver at night. But, she was so disturbed every time she heard sirens going by, she had to shut the windows. In the Midwest in October, it could be eighty degrees one day and fifty the next, but it could have been one hundred degrees at night, and she still would have kept the windows shut.

I was completely drained. I looked so bad, even a stranger could have looked at me and known that something was terribly wrong. But, I wasn't ready to say anything to the kids about the nightmares, and they didn't point out the obvious either. I don't know what possessed me, in that sleep-deprived state, to suddenly decide I was ready to look at family photos, but I did.

It happened in the middle of the night, when I was afraid to go to sleep. I sat in the middle of the living room floor, hundreds of photos surrounding me.

There we were, just to the two of us, looking so young and innocent, in high school.

There was the entire family in so many photos capturing holidays and vacations and everyday moments. I sat and sobbed with a strange combination of happiness and sadness, trying my best not to ruin the photos with teardrops. It was two or three o'clock in the morning, and I had to get up at five o'clock to go to work, but I didn't care. It was worth it. There were so many happy times captured in those photos. It was easy to understand why the kids had enjoyed looking at them.

That was a Wednesday night. The next day, I felt a profound shift. I had stopped disowning parts of my life just because it was painful to see them pass. I was filled with a sense of gratitude for all that I had been given. Not even tragedy or death could take that away from me. It was mine to keep.

I also had the awareness that this new life was my life now, and even though it was different than it had been before, it was still filled with happiness. I was back in my gentle warrior mode—ready to soldier on and meet happiness along the road, wherever I might find it.

What about the kids? What would they take with them into the future—what memories?

One day, when Payton and I were home alone, I asked her to share with me some of her favorite memories of her dad.

She said, "I was about seven years old…"

It was springtime, and Dylan was involved in baseball. I'm not sure where I was at the time, but Bill had taken both kids to the batting cages for Dylan to hit some balls. It was that time of year in the Midwest when we experience intermittent thunderstorms and tornadoes. When the rain started coming down, Bill and the kids had to quickly leave the batting cages, and try to race home before they got totally drenched.

By the time they got home, the sky had blackened, and then turned a grayish-green color that meant a tornado was coming. They just barely made it inside the front door when the tornado sirens went off. Payton was understandably petrified. Any time the sirens went off when she was little, she tended to panic—rushing around trying to hurry the cat, the dogs, and the rest of us downstairs.

My approach with her at those times was always to say, "Payton, you need to calm down and stop crying! We've got to get downstairs!"

In this particular instance, her dad was there instead of me, and he took a different approach with her. She explained, "He comforted me, and told me everything was going to be fine. He told me not to worry because the cat already made it downstairs. Then he got me something to drink, and we went downstairs and played videogames until the storm passed. He was the only one who ever did that for me."

I am the taking-care-of-business type that says, "Snap out of it! There's nothing we can do but deal with it." But that day, her dad really understood her craziness, and comforted her.

As she told me about this memory, she had tears in her eyes, and I started crying too. "Daddy was the only one who ever understood me," she said. "Last month when we had the storms and I was freaking out, Dylan got mad. Daddy never did that."

With tears in my eyes, I promised, "I'm sorry, Sweetie. I'll never do it again."

Her story ended with her saying that after the storm, they all went upstairs, opened the door, and saw that the sky was a beautiful orange-pink, like sherbet.

Payton asked, "So, who is going to be our protector now, Mom?"

I said, "I am, Silly!" What I didn't tell her was that I had asked myself the same question many times since Bill's death.

Payton's memory reminded me of something.

Every spring, during the weather season, Bill tended to sleep very lightly, if at all. As the man of the house, he felt it was his job to be awake enough to get us all downstairs if the tornado sirens went off. So he slept lightly enough that he could hear the sirens, and kept the TV's on all night, so he could listen to the weather updates.

One particular night around 2005, he woke us all up and had us sleep in the living room, so we could get down to the basement quickly if the tornado got too close.

That same protector instinct in Bill led him to want a gun. During our entire relationship, I never heard the end of it. He had been around guns since he was a kid. "We need to have a gun for protection! We can keep it locked up safely away from the kids."

I had never been around firearms, and I'd heard too many news stories of young kids who were in the wrong place at the wrong time when the gun which had been kept in the house "for protection" accidentally fired.

Our kids were still too young. So I put my foot down and said, "Absolutely no guns."

Then, about four years ago, a rifle ended up in our house. Bill confessed that a friend from work who collected firearms had given him the gun. It had been in the top of the closet at one point, and at another time, it was under the bed.

I don't know how long he had it there. Knowing what a protector he was, it didn't really surprise me, but it did infuriate me. I lost my temper, ranting and raving about having children, and needing to get that f***ing gun out of the house.

The next day, the gun was gone—as far as I know. I saw Bill leave with it, anyway.

Why he suddenly felt he needed to have a gun in the house despite my objections, I will never know. For whatever reason, his need to protect us became greater than his need to honor my objections.   Was it paranoia? A sense of foreboding? Garden-variety anxiety? In any case, he could never keep a secret from me for very long. Soon after he got the gun, he told me it was there.

I asked Payton if there was anything else in particular she would remember about her dad. She told me about a dream…

She keeps next to her bed a really cute picture of her and Bill. In the photo, they are sledding around the neighborhood after a snowstorm. She told me that every night, she says goodnight to the picture, and one night, while looking at it, she said, "I wish I could see you just one more time." She fell asleep with that thought in her mind, and she had a dream about Bill.

She didn't remember much of the dream. Bill, the kids, and I were sitting in a booth in a restaurant. Dylan had a girl with him that Payton didn't recognize. Bill and I were seated across from Dylan and the girl. Payton walked up, crying. "See?" Bill said. "Everything is going to be okay."

I said, "Was that your first dream about your dad since the accident?"

"No," she said, "but the others were different. With this dream, when I woke up, I felt like my wish came true. I did get to see him!"

Payton shared one last happy memory with me….

In 2007, we bought the family truck. For many years before that, Bill had a conversion van—one of those big luxury vans with bench chairs, captain's chairs, and a TV inside. We had bought it new during the BMX years because we were on the road so much, and it was a great vehicle for traveling.

That van is the vehicle Payton remembers growing up with; she has so many memories of that van. She did not come on every BMX trip with us; sometimes she stayed with my mom and dad. But, she did have a lot of memories of the BMX riders and trips taken in that van. We didn't realize until we sold it how attached she was to it. We pushed it as far as it would go, so it was truly on its last leg when we got ready to sell it.

The four of us were in the parking lot of the truck dealership, and Bill was cleaning the last few personal items out of the van when Payton burst into tears. We asked her what was wrong, and she told us how much she was going to miss the van, and how many good memories she had of BMX and the boys. She didn't want us to get rid of it.

For some reason, we were all tickled by her attachment to the old van, and we couldn't help it—we started laughing hysterically. Then, she got the giggles right along with us, and she had to agree that she was being kind of ridiculous. The story ends with the four of us driving off the lot in our new truck, headed for home.

"That's a funny memory, Sweetie," I said. "Why do you think it stayed with you?"

"I don't know," she said, "I guess just because of the part about the memories. And all of us laughing together."

I said, "I'm surprised you didn't mention the time you and your dad went sledding—the time in the photo by your bed."

"But Mom," she said, "we went sledding all the time."

~Late October~
Everything Happens For a Reason

Alice: "Would you tell me, please, which way I ought to go from here?
Cheshire Cat: That depends a good deal on where you want to go.
Alice: I don't much care where...
Cheshire Cat: Then it doesn't matter which way you go."
Excerpted from "Alice in Wonderland"

~by Lewis Carroll

Since the accident, I had been trying to convince myself that the divorce happened for a reason—so I wouldn't be on the motorcycle with Bill as he met his destiny, and the kids wouldn't be left without both parents. Now I knew it from the bottom of my heart. As tragic as it all was to lose Bill, it happened that way for a reason.

The next step was to remember that the accident was Bill's destiny—not mine. I needed to remember that so I could go on with my life. *That* was my destiny—to go on with my life, and to help the kids go on with theirs!

It seemed like a higher power had orchestrated things to unfold the way they did—first the divorce and then the accident—to help ease our suffering. Even though we went through all that pain and anguish from the divorce, it was nothing compared to the blow we would have been dealt had there been no separation. I would have simply been a married woman receiving a phone call telling me that my husband—and the kids' father—was gone.

And, because of the divorce, the process of moving Bill's things out of the house was well underway. It would have been so much more painful to do after the accident.

I started telling my friends and loved ones what I was thinking, and asking them, "Does this sound crazy to you?"

No one accused me of being crazy, and the more I thought everything through, the more it made some kind of crazy sense to me. Even the fact that I was the remaining parent made sense to me. If God had to take one of us, and one of us had to stay, I could see how it might make sense to a divine being to leave the mother rather than the father—maybe not in every family, but definitely in ours.

I was still unsure if the divorce would have happened if Lisa had not been in the mix. Ultimately, I decided that destiny may have been *delayed* if she had not been around, but it would have eventually come to pass.

I am a true believer in the concept that things happen for a reason. We may find out the reason tomorrow. We may find out in twenty-five years. We may never find out. Sometimes you get lucky, and you are given a glimpse of the reason. I felt like that's what had happened for me. I now understood why my divorce had to happen.

Meanwhile, I found out that I wasn't the only one having meltdowns in the shower. Payton had been confiding in my mom that she often cried when she was alone—especially in the shower. It made me sad to think of Payton crying in the shower. That used to be her happy time.

I related so much with that. Sometimes, in the shower, I would be washing my feet and I would think of Bill. He was obsessed with my feet. I have cute, little feet, and he always loved them—especially with a fresh pedicure. Most women have to beg their husbands to rub their feet, but not Bill. We would be watching TV, and he would grab the lotion and start giving me a foot rub. Those were some of my favorite memories of him—when he was rubbing my feet.

I wanted to say something to Payton without making her feel spooked about talking to my mom in confidence. It was important to me that she continued to feel safe sharing her feelings with Mom.

I chose my moment with Payton, and gently said, "You know, Sweetie, how when you are in the shower, you start to think a lot because you're alone? I'm thinking maybe you need to get a shower radio. Then, when you're in the shower, you can just play the radio and sing along. You know how you love to sing!"

She loved the idea, and wanted to go buy one right away. Having music playing on the radio seemed to help her deal with her alone time. She was still in the mode of absorbing everything that had happened, and was not talking to me much about things. But, I knew she was processing her feelings on her own in the shower and in her room.

I knew that her healing journey was something she had to take on her own, but I wanted to be able to help in any way that I could. I was happy that the radio idea helped her deal with alone time. To this day, we still have that shower radio, and she still blasts it when she's taking a shower.

Time spent alone in the shower, and alone in bed while trying to fall asleep, have been hard for me, as well. That's when my mind starts to wander.

One night, I was thinking over everything, and I remembered a time when I was seventeen and Bill was eighteen. We would often go down for the weekend to Cuba, Missouri, to Bill, Sr. and Judy's place. The fact that their house is on several acres with a lake made it the perfect place to take a group of friends and camp overnight in tents. I was never the outdoorsy type, but I knew the house was right there, in case it rained or I needed to use the bathroom.

We took a group out there several times. Sometimes there were ten or twenty of us—some girls, some guys, some couples. During the day, the guys fished and the girls sunned themselves. Sometimes we rode dirt bikes. At night, we would build a bonfire, and just hang out, telling stories, drinking a little bit, and enjoying the night air. It was so beautiful to be in that lake setting. At night around the bonfires, Bill would always pull up a lawn chair, and I would sit on his lap.

I loved those times. We were so young and carefree, without a worry in the world. That young love was so innocent and refreshing. We hadn't yet gotten old enough to have adult concerns over kids and work. Bill was always very attentive, loving, and caring with me, making sure the bugs were not attacking me. He really looked after me.

Whenever I pictured us at the lake house, I always fell asleep with a smile on my face, and sometimes a bittersweet tear in my eye.

On October 21st, an appointment I'd made the first week after the accident finally rolled around—the dreaded trip to the Social Security office. I expected that it would be a nightmare, just like visiting the DMV. From the moment I first got them on the phone, it was stressful.

First, they told me very specifically that I absolutely had to bring certain documents with me to my appointment.

But, then I asked, "What if I haven't received the death certificate yet? Then, what?"

And they said, "Then come without it!"

Huh?

I said, "But you just told me…"

I'd dropped it. There was no point in arguing with them.

I arrived at their offices fully expecting a gray, military looking facility, devoid of personality. I was pleasantly surprised to find that it looked very much like a bank. It was a tastefully decorated, open area with floor plants, and windows letting in plenty of light.

I had also fully expected to be the youngest person there. Why wouldn't I be? Only older people would have any reason to visit the Social Security office, right? I was only forty.

I couldn't have been more wrong.

Once I made it past the security officer who searched my purse, I found that the average age of the people around me was about forty-five. What was going on?

As I sat in my seat among the rows of chairs, I got my answer from snippets of overheard conversations. It turned out that people went there after their unemployment benefits ran out. There were also others like me, who were there to inquire about benefits, after losing someone in their family.

They called my name and took me back to a cubicle. I sat down and immediately disclosed that I did not yet have the death certificate, but I had my birth certificate and social security card.

"Oh, don't worry," she said. "We already have the paperwork from Baue Funeral Home. So, we can proceed."

That explained why the person I initially spoke to on the phone told me to keep my appointment even if I hadn't yet received the death certificate.

As she read the document to herself, she paraphrased some of the facts, and repeated them out loud. "I see he died in a motorcycle accident. I'm so sorry…"

She then explained to me that because we were already legally divorced, I was not entitled to any of Bill's benefits—which confirmed what I'd initially been told on the phone. If we would have still been married—or even if we had been separated rather than fully divorced—I would have been eligible.

All of my rationale about how it was meant to be that we'd been divorced before the accident suddenly evaporated. If not for the divorce, I would have had social security income to help with all the financial responsibilities I was facing.

Then, she told me about a law that stated that any spouse—even a divorced one—who was married to the decedent for ten years or more would be entitled to benefits.

Great news!

Not so fast…It turned out that the salary I earned was high enough to disqualify me.

Now I was being penalized for having a good job?

I was totally overwhelmed with all the financial responsibilities on my shoulders. I lost it, and started crying. I felt terrible for the poor woman helping me, but I'd reached my breaking point, and I couldn't stop the flood of tears. A person can only keep it together for so long under the kind of stress I had been experiencing.

"Wait, I think I do have some good news," she said. "Your children qualify for benefits. So that money is there to help you with them. The only downside is that the benefits stop when they turn eighteen." She was very compassionate and comforting.

The amount of the kids' Social Security benefits was comparable to the amount of child support I would have been receiving from Bill, so that would help somewhat. But, what was I going to do when Dylan and Payton entered college? That scenario would be coming up for Dylan before I knew it. Was he going to have to go into debt that it would take him a lifetime to repay because his Social Security benefits from Bill stopped when he turned eighteen? I had the same concerns for Payton.

All in all, my experience in the Social Security office was very different than I had anticipated. I had truly been expecting to deal with a monster, and instead, I met a lovely woman with a big heart.

~Late October II~
Limbo

"Ouiser: Yes, Annelle, I pray! Well, I do!
There, I said it. I hope you're satisfied.
Annelle: I suspected this all along.
Ouiser: Oh! Well, don't you expect me to come to
one of your churches or one of those tent-revivals with all those
Bible-beaters doin' God-only-knows-what!
They'd probably make me eat a live chicken!
Annelle: Not on your first visit."

~From "Steel Magnolias"

O ne day, Randa called to inform me that there was a memorial page set up on Facebook for Bill and Lisa *together*.

"You really need to take a look at it," she said. "I can't believe this."

I understood that Lisa's family and friends, and my family and friends, were all experiencing a profound sense of loss. But, I could not believe they would put up a memorial page on Facebook. It felt so inappropriate. I wanted to call someone and say, "Tell me, did you sit and think about everybody involved before you made this decision?" It was outrageous.

I was so bothered by the thought of it, I had to see it. I took a deep breath, logged onto Facebook, and easily pulled up the memorial page. The main photo showed Bill and Lisa standing there together, as a couple. I could not let my kids see that. Sure, they both knew about her, and Dylan had even met her, but neither one of them had wanted anything to do with her once they found out about the affair.

How could grown adults think that memorial page was appropriate? That was something they should have done privately, not in a public forum where Bill's children could see it.

There were several other photographs of Bill and Lisa together, and some of Lisa by herself. The memorial page had over one hundred friends, about ten of whom I knew by name. The other ninety were Bill's "new friends."

People had written comments to the effect that they had known Billy and Lisa their whole lives and would miss them dearly. They talked about them being happy in Heaven, riding off into the sunset together. Others talked about raising a glass to Lisa here on earth as she raised one to them on the other side.

Seriously? How could they post something like that, knowing there was a question about whether alcohol was a factor in the wreck?

Some of the comments seemed very sincere, but from my perspective, the entire memorial page was grossly inappropriate. If it had been on a site that my children could not access, I still would have thought it was tacky, but my attitude towards it would have been, "Whatever."

Whether it was then, or ten years from then, I didn't want my poor kids to see it—kids who were grieving the death of their father, and still trying to process all their emotions over his affair and our divorce.

I was enraged—and on a mission to get the page shut down.

It was a real eye-opening education to try to penetrate Facebook, and find a real person to talk to. My only option was to file an online complaint. When I did that, and stated that I wished to shut down a page, a box popped up, asking me why.

There didn't seem to be a category to match my situation.

Were there illegal photos? Or, did I find the page offensive? If so, in what way?

The "offensive" category seemed to fit best. So, when the box popped up asking me to elaborate about my reason, I said that Bill had passed away, I was named executrix his estate, and I had not given them authorization to use his name. I pushed the button and watched my complaint disappear into cyberspace, frustrated that Facebook did not provide the option to talk to a live individual.

I didn't get any sort of immediate response, so that was that. Now, I just had to wait and see what happened. From time to time, Randa or I would check the page to see what people were saying, and to see if any action had been taken. I was shocked to see the kinds of personal thoughts people posted. Did they really want the entire world to see their innermost thoughts and feelings?

I was tempted to post something on there saying, "Come on, people! Write these thoughts in a journal!!! Not on a public site."

While I waited to see what—if anything—Facebook would do about my complaint, I had the comfort of knowing I had already blocked Payton from Bill's page. Even if she was on someone else's page, she wouldn't be able to see him. But I also knew that she had plenty of friends on Facebook, and they would be able to see it.

I was anxious for the page to come down right away.

While I was on the computer, I was also following the progress of Passenger X on her Caring Bridge page. Although she remained on a ventilator due to her pre-existing cystic fibrosis condition, the doctors were now certain she was going to live. For the first week and a half, it had been touch and go, and the doctors really weren't sure she would make it.

I am struggling to put into words the tapestry of emotions I felt whenever I thought of her lying in that hospital bed. It was so much more involved and complicated than simply feeling relieved that she had not died.

The fact was, Bill's motorcycle insurance policy would not pay very high benefits for Passenger X. I knew that, in just a couple of days in the hospital, she would have racked up more medical bills than the policy would pay her. I was very aware how common it was for people to sue when they were in an accident.

As I already mentioned, I was afraid that, as Bill's widow, I could somehow share liability for her injuries. I knew that, because Bill and I were divorced, Passenger X couldn't attach a lien on my house because Denny had already told me that much. But, I was still up in the air about life insurance benefits that might be designated for the children, and whether or not those could potentially be lost in a lawsuit. I wouldn't know anything for sure until I received the death certificate. Until then, I was in a very uncomfortable limbo.

Bill and I had our main life insurance through our employers.

After Bill got out of the Navy, he also took out a very inexpensive military life insurance policy, which I paid annually. Other than the policy through my employer, I didn't have a separate policy on myself.

Going through this process turned me into a rabid believer in the importance of life insurance. Every chance I got, I told my friends and loved ones, "You never really know what's going to happen. Don't think the fifty thousand dollar policy you have through your work is going to help very much with supporting your kids—it's not! You need more."

I was fairly sure that on Bill's life insurance policy through the City of St. Peters, he had named the kids as his beneficiary, but I wouldn't know for sure until I got the death certificate.

I needed that document for everything!

No wonder Baue Funeral Home had stressed the importance of it. Every single bit of paperwork that needed to be handled, and every single conversation I needed to have with anyone related to Bill's accident, hinged upon the death certificate. Without it, no action could be taken.

When someone dies because of an illness, the surviving spouse gets the death certificate within a week or two of the death. But because it was an accident—and because the accident potentially involved alcohol—it needed to be investigated. And, the investigation, I was told, could take months.

I was beside myself. I needed the death certificate already!

And I needed that crazy memorial page to come down.

Nothing was happening fast enough—except the one thing I wished I could delay forever. Randa's procedure to remove the tumor was set for October 23rd. It would be performed on an outpatient basis. She would be under for a few hours, and if all went well, she would then be able to go home.

The night before, I brought to her house several "good luck" balloons, a bouquet of flowers, and a six-pack of Bud Light—her favorite beer. When I got there, her oldest was in the room. I had a momentary feeling of panic, thinking, oh, no, maybe I shouldn't be making a big deal of this in front of the kids.

Randa noticed my expression. "Don't worry. He's thirteen. He knows what's going on."

I said, "Are you sure? Maybe I shouldn't have done this…"

"No," she said, "Really. They are beautiful! Thank you so much. That was so thoughtful."

She was in good spirits, which was good for me to see. I thought she might want me with her at the hospital, but she said that between her husband, John, and her sister, who was coming into town to help look after the three boys, she had her bases covered.

"Okay," I said, "but I'll be there if you need me."

I was praying that the procedure would be successful in terms of removing all the cancer. I'd heard too many stories where they don't get it all the first time. My thinking was, let's just get the tumor out and get on with radiation, so she can get on the other side of this as soon as possible.

Randa was so young, such a good person, and the mother of young children. It seemed so unfair that she, of all people, would get cancer—not that anyone ever deserved cancer.

Of course, I wanted to make sure I could be there for Randa in any way she needed me to be, but after all that had happened with Bill, I wasn't sure I could have handled it if anything went wrong with her surgery.

Thankfully, all went well.

Her husband, John, who is not a texter, tried to send me a text telling me that everything was fine. It was very cute—a little hard to decipher, but I got the gist of it.

When I stopped by after work, I found John and the kids running around, as usual. Other than Randa's sister Debbie being there, and the fact that Randa was not allowed to get up off the couch, it could have been any other day in their household. That was exactly what Randa wanted—for things to stay as routine as possible.

Of course, Randa was in pain, and her wounds were all wrapped up.

In my mind, I was thinking, okay, great, we got her through surgery; now all we need is a clean bill of health so she can start radiation. Provided the pathology report did not show anything out of the ordinary, she would be starting daily radiation in four to six weeks. Sadly, that would fall right around the holidays, but there was nothing anyone could do about that. Cancer did not take holidays off.

I clung to the belief that all would be well. We just had to wait for the report to come back.

~Late October III~
Seeing Ghosts

"...Like the layers of the sunset as they melt down the horizon
Are the pieces of the puzzles of the past.
Did it scare you when they shattered?
Did they cut you? Did it matter?
Did the sharpness of their edges make you bleed?
Will you find your way from here, through the images of fear?
Do you know your way around the broken glass?"
"Broken Glass"

~by Vivien Kooper

During the entire month of October, I was in constant contact with both the life insurance and the motorcycle insurance companies. I occupied myself by organizing everything in an accordion file, so that when I finally received the death certificate, I could easily set everything in motion. Not only did it feel good to be prepared, but it helped to keep my mind off thoughts of Bill.

And keeping my mind off Bill was growing harder. I was suddenly seeing ghosts!

Just like when I had begun noticing the dogs jumping up and running to the door at the sound of motorcycle, I was beginning to notice other things—some of which were not actually there. I was starting to feel like a character in the movie *Ghost*.

Any time I would see a silver Silverado truck, with a driver wearing an orange City of St. Peters shirt, my mind would play tricks on me. I would think, "Wait! That was Bill!" I would be gasping for air as my mind was telling me, "See! Bill did not really die!"

256

I would swing my head around for a second, and then continue watching in the rearview mirror until the truck was out of sight. A couple of times, while I was looking backwards at the driver of a truck that just passed, I went off the road, and had to yank the steering wheel back. Each time I narrowly missed an accident because I'd had a Bill sighting, I told myself, you can't do this. Bill is not here!

The same thing happened whenever a motorcycle that remotely resembled Bill's Harley would pass by. I would look to see if it was Bill. My logical mind knew good and well it wasn't, but I could not help myself. What was wrong with me? This definitely was not typical behavior for me! I am someone who is very grounded in reality.

I was wondering what the kids might be going through. I didn't have to wonder for long. One evening in late October, Dylan and I found ourselves having a heart to heart conversation.

He was sitting in the recliner chair, and I was sitting across from him on the couch. We were talking generally about how he was doing and how everything in his life was going. He was giving me perfunctory answers, but he was fidgeting so much, I could tell he needed to share something deeper with me.

When he was finally ready to spill the beans, Dylan looked at me with an expression of seriousness, concern, and love I will never forget. He said, "I need to tell you something…and please don't think I'm saying I'm glad this happened to Dad, or I wanted it to happen. But, I think this all happened to us so Payton and I wouldn't have to suffer the rest of our lives. We are suffering right now, but we will be able to move on. With the way Dad had been acting, we would have suffered for the rest of our lives."

I instantly burst into tears. My God, I thought, my sixteen-year-old is so deep, and in tune, way beyond his years.

"Of course, Dillie," I said, "I know that never in a million years did you wish this, or want it to happen, and I know how sorry you are that it happened to all of us. But, I think your insight is very good."

He had needed to get that off his chest, but had worried that I would judge him. Once he realized that I understood what he was saying, he seemed to feel much better.

Once he had shared that insight with me, I was also able to make some sense of the way he had been responding to the accident. Prior to that conversation with him, I had been deeply concerned about the way he seemed to be handling the pain of the situation. I thought for sure he was sweeping everything under the rug, emotionally. But now I understood.

It seemed like I now had a window into Dylan's approach to grieving. He seemed to have reconciled it by telling himself, the divorce and the accident happened. I can't change those things. I miss my dad, but this is the way my life is now. I just need to accept it and trust that everything happens for a reason.

I was so relieved to have a better sense of what was going on inside him.

Later, I asked him for a couple of his favorite memories of his dad.

When Dylan was fourteen, Bill and I became concerned that Dylan didn't have an after-school sport. We told him we didn't want him sitting around playing videogames all the time. He told us he had been going over to his friend Sean's house quite often and riding bikes with Sean and their mutual friend Mike. The three of them rode their bikes everywhere.

Whenever we brought up the issue of not wanting Dylan sitting around the house after school playing videogames, he said, "But I'm not! I already told you—we're riding bikes."

Bill really gave him the third degree, trying to determine if the boys were riding their bikes as hard as they claimed they were.

One weekend, Bill agreed to take the boys to South County, where they had a big outdoor park with dirt jumps. I had never liked the place because it wasn't supervised and the riders were not required to wear helmets.

When they got there and Bill saw how big the jumps were, he started teasing the boys, saying, "I don't know, guys. There's no way you are going to be able to do these jumps. You can't have been riding your bikes as much as you claim."

Well, Dylan was really nervous as he contemplated one of the biggest jumps, but he was bound and determined to show his dad that he had been telling the truth. What happened next with his dad was something Dylan would never forget.

Bill watched Dylan do the jump and told him how proud he was of him, saying it was obvious that Dylan really had been doing a lot of riding with Sean and Mike. Then, Bill apologized for doubting him. Dylan was really touched.

My son also had fond memories of his first motorcycle ride on Bill's Harley. He had always heard his dad say, "When you're riding your motorcycle, it's like you are free. The wind is blowing in your face, and nothing can stop you." But, Dylan had never personally experienced what his dad was describing, because he had only ridden dirt bikes.

In 2005, Dylan finally got to ride with Bill on his Harley. Dylan said there was nothing special about the ride—it was just him and his dad, out and about. But, the thing that stood out for Dylan was that he could actually feel the love of riding his dad felt when he was on his Harley.

"I finally knew what Dad was talking about," Dylan explained. "The wind was blowing on me, and I felt like I was free. It was great that I got to experience that with Dad—but I still don't want a street bike."

Dylan—thank God—was perfectly content with his dirt bikes.

Dylan also reminded me of the "quitting football talk" he had with his dad, and mentioned the first time his dad had taken him to Chris's shop with him. He said that those were also some of his favorite Bill memories.

Then, he talked about a hot air balloon race in September of 2008—an annual event at Forest Park in St. Louis. Every year, crowds gather as the balloons are fired up, and glow against the background of the night sky. That particular night in 2008, it had rained, so we didn't go. But the next day was the balloon race. Families brought a blanket and a picnic basket, tried to ignore the fact that the grass was still damp, and watched as the balloons raced each other to a designated finish line. Whichever balloon arrived first was the winner.

It was spectacular to be up close to the balloons and watch them all take off at once—seventy-five to a hundred of them.

"Dad was so relaxed," Dylan remembered. "And he really wanted to be with us. I didn't feel like we were putting him out in any way. He didn't seem like he would have rather been working on the race car or hanging out at the computer. He really seemed like he was happy to be around his family."

I knew what my son was getting at—and it broke my heart to hear him say it. In the last year before the divorce, as Bill was working his way up to saying goodbye to us, he increasingly wanted to do his own thing, and pouted when he couldn't. Until Dylan told me about that memory, I didn't realize the extent to which my kids had noticed it too.

When we were done reminiscing, Dylan and I went on with our evening, but I was deeply moved by our conversation, and it started me thinking about the difference between the two kids.

Dylan was grounding his suffering and hurt in realism, and processing everything much like an adult would. In some ways, I felt his wisdom about the situation even surpassed mine. His sister was a whole different story. She was still so young. She seemed to have completely forgotten all about the divorce and the affair. All she knew was that Bill was gone forever.

That night, I went to bed talking to Bill in my heart. "Did you hear what Dylan had to say? Did we really have to have this outcome? Couldn't we have avoided your destiny by little things changing? Why do this to Dylan and Payton? Why do this to me?"

There was no answer back—only the loneliness. So, with my mind and heart full of questions answered only by the heavy silence of night, I drifted off.

~Late October IV~
What If...

"Welcome to the jungle
We take it day by day
If you want it, you're gonna bleed
But it's the price you pay..."
~"Welcome to the Jungle"

by Adler/Hudson/McKagan/Rose/Stradlin (Guns 'n' Roses)

Ever since the accident, the most unlikely person of all had stepped up—Kenny!

He was amazing. Just as he promised he would, he was calling the house several times a week and calling the kids on their cell phones, checking to see if everyone was okay, and whether we needed anything. He made a point to give the kids the one-on-one attention they needed. I found it fascinating to see this man being so giving to my children when he didn't have—and perhaps didn't want—children of his own.

As surprising as it was to see him reaching out in this way, I was very happy about it. It felt good to talk to him. During times of tragedy, we all need different types of people to talk to, and he was my outsider. He knew Bill, and yet he really knew very little about me.

I so appreciated his support of the kids and me and yet at the same time, I was confused by it. Why was he being so thoughtful and nice to us? Why did he feel like he had to do that for the kids and me? I began to wonder if I'd misjudged him.

I decided to roll with it.

Kenny connected with Dylan right away. It was a guy thing. They talked about cars and bikes. Dylan could go over to Kenny's and ride four-wheelers with him, so right away, they had that connection.

260

Kenny also made sure he gave Payton one-on-one time as well. Sometimes he brought remote-controlled cars for both kids, but without fail, every time he came over, he made sure he brought something just for her—a rose, a stuffed animal, a special treat he had picked up for her on the way over. He didn't just give her gifts. He made sure he sat and talked with her.

I would sit across the room, and watch in amazement, wondering if he had any idea how much he had to offer a wife and children.

Kenny decided that, since he'd been spending so much guy time with Dylan, it was time to take Payton and I to the park to take pictures. He knew how much she loved her camera, and thought that would be a great outing for us. The park had a lake, which was beautiful, and it was late fall, so the trees were changing colors. It was the ideal day for taking pictures. One of Payton's photographs was used for the cover of this book.

Kenny was so sweet with Payton, and it shook me up a little to see how she was soaking up the male attention. Until I actually saw her around Kenny, I had not realized just how much she must have been yearning for that male presence in her life. She lost that on July 5th when Bill left the house.

I felt the same way. When we got back in the car to head home, Kenny opened the car door for me, and I was startled. It had been a long time since anyone had done that for me, and I thought, gosh, if I feel this way, I can only imagine how my little girl feels.

Her dad was gone. Here was Bill's friend talking with her, listening, bringing her gifts, teasing her in that good-natured way that can only come from a guy. I was suddenly so sad for all of us.

I started thinking of stories I'd heard about girls who had lost their fathers getting attachments to the wrong people, and I became frightened. In today's world, such possibilities were even more frightening.

Yet, I did feel safe around Kenny. He was a surprising blessing—just what we all needed. My friendship with him reminded me of my friendship with Bill in the very beginning of our relationship, before it turned romantic.

When he left, he gave us big hugs of concern, which felt good, and completely appropriate.

During this time around the end of October, I was inundated with paperwork related to the accident, and I was on a mission. Every time I spoke to a friend or loved one, I continued to remind them about the necessity of having a "what if" file. I am a very organized person. Yet, when tragedy hit, I was unprepared.

Did they want to find themselves unprepared? When tragedy hits, everyone is so emotionally exhausted and devastated, it's much harder to try to gather the necessary documentation. It's better to do it in advance, when you are still thinking clearly.

Of course no one thinks tragedy is going to hit their lives. But, now I knew better. I had struggled so much, and didn't want to see anyone else have to go through the same thing.

I began to preach about the importance of keeping all your important paperwork in one file—birth certificates, social security cards, your Will, your car titles; and not necessarily the entire policies, but the name and number of your health, life, and auto insurance companies. Not only does everything need to be in one file, but a family member or someone you trust needs to know where it is. The designated person should not be your spouse. If you were both in an accident together, no one would be able to find the file.

If you're going to put those important papers in a safe deposit box, keep in mind that the safe deposit box can freeze upon the event of your death, unless you specifically designate in advance that your spouse (or another family member) is to have access to it in the event of your death.

Nobody wants to think about such things. It's human nature to put them out of your mind. But, if you have the file prepared in advance, your poor family members won't have to ransack your house when tragedy hits, looking for the paperwork they need. You can save the survivors so much agony and stress.

It is especially important to have a Will if you have children, and everyone should not only have one, but make sure it is updated. Ours were not. They were created before the children were born, and despite the fact my uncle is an attorney, we never thought about updating them.

Luckily, because we were legally divorced, we had a divorce decree stating that the surviving parent automatically became the legal guardian of our children if the other parent died. But, without Wills having been updated to reflect the fact that we now had children, there's no telling what would have happened if Bill and I had died together. Family members would have been fighting over the kids. It's so much simpler for everyone to spend a couple of hundred dollars to get a current Will—or do it yourself online for free.

It's also important to have a living Will. It is the only way to ensure that your wishes will be carried out in the event of your death or incapacitation.

In my case, for example, Bill died almost instantly. But, what if he hadn't? He might have been kept alive on a breathing machine—which is not something Bill would have wanted. I knew what his wishes were in regards to being kept live by artificial means.

And, what about issues of organ donation? Those are things you definitely want to designate in advance. Otherwise, if something happens to you—or your loved ones—it is anyone's guess as to what could transpire.

I was on a rampage. Every time my phone would ring, the poor soul on the other end would get an earful. "Maggie," I would say, "do you have your

Will done? Better make sure it's updated!" Or, "Randa, you have three children. Better make sure you have enough life insurance to cover you in case something happens."

I passed along what I'd been told—that when it comes to life insurance, it's good to get a policy where the payout is seven to ten times your annual salary.

I'm sure everyone thought I'd lost my mind. But later, they would come back and tell me that they had taken my advice to heart—if only in some small way.

I also reminded everyone that we tend to think about something happening to our spouse, but the reality is, we also need to consider what advance preparations we might need related to our aging parents.

I would say, "Think how much fun it would be hunting for the insurance policy of your parents! Better make sure you know in advance where all of their paperwork is kept."

If I had known all of this in advance, I could have simply grabbed my folder, and saved myself an immense amount of heartache and stress. But, I figured, I was forty years old—too young to be dealing with such things. I found out the hard way that tragedy can—and does—strike when you least expect it, and it's no respecter of age.

As I was dealing with this never-ending paper trail, I was shocked to discover that I wasn't the only one who was aware of our family's tragedy. Once Bill's death became public record, the bloodsuckers came out of the woodwork. It seemed that every attorney and realtor in the greater St. Louis had our name, number, and address, and they thought that post-tragedy was a good time to try to get our business!

I was mortified. The most appalling part of receiving solicitations by mail at such a time was the fact that they were often addressed to Dylan and Payton. Apparently, in the legal documentation naming someone as the executor or executrix of an estate, the children are also named. And the fact that such information was accessible by any businessperson who wanted it was evidenced by the offensive junk mail we were receiving.

Was Dylan considering buying a home? They were terribly sorry about his loss, but perhaps a change of scenery might help.

Or, maybe Payton found herself in need of legal counsel to help her sort through all the paperwork related to the recent tragedy she suffered.

As I sorted through the mail, I couldn't believe my eyes.

One day, I asked my mom, "What in the world are these ambulance chasers thinking?"

I got so angry at one point, I called one of the realtors who sent us a solicitation suggesting that Payton might like to sell them her home, and I said, "Okay, fine! You want to buy our house—now when it's been on the market for ages? Great! Then buy it! But why are you sending this mail to my twelve-year-old daughter? Are you thinking she's the one who is going to sell it to you?"

Needless to say, she was stunned—and apologized.

I know that people need to drum up business, but there has to be a better way.

Around this same time, I was talking to friends of Bill's, in an attempt to make sense of the divorce, the affair, and the tragedy that ensued. I needed deeper insight into Lisa's character. I was also hoping to get a deeper understanding of the change in Bill that led him down the road he took.

One man I talked to had worked with Bill for many years, and also attended junior high school with him. The guy really looked up to Bill, and envied the fact that he had a lasting marriage and two children. The man himself was divorced and seemed to feel he had taken a wrong turn in his own life. He shared with me the fact that when Bill told him he was leaving me, he tried to talk him out of it.

The guy told me what a good friend Bill had been to him, and how much he appreciated being able to confide in Bill without feeling judged. Bill was also a good listener. The fact that he—a guy who was not as together as Bill—was questioning Bill's judgment took me aback.

He told Bill, "Dude, have you really given this enough thought? You have invested twenty-four years of your life in this!"

Here was a guy who, by his own admission, had messed up his life. Yet even he could see that what Bill was doing with Lisa wasn't right.

Another friend of Bill's—a guy who shared Bill's love of racing—invited me to have dinner with him and his wife. I had talked to him at the funeral and we'd promised we'd get together.

Knowing they had likely gotten together socially with Bill and Lisa as a couple, I was a little uncomfortable about getting together with them. We met at a restaurant and I ended up having a great time with them. We reminisced about our BMX days, and all the goofy antics of Bill and the kids.

Suddenly the mood turned serious, as his wife shared with me her concerns over Bill being with Lisa. She shared with me how heartbroken they both were to see Bill leave me and the kids. She became very emotional, and started crying.

The evening took a strange turn. Apparently, there was another couple with whom they had socialized as well—and that couple also knew Bill and Lisa. Something must have gone wrong at a social gathering because, while the three of us were having dinner, the wife made it clear that she never wanted her husband to bring the other couple to her home again—ever. She was very emphatic.

The general impression I got was that Bill and Lisa's relationship involved a lot of partying and wild friends. I was unclear about the specific incident that had caused the wife to be so upset, but it was clear that she did not enjoy watching Bill's life unravel.

Between the different friends I talked to, I got confirmation that I wasn't crazy. Bill really *had* been acting strangely before the accident—and that was from the perspective of friends that I knew for certain really loved and admired Bill. That gave what they were saying even more weight.

I was now completely convinced that Bill had undergone a midlife crisis precipitated by a severe chemical imbalance. He must have had the most extreme case possible, because it had blocked his ability to make rational decisions. Everything I'd read confirmed it: "The person you love will, all of a sudden, make erratic, overnight decisions and changes, and treat them like they were no big deal."

~Halloween~
A Few More Answers

"And when I'm gone, just carry on, don't mourn
Rejoice every time you hear the sound of my voice
Just know that I'm looking down on you smiling
And I didn't feel a thing
So baby don't feel no pain
Just smile back..."
"When I'm Gone"

~by Luis Edgardo Resto and Marshall Mathers, III (Eminem)

The day before Halloween, I received notice that I could finally pick up the official document appointing me the executrix of Bill's estate, which was in the judge's chambers being signed. I could now go to Bill's storage unit, and I had very mixed feelings about it. I imagined that going through Bill's belongings might be emotionally trying for me—and I was pretty sure I was going to find some of Lisa's belongings in there, as well. I knew that wasn't going to be easy.

I immediately called Randa. "I'm going to pick up the official papers proving that I'm the executrix of the estate. Is there any way you could get off work early and meet me at the unit?"

Unfortunately, Randa was busy with patients, and couldn't get away.

So, I called Kenny and asked if he could meet me. I knew he owned his own business, so I figured it would be easier for him to get away.

No luck. He had meetings. But, he told me he could go the following day. I thanked him, but said I really had to go right that minute.

Obviously, I was meant to go by myself. As I was driving there, I wondered what I was going to encounter—a unit the size of a double-car garage or the size of a closet? As you've no doubt noticed by now, I'm someone who likes to have a plan, so going into the unknown was making me nervous.

When I arrived at the storage facility's office and showed them my papers, they told me that they didn't have the key to Bill's unit. They would have to weld off the lock.

I stood there, watching the guy holding his welding torch with a puddle of rainwater at his feet. Oh perfect, I was thinking, all I need now is for this man to get electrocuted. But he was fine, the lock fell off, and he left me standing in front of the open door of the unit.

I started taking deep breaths, trying to prepare myself for whatever was on the other side of the door. When I felt I was ready to open the door, I gave myself a little pep talk, saying, well, whatever is here is here, and it's time to get it all organized. I figured there would be some things I would want to keep, and other things I would take to the Goodwill. And, then I'd have to figure out what to do with Lisa's belongings.

In any case, I was not about to continue paying seventy-five dollars a month to store everything. It had to be dealt with now.

I had to yank hard on the door to get it to lift open. Things were stacked to the very top of the unit—boxes and plastic bins.

The very first thing I saw was an open box with a lacy, white satin photo album. I did a double-take. What the hell? It was definitely nothing I had ever owned, so it had to be Lisa's. Okay, now I knew for sure—Lisa's belongings were in the storage locker, too.

I grabbed the box with the photo album. Looking more closely, I could see that it was a wedding photo album. Judging from the age Lisa appeared to be in the photos, I figured it was from her first marriage. I thought, this is weird, leaving this photo album in an open cardboard box like this, totally unprotected. I will cherish all of my pictures forever.

I found myself getting angry and upset all over again at the thought of Bill and Lisa. Was it really necessary to torture me by making me look at all these pictures?

I started wondering about Lisa's character again, and asking myself questions that were impossible to answer. In response, I was making all sorts of assumptions, none of them good. My anger motivated me to plow through the contents of the storage locker as quickly as I could, so I could put it all behind me.

One thing I did learn about Lisa was that she loved dolphins. I found boxes of all kinds of dolphin knick knacks, and even a glass dolphin table— definitely not to my taste, surprise, surprise.

I also found boxes of her clothing and paperwork. Why would someone put paperwork in a storage shed?

What I did not find was the naval discharge paperwork I had been looking for. I never would get my hands on that file. Thankfully, I hadn't needed it for Jefferson Barracks. But, the file contained certificates of military achievement, and other keepsakes that I thought Dylan might appreciate.

After about two hours, I had everything more or less organized into categories. I was so filled with adrenaline, I was able to heave the boxes around like a truck driver. In that moment, I probably could have hoisted a car over my head, like in those stories you hear on the news where someone is so pumped with adrenaline, they are momentarily imbued with superhuman abilities.

I went back to the office at the storage facility and they gave me another lock. Then I put some things I was planning to keep in my car, and shut the door to the storage unit. As I turned the lock, I had one of those moments you get after you've survived something traumatic. During the event, you just grit your teeth and bear it. But afterwards—that's when it hits you. My God, I thought, I just touched some of Lisa's things!

I was okay. I had survived the ordeal.

On the way home, I contemplated calling Lisa's mother and letting her know that she could come get Lisa's things. I knew that Bill, Sr. and Judy had her phone number. I called some friends of mine who knew friends of Lisa's, and ran the whole idea by them.

They were saying, "Why do you care? Throw everything away! Or, better yet, burn it!"

I knew that on Lisa's side as well as our side, everyone had suffered a tremendous loss. I may not have liked her—or the idea of her, which was all I really knew—but I still wanted to do the right thing. I was clear in my own mind that whoever was going to pick up her things better come right away. I wanted it over with as soon as possible.

When I got home, I called Judy. "What do you think?" I asked her. "Do you think I should call Lisa's mother or her friends?"

She said, "Well, you're a better person than I am. I would just burn it all."

I said, "Go ahead and give me her mom's number before I lose my nerve. I'm going to call her."

She said, "Are you sure you want to do this?"

I said, "Yeah, I need to do this for me."

I didn't really want anyone in Lisa's camp having my cell phone number. So, I made a point to call from my home phone, figuring the number was listed anyway. It was clear by the way she answered the phone that my name came up on her caller I.D.

She said hello in a very standoffish voice.

I told her who I was and she asked me what I wanted.

I explained that I'd just received the executrix paperwork that day and had gone to Bill's storage locker, where I'd found some of Lisa's belongings. I went on to say that I knew what it was like to lose somebody, and to acknowledge that we had both lost someone we loved in a very convoluted tragedy.

"Being a mother myself," I said, "I can imagine how you feel, and I figured you might want these items of your daughter's. Among her things are some photo albums from her wedding."

When I said, that, her entire demeanor changed. She told me she was very thankful that I had called, and promised she would make arrangements for someone to meet me at the storage unit the next day.

I hung up feeling good—like I had definitely done the right thing. I could feel that she, too, was in a lot of pain.

Then, I called our friend Chris, and asked him if he could bring his truck to the storage facility the following day. He said that he would come, and that he would call another friend with a truck and ask him to meet us there, as well. Randa and my brother were going to meet me there first, to help get everything more organized, and to take back to the house any boxes that wouldn't fit in my car. Chris and his friends would show up afterwards. At some point, whoever was coming from Lisa's side would meet us there.

It was all arranged for the following day—Halloween. It somehow seemed fitting.

The next day, Mitch met Randa and me there. We dove right in, started sorting through everything, and made good headway before anyone else arrived. When Chris got there, he told me that the couple coming to pick up Lisa's things was the very couple mentioned the night I had dinner with those friends of Bill's. Remember? The wife had said she never wanted this particular couple in her house again—and they were coming to the storage locker! Not only that, but they were coming in a car, not a truck. I didn't see how everything was going to fit into their car.

I don't know who I expected to show up, but definitely not them. I felt very nervous about seeing them, and suddenly I wasn't sure I could go through with it. Before I could plan an escape, I got the phone call that they were there and needed to be buzzed in. I was trapped—and I didn't even have Randa or my brother to hide behind, because they'd already left. I had a fleeting thought that maybe I could just jump in my car and speed away, but it passed.

When the couple pulled up, the woman said a pleasant hello to me, and I said, "There's her stuff." Then I made a hasty retreat into the background, where I stayed.

Chris and his friend decided to put all the things going to the Goodwill in the same truck as the things coming back to my house, and use their other truck to help Lisa's friends, whose car was not going to hold everything.

Chris and I said our goodbyes, and the trucks and the car pulled away. The storage shed was taken care of.

As I left, I felt no emotion other than a feeling of being glad that the mystery of the storage shed was now behind me, and the satisfaction of knowing I had done the right thing by Lisa's family.

~November~
Time Marches On

*"The best thing about the future
Is that it comes one day at a time."*

~Abraham Lincoln

I pulled into my driveway, aware that it was Halloween night, my second favorite holiday of the year, after Christmas. I love to fill my house with decorations—the more creepy and disgusting, the better. Unfortunately, since our house was on the market, I'd had to restrain myself. I didn't want to scare off potential buyers. I could have dressed up, at least, but for the first time in years, I didn't feel like it. The day at the storage unit had already been frightful enough.

So much for Halloween festivities.

I decided to log on to the computer.

It had been awhile since I had checked on Passenger X's condition, and I wanted to see how she was doing. The update on her Caring Bridge site stated that she was beginning physical therapy to rehabilitate her vocal chords, which had been weakened by the tracheotomy. She was talking and progressing very well.

Then I read a sentence that gave me a cold chill. It said something to the effect that, the day before had been a very difficult day for her because she finally found out all the details of the accident. She must have suffered some memory loss, and was just finding out that Bill and Lisa had died. Her family wrote in a public area of the website that she was very shaken up and saddened, but would get through that difficult time with the love and support of friends and family.

I still had the overpowering feeling that Bill, by deciding to lay his bike down on its side, had probably saved her life. I still desperately wanted to say to her, "Do you realize how lucky you are?"

271

Sadly, I had to put prudence above my human need to connect with this woman who had been with Bill in the last hours of his life. I had to be very careful what I said to her, because there was little doubt in my mind that she would find herself in a position where she felt she had to sue Bill's estate. Her medical bills were bound to be astronomical, and her insurance would only cover so much.

I had such mixed feelings when I thought about that. On the one hand, I understood that she had medical bills, and I knew what I would likely do in the same situation. On the other hand, I felt like *Bill saved her life!* So, why sue the estate benefiting his children?

At this point, I still didn't have the death certificate signed by the judge, so I didn't know what the life insurance benefits were going to be.

It was so strange to think that this woman would be indelibly stamped on my psyche because of her involvement in Bill's accident—and yet, she didn't know me from Adam. For that matter, she barely knew Bill. She had met him for the first time the day of the accident. She was someone that Driver X—the man driving the other bike—knew. She may not have even known Lisa.

You, along with three others, are heading out on the road for an afternoon motorcycle ride. Ten minutes before the fatal accident that will take the lives of two of the four riders, you decide to switch cycles. You don't die—but you might have been one of the two who did. Your odds were fifty-fifty. Two lived,   two   passed   away.

I will always wonder what factored into Lisa's fateful decision to switch motorcycles. What if she had *stayed* on the back of Bill's bike? What if Passenger X had been on the back of the other motorcycle and died—and Lisa had lived?

It was mind-boggling to consider. Had it played out that way—where Bill died and Lisa lived—the whole horrific journey following the accident would have been that much more difficult for me to bear. I am definitely not saying that I wish on Lisa the tragedy that occurred. I certainly do not.

But, it would have been so hard for me to live with the knowledge that by laying his bike on his side, Bill had saved Lisa rather than Passenger X. I'm sure that Bill was hoping he would save *both* his passenger and himself by laying down his bike, but he took the brunt of the weight on himself, and that accounted for his fatal injuries.

Had Lisa survived, I might have spent the rest of my life blaming her for the accident—not that it would have been logical or fair of me to do so. But, I already felt betrayed over the affair, so I probably would have blamed the whole situation on her—the divorce, Bill's death, everything. I could envision telling myself that maybe, if she had not been in the picture, he wouldn't have been on the road that day.

I probably would have made her responsible for all my misfortune, the scapegoat for all my pain and misery.

Life did *not* go that way. Lisa did *not* survive. Bill and Lisa both passed away. Because of the way it played out, I do not blame Lisa for everything. I realize that Bill was partly to blame.

Again, it seems like this was the way it was supposed to happen for my life—and my children's. Because, although I have never, and would never, bring it up with them, I have a feeling they would have blamed Lisa, too.

The first week of November arrived.

I still did not have the signed death certificate, and I was getting very anxious. It had been nearly a month since the accident, and my compulsion to want things organized was in full swing. Without that one important document, I could not move forward. As I was expressing my frustration over this to someone—I can't recall who it was—they suggested I call the state police to see if I could find out what was happening with the investigation, and call the courthouse to ask about their protocol in expediting the death certificate.

So, I started calling around. I talked to the nicest Illinois police sergeants and detectives. I was a little nervous and intimidated at first, but they were so helpful and kind. Because I had an accident report number, I had somewhere to start. I explained that I was following up, and after being passed around to a few people, I finally got a very helpful detective who said he was handling the case. He was very informative and told me that my best bet was to contact the Madison County courthouse and coroner's office.

The life and motorcycle insurance companies were going to need not only the death certificate but all documentation concerning the accident. I knew I was going to need copies of the ambulance bills, so I had to call the hospital.

The red tape was unbelievable. Thankfully, because I work in the medical field, I had a better sense of what would be needed. And, I was lucky enough to talk to some very helpful people.

One of the first things I received was the accident report. It was the first time I had ever seen one, so I hadn't known what to expect. The document listed everyone involved, all the witnesses, the makes and models of the motorcycles and the truck. Up until that moment, I had known that there were small children in the truck, but that was all I knew.

The report listed their names and ages. That took me completely off guard. I replayed in my mind what I knew about the accident, and then I tried to imagine these children seeing it—at four, seven, and nine years of age.

A seven-year-old and a nine-year-old definitely would have known what they were looking at when they saw people lying in the road. I pictured their dad getting out of the truck to try to help Bill and the others, and the children waiting in the truck, and watching. My heart hurt for everyone involved.

The accident report also listed other witnesses. Situated between the two motorcycles and the truck they hit were the car they were passing when they crashed, and an oncoming car. There were witnesses in both vehicles, and the report contained statements from them. There was also a typed statement from the on-the-scene officer as to what he considered to be a probable scenario for the accident.

It was then that I realized that there was an investigation being done. I had assumed that there would be an investigation, but now I knew for sure. I had the report, the report number, and a notation that "due to the fatal injury of passenger one [Lisa], will be conducting investigation." Apparently, when a passenger dies but the driver survives, the driver is investigated. I thought to myself, poor Driver X; he has a long road ahead of him.

The first page of the report hit me hard because of the descriptions of the children in the truck. So did the last page. The policeman had drawn a diagram of the accident, using dashes to indicate the cycles from position to position, and then to their final resting position. Bill's cycle was called "unit two." I could see where it ended up laying on the road. The other cycle—"unit one"—was in a grass ditch. Looking at that took my breath away.

I had worked in the medical field for seventeen years, and I had read countless charts and various reports, but emergency room reports were one of my specialties. I called the hospital where Bill had been taken. They told me that it was no problem—if I faxed over my legal paperwork, they would fax me the medical records. At the time I made the request, I didn't anticipate how difficult it would be for me to read the emergency room records, but when they came in the next day, and I was actually holding them in my hands, I froze.

Okay, Shelly, I said to myself, you wanted to know what this says; now here's your chance. But, I couldn't bear to look. Finally, after telling myself I was being ridiculous, I opened it and started reading. There was the usual chicken scratch, which I had learned to decipher over many years in the medical field...

History and chief complaints: Unconscious. No complaints.

I started remembering being at the hospital that night.

Patient arrived in full cardiac arrest…CPR performed between accident site and emergency room.

So, they had not stopped doing CPR from the time of the accident all the way to the hospital.

Pupils dilated and fixed.

They had tried to put in a chest tube but there was too much blood.

As I read on, I started shivering and shaking. So many times I had read similar descriptions—thousands of times, in fact. But this time, the report was referring to Bill. It was so hard to wrap my brain around. I kept glancing up at the name on the report because my mind could not accept it.

The accident occurred between 7:00 and 7:15 p.m. Bill arrived at the hospital at 7:33. The time of death was listed as 8:30 p.m.

The remainder of the report set forth very basic information—until I got to the last several pages, where I found eight EKG strips, the last of which showed a flat line. I dropped all the papers on my desk. I was not prepared for that. Yet, I should have been. The EKG strips showed that the needle was going up and down, which meant they were administering CPR. That should have told me what I would find on the last page. But, when I turned the page and saw the flat line, it was devastating.

I got up and shut my office door, then sat back down, with tears rolling down my face. How could I have thought that because I was so accustomed to reading ER charts, it wouldn't have an effect on me?

It's very different when it hits so close to home.

~Early November~
Bad News/Good News

Buzz: "Sheriff, this is no time to panic."
Woody: "This is a perfect time to panic!"

~from "Toy Story"

On November 4th, Randa found out bad news. Her doctor was unhappy with the results from the pathologist. When they took out the tumors, they took out some of the tissue in the surrounding area. When they tested, they discovered they hadn't removed enough of the margins. They wanted to take out a little more. Better to be safe than sorry.

That meant that instead of being able to schedule and begin radiation, she had to schedule a second surgery. We were trying to find the silver lining.

I pointed out, "Well, at least you'll be able to get through the holidays without radiation."

At that point, she was seriously wondering whether she should just go ahead and have a mastectomy. She did not like the idea that they were going to keep cutting on her. But, I cautioned her not to overreact, and pointed out that her upcoming procedure was not as big a procedure as the first one.

She was fine with them taking out a little bit more of the margins. But, she'd already gotten herself into the mindset that she was on her way to recovery, and now she had to return to square one.

On November 6th, I talked to the Madison County Coroner assigned to Bill's case. It took me about five minutes on the phone with him before I realized who I was talking to.

I said, "Wait a minute. I remember you—you are Shane, the same coroner from the hospital!" When we were at the hospital, I had just assumed he was the one on call; I didn't realize he had actually been assigned to the case.

276

He remembered me as well, and told me that the night of Bill's accident was a night he would never forget.

Over the phone, I was every bit as impressed with him as I had been on the night of the accident. He was so helpful, explaining the death certificate process to me. He told me that when someone dies of natural causes, the surviving family gets the death certificate within a few days. But, because there was a toxicology report ordered, it could take months. Apparently, there was a big backlog of toxicology reports—a fact that was exacerbated by cutbacks.

He kept my hopes up by saying, "Just stay on top of it. It will come eventually, but don't hold your breath. It might be December or January."

December or January? I had been hoping the whole ordeal would be over by year's end.

Shane also explained that there would be an inquest with a jury. Because the death certificate was being submitted to the court for the judge's signature, it had to be determined whether Bill's death would be ruled an accident or suicide.

Suicide?!

I could not understand why a jury had to get involved, but he said that whenever someone dies of a questionable cause—as opposed to a natural cause—this was the protocol.

A questionable cause? I was blown away. It was clearly an accident!

Apparently, in the event of a vehicle accident, there was always an inquest at the courthouse. Then, and only then, would the death certificate be issued—provided that the jury determined it was an accident, and the judge signed off on it.

Before we hung up, Shane shared with me some of his own personal feelings over the death of a close friend. He said he knew how hard it was to go through the grief, encouraged me to hang in there, and told me it would all work out.

He was so kind and empathetic, just like he had been at the hospital. I was overwhelmed by how much compassion someone so young was able to express. He even gave me his cell phone number and invited me to call any time, day or night, if I had questions or concerns, or simply wanted any update. He also promised he would call me as soon as he heard anything. I really needed someone to show me that degree of kindness. I felt like I was in good hands.

I felt grateful to whoever it was that suggested I start making those phone calls, and I wished I could remember who they were so I could thank them properly. If I hadn't made those calls, I would never have talked to Shane, and I would never have known to go to the inquest.

I knew that the inquest wouldn't be any time soon. All I could do was wait.

In the meantime, I started preparing myself to deal with the new realities of my life—financial and otherwise. My uncle helped me recognize the things that were within my control, and he began giving me assignments. He knew I needed to stay occupied, and feel like I was moving things forward.

First, I had to go to the bank, let them know that Bill had passed away, and take whatever steps were necessary to get the balance for the estate. When I went in and told them about my situation, they were very helpful. The things I learned from them confirmed for me that I'd done the right thing by getting my divorce over with quickly. Bill had not been making the greatest financial decisions, which I had figured.

Then, on the 9th, I got a message from Shane telling me that the toxicology report had come back. I couldn't believe it! It was only three days since we had spoken, and he had been preparing me to wait months. He also told me, off the record, that *the report showed Bill had been under the legal limit for alcohol, and showed no sign of drugs in his system. In Illinois, the legal limit is .08, and he was at .052.*

When I heard that, I had the overwhelming desire to jump up and cheer. I knew in my gut that the report would show he wasn't drunk. I was tempted to call every person who had insensitively mentioned "drunk driving" in relation to Bill, and set them straight, starting with the writer of that article in the paper.

I couldn't wait to get home and tell Dylan and Payton because they, too, were certain the accident couldn't have been alcohol related. When I told them the news, they had the same reaction I did.

"That's it!" Dylan said. "I'm getting on the computer…"

I stopped him. "No, we are better people than that. We don't want to stoop to that level."

We all felt validated. Bill may have lost his mind in some sense, but, as sure as I knew my own name, I knew he would not be driving his motorcycle while he was drunk.

I called Bill, Sr. and Judy, as well as Jan, and everyone had the same reaction of excitement and outrage.

I also found out that the date for the inquest had been set for November 18th. I didn't have to go, but if I did, I could potentially walk away with the toxicology report and the signed death certificate. There was no question in my mind that I needed to go. The coroner and the detective would be getting up and talking about what happened during the accident, and I needed to hear what they had to say. My mom, God bless her, decided to come into town to be with me for the inquest. Everyone who loved me agreed I should not go alone.

A few days later, more good news! Passenger X was finally going home from the hospital. She would be getting a lot of physical therapy down the road, but at least she was going home. That was wonderful news, courtesy of her Caring Bridge page, which I had been following regularly.

Randa's second surgery ended up being set for the 20th of November. We were grateful that it wasn't set for the same day as the inquest, that it was scheduled before Thanksgiving, and that she'd be able to start radiation right after the holidays.

On the one hand, I suddenly felt like I was in the flow of life again, and things were starting to go well. I was excited about getting the final paperwork I needed. On the other hand, I was down in the dumps over the fact that my house still hadn't sold. The holidays were coming up, and I wanted to be able to relax in front of the Christmas tree lights without worrying whether there was a dog hair or a speck of dirt somewhere in the house that could potentially offend potential buyers.

~November 18th~
The Inquest

*"I've come to believe that each of us has a personal calling
that's as unique as a fingerprint,
and that the best way to succeed is to discover what you love
and then find a way to offer it to others in the form of service..."*

~by Oprah Winfrey

S hane had warned me to arrive early for the inquest, which was an hour and a half away in Madison County. He said that if I didn't get there early, I might not be able to find parking. I imagined a small town courthouse. How many people could there be?

When Mom and I pulled in to the parking lot, we started circling to find the right building, and noticed a line of about a hundred people out front. We were flabbergasted. Now, I understood why Shane had told me to wear good walking shoes.

We ended up having to park several blocks away in a bank parking lot. Then, when we finally found the right building and went inside, the guy in front of us in line tried to pass through the metal detector with an enormous fishing knife. Then, Mom set off the metal detector with her boots.

I was rattled before we ever got to the upstairs courtroom.

There was a case ahead of us. As we waited our turn outside the courtroom, we could hear traffic cases being called. We peered over the balcony onto the first floor to see the huge crowd that had been standing around outside, waiting to make its way inside. That explained the line around the building—traffic cases. Every so often, we peeked through the tiny glass window in the door to our courtroom, and could see the judge sitting at the bench.

We kept checking our watches, wondering what was taking Bill, Sr. so long to arrive. He really wanted to be there for the inquest, and it was getting closer and closer to the time for our hearing.

While we were waiting on Bill's father to arrive, a clerk approached us and asked who we were. The fact that we didn't know what we were doing must have been written all over our faces. I explained that we were there for the inquest, and he assured us that we were in the right place. Then, he introduced me to the detective I'd been talking to on the phone, who was very warm and comforting. It was good to put a face to the voice.

He explained what would happen during the inquest:

He would approach the bench and go over the police report. They would discuss the other motorcycle driver and what happened with him. But, he assured me that they were two separate cases, not related in any way. The other man was being investigated by the homicide division because of the death of Lisa. Since Bill died and his passenger lived, there was no homicide investigation.

I already knew much of what he told me, but I was stunned by the word "homicide." I asked him to clarify.

He explained that because the other driver's passenger, Lisa, had died, they had to wait on the toxicology report to determine whether he was intoxicated, and whether they would charge him with a crime.

He reassured me again that even though Bill and the other motorcycle driver had been riding together, Bill would not in any way be the subject of the investigation of the other driver. It had already been determined that Bill didn't cause the other guy to crash, and the other guy didn't cause Bill to crash.

The jury would consist of eight people who would listen to the coroner's report and the oral testimony of the detective, and then determine the cause of accident—which would then be stated on the death certificate. He also told me that the coroner would be reading his report in detail.

After his explanation, I realized that Bill's case really was cut and dried, but they had to go through the red tape because it was proper protocol.

Shane had already told me that, as much he would have liked to be at the hearing, he wouldn't be able to attend. He said that a colleague would be appearing in his place. He apologized and expressed regret over missing it, but said that he had worked all night and couldn't function.

The detective explained where we would sit in the back of the courtroom.

Still no Bill, Sr.

The detective wanted to know if anyone else was coming, and I said we were waiting for Bill's dad, who was on his way. He said, "Well, we've got to get started."

I said, "Okay, you're the boss," and into the courtroom we went. I was very nervous. There were other people sitting on benches in the same section, and knowing they had stayed in there from the previous case, I concluded that they must be trainees of some kind.

I did recognize one man as the chief coroner of Madison County, and I wondered if he would be speaking. I knew it was him because I'd seen him online when I had done a search for his email address. I emailed him a letter saying how Shane had gone above and beyond the call of duty the night of the accident. The chief sent me a lovely response, thanking me, and telling me that they don't hear positive comments often enough.

The judge began addressing the jury. He spoke in a very formal manner, saying, "This is the inquest of William… You are here to determine the cause of death—homicide, suicide, or accident. We have family members here today with us. We have the detective here, and the coroner investigator. Detective?"

The detective read his report—which was similar to the language in the accident report. He then spoke about the fact that another driver was involved, but that they were completely separate incidents. His conclusion: Bill's death was a horrible accident. Bill was not under the influence of alcohol. He lost control of the motorcycle.

None of this was news to me.

Then, the chief coroner started reading from the coroner's report. It was more detailed than I was expecting, and although I had never seen any photos, it came to light that some had been taken. They reviewed the photos and stated that the investigator, Shane, had taken the photos, examined Bill's body, and reviewed the x-rays. Before that, I had only a vague sense of what a coroner did; once I heard the details, I was even more impressed that someone as young as Shane had the knowledge, the intelligence, and the equilibrium to handle all that.

They talked in detail about Bill's chest injuries. It was nothing they hadn't told me at the hospital, but when I heard them read it in person, my hands started to shake and sweat. My mom took my hand.

So many cc's of blood were lost…the chest tube wouldn't go in because there was so much blood and damage…

Of course, I knew Bill had been hurt very badly. But, when they read about all the internal damage done from the weight of the motorcycle and the impact, as well as the details of the compound fracture in his leg, it was almost more than I could stand.

Two females members of the jury kept looking my way sympathetically. I wondered whether they thought I was Bill's wife. They were probably very confused, knowing the female passenger on the back of Bill's bike was not his wife. The passenger was referred to as "an unrelated person, not a family member" who survived the accident and recently went home from the hospital.

Listening to the report being read, I felt sick, and tears were flowing down my face. Mom was crying, too. It was so different hearing it read aloud in so much detail.

The judge then gave jury instructions to the jury, reminding them to keep in mind the fact that Bill was not under the influence. I found that curious, and didn't understand why they were stressing that.

The judge then dismissed everyone so the jury could enter into deliberations.

Although the proceedings were excruciating to me, they had taken no more than fifteen or twenty minutes.

Out in the hallway, the detective approached me to express again how sorry he was, and to invite me to call him if I had any questions.

I told him I'd expected the inquest to give more detail about what happened on the actual day of the accident—the events that had led up to the crash.

He told me that Driver X had already sought representation by an attorney, and had been advised not to discuss the accident. He also told me that they had not yet spoken to Passenger X, but would be talking to her. Without speaking to Passenger X, and without Driver X's willingness to discuss the crash, they didn't really know what happened that day, other than what they could surmise.

"I know you need that information for closure," he said.

I said, "Yes, and my kids also need to know."

"I understand," he said, "and I will make sure you get that information as soon as it becomes available." He seemed to sympathize with me completely.

We were out in the hall no more than ten or fifteen minutes before they called us back in.

The jury had reached their unanimous conclusion: *Accidental death due to chest trauma.* That would be the official statement issued on the death certificate.

I was not surprised, but I was relieved that it was official, and no longer in dispute.

I couldn't wait to finally get my hands on the death certificate and a copy of the toxicology report. When I asked the detective about it, he told me that I'd have to go next door to the coroner's office for the toxicology report, but I would not get the death certificate yet. He said I should have it by the end of the week.

I couldn't believe it. I was so sure I would walk away from the inquest with both of those documents.

He explained that because the accident had occurred in Illinois, and Bill's body had been released first to a funeral home in Illinois, the death certificate had to go there first. They had to sign off on it before it could be sent to Baue Funeral Home.

"But don't worry," he said, "it shouldn't take more than a few days. It's all done electronically through their system. So, be sure to call your funeral home and alert them that it's on its way."

At least I could get the toxicology report. Then, I only had to wait a few more days.

Before we left the building, Bill, Sr. arrived. He had gotten caught in traffic, and was beside himself that he had not gotten to hear what was said in the courtroom. My mom and I tried to comfort him. "You know how we thought we were going to learn what happened that day? Well, you didn't miss anything. They explained more about the physical trauma to Bill's body…"

He gave me a big, sincere hug, expressed how concerned he was for the kids and I in terms of our financial situation, and wanted to know if we were in need of money.

I was so touched. As I've said, he is generally a very reserved man.

I thanked him profusely but declined, telling him I'd let him know if we needed his help in the future. I also told him I was hopeful that the social security benefits for the kids would be coming in soon to help ease the burden.

He was so dear.

The three of us walked out, my mom and I heading to the other building for the toxicology report. When we got to the coroner's office, I inquired as to whether we would need extra certified originals of the toxicology report, and they said no. I figured I'd better check because I had been surprised to discover that we needed several originals of the death certificate. It's like a birth certificate—everyone wants to see an original. Luckily, when I'd stepped out of the room during the "arrangements" meeting at Baue, it was decided that we should get ten originals of the death certificate. Had I been present, I'm sure I would have ordered only one.

Driving back home, my mom and I reflected on everything that had happened in the last month, and how unreal it all seemed. It was the first time I was sharing my deepest emotions with someone other than my counselor.

Mom was so great. She sat and listened, and continued to reassure me that she and my dad would be there for whatever I needed. She even told me that they would come live with the kids and me for awhile if that's what we felt we needed. I felt so blessed to have a mom and dad who were willing to give up everything for me and whatever I might need.

At the same time that she let me know they'd be there for the kids and me, she said, "You can figure this out, Shelly."

That's the way they raised me—to know they were always there for me if I needed them; and to be able to figure things out on my own.

~Late November~
Thanksgiving

"Would you tell me I was wrong?
Would you help me understand?
Are you looking down upon me?
Are you proud of who I am?
There's nothing I wouldn't do to have just one more chance
To look into your eyes and see you looking back..."
"Hurt"

~by Aguilera/Perry/Ronson (Christina Aguilera)

After the inquest, I had two things on my mind—Randa's surgery, which was set for November 19th; and the death certificate, which I'd hoped to pick up at the inquest.

When I found out I wouldn't be getting the document at the hearing, I was encouraged by what the detective told me—that it would be sent electronically. To me, that meant instantaneous delivery. So, what was holding it up? Why couldn't the funeral home in Illinois push a button and send it to Baue for me?

When I called the funeral home in Illinois, the lady I spoke to explained to me that it was electronic *within* the state of Illinois, but, from state to state, it was all done manually.

I lost it. I started crying, and explaining to her that it was the last piece of paper I needed in order to move on.

"Well, the best we can do," she said, "is overnight it. But first, the judge needs to sign all the copies."

Okay, they were going to overnight them to me. Wonderful. I immediately called Baue and asked them to call me the second they arrived. I needed to get copies to my attorney, so he could get the ball rolling on all the things he had been delaying while he waited for the death certificate.

On the 19th, I got the usual three-word text from Randa's husband John, "Everything is fine." He was so cute. As I said, he wasn't a big texter, but he made the effort so I could have peace of mind.

Right after I got that text from John, I got a phone call from Baue, letting me know that the death certificates had finally arrived, and I could go pick them up!

I raced over there.

As I turned the corner and saw the funeral home, my stomach dropped, and my forearms, which had a white-knuckle grip on the steering wheel, started shaking. I had been so anxious for the death certificates to arrive, I hadn't really thought much about the fact that I'd have to pick them up at the funeral home where Bill's services were held. Now that the moment had come, I wasn't sure I could walk in there.

I sat in my car, debating. Maybe I could call them from the car and ask them to bring them out to me. Then I thought, this is ridiculous! You can do this! Just go one step at a time. So, in slow motion, I walked up there. Before I even had the door completely open, I was assaulted by the familiar smell. I had to talk myself into proceeding. Okay, I told myself, the papers are right there at the front desk. You are just going to grab them and leave.

Thankfully, the lady was sitting right there at the desk, and handed me my envelope. I said, "Great, thank you very much!" And, then silently, I said, "And bye-bye!"

As I left, I let out a big exhale. I had been holding my breath because I didn't want to smell that super-sweet fragrance one second longer than I had to. I've been to three funerals since Bill's, and they were tough enough; had they been at the very same funeral home, I don't think I could have handled it.

I rushed to my car, and then I was out of there.

I went right to my uncle's and gave him most of the originals, keeping a few for myself. After handing them over to him, I let out a huge sigh of relief. Now, Denny could take over. He had everything already prepared to mail to the insurance companies, and now, at last, he had the green light to move ahead.

I had been so focused on getting the death certificates. I was finally able to let go, and not have to worry anymore.

Now, what was I going to do? I had to find something else to fill my time.

Wait! I knew what to do! Once Denny mailed the death certificates, I could go into follow-up mode. Perfect. That would keep me from losing my mind.

That evening I called Randa, asked her what kind of food she was in the mood for, and brought her dinner. When I got there, she was in much better spirits than after the first surgery. Still, we couldn't believe she'd had to go through that again—the ice packs, the soreness. The doctors had told her they would be checking all the cells again to make sure there were no cancer cells in the new margins. They didn't expect there to be. Provided everything went well, Randa could start radiation as soon as she healed. She was not a candidate for chemotherapy because the cancer was not very advanced.

We had a nice visit, and then I left her in the good hands of her husband, who was doing a great job of keeping the kids out from under foot so she could get some rest.

I was so thankful that she had made it through surgery with no apparent complications.

Next on the agenda—Thanksgiving.

The kids and I had a powwow and agreed that if we were going to be in our old house for Christmas, at least we should get new Christmas ornaments. Payton and I came up with a lime green and silver color scheme, went shopping for the tree, and true to family tradition, made sure we put it up before Thanksgiving. That's how we have always kicked off our holidays.

None of us were fooled into thinking that we were about to have a Norman Rockwell Christmas. The loss of Bill made that impossible. But, we did have to admit that the tree looked beautiful. In fact, everyone was saying it looked so good, it could have been in Macy's.

I couldn't have agreed more. I like a lot of lights on my tree, and that year, we went all out. It was so nice to kick up our feet in the evenings and just watch the tree flicker.

We had a beautiful Christmas tree. Now, we just had to figure out how to get through the holidays without Bill. "Don't worry," everyone was saying, "you'll get through it, just like you'll get through all the other firsts. There will be a first for everything."

The one saving grace was that Thanksgiving—which wasn't a big deal in our family—came before Christmas, which was a big deal. For Thanksgiving, our only tradition was dinner with the whole family. It seemed like a good "practice" holiday.

For many years, the BMX racing Olympics were held over Thanksgiving weekend, and we weren't even in town for the holiday. The fact that we knew there was a big event that would keep us out of town for the Thanksgiving holiday helped to make it less of a big deal for us. When we were in town, we usually went to my brother's house. Mitch and Theresa's house was the perfect place for a big gathering, because they had plenty of room.

For Thanksgiving 2009, along with the kids and me, the cast of characters included my parents, Uncle Denny and Aunt Vickie, and my grandparents, who were in town from Arkansas. Granny Franny loves to cook with Crisco, and she usually brings an outstanding homemade pie or two. Everyone looks forward to her delicious pies.

Dylan and Payton both seemed to be in fine spirits as we got ready to go over to Mitch and Theresa's, and I actually thought we might slide through the day with no problem.

Whenever my family gets together, there's usually a friendly game of chance, and this year it was a Texas Hold-em tournament. Dylan plays, and he was really looking forward to wiping the floor with his relatives. Last year, the competition came down to him and my brother. Mitch won. Dylan was planning his revenge.

Later, I was teasing Mitch. "You're a horrible uncle! You should have let your nephew win!"

"Well, I may have won," Mitch said, "but you seem to have forgotten that I gave Dylan half my winnings!"

"Good! You better have given him half the money," I said. "You should have let him win!"

We got there, everyone started talking, and the adults started breaking out the hard stuff. It was about three o'clock in the afternoon. Since we only lived ten minutes away, I felt safe having a drink. So, I was drinking a glass of wine, and thinking, oh, my gosh, we are actually going to pull this off.

Everyone was acting as if nothing had ever happened. I thought, well, if that's the way we have to do it, then that's the way we'll do it. Then, when we were all gathered in the kitchen, and just about to sit down to dinner, Payton started sobbing.

My mom and I were standing nearby. "What's wrong, Sweetie?"

She said, "I miss my daddy! Why isn't he here? I hate this! It is so unfair."

I immediately started to cry right along with Payton.

My mom had the presence of mind to take over, inviting Payton to go into Mitch and Theresa's room with her to have a talk. I was so thankful she stepped in. Otherwise, Payton and I would have both been crying hysterically, amidst a house full of people.

About ten minutes later, Payton and my mom came back out and joined the party. Payton's tears had dried, and she took a seat by my side at the table, and started eating. I didn't know what Mom had said to her, but Payton had obviously found it comforting, and was clearly feeling better.

I never mix champagne with anything else—but I had started the festivities with mixed drinks, and then someone opened a bottle of champagne with dinner. Every time I turned around, my glass was full. By the time the after-dinner card game started, I was feeling no pain. I was definitely drowning my sorrows—drinking to cover my pain and sadness. That is not my usual behavior around alcohol, but, on that first holiday since Bill's death, it was the best survival mechanism I could muster.

I was completely trashed to the point where I was giggling and mumbling—or so I was told later. The last thing I remembered of the evening, Dylan was winning at cards.

Somehow, seeing their mom wasted turned out to be a good thing for the kids. They were able to have a good laugh, and enjoy watching their mom act like an idiot. They had never, ever seen me in that condition, and they thought it was hysterical. Oddly enough, my drunkenness lightened the mood, and helped them get through what could have been a dark holiday.

Dylan won the card game, and then drove Payton and me home. He was so excited—eighty dollars in his pocket, and a chance to be the adult behind the wheel of the car.

When we got home, the kids had to help me upstairs. I got in the shower, and apparently Payton listened for the water to turn off, worrying that I might never make it out of the shower.

The next morning was Black Friday—the perfect name for how I woke up feeling. I was supposed to pick up my mom to go shopping. We had learned by then that our days of getting up at four o'clock in the morning were behind us, so we usually went at seven. Around eight o'clock in the morning, my phone rang. It was Mom, saying, "I guess you're not coming to get me."

I groaned. "Why did you guys let me drink so much?"

Mom said, "We figured you needed it."

I had a killer hangover. I couldn't even get any relief over the porcelain bowl.

What was worse, in addition to our now ruined shopping plans, Kenny was supposed to be coming over to spend some time with Payton. As I've mentioned, my daughter is obsessed with the *Twilight* movie series, and the three of us were supposed to go see *New Moon*. Because Kenny had not yet seen the first *Twilight* yet, we were supposed to watch the DVD, go have lunch, and then go see *New Moon*.

How in the world was I going to make it through the day?

I decided to put one shaky foot in front of the other, and take it nice and slow. First, I took a shower. Then, I went in search of my hangover remedy: real—not diet—Pepsi, specifically from a fountain, not a can.

I actually started to feel vaguely human after the shower and the Pepsi.

That's when my kids started reminiscing about my antics, and sharing with me what a great time they had the night before. Watching their drunken mother allowed my kids to share a good laugh. And, being blasted got me through our first holiday without Bill. All in all, I was embarrassed, but grateful we had made it through that hurdle. Hopefully, Christmas would be less of a fiasco.

Once I was feeling more functional, I started preparing for Kenny to come over, and Dylan took off to hang out with friends.

Kenny spent the day with a twelve-year-old and her hung-over mom. We all had a wonderful time. I even began to think of Kenny as my "fix." He was totally catering to us—opening doors and paying a lot of attention to Payton.

After her Thanksgiving meltdown, she really needed that.

At the end of the day, he made us promise to see *Eclipse* with him when it came out.

"Just let me know when you want us there," I said.

What a great day it turned out to be. Life was definitely unfolding in a surprising way.

Meanwhile, I was checking the mail every day to see if we had gotten responses from the various insurance companies. One day a certified letter came in the mail. I thought, oh, no, this can't be good. I had to go the post office to pick it up, and when the postal clerk handed me the envelope, it had the return address of an Illinois lawyer.

"Do I have to accept the letter?" I joked.

The postal clerk was not amused.

As I walked to the car, I knew I was about to find out that Passenger X was suing Bill's estate. I opened the letter. Sure enough!

I called Denny right away. He told me to fax him the letter, and promised to call Passenger X's attorney in the morning, and tell him there was really nothing *in* the estate to help cover her medical expenses. What *was* in the estate would cover the costs of Bill's funeral and attorney's fees, but barely.

As to the insurance policy money, thank God, it turned out to be untouchable because the kids were the named beneficiaries, after all. Whenever there is a named beneficiary, that money is also protected. Only assets without beneficiaries—like a house—go into an estate. Because I was legally divorced, and the house was granted solely to me in the divorce, it was not part of Bill's estate.

Bill had debt in his own name, and that debt would go against any money in the estate—unless there was nothing left in the estate, in which case the debt would be written off. I was horrified to discover that the joint debt we would have been splitting between us according to our divorce decree, now fell entirely on my shoulders because Bill was deceased.

If we were simply divorced, I would have only been fifty percent responsible for our joint debt, but since Bill was deceased, I was one hundred percent responsible? That meant that creditors were willing to accept a certain amount of money from me, the ex-Mrs.-So-and-So towards the debt. But, if they couldn't get the rest of the money from my ex-husband due to the fact that he had died, then they were perfectly prepared to come after me for the entire amount. If it hadn't been happening directly to me, I would never have believed it.

Denny got involved. He called the creditors on the joint debt we owed, and tried to get them to accept the same fifty percent I would have been liable for had Bill lived. No dice. Only one was willing to go along with that arrangement. They did not consider our divorce decree to be a legally binding legal document. As far as they were concerned, if Bill was alive to pay his share of the debt, great; if not, someone had to pay it, and that someone was me.

As for the certified letter from the attorney, I was again filled with the same mixed feelings I had been experiencing all along. On the one hand, I understood that she needed to get her medical expenses covered. On the other hand, I wanted to ask, "Why are you going to try to take money from the estate of a divorced man with two children? All they have left of their father is the money from his estate. You are alive and their dad is dead!"

Denny assured me that there was nothing to worry about.

~December~
Playing it by Ear

"I'll be right here where you need me
Anytime, just keep believing
and I'll be right here,
If you ever need a friend,
Someone to care and understand
I'll be right here,
All you have to do is call my name
No matter how close or far away
Ask me once and I'll come,
I'll come running,
And when I can't be with you
Dream me near,
Keep me in your heart
And I'll appear..."
"Right Here"

~by James/Cyrus/Amato (Miley Cyrus)

B y early December, all of the financial and insurance matters were pending completion. Once I'd sent in the death certificates, I began the process of following up, as I'd promised myself I would.

Before Bill's death, his employer had always been the provider of our family's health insurance. Now, I had to find new insurance for the kids. Time to educate myself on the subject. It was kind of funny—I work around insurance all the time, yet, thanks to the City of St. Peters, I'd never had to give it much thought.

What now?

My employer offered health insurance, but it was costly. I was accustomed to paying practically nothing for all four of us to be on Bill's policy through the city. After the divorce, the kids stayed on Bill's policy—but their policy through the city was only good through the end of the year.

Even though I had dealt with insurance extensively through my job, I was now on the other side of the equation. The first few inquiries I made showed me how expensive it could be. I realized I was going to need to shop around to get a reasonable price. If you take the time to really do your research, you can find a fairly decent policy for your kids. This is what I recommend to any parent who pays for their own insurance through their employer and is considering adding their children to their policy: make sure you really shop around; if you do your research, and really compare rates, you can save yourself money.

I was able to save three hundred dollars a month over what I would have paid to have the kids on my policy at work, and I got a policy that really matched my kids' needs. I was thrilled to death—and I learned my lesson about shopping around to get better pricing. In the beginning of doing my research, it looked like I would go broke just getting health insurance for the kids.

The kids and I were still seeing our counselor, Marcy. Payton and I were going every two or three weeks and Dylan, who felt he was really doing well, was seeing her only on an as-needed basis.

Payton was very comfortable with Marcy, who had kids of her own. Marcy wasn't able to reveal much to me because of doctor-patient confidentiality, but in giving me the broad brushstrokes, she told me that therapy really seemed to be helping Payton. She was opening up about everything—not just Bill.

My sessions with Marcy were definitely centered around my feelings over Bill, and how much I needed to work on expressing my emotions. I tend to keep everything real close to my heart. I was never going to be as expressive as someone with a different personality type, but we were making progress.

I'd had some little meltdowns in front of her in the beginning, but I was really starting to feel better. Now, I enjoyed seeing her, but I didn't feel like I needed it quite as badly. Even my shower meltdowns were becoming less frequent—not that they were gone entirely.

One thing heavily on my mind was the upcoming Christmas holiday. I had no idea how to handle it. Should I talk openly and freely about Bill? Should I wait for the kids to say something to me? More than anything in the world, I did not want my children to hurt anymore. I needed one of the wise men from those nativity scenes to magically come to life, and tell me what to do!

Being up in the air over Christmas was eating away at my soul and making me a nervous wreck.

Finally, after a lot of sleepless nights, I started to hear a little voice in the back of my mind, telling me there was no wrong or right way to do things. I realized I had no choice but to play it by ear.

In the weeks leading up to Christmas, I dropped little comments about how pretty our tree looked, and how glad I was that we had done something different this year, because our lives *were* different.

If the kids chimed in, then I might run with that line of conversation a bit more. If they didn't, I backed off.

In the past, we had always gotten a real Christmas tree. As much as I truly loved the lime green and silver tree we picked out, and as much as it seemed fitting to have something different now that Bill was gone, I missed the smell of pine. So, I pulled out the pine candles I had squirreled away, and kept them burning nearly twenty-four/seven. The minute I got home from work, I would light a candle, and it would put me in the holiday spirit.

The kids got to the point where they were saying, "Alright! Enough already with the pine candles," but I couldn't give them up.

I also felt that we needed to find a way to acknowledge Bill at Christmas. It was such an important holiday for our family. I asked the kids what they thought about getting some sort of memorial candle for Bill, and told them I knew of a specialty store in Old Town St. Charles, where they could surround a candle in hurricane glass, and put memorabilia around the glass. I discussed it with Randa, and we talked about the kinds of memorabilia we could include—something to remind us of Bill's Harley, and the St. Louis Blues hockey team.

I was surprised when both kids said that they absolutely hated the idea. They did not explain themselves—they simply said they didn't want that candle around.

I really wanted to make it as good a Christmas for them as I could. I had always overindulged them with gifts, making sure I got them at least one big thing off their wish lists. I loved seeing their faces as they opened the gifts. It was priceless.

Now, I was really torn. The part of me that loves Christmas wanted to spend every dime I could on the kids, so they would have a special Christmas. The realistic side of me was aware that we only had one income, now, and we needed to be careful. The problem was, if the kids didn't get their usual over-the-top Christmas, they would remember it not only as the year they lost their father, but the year that Christmas started to change.

I decided I would tell everyone in my family that any gift money I had was going to my kids. Everyone said, "Of course! Absolutely!"

I watched for sales in advance of Christmas, and tried to pick up things when they were discounted. Doing Christmas shopping helped me feel a little better about the holiday. There was no getting around the fact that it was a different kind of Christmas, but at least shopping gave me a place to focus my attention and energy. I didn't try to make up for the absence of Bill by purchasing *extra* gifts for the kids. I just bought the usual amount.

I felt good that even in the midst of a difficult time, I had been able to purchase the gifts Santa would need to make the tree look special. I had no control over the fact that my children's father would not be there on Christmas morning when they came down the stairs, but at least I could control what they saw around the tree.

We always celebrated Christmas Eve with the whole family at Mitch and Theresa's house. Then, my mom and dad—who live at the lake house—would sleep over and wake up with us. On Christmas Day, we would all congregate at our house, and invite Jan to join us, so the kids could stay at home with their gifts, rather than having to leave the house to be with her.

The week before Christmas, we got the news that Randa needed a third surgery. The doctor told her that even though he had taken out extra margins, he wanted to go a little further out. At this point, I was hoping she would get a second opinion, but I knew how discouraging it would be to have to start over from square one with someone new. She was, understandably, very down. She decided that at some point, she would just tell them to do a mastectomy so she could have it over and done with, once and for all.

Her third surgery was set for January 8th—which meant we had to get through the holidays with that hanging over our heads. We all tried to stay busy and upbeat, but it was in the back of our minds.

Meanwhile, with Christmas around the corner, we were all watching the weather. We hadn't had a white Christmas in several years. As I've mentioned, a white Christmas had always meant one thing for our family—Bill would have to work, plowing the streets.

Now, I wished for snow.

~Christmas~
The Holiday Spirit

"Long you live and high you fly,
Smiles you'll give and tears you'll cry,
All you touch and all you see
Is all your life will ever be..."
"Breathe"

~by Pink Floyd

O n Christmas Eve, we went over to Mitch and Theresa's, where my entire family and Theresa's entire family gathered around tons of presents. I had called Jan in advance, and made arrangements for us to meet at her house after Christmas, so she was not with us.

We managed to enjoy Christmas Eve without tears—perhaps because we had gotten our breakdowns out of the way at Thanksgiving. Now that the same people were gathered together again, there was no doubt in my mind that everyone was having their private moments of sadness and grief. But, there wasn't a dam waiting to burst.

We sat down to dinner. There was ham for the meat-eaters, and for us vegetarians, pasta with red sauce. Usually, we linger over the dinner table, but that year, we didn't want to make the kids wait to open their presents.

When Bill was still alive, he, Uncle Denny, and Mitch used to be the ones to hand out gifts to everyone. That night, Dylan stepped in for his father, and started passing out presents.

My grandmother, God love her, is a complete character, and every year, we wait with bated breath to see what unusual gift she is going to give. Sometimes she comes up with something truly surprising. Other times, she embroiders quilts and gives them to the kids.

297

One year, Bill teased her, saying, "Hey, where is my quilt? You never gave me a quilt!" The next year, she presented him with his very own quilt.

When Randa and I were packing up his things after the divorce, I said, "Make sure to put that in the box for Bill."

Randa said, "Why let him have it? Your grandmother made that!"

I said, "Yeah, but she made it just for him."

Sure enough, when he came to pick up his things, he made a point to ask which box the quilt was in. I shared that story with my grandmother on Christmas Eve, so she would know that the quilt had meant a lot to him.

Everyone had fun watching each other open their gifts. There was plenty of egg nog, wine, and beer for the adults, and soda for the kids. When everyone started getting sleepy, we loaded up our car with gifts, and so did Mom and Dad.

My grandparents, who live in Arkansas, were staying at Vickie and Denny's. They would stop by our house the next day before heading back home.

Mom and Dad headed over to my house, where we all unloaded the kids' gifts into the living room, so they could enjoy them again on Christmas morning.

It was about eleven o'clock at night. The weather forecast was predicting a light dusting of snow. It was already misting outside. The temperature just needed to drop enough for it to snow. Just like I always know by the scent of the air whether or not it is going to rain, I could tell that snow was on its way. My fingers were crossed.

It was the one night of the year that the kids couldn't wait to go to bed. They ran upstairs, anxious to take a shower and hop into bed. They have a tradition where, on Christmas Eve, Payton always sleeps on Dylan's floor, so whoever awakens first can wake up the other one. It never fails that they wake up before the sun rises, wake us up, and tell us it is time to go downstairs.

Once the kids showered, they made a pallet on Dylan's floor for Payton. My dad also went off to bed.

Mom and I still had to collect the Santa gifts from their hiding places around the house, and wrap them. That year, Dylan's wrapping paper color was dark blue and Payton's was light blue. They each had a stocking with their name on it. Once I was sure the kids were asleep, I started bringing everything downstairs to wrap.

Mom's back and leg were acting up, so I sent her to bed. I knew I could handle the wrapping by myself. About an hour later, as I was finishing up, I could feel the sadness brewing inside. I turned off all the lights except the Christmas tree lights, sat on the couch, and sobbed.

What happened to my life? How had I become the only Santa in the house? I missed Bill tremendously, and felt overwhelmed by sadness and loneliness. A moment later, I felt angry at the way he had hurt the kids and me. A moment later, the longing and heartache returned. As my tears flowed, I reflected on so many wonderful Christmases together.

When I couldn't stand it any longer, I headed upstairs. I left the Christmas tree lights on so that when the kids got up with the roosters, they would see the tree all lit up. It was one-thirty by the time I fell asleep, knowing full well I would be awakened in a few hours by my excited son and daughter, anxious to greet Christmas morning.

The next thing I knew, my lovely beagle, Mia—who happens to be the perfect height to put her head on my bed—was staring me down. She does that every morning. It is her way of signaling that she needs to go out. She is too ladylike to bark, but she doesn't need to make a sound. I can feel her staring at me, and it wakes me up.

I was startled to see that it was light outside. What was going on? Why hadn't the kids gotten me out of bed? Surely they were not sleeping at seven o'clock on Christmas morning. I felt like a new mother as I tiptoed down the hall to make sure they were still breathing.

They looked like two angels at rest, so I went downstairs, plugged in the rest of the lights, lit all the candles, and got the coffee started. As I passed by the flag we had been presented with at Bill's funeral, I noticed the candle I had placed in front of it but never burned. In that moment, I decided that candle would be the memorial candle I'd been longing for.

"This is for you, Bud" I said aloud as I lit it. "I miss you. You will be in my thoughts all day today."

I went back upstairs and snuck into Dylan's room, where I found a couple of fakers giggling under the covers. Once they were out of bed, we woke up my mom and dad, and went downstairs.

Mom started cooking breakfast, and I basked in the glow on the kids' faces as they opened their gifts from Santa. Normally, it would have been Bill cooking, and joining me in drinking a mimosa.

Every so often, I would glance over at one of the kids as they opened a present, and smile to myself. I could feel the presence of a higher power, letting me know that Bill was right there with me, taking comfort in knowing I had done a good job in getting us through the aftermath of the tragedy, and our first holiday season without him.

I could almost hear Bill saying, "You did it, Shell. You pulled off the holiday season."

It was true. The kids *were* doing pretty well.

I decided to leave the memorial candle burning for him all day long.

At one point that morning, as I let Mia out the door to do her business, I gasped. It had snowed!

It was one more sign that this Christmas was different in every way. It was just a light dusting of snow, but it would have been enough to send Bill off to work on the snowplow. Not this year. Finally, he could rest.

We all spent the day lounging in our pajamas, eating, drinking, hugging, talking, laughing, and watching the kids with their gifts. Payton even treated us to a fashion show of her new clothes. It was a very relaxing day, and before we knew it, night had come. The following day, I would be taking the kids over to Jan's to spend some holiday time with her.

Christmas passed with no outward expression of sadness from the kids. But, as we looked out at the snow on the ground, I knew we all shared the same thought: Any other year, Bill would have been out there doing his duty for the City of St. Peters, clearing the snow off the roads for those families who were heading home to their loved ones for the holiday.

It was so strange to think that Bill would never be coming home to his own family again.

~January, 2010~
A New Year

"If ever there is a tomorrow when we're not together,
there is something you must always remember:
You're braver than you believe,
stronger than you seem,
and smarter than you think.
But the most important thing is,
even if we're apart,
I'll always be with you."
(Christopher Robin to Pooh)
"Winnie the Pooh"

~by A.E. Milne

Bill and I were very aware of what could happen on the roads on New Year's Eve, so our plans always kept us close to home. We usually went to a local restaurant and a movie, had friends over, or went to a friend's party, as long as they lived nearby.

Since his accident, I was more inclined than ever to stay off the roads.

For New Year's Eve 2010, the kids were each going over to a friend's house, and I was going to Randa's for her annual New Year's Eve party and lobster race. Yep—every year, she orders fresh lobsters, brings them home, and lets the kids have lobster races with them on the kitchen floor before the crustaceans become dinner for her family and friends.

Randa's father started the tradition when she was little, and she has kept it up throughout the years. She is the most wonderful cook, and day in and day out, her kids eat better than any kids I know. But, on New Year's Eve, she really goes all out.

301

Being a vegetarian, the whole concept of lobster is lost on me. I'm not about to dip a lobster tail in butter and put it in my mouth. And, watching them crawl across the kitchen floor on the way to their death makes my hair stand on end.

But, I always get a kick out of how much Randa enjoys the whole spectacle. And, other than the lobsters giving me the willies, we had a lovely evening. I even got to meet some friends of Randa's for the first time.

Randa and I made a pact. "We have to make 2010 a good year for us both. We have been through so much already, and we still have more to go through, but we will make it through whatever is to come, just as we've made it this far."

A little bit after the stroke of midnight, I decided I better head home. I didn't want to be out driving too late. The mere thought of getting pulled over gave me a heart attack—not that I was drunk; not by a long shot. In fact, my mind was clear, and I was reflecting upon how much I was looking forward to putting 2009 behind me.

Suddenly it hit me—I was looking forward instead of backward! Hope was returning.

January 1st is my dad's birthday. Mine is on the 4th. So, on New Year's Day, we did a joint celebration with the whole family, just as we did every year. When I was growing up, my mom did a really good job of separating our birthdays so we each felt like we had our own special day, but when we became adults, it just made sense to celebrate together, with the whole family present.

On January 3rd, the kids and I headed down to Bill's parents' house in Cuba, which, as you know by now, is an hour and a half away from us in the country. Every year for twenty-four years, Bill and I had seen his parents after Christmas, and the kids and I were looking forward to relaxing with that side of the family. Bill, Sr. and Judy had already sent the kids a cash gift for the holiday, so this visit was just a chance to be together over a meal.

Bill's half-sister and brother, Jeri Ann and Michael, were there, as always. Traditionally, Judi, Jeri Ann, and I spent the day chatting while Bill, his dad, Dylan, and Michael spent the day outside messing around on four-wheelers. Despite the fact that Bill wasn't with us, the visit unfolded in much the same way.

Naturally, everyone seemed to be experiencing their own personal moments of remembrance and grief, but all in all, we had a great time.

On the drive back home, the kids fell asleep. I was happy we had honored the tradition, and made the trip. And, I reflected on how good it felt to be with everyone in a setting other than the funeral. We needed that happy time together.

As I was driving, it grew dark, and I thought, wait, this isn't the way it's supposed to be. I'm not supposed to be the one driving. I'm supposed to be sleeping along with the kids while Bill drives.

I couldn't get over how profoundly everything had changed from one year to the next. Here it was, the beginning of January, and I was looking forward to whatever 2010 might bring like I had never looked forward to anything in my life. It couldn't come fast enough for me.

It seemed like an eternity ago that I had been looking forward to 2009 and all the milestones it would bring—including my fortieth birthday. That's when it hit me. My forty-first birthday was the next day! Because we had already celebrated it along with my dad's birthday, I'd totally forgotten.

Since I had already had the joint celebration with my dad, January 4th was uneventful. I barely gave a thought to my birthday. I was totally focused on Randa's upcoming surgery.

The evening before each of her surgeries, I had brought her dinner and a little gift. Now, she was on her third surgery. Thankfully, the surgery went wonderfully well. Because the operation was on a Friday, we had to wait until Monday for the pathology results—which came back right on time.

Everything was fine! At long last, she could schedule radiation and we could begin to put the whole thing behind us.

Also in January, Payton and I went with a group of families to a gymnastics meet in Florida. I really needed to get away, and I always loved being with the other families. It reminded me of the BMX days. I was also looking forward to four days of lounging on a warm beach. Since we had chosen to go to Seattle, rather than a beach destination, on our last family vacation, I was ready for the beach.

Payton did very well in her meet, and we both had a great time. There was only one odd moment. One of the gymnastics dads did not know my whole story. The last he had heard, I was divorced. So, in a very upbeat voice, he asked me, "So, are you ready to start dating?"

I said, "Wow, you're the first one to ask me that. No, I'm really *not* ready."

His wife apologized, saying, "Don't blame him. He didn't know."

I wasn't offended—just startled. For the first time in twenty-four years, the "D" word was going to become part of my vocabulary—dating! The concept scared me to death. It seemed like a good time for some healthy denial. I would think about dating later—much later.

Meanwhile, just as I was starting to relax, there was more Facebook drama. Just what I needed.

It happened on the evening of Wednesday, January 20th, while Dylan and I were watching TV. It was after 9:00. Payton was already upstairs in bed.

The home phone rang, which was unusual. If someone was going to call at that hour, they usually called on my cell phone.

I picked up, and heard a woman yelling at me. At first, I could only understand bits and pieces of what she was saying.

"You are such a bitch," she yelled. "You don't even realize what you've done!"

I was dumbfounded, staring at the phone. Dylan noticed that something funny was going on, and started staring at me.

Her last words to me were "Watch your f***ing back!" Then she hung up.

What in the world? I had not been able to get a word in edgewise.

Dylan said, "Mom? What was that?"

I said, "Dyl, is there anything you need to tell me? Are you having problems with anyone?"

That was the only thing I could figure—that something had happened with the kids. There was sure as hell nothing going on in my life that would have brought on a phone call like that.

It took a few minutes to get over the fact that some stranger had just called me a bitch. Then, Dylan and I went back to watching TV.

The phone rang again. This caller started off the same way, and ended with, "How dare you think you can shut down our site?!"

I was still in the dark as to what they were talking about.

Dylan suggested, "It's probably Payton. Maybe she's in a fight with someone."

Then it occurred to me what was happening. "No," I said, "I think it's Facebook. Lisa's friends created a memorial page on there, mainly of Lisa, but with some pictures of the two of them. I filed a complaint."

He said, "Oh, my God! *Whatever.*"

I went over to the computer, and tried to pull up the memorial page on Facebook, but nothing came up. Ah, I thought, that must be why these people are beside themselves.

I called Randa. "You're never going to believe this. I'm getting prank phone calls and threats from these crazy people. How can they not understand that my kids don't need to see Bill and Lisa drunk together on that memorial page?"

Randa got on Facebook and started fishing around. She found someone who had posted something on their wall to the effect of, "I have this f***ing bitch's phone number. Who wants it?"

I could not believe these women in their mid-forties were carrying on like this. I became outraged. Bring it on, was my attitude. You put my number up there and I will call the police!

Randa read me some other threatening posts along the lines of, "Give me her number. By the time I get done with her, she'll have to get her number changed."

It was surreal. I was in complete amazement.

I called my mom, who suggested I take the phone off the hook. Before I had a chance, another call came in. This time, I was ready. The caller started accusing me of having no sensitivity towards the mourners who needed a place to share happy thoughts about Lisa and Bill. Then, she proceeded to tell me she had known Bill for his whole life.

That put me over the edge.

"Oh, no you have not!" I said, "You knew him in grade school, and in the last ninety days of his life. What about the thirty years in the middle? I bet you did not give him a single thought in all that time!"

Then the woman brought up Lisa's mother, and suggested I was hurting her by having the site removed, and I said, "Then Lisa's mother is not the mother I thought she was. I don't know any mom who wants to see pictures of their drunken daughter. And how dare you act like *I'm* a bad person, and blame *me* for asking to have the page shut down! It was on *you* to make the memorial page private. It so happens that I contacted Lisa's mother and returned her belongings, which is more than any normal person would have done in this situation."

"For over twenty years," I continued, "Bill was a devoted family man…His children do not need to see that memorial page…You have a lot of nerve calling my house and harassing me…You need to grow up."

"Well, then," she said, "if you are just trying to protect your children, why not block them from that page?"

I asked if she had children of her own, and she said she did.

"Then you know that if I block my kids on our home computer, they will simply go over to a friend's house to see it!"

I suggested that maybe she would like to wake up her own children, take them over to her computer, and show them pictures of their daddy and his girlfriend.

As a friend of Lisa's, she didn't go so far as to agree with me. But, she admitted she'd also been married a long time, and by the end of the conversation, she agreed that there were two sides to every story.

I felt satisfied. Even though she didn't apologize or back down entirely, she did seem to see and understand my point.

For the next several nights, I left the home phone off the hook. That did the trick. The harassing phone calls stopped.

Lisa's friends did put the memorial page back up, but this time it didn't have Bill's name on it, and was accessible by permission only.

It took some investigating, but I figured out how everyone knew it was me who had shut down the original page. When I filed my complaint with Facebook, I had to submit my name. When Facebook acted on my complaint, a message was sent out to the effect that I had found the memorial page offensive, and after looking into the matter, Facebook determined that I had good reason. So, they were shutting down the page.

And they mentioned me by name!

I was horrified. For the next several days, I tried to get Facebook to see that revealing my name was dangerous. I got nowhere with them. But, at least they took down the page.

Best of all, I had gotten someone in Lisa's circle of friends to listen to my side of the story. The things I pointed out to her were things I'd been itching to say for so long.

Randa wanted the chance to give them a piece of her mind, as well, and I loved her for it. But, I felt like we were better off not climbing back into the sandbox with those people. No good would come of it.

So much for 2010 being my drama-free year. I was only twenty days into it, and already, my head was spinning.

~February—March~
A Brand New Year, Take Two

"It is only with the heart
That one can see rightly.
What is essential is invisible to the eye."
"The Little Prince"

-by Antoine de Saint-Exupery

February would bring my brother's birthday on the sixth and my mom's on the fifteenth—tax day! It was time to prepare my taxes.

For the previous two years, we had filed online, but I figured this year was going to be more complicated. Between Bill being gone, and the kids having already received their money from the estate, I knew it wasn't going to be a typical tax year for our household.

I called the ladies who usually did our tax preparation and made an appointment for the fifteenth. They knew nothing about the divorce or Bill's death. Once I filled them in, they said, "You know you're going to have to file taxes for Bill."

I couldn't believe my ears!

"Are you kidding?" I said. "I have to file taxes on someone who has died?"

They told me that either I had to or the estate had to—which meant that either way, I wasn't going to be able to get out of it.

I called my uncle. "What happens if he owes money?"

Denny said, "They will try to take it out of the estate."

I was so bothered by that.

Meanwhile, Valentine's Day was also coming. In our house, it was never truly a lover's day for Bill and me. If we did anything romantic, it was dinner and a movie, but it was more of a family holiday for us. Cupid would visit the kids in the middle of the night, and leave a gift (usually something red) wrapped in pink and white paper at the foot of their beds.

So, I wasn't feeling a big loss on Valentine's Day. I was busy preparing for my mom's birthday celebration, and preparing for tax day. There was also a birthday party planned for Jeri Ann's son, Jackson, on Valentine's Day. He was turning one year old. I made a point of taking the kids to that, to make sure we were doing something upbeat on Valentine's Day. It felt good to be in happy surroundings.

On the fifteenth, I decided to take the whole day off work. I asked the kids if they would like to go to the cemetery. We hadn't visited since the burial, and I wanted us to see the headstone. Payton said she would go, as long as she could bring two of her friends from gymnastics, which was fine with me. Dylan was fine with the idea. He had always been willing, but was waiting until Payton was ready.

When we woke up that morning, I discovered a light dusting of snow on the ground. When it snows, especially when it snows just a little bit, the traffic is always a nightmare. All morning, I was debating—do we go or not? I was envisioning rows of frosted tombstones, and decided we'd better postpone our trip.

My meeting with the tax preparer went very well. She was extremely helpful, experimenting with different avenues until she finally found the one that made the most sense. Bill still ended up with a small tax obligation, which would be given top priority by the estate, and be paid before any other creditors. I also had to pay a couple hundred dollars for tax preparation for him.

I was grateful to have the tax returns out of the way, but I was still in disbelief over the fact that I'd had to file tax returns for someone who was deceased.

When I'd explained to the tax preparer all that had transpired over the past year, she was amazed. "Wow," she said, "you've been through more in the past year than most people go through in a lifetime."

Tax day was also the day that Randa was starting radiation. They had her on a grueling schedule—Monday through Friday for six weeks, in fifteen-minute intervals. They warned her that it would take a few weeks before it really took a physical toll on her, and that would turn out to be true. Towards the end of the six weeks, she would start to really feel depleted, but being a trouper, she continued to go to work. Her kids never knew anything was wrong.

The following night, February 16th, was a big night for Dylan. Since the day he turned sixteen, he had been imploring us to let him get a foreign car he could fix up and "drift." I knew that his drifting hobby would keep him occupied. If he was working on his car all the time, how much trouble could he get into?

Once we agreed, he put his heart into finding just the right car, and found a guy right in our area. The car Dylan wanted was a Nissan 240SX.

"Let me get this straight," I said. "You would rather have a 1989 Nissan than the 2004 Ford we gave you? Do you realize how old this car is?"

He said, "But, it's the car I've always wanted, Mom, and it's such a good deal, I can't pass it up!"

He had been saving birthday and Christmas money and had more than enough to buy the car.

I made a deal with Dylan—he could get the car only if either Kenny or Chris verified that it was a good car.

After about fifteen tries, Dylan finally got Kenny on the phone, and explained the whole situation to him.

"Okay," Kenny said, "I hear you. Now let me talk to your mom."

"Listen," Kenny said, "I know absolutely nothing about foreign cars! Remember me? I'm a muscle-car guy!"

I laughed. "Well, you still know more than I do!"

Kenny promised to come over the following night, and to bring a friend with him who was familiar with foreign cars.

The next night, Kenny, his friend, Mike, and Dylan were like three little kids in a candy store as they hovered over the computer, excitedly discussing what parts they could buy and all the things Dylan could do to his car. Boys and their toys!

As I watched those grown men interacting with Dylan with such excitement, all I could think was, this is supposed to be a moment Dylan is sharing with Bill. Getting a racecar he could drift was something Dylan and Bill had been discussing—and now there were two other men sitting in my house, standing in for Bill.

It made me so sad. And so happy to know that Dylan had someone to be there with him in his excitement.

They all went and looked at the car, and before I knew it, my son was the proud owner of his dream car, "Zinky," a 1989 Nissan 240 SX. When they got back to the house, Kenny whispered to me, "Dylan is really excited about this car, so be sure not to do the mom thing too hard. It will be tempting to comment on what it looks like, but just make sure you let him how much you like it."

Oh, my God! What did this car look like?

As it turned out, it wasn't as bad as I feared, and at least Dylan was happy—ecstatic, in fact. If the weather had been warmer, I'm sure he would have camped out in the car.

He kept the car a secret for a couple of days, and then Kenny drove Dylan over to see his two best friends and surprise them.

"I can't believe he kept this a secret!" Kenny said. "I would have been telling everyone who would listen."

It made me feel so good to know that Dylan now had something he could truly love and pour his attention into.

By the middle of March, he also had something else that was going to occupy a lot of his time—his first job! It wasn't a job in a car repair shop, which would have been his dream job, but his job at McDonald's meant he was getting a regular paycheck, and there was no arguing with that. He now had a way to pay for all the parts and gadgets he needed for his car.

I was starting to see some of the positive changes I was hoping for in 2010.

Just as Dylan was starting his new job, his sister decided it was time to retire from gymnastics.

I said, "But, I don't understand! Gymnastics taught you so much…"

Then, a friend of mine gave me a different perspective on the situation. "Maybe Payton is ready for something new. Gymnastics was always something she associated with you and Bill."

It was true. Bill had gone to all of Payton's gymnastics meets, and helped out in any way he could.

There was also the fact that Payton was going through a growth spurt, and that may have factored into her decision.

She clearly gave the whole thing a lot of thought before coming to me. "Instead of twenty hours a week in gymnastics, I will still do tumbling. But, I also want to try cheerleading, swimming, tennis, and acting in plays at school."

My daughter is a smart cookie. We have raised the kids right, and she knew that if she came to me without a plan, I would have objected to her quitting gymnastics. Coming home from school every day and doing nothing was not an option for either one of them. But, how could I argue with her when she had such a well-rounded schedule planned out?

Payton played tennis once in awhile with her dad; and she still held her nose when she jumped into a pool. So, it was going to be interesting to see how these various activities would play out in her life.

March ended with dinner at a restaurant with Jan, and a weekend trip out to visit Kenny in the country. Both visits were fairly successful.

2010 was definitely looking up. Who says the new year has to start in January?

~April~
The Promise of Springtime

"To everything there is a season,
And a time to every purpose under Heaven."
Ecclesiastes 3:1

~The Holy Bible

I am a romantic at heart, and I loved the idea of spring returning. I knew I was going to suffer with allergies, but watching the trees come back to life, and smelling all the flowers in bloom is irresistible. I keep the windows flung open wide, and allergy pills handy.

The kids and I were having a good run. Our tragedy had brought us even closer, and we were moving through this new world in which we found ourselves as a tight unit. I still had to manage the typical teen issues that came up from time to time, but all in all, we were bonding in a way we might not have been had we found ourselves in a normal situation.

I was feeling really good for the first time in ages.

I was beginning phone interviews with a writer, so she could collect the notes to write my story. I had no idea that telling someone my story out loud would be so therapeutic. I felt so good after each phone session with her because I was able to share things I hadn't even been able to share with my counselor. My mom and Randa loved knowing that one of the phone sessions was set up, because I felt so good afterwards.

Not only was I helping myself by telling the writer my story, I was starting to believe someone else might be helped by reading it. I also knew the day would come when Dylan and Payton would read it, and when that day came, they would be blessed by having our story in a book we could treasure for all time.

I had been living for so long without hope, and now it was coming back. I was also beginning to dream again. The future—which had seemed so bleak—was beginning to seem like a blank canvas on which the picture of my new life was appearing, one brush stroke at a time.

From day one, I've said, "If I can help just one person with this book, it will be worth everything I've invested in it."

In April, Payton turned thirteen years old. It was a little bit scary, watching my baby turn into a teenager, but it was also exciting. I am totally enjoying this young adult phase of the kids' lives. I also loved their younger years, of course.

The Supercross tour was coming to St. Louis. Every year, Bill and his half-brother Michael would take Dylan and Bill, Sr. to see the professional motorcycle riders race at Supercross. This year, Bill, Sr. and Michael took Dylan. Of course, it crossed Dylan's mind that his dad was not with them, but even though he missed his father, he still had a good time. It was an event he had shared with his dad for so many years, he could feel his dad beside him in spirit.

As for me, I decided it was time to spread my wings a bit, so I planned an all-girls weekend in Chicago. My parents stayed with the kids, and three of us girls from St. Louis (Randa, Regina, and me), and one from Houston (Tanya), all flew to Chicago to visit my grounded-in-reality friend, Ann. She is a single physician who lives in a beautiful, three-level condo in downtown Chicago, with a view of the skyline. I felt like we were in a mini New York. I loved being away from the suburbs for the weekend.

We all played hooky from work on Friday, and spent the weekend eating, drinking, partying, and shopping. It was a grown-up slumber party, as we sat up until four o'clock in the morning, talking.

It was so good for me—especially the ratio of three single women and two married. For the first time in a long time, I was hanging out with single people, and letting them teach me the ropes. I needed a lot of guidance because, frankly, I didn't have the faintest idea of how to act. The idea of being a single person was still totally novel—and frightening.

How could I think about even talking to a strange man, much less dating one, after twenty-four years with the same man? Would I be able to tell the difference between a normal man and a psycho?

I don't want to be alone. I want to share the rest of my life with someone, so I am going to have to figure it out. And I believe I will. Someday that somebody new will come along—no doubt when I least expect it.

Strangely enough, as I was thinking more and more about the future, both kids and I were getting less interested in a brand new house. Our house had been on the market forever, and the looky-loos were making our lives hell.

I couldn't take it anymore.

Payton had no interest in leaving her school district and starting over somewhere.

Dylan wanted to turn the basement into his man cave.

And, to top it off, I wasn't too thrilled with my choices in terms of a new house we could afford.

So, one day, I tossed an idea out to the kids. "What if, instead of moving, we stayed in our house, and put the money I saved towards remodeling? We could get all new furniture, and make it feel like new."

When the subject had first come up, they were dead set on moving—and they weren't the only ones. Back then, everything seemed too familiar, and we all wanted out. Over time, the determination to move had faded a bit.

The kids were both on board with the idea.

In order to pull it off, I was going to have to enlist my dad and brother as unpaid laborers. Luckily for me, I have the greatest family in the world, and they agreed to help me. It felt so good to pick up the phone and tell my realtor that I was taking my house off the market.

Little by little, one room at a time, we are transforming the house—and our lives.

I had this dream…

Bill and I are in a moving vehicle of some kind—maybe a truck. He is sitting in the driver's seat, but he's not driving. We are sitting there talking.

"How could you let this happen?" I ask. "You're such a good motorcycle rider."

He says, "It happened so quickly. We had been riding all day…Wham, wham. It was over."

Then I get very angry. "You're watching over us and you see how much pain we are in. If you wouldn't have left me, none of this would have happened!"

He says, "Something was going to happen, Shell. This was the way it was supposed to be…But, you are the only one I ever loved. You were the only one that was always for me."

Was it a visit from Bill? The spiritual side of me says yes. The logical side of me says that it was just my mind, telling me to move on.

Bill always told me he was not going to live past thirty. Then, he hit thirty and said, "You know, I'll be surprised if I live to be forty."

He seemed to have a premonition that he was not going to live to be an old man. He knew that.

I would always say, "No, you're crazy! We will grow old together. I will be pushing you around in a wheelchair."

I feel so blessed to have had Bill for over half my life. I had what many don't get ever in a lifetime—a best friend that happened to be my husband, and two amazing kids.

Bill and I literally grew up together and experienced so much as a couple and as parents. I wouldn't change that—ever.

Yet, I hate every second of what happened in those last few months—having to watch the life we had slip away and get lost. I had the perfect family of four, a marriage of twenty years, and to watch it unravel before me like that was agonizing.

At the same time, I was lucky to have experienced every bit of it—the twenty-four years with Bill, as well as the last few months before he died. It seems strange, considering all that came to pass, to call myself lucky.

Yet, I know, that in some weird way, we had to experience the months before Bill's death in order to be able to cope with the ultimate loss of him from our lives…and in order for the bear inside of him to experience its last journey on earth.

For although I lived more than half my life with Bill, and fully believe he gave me all the time he had to give to a wife, I also believe that, just like in the film, *Legends of the Fall,* Bill had a bear living inside of him. And, before he left this earth, he needed to release it. Just for a moment in time, he needed to live the carefree life he never had because we married so young.

He wanted to be the perfect "Brady Bunch" family, where we did everything together. And that's what we were. We gave everything we had to our kids. He was so happy with his decision to live that life with the kids and me.

But, as the time to make his transition was getting closer, he started doing things that were outside of the family norm—going on motorcycle weekends with his friends, or racecar trips. At the time, I couldn't understand the change in him, and I just found it irritating.

Now I see that it was the bear inside of him, beginning to come out of hibernation and take over, like he always knew it eventually would.

I believe Bill loved Lisa—the freedom that she represented. And they may have even talked about getting married, but I truly believe he knew it was never going to happen.

He saw the end coming around the bend. And, he knew that he would soon be taking his final drive.

About the Author

Shelly Hess is a proud mother who loves nothing more than spending time with her family, and teaching her remarkable son and daughter the value of the family bond. She is also an animal lover, whose two dogs love to take her for a walk in the park on a beautiful fall or spring day.

When Shelly is not spending time with her extended family, or at work in the medical billing industry, she often enjoys a good glass of wine while contemplating a serene lake or the sound of the surf on a beach vacation.

The author firmly believes that everyone has a story to tell, and no matter how wounded we may be by circumstance or tragedy, healing can come in the telling of our story. It is her hope that in sharing her tragic experience, she can encourage and inspire those who are facing challenges of their own.

Shelly Hess lives in a suburb of St. Louis, where she awaits a golf teacher with the patience to teach her the game. She firmly believes that everything happens for a reason, and trusts in the ancient Buddhist proverb: "When the student is ready, the teacher will appear."

LaVergne, TN USA
25 March 2011

221705LV00001B/57/P